POWER FAILURE

Two Israeli jets flying CAP over Haifa at twenty thousand feet suddenly lost all radio contact with the ground and with each other. Both craft flamed out as all electronic components on them failed in a smoking mass. With little lift in their short stubby wings, the planes dropped toward the ground with a hard-won glide path that topped out at forty percent. The pilots tried to restart their engines, but nothing worked. Not even the altimeter functioned, and the pilots desperately made their last move. They hugged their arms to their sides and pulled the ejection handle. The shotgun-shell-like devices exploded, which set off the solid fuel rockets that blasted the ejection seats high away from the doomed F-14 Tomcat fighters. The parachutes opened and the pilots drifted down toward Israel having no idea why their planes failed.

SEAL TEAM SEVEN
FIELD OF FIRE

KEITH DOUGLASS

BERKLEY BOOKS, NEW YORK

Special thanks to Chet Cunningham
for his contributions to this book.

This is a work of fiction. Names, characters, places, and incidents either are the product of the author's imagination or are used fictitiously, and any resemblance to actual persons, living or dead, business establishments, events, or locales is entirely coincidental.

SEAL TEAM SEVEN: FIELD OF FIRE

A Berkley Book / published by arrangement with
the author

PRINTING HISTORY
Berkley edition / June 2003

Copyright © 2003 by The Berkley Publishing Group
SEAL TEAM SEVEN logo illustration by Michael Racz.

For information address: The Berkley Publishing Group,
a division of Penguin Group (USA) Inc.,
375 Hudson Street, New York, New York 10014.

ISBN: 0-425-19068-4

BERKLEY®
Berkley Books are published by The Berkley Publishing Group,
a division of Penguin Group (USA) Inc.,
375 Hudson Street, New York, New York 10014.
BERKLEY and the "B" design
are trademarks belonging to Penguin Group (USA) Inc.

PRINTED IN THE UNITED STATES OF AMERICA

10 9 8 7 6 5 4 3 2 1

*This work of fiction is sincerely
dedicated to all those who perished
in the September 11 murderous atrocity,
in the Pentagon attack, the World Trade Center
disaster, and the fourth plane crashed
by suicidal terrorists.
No society or rational people
should have to experience
such demented actions
by worldwide criminal elements.*

SEAL TEAM SEVEN

THIRD PLATOON*
CORONADO, CALIFORNIA

Rear Admiral (L) Richard Kenner. Commander of all SEALs. Little Creek, Virginia.

Captain Harry L. Arjarack. Commanding Officer of NAVSPECWARGRUP-ONE, in Coronado, California. 51.

Commander Dean Masciareli. Commanding officer of Navy Special Warfare Group One's SEAL Team Seven in Coronado, California. 47, 5' 11", 220 pounds. Annapolis graduate.

Master Chief Petty Officer Gordon MacKenzie. Administrator and head enlisted man of all of SEAL Team Seven. 47, 5' 10", 180 pounds.

Lieutenant Commander Blake Murdock. Platoon Leader, Third Platoon. 32, 6' 2", 210 pounds. Annapolis graduate. Six years in SEALs. Father an important congressman from Virginia. Murdock has an apartment in Coronado. Owns a car and a motorcycle. Loves to fish. Weapon: Alliant Bull Pup duo 5.56mm & 20mm explosive round. Speaks Arabic.

ALPHA SQUAD

Timothy F. Sadler. Senior Chief Petty Officer. Top EM in Third Platoon. Third in command. 32, 6' 2", 220 pounds. Married to Sylvia, no children. Been in the Navy for fifteen years, a SEAL for last eight. Expert fisherman. Plays trumpet in any Dixieland combo he can find. Weapon: Alliant Bull Pup duo 5.56mm & 20mm explosive round. Good with the men. Speaks German and some Farsi.

*Third Platoon assigned exclusively to the Central Intelligence Agency to perform any needed tasks on a covert basis anywhere in the world. All are top-secret assignments. Goes around Navy chain of command. Direct orders from the CIA and the CNO.

David "Jaybird" Sterling. Machinist Mate First Class. Lead petty officer. 24, 5' 10", 170 pounds. Quick mind, fine tactician. Single. Drinks too much sometimes. Crack shot with all arms. Grew up in Oregon. Helps plan attack operations. Weapon: H & K MP-5SD submachine gun.

Luke "Mountain" Howard. Gunner's Mate Second Class. 28, 6' 4", 250 pounds. Black man. Football at Oregon State. Try-out with Oakland Raiders six years ago. In Navy six years, SEAL for four. Single. Rides a motorcycle. A skiing and wind surfing nut. Squad sniper. Weapon: H & K PSG1 7.62 NATO sniper rifle.

Bill Bradford. Quartermaster First Class. 24, 6' 2", 215 pounds. An artist in spare time. Paints oils. He sells his marine paintings. Single. Quiet. Reads a lot. Has two years of college. Platoon radio operator. Carries a SATCOM on most missions. Weapon: Alliant Bull Pup duo 5.56mm & 20mm explosive round. Speaks Italian and some Arabic.

Joe "Ricochet" Lampedusa. Operations Specialist First Class. 21, 5' 11", 175 pounds. Good tracker, quick thinker. Had a year of college. Loves motorcycles. Wants a Hog. Pot smoker on the sly. Picks up plain girls. Platoon scout. Weapon: Colt M-4A1 with grenade launcher, alternate Bull Pup duo 5.56mm & 20mm explosive round.

Kenneth Ching. Quartermaster First Class. 25, 6' even, 180 pounds. Full-blooded Chinese. Platoon translator. Speaks Mandarin Chinese, Japanese, Russian, and Spanish. Bicycling nut. Paid $1,200 for off-road bike. Is trying for Officer Candidate School. Weapon: H & K MP-5SD submachine gun.

Vincent "Vinnie" Van Dyke. Electrician's Mate Second Class. 24, 6' 2", 220 pounds. Enlisted out of high school. Played varsity basketball. Wants to be a commercial fisherman after his current hitch. Good with his hands. Squad machine gunner. Weapon: H & K 21-E 7.62 NATO round machine gun. Speaks Dutch, German, and some Arabic.

Bravo Squad

Lieutenant (j.g.) Christopher "Chris" Gardner. Squad Leader Bravo Squad. Second in Command of the platoon. 28, 6' 4", 240 pounds. From Seattle. Four years in SEALs. Hangglider nut. Married to Wanda, a clothing designer. No kids. Annapolis graduate. Father is a Navy rear admiral. Grew up in ten different states. Weapon: Alliant Bull Pup duo 5.56mm & 20mm explosive round. Alternate: H & K G-11 submachine gun.

George "Petard" Canzoneri. Torpedoman's Mate First Class. 27, 5' 11", 190 pounds. Married to Navy wife Phyllis. No kids. Nine years in Navy. Expert on explosives. Nicknamed "Petard" for almost hoisting himself one time. Top pick in platoon for explosives work. Weapon: Alliant Bull Pup duo 5.56mm & 20mm explosive round.

Miguel Fernandez. Gunner's Mate First Class. 26, 6' 1", 180 pounds. Wife, Maria; daughter, Linda, 7, in Coronado. Spends his off time with them. Highly family oriented. He has family in San Diego. Speaks Spanish and Portuguese. Squad sniper. Weapon: H & K PSG1 7.62 NATO sniper rifle.

Omar "Ollie" Rafii. Yeoman Second Class. 24, 6' even, 180 pounds. From Saudi Arabia. In U.S. since he was four. Loves horses, has two. Married, two children. Speaks perfect Farsi and Arabic. Expert with all knives. Throws killing knives with deadly accuracy. Weapon: H & K MP-5SD submachine gun.

Tracy Donegan. Signalman Second Class. 24, 6' even, 185 pounds. Former Navy boxer. Tough. Single. Expert tracker and expert on camouflage and ground warfare. Top marksman. Platoon driver, mechanic. Speaks Swahili and Italian. Weapon: H & K G-11 with caseless rounds.

Jack Mahanani. Hospital Corpsman First Class. 25, 6' 4", 240 pounds. Platoon medic. Tahitian/Hawaiian. Expert swimmer. Bench-presses four hundred pounds. Divorced. Top surfer. Wants the .50 sniper rifle. Weapon: Alliant Bull Pup duo 5.56mm

& 20mm explosive round. Alternate: Colt M-4A1 with grenade launcher.

Wade Claymore. Radioman Second Class. 24, 6' 3", 230 pounds. Unmarried. Played two years of Junior College football. A computer whiz. Can program, repair, and build computers. Shoots pistol competitively. Lives in Coronado. Weapon: Alliant Bull Pup duo with 5.56 & 20mm explosive round.

Paul "Jeff" Jefferson. Engineman Second Class. 23, 6' 1", 200 pounds. Black man. Expert in small arms. Can tear apart most weapons and reassemble, repair, and innovate them. A chess player to match Ed DeWitt. Weapon: Alliant Bull Pup duo 5.56mm & 20mm explosive round.

1

Lebanon
Eight miles into the buffer zone

Something moved out there in the darkest night that Corporal David Aharon had ever seen. They were black-on-black ghost shadows fading away, drifting back, filtering through his sharp night vision like holographs on the inside of an eternally sealed tomb. Aharon tacked one of the fuzzy mirages with his Uzi automatic rifle, then squeezed his eyes shut for a moment. When he looked back, the dark apparition had edged closer. He kicked his best friend in the whole Israeli army, Jacob Zared. The slender soldier, not long from Chicago, came awake instantly and pushed his Uzi over the lip of the bunker.

"Something's out there," Corporal Aharon whispered. "Near that rock, twenty feet on the left. That's on the only access to this position."

"I don't see nothing, Aharon," Zared grumbled. "You're just trying to get me up early to relieve you on guard. I got me an hour to sleep yet."

"Look closer, damnit, that shadow is moving."

"Then shoot it."

"Yeah." Corporal Aharon aimed and sent seven rounds of 9mm Parabellums into the moving shadow. At once a scream echoed off the stark, dry hillside. The stuttering of submachine guns replied with counterfire. Before the echoes of the rounds quieted, more dark ghostly shapes moved in the blackness. Then fingers pulled pins out of grenades and the deadly hand bombs sailed through the air from only twenty yards away.

Before the grenades hit, both Israeli soldiers were firing on full automatic with their Uzis, spraying the slight downslope in front of them. They knew where the rocks were, none large enough to hide a man. They emptied their forty-round magazines, jammed in new ones, and had started to use them when the first grenade went off just outside the sandbags. It blew dirt and sand into their faces and they sagged down behind the parapet into the safety of the bunker.

The next grenade exploded just inside the sandbags and shattered Aharon's right leg. The third bomb went off with a terrifying roar, the exploding shrapnel from the steel casing tearing into Zared's neck and head, dumping him half over Corporal Aharon and dead before he hit the ground.

Aharon pushed his friend off his legs and lifted his Uzi just as the first attacker looked over the sandbags. Even in the darkness, the corporal could make out the angry face of the Arab. Aharon pulled the trigger, blasting six rounds into the soldier's face, slamming him off the bunker. Corporal Aharon edged up so he could see over the top of the canvas bags. More moving shadows. He drilled them with spaced six-round bursts. Two weapons sent counterfire, but they missed. He fired until his magazine was empty. He hit the release and reached for a filled one. It was right beside his knee. He jammed it in, pulled the arming handle, and edged up for another look.

An enemy soldier crawled toward the bunker, dragging one leg, his submachine gun cradled in his arms. Aharon blasted him into a meeting with Allah, as six rounds ripped into his head, splitting his skull open and spraying the rocks and gravel with brains, blood, and gray matter.

The sudden quiet startled Aharon. He could see no one else moving. No shadow lifted to throw a grenade. No rifle or submachine gun chattered at him. Gone. Or dead. He wiped his face and his hand came away sticky. Then he smelled the blood. Jacob Zared's blood. A sudden rush of fury flooded over him and he lifted up and emptied the magazine in two long bursts into the area where he had seen the ghost shadows. If only he had fired when he first noticed them, Zared would be alive. He thought of the other man in the bunker. He hadn't made a sound. Was he sleeping?

Immediately Aharon shielded the narrow beam of his pencil light and checked the rest of the bunker. It was nothing more than an eight-foot-long arc built up by sand-bags, with a small cave behind it carved by some ancient people into the nearly vertical wall of rocks. He hadn't counted on grenades. On the first sweep of the far side of the bunker, he found the new guy, Elkan. He didn't even know his first name. He had come into the squad yester-day as a replacement for a man who had been seriously wounded in a street bombing last week. Elkan lay where he had been sleeping. It looked like he had lifted up when the first firing came, then before he could get turned around to use his weapon, a grenade had jolted hot steel shards into him in a dozen vital places.

Corporal Aharon reached for the squad radio that he had positioned on a small shelf in back of the shallow cave to keep it safe. He grabbed it and punched the on switch and then the send button. No red light came on. He shook it to move the batteries slightly so they would make better contact. That had worked before. Not this time. He used the light again with his back toward the front of the bunker. The radio had been chopped up by half a dozen pieces of a grenade.

He had to report the attack. So he would walk. Could he walk? He used the light to check his right leg. The explosion had gouged a six-inch strip of flesh off his calf. It was so deep he could see the white bone. He pulled open his belt first-aid kit and took out an ampoule of morphine and injected it into his arm. Then he used a roller bandage and tried to wrap up his leg. It took him a half hour fighting the pain that the drug couldn't deaden. At last he used a large red handkerchief and made a final outer wrap on the six-inch-long wound. He made it so tight that he keened sharply with pain.

He stood, testing the leg, hoping that none of the at-tackers still watched the bunker. No one shot at him. He took a step over Zared's body, then back. He did it three times, and nodded. Yes, he could walk. It was only six miles back to the closest bunker and then to the border. They would have a radio. They might even have heard the firing. Ten soldiers manned that position.

Corporal Aharon picked up the three Uzis and then his small pack and sat on the edge of the bunker. He ground his teeth and scowled as he swung his legs up and over the sandbags. They made it and he took a deep breath. Then he tightened his legs and belly and eased his feet slowly to the ground. The searing jolt of pain when his right boot touched the ground brought a gasp and then a long shiver over his whole body. It hurt like hell. Yes, he could do this. He had run marathons. Once he ran forty miles just to see if he could. He could do this damned six miles.

The first three miles filled him with anger and pain. Why had they attacked? It had to have been expert raiders, commandos, and the elite of either Lebanon or Syria. He didn't even know if Lebanon had any special troops.

The next two miles filled Aharon with a deadly, suppressed fury that dulled his pain as he concentrated his mind on plain, old-fashioned revenge. That wish, those plans, spurred him on with enough adrenaline to make it through the last mile. A sentry heard him coming when he was a hundred yards away. A password saved him, and the sentry helped him limp into the command post in one of the three bunkers, where he waved at the sergeant in charge. Then Corporal David Aharon promptly passed out.

Less than a half mile from the border on the Lebanese side of the buffer zone, Captain Jarash Rayak lifted his submachine gun and aimed it at the noise he heard out front. The clouds had cleared away from a half moon, and soon he saw two men supporting each other as they limped slowly forward. Only one of them had a weapon.

"Password," the captain snapped.

"Moon shadows," the word came back. Captain Rayak relaxed. He waited for the two men to come to him, told them to sit down, and then he questioned them thoroughly.

"Yes sir, Captain. It went as we planned. We got close enough to use grenades in the dark and fired our weapons. We must have killed all of them in the bunker. I watched for twenty minutes and nobody came out. We lost five men. Private Dasht here is severely wounded. Can we get him back to the hospital?"

"In due time." Captain Rayak smiled. Yes, this should be enough. They would return to the Lebanon defense center, where he could call his colonel with the good news. Colonel Madinat would be pleased. Now if the Israelis followed through the way they usually did, the stage would be set.

He brought up a jeep and took the two enlisted men back to the defense center, where they were quickly taken to the hospital. Making the phone call to the colonel was pure pleasure.

Less than twelve hours after the attack on the border Israeli bunker, Israeli jets streaked over the buffer zone with full loads of bombs and rockets. The six American-made F-18 fighters slanted down just past the safe zone and destroyed a small Lebanese military post, then blasted apart four houses usually used by Lebanese line crossers. They continued on to the next small town in Lebanon, where they wiped out a large electrical substation, six train cars on the main line north, and more than a dozen business firms and small manufacturing plants.

Ten minutes after the aircraft attack, the Israeli radio and TV came on the air with a statement from the minister of defense. "One of our forward observation posts in the buffer zone between Israel and Lebanon was viciously attacked last night by elite line crossing troops from Lebanon, killing two soldiers and seriously wounding the third.

"This morning Israeli fighter aircraft destroyed several military targets in southern Lebanon in retaliation for the unprovoked attack on our armed forces. Any future missions that Lebanon or Syria run into the buffer zone, or into Israel, will be dealt with at once and with deadly force. Our purpose is to live in peace with our neighbors to the north. It is our hope that they will observe the civilized actions that will permit this."

Damascus, Syria

General Mahdi Diar looked up at a small TV screen as the Israeli defense minister gave his warning.

"Yes," he shouted. "Yes, they have taken the bait. They have played it exactly as we planned." He turned to an aide. "Make sure that the bodies of the five rangers who were killed in the raid are recovered. They each will receive a medal and their burial costs will be paid for as well." He looked back at the three-dimensional layout of a long swath of land extending south from the Lebanese-Israeli buffer zone and smiled. As most military men do, he was working on a grand war game strategy. This one would bring Israel to her knees begging for a just peace before her population was pushed ingloriously into the Mediterranean Sea. This war game could quickly turn into something more deadly. General Diar looked around and waved at another aide.

"I must celebrate. Bring me a tall glass of lemonade from my special supply." The aide grinned and left the room. General Diar was short and square like a Lebanese cedar fence post. His black hair was cut close and he wore a tailored uniform that hid a layer of fat around his midsection. He used glasses and now peered over them at the display in front of him. He moved a symbol for a company of tanks up to the Israeli border. Again he smiled from dark eyes and showed stained teeth that he could never get clean. His round face held puffy cheeks, dark brows, and a nose that was both sharp and long, giving him a wolfish appearance. The smile tempered; then it faded as he looked at the symbols for the mass of troops and equipment that would be held at least fifty miles north of the Lebanese-Israeli border. It must be done. It had been all arranged, and now the bait had been cast and Israel had swallowed it hook, line, and new bomb.

General Diar laughed softly as he lifted the chilled glass

of lemonade that contained a generous portion of vodka. Yes, soon now. So very soon and it would begin. Then with any luck and with an overwhelming victory, he would be a national hero, and who knew, he might soon be president of all sixteen million Syrians.

2

Near Boulevard, California

Third Platoon of SEAL Team Seven, based in Coronado, California, hadn't been on a live fire training exercise in more than a week.

"We can't let you guys get rusty," Lieutenant (j.g.) Chris Gardner said on the eight-mile hike into the far outback of a ranch in East San Diego County. The owner had long ago agreed to let them use some of his land for live firing practice. They were in the edge of the Laguna Mountains and near the southern section of the Anza-Borrego Desert State Park. There wasn't a building or a road within fifteen miles of them in any direction, and thirty miles in others. Here they could practice their automatic weapons, their 20mm rifle air bursts, and stage small wars all their own without bothering anyone, and usually without anyone ever hearing them. All they had to do was close any gate that they opened, and pick up their brass so the hot southern California sun didn't magnify off it and start a range fire.

Platoon Leader Lieutenant Commander Blake Murdock let Gardner lead the pack today. He planned the exercise, primed the troops, issued the weapons, and would run the whole thing. Murdock had been breaking in this new second in command for several months now, through retraining and on at least two hot fire missions out of country. The more experience he had with the men under combat conditions the better. Then he would know about how the men would react, and they would know his moves and gain respect for him as the team leader. At all times he was the leader of Bravo Squad.

Gardner jogged up to the head of the strung-out combat patrol and waved at Operations Specialist First Class Joe "Lam" Lampedusa.

"Speed it up a little, Lam, we're running late. We need to be to the spire over there in twenty minutes."

Lam nodded. He had wondered about the pace, but let the officer in charge do the changing. He shifted into a slightly higher gear, lengthened out his stride, and saw the men behind him respond to keep their five yards distance from each other just like on a real combat mission.

Eighteen minutes later the platoon knelt down at the edge of the spire they had used for years as a key point of the landscape.

The JG nodded at Lam and faced the troops. "So far, so good. We're warmed up now. Our next little mission is for each man to laser two shots from our twenties at our favorite oak tree snag over there eight hundred yards. We have six twenties along today. One is in the repair shop, so we'll trade off. I want a defensive line along here for you six with the Bull Pups. Now."

The six SEALs with the 20mm shoulder-fired weapons jogged up to the imaginary line the JG had drawn in front of him and went prone with the weapons. "Fire when you're ready. Two rounds each, laser on that old snag. Go."

The 20mm shoulder-fired rifles were not yet operational in the U.S. military. In fact Murdock had wrangled seven of them out of the CIA to "field test." The weapons would be fully developed and made available to the armed forces sometime during 2005. The weapon has a 20mm barrel on top, and above that a laser/telescopic sight; it can laser up to a thousand yards away. When the gunner pulls the trigger, the laser shoots back the distance to the laser sight, which sends the data to the arming mechanism. There the weapon sets the round's fuse for the number of rotations the slug has to make to reach the target. At the lasered target the round explodes in an air burst. The weapon is awesome, turning a dog soldier in combat into a walking field artillery piece. The barrel below the 20mm one is for 5.56 rounds. Each barrel has a magazine but the rifle works with one trigger. The 20mm magazine holds five rounds. Unloaded, the Bull Pup twenty is slightly lighter than the same configuration of the M-16. Four major companies are working on the project that the military has approved. Heckler and Koch in Germany is one of the prime contractors.

Two SEALs fired the 20mm rifles immediately. They made a different sound than the troops had been used to. Both the first two rounds exploded in airbursts directly over the snag. The next four came close enough for a killing spray of the highly dangerous airburst that showered everything below it with deadly shrapnel.

The men changed places as they finished their rounds, and soon all sixteen men, including the two officers, had taken their shots at the old snag.

"Back in squad order," Gardner called. "I want a skirmish line by squads. Every other man prone and ready to fire his TO weapon. The men standing will charge forward twenty yards and go prone. As soon as the forward man starts firing, the prone man will come to his feet and surge to his partner and then twenty yards forward. Keep your five yards distance at all times and let's try not to kill anybody in our platoon this afternoon. Basic fire and cover, advancing on an objective. You men with the twenties, use the 5.56 configuration. Let's do it. Commander Murdock will hold the far end of the line; I'll be on this end. Keep your twenty-yard runs as even as possible with the other half of your squad and the other squad. Any questions?"

"What happens if my partner slants out of his lane and gets close to my line of fire?"

"You kill the bastard," Machinist Mate First Class David "Jaybird" Sterling cracked.

"You do and you carry the body on your back for the next week of training," Gardner gunned back. Everyone roared. Murdock stood back and watched. So far he had been pleased with the way Gardner had eased into his role as second in the platoon. He was handling it just right. He didn't have a lot of field experience under fire, but that would be solved soon enough.

Murdock took his position with Alpha Squad, teaming with Lam, who walked right ahead of him in most combat patrol situations. They understood each other, had been in tough firefights more times than they could remember in the past three years. Men with the Bull Pups fired the 5.56 second barrel on the weapon that was located right under the 20mm top tube. Even with the laser sight and the telescopic sight, the Bull Pup was easy to carry and to fire.

Gardner checked the lineup, then fired three rounds from his 5.56 barrel and the men began to fire. In combat they would key on the leader's weapon. When he fired, they fired. Murdock was prone as Lam rushed ahead for twenty yards. Murdock's rounds slammed across the windswept, dry mountainous terrain five yards from Lam. When the lead scout hit the deck and began firing, Murdock moved up, went past him twenty yards, and bellied down with his Bull Pup out front spitting the 5.56 rounds forward.

When each man had fired and supported four times, Gardner blew his whistle. He grinned. "Got your attention, right? I won't use it in a combat situation. But there you'll have one eye on me or Commander Murdock and get an arm signal to cease fire. Any questions?" There were none. "Okay, you guys. Find a rock and break out your MREs. If you didn't bring one this morning from the bus, you're out of luck. We have twenty minutes to chow down. These are the new MREs with the heat pouch, so we can all get a hot meal. Most of them are pretty good. No lima beans or corned beef hash here."

"What were they?" Hospital Corpsman First Class Jack Mahanani asked.

"During WW two and Korea they had the old C rations that came in cans. Ham and lima beans and corned beef hash were the dogs of the trading table. Beans and franks were the top of the heap. Some guys actually liked the hash. We have eighteen minutes more."

Murdock heated up his entree in the heat pouch, some kind of chemical combination that produced heat and did away with the little stoves they used to have in C rations.

The new MREs were much better than the old ones. They still had all the small goodies in them such as Tabasco sauce, peanut butter, cocoa powder, cold beverage powder, crackers, salt, sugar, creamer, moist towelette, instant coffee, a matchbook, salt pills, and a plastic spoon. Murdock finished his, stuffed the residue and unopened parts back into his backpack, and watched his second.

JG Gardner stood up on cue and looked around. "We move in two minutes. If I see a scrap of any litter on the deck, there will be a twenty-mile run this afternoon with full field equipment."

It was one warning the JG didn't have to make. The platoon had never left a mess in its wake. In combat a scrap from an MRE could be enough to identify them and track them in some foreign country. The President and the chief of naval operations didn't like that to happen on a covert mission.

They moved into combat patrol formation, two large eight-man diamonds with Lam out in front of the first one as lead scout, Murdock leading Alpha Squad behind him and the JG with his diamond formation a hundred yards behind Murdock's squad.

They headed generally back toward the bus. After two miles, the JG called that an attack had hit them from their right flank. He ordered the men to swing to the right in a line of skirmishers and go to ground. When the SEALs were in place he fired three rounds to the front, and the fifteen men joined in live firing with their personal weapons. After twenty seconds he called it off with hand signals. Only one man missed the hand signal and he fired two bursts after everyone else stopped.

"So, Signalman Donegan, didn't you get the signal? Keep one eye on me or on the man beside you. Those two extra bursts might have cut down some friendlies you didn't even know about."

"Aye, aye, JG. I got it."

The JG looked at his watch. "A little after fourteen hundred. We have a demo scheduled at the bus at fourteen-thirty. A mediocre marathon runner can do a mile in five minutes all day long. We're how far from the bus?"

"About six miles, JG," Lam said.

"Close enough. If we did a six-minute mile we could be at the bus nearly on time."

"Never happen," Jaybird said. "We're downhill on loose rock and gravel. If we run we have a high probability of some sprained or broken ankles. I'd opt for an eight-minute mile and come in a little late."

"Any other bids?" the JG asked.

Nobody spoke up. The JG grinned. "Hell, I was thinking more like a ten-minute pace, but if you really want to hit the eight-minute one . . ."

He was shouted down and Gardner grinned. "On your feet, single-file patrol formation. Lam in front and set it at ten minutes to the mile. The demo at the bus can wait a half hour, since our very own Commander Murdock is going to be making the presentation."

Lam fudged a little and moved them out at near a nine-minutes-to-the-mile pace and brought the troops into the bus where they always parked it in just over fifty-one minutes. It was August and the mountain was hot and dry. The area was in a one-hundred-day run without a one-hundredth of an inch or more of rain. The SEALs took off their floppy hats and shrugged out of packs and hit their canteens. There was no water control. If you drank too much and ran out, it was your problem.

Murdock went into the bus and brought back a folding card table and two boxes. He took out of one of them a stack of papers that he anchored on the table with a magazine from his Bull Pup. The second box held a plastic-wrapped item he lay on the table and beside it he put a series of long tube-like devices of different diameters.

"Okay, men, gather round and relax," Murdock said. "What I have to show you here today, some of you won't believe. But it is true. What's the fastest gun in the world?"

"The AK-47 will go six hundred rounds per minute," Bill Bradford said.

"The M-16 cranks out seven hundred and fifty per minute," Miguel Fernandez said.

"Any other bidders?" Murdock asked.

"The Colt Commando will go from six hundred to one thousand rounds depending on the ammo," Paul Jefferson threw in.

"Now we're getting somewhere," Murdock said. "I thought you guys knew weapons. What about the good old Armalite AR-18? No takers? It will do eight hundred rpm. Then the Famas from France will spit them out at nine hundred and fifty rounds a minute. Not bad." He picked up the padded plastic-covered item from the table. "Here we have a little item that puts all those submachine guns to shame. Yeah, this is a handgun, a little bigger and heavier than you're used to, but it's the fastest gun in the Old West or the new east or anywhere in the world."

Murdock slowly unwrapped the weapon from the concealing covers. It showed up about twice the size of a Colt .45, all black and what looked like six barrels coming out of an oblong shielded muzzle.

"A handgun?" somebody asked.

"Yep, just a handgun. This little dandy can fire a hundred and eighty rounds in less than one-hundredth of a second. For those of you who were not math majors, that's eighteen thousand rounds in a second. Jaybird, how many would that be fired in a minute?"

Jaybird frowned a moment. "Hell, Commander, that would be well over a million rounds a minute."

"Told you it was fast. The only problem is you couldn't load that many rounds in a weapon this size. But look at the muzzle. There are seven barrels inside that housing. One is a forty-five-caliber, one is a thirty-eight-caliber, two are nine-millimeter and the other three are twenty-two-caliber."

"Yeah, but how can it shoot so damned fast?" Omar Rafii asked.

"I've been hoping somebody would ask that. The rounds are held together with small wads of propellant. No casing, no primer, nothing but the round and the propellant and they are jammed together in one long connection that is inserted into the barrel. Then, when triggered, the rounds are fired electronically. No moving parts, not a damn one. That's why they can be fired so fast. Now, this weapon is not ready for combat yet, even on a trial basis."

"Yeah, but that doesn't stop us from taking one along," Jaybird chirped. They all laughed thinking about the other "experimental" weapons they had tested in combat situations in the past two years.

"This model will be the O'Dwyer VLE, which stands for Variable Lethality Law Enforcement. It's a handgun. Mike O'Dwyer, an Australian, is the inventor through his company there. This model aimed for police and military use has a selector on the hand grip for the barrel you want to fire, and has a fingerprint user ID system to limit the use of the weapon to a single person or to two, three, or five people.

"Right now the weapon is set up to fire fifteen rounds faster than you can spit. The only rounds we have for it are the nine-millimeter. They have been slightly altered to fit the bore, so not any nine-millimeter would work. The stacked rounds are loaded from the rear of the weapon. No three-round burst here. You touch the trigger and all fifteen rounds spurt out faster than you can blink."

"Will this one fire?" Ken Ching asked.

"Yes. We have six tubes of rounds, so just six of you get to use it. The JG and I fired it last night, and we strongly suggest that you use a two-handed grip and don't touch the trigger until you're ready to kill off a few terrs. Rank has no privilege here. You six guys on this end of the group will fire. Step right up."

Jaybird Sterling was first in line. He hefted the weapon, held it in one hand, then used two hands with a wide-open stance. He looked at Murdock. "Is it loaded and ready to go?"

"Yes. I've touched the button for the right barrel. All you have to do is try not to shoot your foot off as those fifteen rounds come screaming out of the muzzle."

"What about the range?" Jaybird asked.

"I have no idea. We fired out to sea last night. See that

whitish rock out there about a hundred? Take a shot at
it."

Jaybird held the weapon in his right hand, then brought
up his left hand gripping his right in the best police stance.
He aimed through the groove in the rear sight to the tall
sight on the front of the top housing—and touched the
trigger.

The sound came in a splat, a jolting, instantaneous,
lightning-crack blast of fifteen 9mm rounds going off at
once. The sound billowed out and then quieted in an instant. Only the echoes rolling through the hills lasted more
than a microsecond. Then they were gone and Jaybird
stared at the white rock. Fifteen spurts of dirt and rocks
kicked up below and to the right. Jaybird wet his thumb
and first finger in his mouth, then reached out and washed
down the front sight. "Goddamn," he whispered. "Looks
like this weapon fires a little low and to the right."

Murdock took the handgun, opened the rear of it, inserted another fifteen stacked rounds, and passed the
O'Dwyer to the next man, Luke Howard. The gunner's
mate second class looked it over, then lifted it and fired
it with his big right hand. As the same sound belched from
the muzzle of the weapon, it climbed to a forty-five-
degree angle, and Howard snorted. "Yep, this is a two-
fisted little pecker head, no doubt about it."

"Remember this weapon isn't perfected yet. Police are
starting to take notice. They could load it with special
rounds that wouldn't penetrate a body for a second kill.
They could use nonlethal rounds such as pepper balls or
even paint balls. The thinking here is that with seven barrels, you have a lot of shots before reloading. Say you
wasted your first shot with the forty-fives and missed. You
work to the nine-millimeter and give it a try. You still
have two barrels of thirty-eight rounds and three of
twenty-two. The smaller rounds would have more slugs
per tube. Maybe twenty-five in the twenty-two-caliber
barrels.

"Yeah," Canzoneri said. "But you still have only seven
shots out of the seven barrels."

"The talk now is that this can be modified to shoot in

groups of three or five. Which would give you up to five or six times as many tries per barrel."

"I'll take two," Mahanani said. "One for me and one for my uncle who has a pineapple stand out on Oahu."

The rest of the men fired and praised the weapon, then Murdock closed up his dog and pony show. "I'm through here, JG. You have the con."

Lieutenant (j.g.) Gardner looked up at the sun, then down at his watch. "Remember that one-mile measured course we laid out down along the road to the highway?"

The SEALs groaned knowing what came next.

"You're right. Time we had some time trials on this picnic. Strip off your equipment. I only want to see cammie shirts, pants, and boots. This will go on your record. You'll be timed on this one. First man back gets a case of beer. Start stripping."

Gardner took his stopwatch out and handed it to Rafii. "You'll be timekeeper and sit in the shade until we get back. Time each one and write it down on my clipboard. I don't quite trust that leg wound of yours to be completely healed. We've stressed it enough for one day. The rest of us get ready. It's a two-mile run."

Omar Rafii, who came to the U.S. with his parents from Saudi Arabia when he was four, looked down at his right leg. It had taken shrapnel from a hand grenade and had given him a bad time about healing. He'd been to Balboa twice, but this last time they had given him a clean bill and marked him fit for SEAL duty. It didn't hurt anymore. But he admitted that it was a bit sore sometimes after a hike or a tough workout. He had to make it perfect.

Murdock had pulled off his pack and combat harness, but kept on his floppy hat, as did most of the men. He felt light and easy without the usual thirty to forty pounds of gear they packed even on training missions. That could balloon to a hundred pounds on an airdrop.

"Gentlemen, start your engines," Miguel Fernandez said, as they lined up next to the bus's bumper. Murdock and Gardner were in the second row. In the SEAL tradition, every officer in each unit took all of the PT, road-work and exercises that the men did. Every time. It was remarkable the amount of good feeling this brought to the men. Gardner held up his right hand and brought it down, bellowing out, "Go."

Jaybird and Lam led the pack. Both had run track in high school and had a natural stride. They soon put twenty yards on the pack. Everyone else kept up what Murdock figured was about a six-minutes-to-the-mile pace. He had no idea how fast the leaders were running.

It was slightly less than fifteen minutes later when the last of the SEALs galloped over the finish line. He was Luke Howard, and while he was powerful at most things with his six-four, 250-pound body, running fast was not one of them. Jaybird and Lam had raced each other flat out the last fifty yards and hit the tape dead even at 12: 38.2. Gardner laughed when both men asked for a case of beer.

"Hey, we both won, we both get a case," Lam said.

Gardner chuckled. "You guys trying to put me in the poor house? You get a case and you share it." The men paced around to cool down and help their heart rate come down slower. After five minutes, the JG gathered them around. "Any comments or questions about today's exercise?"

"Is it over?" Vinnie Van Dyke asked. Everyone applauded, then watched the officer.

Gardner's face went stern, then he barked out the words. "Damnit, it's over when I say it's over." He scowled at them, then grinned. "Hey, it's over. Everybody, one last policing the area, then it's back on the bus."

During the two days of field training, Murdock had closely watched the new man to the platoon. Frank Victor had been shot up on the last mission with a dangerous wound to his chest. They barely kept him alive getting him choppered to an operating room on an aircraft carrier, where they worked on him for four hours. They finally found most of the pieces of the shattered slug in his chest and repaired the damage of one round to his neck, which had missed his right carotid artery by a half inch. He had stayed on the carrier for two weeks before they felt they could safely fly him to Balboa Naval Hospital in San Diego. He'd been there ever since, over three months now, recuperating and healing. He knew he couldn't function as a SEAL anymore, and had requested a transfer to one of the SEAL service units there on Coronado. He'd be involved, but not in one of the teams.

The new man had good qualifications. Murdock realized that lately he had been selecting bigger, taller, faster men than he had in the past. He decided he'd been influenced by the National Football League, where the linemen were almost all over three-hundred pounds and so fast it made Murdock gasp. They were tall and tough and fast, and Murdock had slued in that direction.

Wade Claymore was the new man in Bravo Squad. He was six-foot three-inches, could run the forty-yard dash in 4.5 seconds, and weighed 230 pounds. He was a radioman second class, twenty-four years old, and unmarried. So far he had blended in well. He'd been in Team Three there in Coronado and had applied four times to transfer into the Third Platoon of Seven. In the interview with Murdock and Gardner, Claymore had impressed them with his maturity and his desire to get into more action than the normal teams got. He said the routine six months tour sitting on a carrier was a total bore and a waste of time. He also had two years of junior college where he played football. Murdock had given him a thumbs-up and Gardner, who would have him in his squad, also approved.

Murdock watched the men as they cleaned up the area for the fifth time, then stepped on board the bus and flaked out on the seats. They were sharp again. They were ready. The last mission had been tough and they had needed some downtime. Now, even with the new man, they were set to go. The only trouble was Murdock had no idea what Don Stroh, their CIA contact, or the CNO might have in mind for his men.

At least he had solved one problem. During their recent three-month hiatus from any action trips, he had talked Tracy Donegan into becoming their driver. He had taken a week-long course in military driving, been issued a military driver's license and then got checked out on the bus they always used for their trips to the desert. Donegan was a car nut, and a mechanic. He'd been the unofficial platoon driver; now he was legitimate.

They should get back to Coronado sometime around 1730. Just in time for a wrap-up and then a great dinner at home. Chris Gardner slid into the seat ahead of Murdock and turned to face him.

"So, how did it go today?"

"Good. No rating, but I loved that line about it's over when I say it's over. Great timing. Also you picked up on that suggestion from Jaybird that a six-minute mile downhill would be too dangerous. Some officers have a hard time taking a suggestion from the men that way, especially when you were wrong." Murdock chuckled. "Hey, don't sweat it. I've been corrected by some of the guys a dozen or more times, and usually it winds up saving some lives. That's why we function the way we do. Okay, you get an A minus. Now don't bother me, I'm going to take a nap." He punched the JG on the shoulder and leaned back in the seat with his head against the side of the bus. He woke up just as the bus pulled into the parking lot outside the Quarterdeck.

3

Murdock peaked his fingers and stared at the training sked
he and JG Gardner had put together last weekend. As with
any good team, now and then you had to go back to basics
to ensure skills, to sharpen timing and to renew dedica-
tion. This was one of those days. Not pleasant, but a task
that had to be done. It was noon on Wednesday, and the
platoon had worked the O course first thing in the morning, recorded the times, then done a six-mile run in the
soft sand at seven minutes to the mile. They had jogged
back with full field gear through knee-deep surf just to
keep their water wings ready.

That afternoon it would be a swim. They would cut
across the arc of the silver strand moving south and come
in at the Navy radio towers just this side of Imperial
Beach. A twelve-mile round trip. About time they
stretched a few swimming muscles. They would go down
underwater on a simulated combat mission. After storming the beach there, they would return on the surface with
one wounded to tow. Yes.

His second in command, JG Gardner, came in with a
huge grin. "Hey, didn't tell you about my flying over the
weekend. Hadn't tried the Black's Beach cliffs for a long
time, the glider port there. Man, what a hoot. The wind
comes up that cliff like a storm and you get off so fast
it's almost scary. But then you can sail and glide and pick
up altitude and come back up on top of the plateau again.
You ever done any hang gliding, Commander?"

"Some, until I almost broke an ankle one day. I sold it and settled for a motorcycle."

"This is perfect country for hang gliding." He looked down at the training sked. "You find any problems with the outline?"

"Nope. Just wondering when Don Stroh is going to be giving us a call. You know what he's trying to do?"

"Haven't heard anything from him."

"He's trying to get our platoon cut out of Team Seven and made an independent platoon answering directly to the NAVSPECWARGRUP-ONE CO."

"He wouldn't do that. Would he?"

"He could." Murdock shook his head. "Masciareli has been giving us some flack again about our orders not going through channels. If Captain Arjarack gets his dander up, he can swing a lot of weight with our admiral, who can yell loudly at the CNO."

"The CNO would have to direct the move. He could do it. Hell, he can do almost anything he wants to with the Navy. Let's say he did push it through. We'd be out of here and into new quarters somewhere. There aren't any spare units available in this lash-up."

"If the CNO said to, they would move in some portables or build us a headquarters. Might be nice."

"Getting out from under Masciareli's thumb, yeah, I know what you mean." Gardner looked at his waterproof watch. "Formation in seven minutes. Full field gear?"

"Just like we meant it."

An hour later the Third Platoon swam fifteen feet below the light chop of the cool Pacific Ocean heading south on a compass reading that would bring them back to land at the Naval Radio Station and antennas just outside of Imperial Beach. Murdock had put Gardner in the lead to set the pace and keep the direction right. So far he was doing a good job. All of the men had the waterproof, underwater-operating Motorolas. It meant the platoon could keep in touch with one another underwater as they moved toward a target. Everything was waterproof—the earpiece, the throat mike, and the unit that hooked on their belts.

Murdock used his radio. "Everyone, let's take a sneak and peek up on top, faces only. I want to count you and see what kind of a spread we have made."

The SEALs surfaced and let only their faces out of the water. Murdock counted, all present, then he checked the distance the farthest SEAL was from the leader. "Who is tail-end Charlie?" he asked on the set.

"Guess that's me, Skipper," Canzoneri said. "Sorry, I'm closing up and will rattle somebody's tail the rest of the way."

"Not a chance. Canzoneri, take the lead. Get the compass board from the JG and move us out when you're ready. You know the target. Move us down there—only this time, we're going down thirty feet. There is simulated firing into the water and we have to go under it. Let's move it, Canzoneri."

They made the objective and lined up in the water near the shore still submerged. Murdock gave the order for two men to hit the beach as scouts. Rafii and Fernandez surfaced and caught a breaker and let it wash them shoreward. Two more breakers deposited them on the beach like two watersoaked logs. They checked the empty beach from one end to the other, then Fernandez used his radio.

"It's a go. All clear. Go."

The rest of the SEALs lifted up and stormed the beach. On a real mission they would be firing as they came. This time they ran up, flopped into the sand, and created a forward defense line. Murdock lay in the sand a moment, then he stood and evaluated the perimeter. "Okay, take ten. Bradford, you were the last puppy up the sand. You getting too old in rank for this kind of life?"

"No, sir, just got my fucking feet mixed up in that last wave. No sweat here, Commander."

"Good. You're our sole wounded man for the trip back to the BUD/S. You were gut shot and may not make it. Mahanani, wrap him up. Distribute his weapon and gear to the other men. We'll go back on the surface. Jaybird has the con with the compass board. Alpha will tow our wounded man. How we going to do it without letting him drown out there?"

"I've got one inflatable I can blow up full of air, but it won't hold up two hundred pounds," Mahanani said.

"Do it," Murdock ordered. "What else?"

"We use his buddy cord under his arms and looped over his chest for a tow rope," Jaybird said.

"What else?" Gardner asked.

"Does it work to tie the legs of pants and fill them full of air and use them as water wings?" Ken Ching asked.

"I don't know," Murdock said. "Take his pants off and try it. It could take two or three pair of pants to keep Bradford from sinking. Mahanani, he's your responsibility. Set things up now."

It took only two minutes to move his pack, combat vest, and Bull Pup to other SEALs. Then Bradford stripped off his pants and tied the bottoms of the cammies with one tough overhand knot. They put Bradford into the water before he started stopping cars on the nearby Silver Strand Boulevard. He lifted the pants high over his head and swung them down. It took four tries before he had enough air in them to do much good. He held the waist of the pants together and put them under his arms, then lifted his feet off the bottom. He floated, feet down, but there was enough air in both units to keep his head and shoulders out of the Pacific Ocean.

Mahanani had the air-filled plastic float tied around Bradford's chest.

"Everyone back in the water," JG Gardner called and the SEALs moved back into the Pacific. Mahanani picked Howard and the new man Claymore to help him with Bradford. Jaybird led out the parade and the SEALs followed in two rough lines in back of him on the surface, moving with an easy crawl stroke.

The two floats worked well at first, but gradually the air seeped out of the cammie pants and they had to pause and refill them. Then Mahanani called for a halt. "Need another pair of pants," he said on the radio.

"Use your own," JG Gardner said and there were hoots of laughter from the others. Mahanani pulled them off and tied the wet pant leg bottoms, then inflated them. They worked better wet than dry. The SEALs swam again.

It took them over an hour and a half to get back to the BUD/S area towing Bradford. Four times they had to stop and reinflate the pants. On the last stop they got a third pair of pants to use for an inflatable. When they straggled up on the beach outside of BUD/S, they flopped on the sand to recover.

Murdock walked around the men, judging their condition. Not bad considering. They almost never would have a six-mile swim to get to a target, and if they did, they wouldn't be towing an injured man. It made good training.

"Okay, guys, that's it for today," Murdock said. "We'll see you bright and ready at oh-eight-hundred. Don't be late, we have a surprise for you."

A half hour later, after the men had cleaned up, changed into their civilian clothes, and left over the Quarterdeck, Lieutenant (j.g.) Gardner looked at Murdock. "What's the surprise for the men tomorrow?"

Murdock grinned. "Hey, JG, that's what you have to come up with between now and then. As for me, I've got a good dinner waiting for me at home. You have fun figuring out the surprise."

In the parking lot, three SEALs checked out a new motorcycle, a Harley Hog.

"How the hell you afford this?" Jaybird asked Lam, who was straddling the machine. "We're talking twenty-five to thirty grand here."

"Sold my car and wiped out my savings account," Lam said. "But she's worth it. I've wanted one of these bikes since I could walk."

"What happens when it rains?" Ching asked.

"Four times a year I'll get wet," Lam said. "Hey, I won't melt. And no, you can't ride her. Not until I get the first scrape or dent in the fenders. Right now I'm late to get down to the dealership. They've got my saddlebags in."

"Saddlebags?" Jaybird asked. "Yeah, she does look a little like a quarter horse at that."

Lam swung at Jaybird, who backed up quickly. "Come

on, Lam, insurance alone is going to cost a bundle on that thing."

"Not much more than my car, about five hundred a year. Now, if there's no more flaming jealous questions, I'm out of here."

Lam started the Hog and turned her into gear, then eased out of the parking lot onto Silver Strand Boulevard and turned left heading for Coronado and the Bay Bridge. He had lots of time. He rolled up to the first light and stopped, putting his right foot down. Oh, yeah, now this was traveling. He might take a thirty-day leave and do the country. Be more fun with another biker. Might be a thought. He'd think it over and look for an another biker.

The Harley-Davidson dealership in San Diego was busy when Lam parked his Hog outside and went in. He got his saddlebags and just had them mounted when three bikers in leather jackets came by and waved.

"Brand-new machine?"

"Hell no, she's three days old," Lam said. They all laughed. The others looked to be in their thirties, maybe one younger.

"You looking for a ride? We've got a short run set for tonight and we need one more man to round out the foursome. Want to go on about sixty-five?"

"Sixty-five, like in miles?"

"Right, up toward the Laguna Mountain area," the redhead said. "Wherever we happen to light. Should be back before midnight."

Lam considered it. The three looked normal enough. All had black leathers but no gang markings. One guy had a full beard that he kept trimmed.

Lam shrugged. "Hey, why not. I haven't had her out on the open road before. Be a kick. When are you going?"

"Just as soon as you get your new Hog wound up. We're all set."

"Let's move," Lam said. The three strode to their bikes, started them, gunned them for show, and then angled out of the parking area to the street and toward the nearby freeway. Lam cruised in beside the back man and they rode in a foursome square onto the freeway and headed out on the U.S. 8 interstate toward El Centro.

"Oh yeah," Lam whispered as they raced along at seventy miles an hour, slanting into the fast lane as one square entity passing everyone in the left lanes, now and then swinging into the number two lane to pass a slower moving rig. They raced through El Cajon and then quickly past Alpine on the freeway. Lance eased the helmet to adjust it a little, glad that the clear plastic shield kept the wind out of his eyes. They rolled up the freeway, edging up to 80mph when the speed limit changed to seventy.

Flying!

Gradually they reduced speed and took the Descanso off ramp. They powered around the corner in front of the Descanso store and kept heading north. Lam didn't ask where they were going. He was too pleased just to relax and ride after a vigorous day of SEAL training. He might have a sore muscle or two tomorrow, but he doubted it. He was in the best shape of his life. What more could he ask for? A great job, a career with the Navy, and now a Harley Hog like he'd wanted for half of his life.

The front bikers slowed when they came to a small store set in a wide place in the road. There was parking just off the pavement, and neon blur that said "Beer" in a sign in the window. The first two bikers swung in, stopped and put down their kickstands. Lam and the other man did the same.

Lam held out his hand to his riding partner. "Hey, I'm Joe Lampedusa." The man with red hair and a trimmed beard took off his helmet and snorted.

"Goddamnit, I hate these fucking helmets, but we got to wear them." He was maybe thirty, built square and heavy with huge arms and an iron-pumped chest. He wiped sweat off his face, rubbed his palm on his jeans and held out his hand to Lam. "I'm Cooley Burdett. Those other jaspers are Woodenhead Woodward and Johnnie Downfield. Not that you'd want to know much more about them."

They walked toward the store where the first two had already stepped inside. "What do you do for a living?" Lam asked.

"I'm manager of a grocery store, a big new Albertson's. We're kicking ass in our area."

They went into the small store. The first two men were already unscrewing the tops of beers. They passed cold ones to Cooley and Lam.

Lam held out his hand to the other two men and found out Downfield was a bank loan officer. He was tall, on the thin side, with long blond hair and dark eyes that tried to bore right through you. He had a three-day beard and must not have owned a comb. Woodward was a personal fitness trainer, he said. He had an athletic build, wide shoulders and narrow hips, and walked like a cat on the prowl. They sat on a bench outside the small store and watched the traffic go by as they tipped their beers. Not many cars on this side road. They talked about their jobs.

"Hate being in the damned bank," Downfield said. "I get all the little old ladies who can't balance their checkbook. Drive me bonkers."

They had another beer and then worked on a third. Lam had watched the men get a little more drunk all the time. He guessed they weren't usually heavy drinkers. They might take these rides to blow off steam. He wondered if they could ride back to town.

Woodward emptied his third beer and snorted. "Had me this old bitch today who wants to be thirty again. She's fifty-five or so and skinny. Now she wants to build up some tone and a little bit of arm muscle. I told her it would take her two hours of work a day and she threw a vase at me. Luckily I caught it. Hell, this is the only way I can blow off steam. All day and half the night I got to be nice to the rich tits."

Cooley had stopped with two beers and he watched the other men with a growing frown. "Come on, guys, we better be getting back to town while you two can still ride," he said. "We don't want to repeat what happened two months ago."

"That was a fucking accident," Woodward said. "Hell, I'm getting another round of beer." He went inside, and a minute later they heard the loud voices.

"What the fuck you mean no more beer?" Woodward

screamed. Cooley rushed inside with Downfield right behind him. Lam hesitated. Maybe he should just ride away.
It could get ugly in there. He lifted his brows and stepped
inside. Woodward had grabbed the shirtfront of the old
clerk and twisted it until the man could barely breathe.
Lam figured the old guy had to be seventy-five.

"Look, granddad. I said we want two more beers. Ain't
my money no good in here? Now, get me the beers."
Woodward let go of the man's shirt and glared at him.
The much smaller clerk cleared his throat, rubbed his
neck, and then slowly shook his head.

"You're on bikes, you get drunk and go down, you
could sue me. No sir. No more beer for you boys."

"You sonofabitch," Woodward bellowed. "You old
fucking bastard. I should knock your head in. We ain't
half-drunk yet. Now get us those beers."

The old man, who Lam decided must be more than
eighty, slowly shook his head and reached under the
counter. He brought up a revolver but held it with the
muzzle pointing down at the floor.

"Guess it's time you boys left," the clerk said.

Woodward shrugged. "What the hell, maybe so." He
started to turn away, then spun back, his fist shot out and
hit the store man on the side of the head and dumped him
sideways behind the counter. The gun went flying from
his hand. Woodward rushed behind the counter and
scooped up the gun, then stared down at the old man.

"I should stomp you good, you dried up old bastard,"
Woodward said. "Pulling a piece on me that way."

"Let's ride," Cooley said. "You put him down, Woodward. Don't mess him any more."

"Bastard," Woodward said, looking down at the old
man still on the floor. "I should stomp some sense into
him." Woodward kicked the old man in the side and he
yelped in pain.

"Come on, Woodward, leave him, let's get the hell out
of here," Cooley said.

"Hell no. He owes me. Pulled a piece on me. I don't
take shit like that off an old cocksucker like this one." He
kicked the old man in the ribs and Lam could hear the

bones breaking. Then Woodward kicked him again and once more.

"I'm out of here," Cooley said.

Woodward looked up. "Yeah, okay. Wonder what's in the damn money till?" He pushed a button on the old-fashioned cash register and it popped open. "Oh, damn, some bills." Woodward scooped them up and grinned.

Lam jolted for the door, ran to his bike, and kicked up the stand. He pushed the Harley down the slight hill, jumped on board, and started the engine. Then he raced down the road. What the hell had he got himself into? That Woodward guy hurt the old man bad, could have put him in the hospital if one of those broken ribs punctured a lung. What the hell was he thinking riding with three guys he didn't even know? He raced away and heard some shouts behind him. Oh, damn. Now the three of them were going to come after him. He wasn't one of them, and he witnessed an attack that could be called attempted murder and robbery. Damn, he had to ride fast and get away from them.

Now Lam could hear the snarl of the heavy bikes behind him on the twisting road. They were gaining. How could he get away from them? The big trouble was all three of them were better bike riders than he was. He had to think of something fast or he would have a tough fight on his hands. Or maybe they would just run him off the road and hope that he died in the crash. He looked back and saw the three bike headlights boring through the darkness. What the hell was he going to do?

4

Lam swept around a sharp curve, gunned the engine, and barely kept on the two-lane roadway. He slashed through the next corner and could hear the engines of the three bikes growling behind him. He looked frantically for a house, a store—anywhere there were people. A California highway patrolman would do just fine. No such luck. No houses, not even any cars coming past. Ahead to the left he saw what looked like a narrow dirt lane slanting off the blacktop. He slowed. Yes, it might work. He turned off and saw a clump of trees ahead in the darkness.

There was a good chance. He killed his engine, killed his lights, and coasted down the slight incline thirty yards into the trees, then pushed the bike deeper into the dark shadows until he was sure no one on the road could see him. Yes, he had a chance. Lam felt his heart pounding in his chest. His blood pressure must be off the scale. Then he heard the wail and whine as the three motorcycles came around the last curve and down the straightaway. He saw the lights; three of them glaring into the night like some strange, vicious, three-eyed beast.

Before he realized it, the three bikes had passed the trail and growled on down the highway heading toward Descanso. He had no idea how far away the small settlement was. His move might just work. His bike was heavier and bigger than the other three. Theoretically it could out perform all of them. When they didn't spot him in Descanso or on the mile or so to the freeway, they just might think that he'd outdistanced them and was away.

Time. They might drop off one rider to wait and watch

for him. He would have to outwait them. Right here was a good spot for a two-hour stop. They would quickly get tired of watching. Riding as well as they were, they must tolerate the booze better than he'd figured they would. He'd had only two beers, so it wouldn't hurt his ability to ride his bike, even though he could drink six beers and hardly feel it. SEAL basic training.

Lam parked the bike and sat down so he could lean against a tree. A small nap might be good. He closed his eyes.

His eyes snapped open and he checked his wristwatch. A quarter of two. They would be sleeping it off somewhere by now. He sat up and then stood and turned his bike around. He started the engine and eased out from the woods to the dirt trail he had come in. At the edge of the blacktopped roadway he paused and watched both ways, then rode out and down the road toward Descanso. He went through the sleeping settlement quietly. There were only a restaurant, a couple of stores, and a filling station. That was about it. When he came to the turnoff for Interstate 8 he paused. He could ride it right into El Cajon and then on to the bridge and home. Or he could take the back route, go east on the interstate to the turnoff due south on S-1 and ride into Campo almost on the U.S./Mexican border. From there it was an easy ride on Highway 94 right into Spring Valley and directly to the bridge to Coronado. Longer and slower, but maybe safer.

He was due at the Quarterdeck at 0800. The time was pushing at 0200. He shook his head and turned west on the freeway. He'd risk that one of them was still watching for him. He doubted it. And anyway he could take one of them with no trouble.

The miles raced by until he came to Alpine. On the ride back a stray thought kept nagging at him. Nobody might find the old man at the small store until morning. He could be in bad shape by then. He had to report it. How? Then he remembered the WETIP phone number. Tips to the police were anonymous and were taken seriously. He turned into Tavern Road just outside of Alpine and found a closed filling station with an outside phone. He sat on his bike and dialed, then gave a concise report about the old man who was beat up in his store above Descanso. There were no questions. He hung up at once and rode away from the booth and back on the freeway.

A short time later he sliced down the freeway through El Cajon and made a straight run to the San Diego–Coronado Bay Bridge.

Then he was home. He put his Harley in the underground storage, wedging it into the individual unit each condo had down there. It was out of sight and safe. Now all he had to do was get three hours of sleep and report for duty first thing in the morning.

The next morning Lam had the TV set turned to the local news station and listened as he tried to eat breakfast. All he could think about was the surprised look in the old man's eyes when Woodward had slugged him and knocked him down. Then the story came on the local TV news.

"East County sheriff's deputies found an elderly man in his wide open small store above Descanso on Highway 79 late last night after a tip came in. The man had been severely beaten and his store robbed. He was conscious for a short time after police arrived and told them that four bikers in black leather jackets had got drunk in his store and knocked him down and then kicked him.

"By the time paramedics arrived on the scene, the elderly store owner had died of his injuries. Police are searching for the four bikers. They have no other descriptions."

Lam closed his eyes. What the hell could he do now? Technically he was part of the group, he was just as guilty of murder in the eyes of the law as Woodward was.

"Oh, damn," Lam said. He looked at the clock. It was time for him to get out his Harley and ride the two miles to work at SEAL Team Seven. He had to go in. He had to act like nothing had happened last night. Nothing at all.

At the parking lot outside the Quarterdeck, he rolled his Hog directly in front of two cars, almost hiding it from a casual view from Silver Strand Boulevard. He waved at the master chief on his way across the Quarterdeck and then eased into Platoon Three and got into his cammies.

In the platoon office, Murdock and Gardner did one last check on the training schedule and made some changes. The phone rang just before 0800 and Murdock picked it up on the second chime.

"Yes sir, this is Platoon Three of the Seventh."

"You guys finally get awake out there? Hell, it's almost lunchtime back here." It was the familiar voice of Don Stroh, their control from the Central Intelligence Agency.

"Should we be talking?" Murdock asked.

"Oh, hell yes. The CNO told me not to worry about what your ringbanger commander out there told you. He and your captain are outranked all over the place. The CNO will send down an assignment through channels, and we'll see how quickly it gets there. Here's the word. You have a special assignment straight from the CNO and my boss. You will be leaving tomorrow morning at oh-eight-hundred in the small business jet for a trip to Washington, D.C. You will take only five men with you. You are to include any Arabic and Farsi speakers, and other men who can pick up a language quickly."

"Arabic? We have two."

"You will have a week of training here, then you'll receive your special assignment."

"I'll bet we won't be going to Switzerland. Six men. That will take some thought. Can you tell me anything more?"

"Not a word. Your Navy orders will be even less specific. I'll see you tomorrow in Virginia."

"That's it?"

"Afraid so. My dance card is all filled up. Best I can do. How's the fishing?"

"You missed the albacore again. Two fish per pole out on the overnight boat. Plus yellow fin, a few Dorado, and some yellowtail. Best fishing here in ten years."

"Thanks for that. Oh, they want you to come naked. No duffel, no bags, no extra cammies, no weapons or combat gear. Just your bodies and your minds. See you tomorrow."

Murdock hung up and looked at Gardner. "JG, I and five men will be flying out tomorrow morning. You'll have the con here. I don't know what the mission is or how long it might last. All I know is that we will have a week's training in Virginia."

"CIA?"

"Good guess. He wants our Arabic and Farsi speakers. That's Rafii and I and who else?"

"I saw in the personnel files that Bradford speaks Italian and some Arabic," Gardner said. "He would pick up Arabic quickly."

"Yes. And Fernandez. With his Spanish, Arabic would be easy."

"For operational efficiency I want Jaybird and Lam," Murdock said. "That makes six. Ask the senior chief to have the master chief cut orders for us and to have those five men meet me here in ten minutes."

Gardner nodded and left.

Murdock stared at the phone. You train and train and wait and wait, and then it all happens overnight. Arabic. So they would be inserted into some Arab country. That wasn't hard to figure out, but which one and why?

They had a minimum training day, doing a twelve-mile hike in full gear and ammo loads, and then went through the kill house. Lieutenant (j.g.) Gardner turned in the best kill ratio with a 92 percent.

"You trying to show off, JG?" Jaybird cracked. "Hell, nobody's ever got a ninety in this league. We've seen some eighties but they were mostly luck."

"Hey, small man with a big mouth," Senior Chief Sadler barked. "Let's show a little respect for a good shooter. You ever shoot that good, I'll shine your shoes for a week."

Jaybird grinned. "Sir, Lieutenant sir. I was just kidding. Congratulations on a fine shoot."

Lam did the poorest he'd ever done on the targets. He had a 53 percent kill score. "Hell, anybody can have an off day," he said.

"Not when it's for real," Murdock said. "That is not when it's for real and you still want to live."

Lam kept to himself. It wasn't unusual. He didn't know what else to do. He hadn't given the police the men's names. He figured he could do that in a later call. Now he was going to be out of the country for a while. What the hell should he do, phone the WETIP tonight? He wasn't sure.

A Navy van met the SEALs in the parking lot at 0730 the next morning.

"Feel naked," Jaybird said.

"Hell, you are naked," Lam jabbed. They all stepped into the van and ten minutes later were at the North Island Naval Air Station looking at one of the small business jets that the military often used for VIPs and select senior officers or groups that needed to move in a rush, like the SEALs. They had flown in this aircraft before.

It was the Gulfstream II, the VC-11. Made by Grumman, it carried a crew of three and could seat nineteen passengers. It was powered by two Rolls-Royce RB163-25 Spey Mk 511-8 turbofan engines. It cruised at 25,000 feet at 581 mph, and had a top ceiling of 43,000 feet. On one tank of jet fuel it could cover 3,712 miles. Originally built as a civilian executive jet, it held first-class-size aircraft seats, a galley, and electronic provisions for laptop computers and other communications equipment.

The crew chief today was a Coast Guard first class petty officer who met them at the door. She had on her class A uniform and smiled.

"Good morning, gentlemen. I know you had breakfast, but if anyone is still hungry, we'll have a snack in two hours and then a hot lunch at eleven-hundred. Our flying time today will be about five hours and twenty-seven minutes if the pilots can hook onto the right jet stream. As you know, the jet stream always flows from west to east, sometimes up to a hundred miles an hour. At least that's what I've heard. Are there any questions?"

"Yeah, are you married?" Jaybird asked.

"That wasn't a question, SEAL, that was an overpowering desire by a poor lost soul who desperately needs to be mothered and protected. Any questions about our flight?"

"Two points scored for a takedown by the lady, and zero points for Jaybird," Lam said. Everyone laughed, including the crew chief. She vanished back into the front of the plane.

The trip went so quickly Murdock didn't have time to think much about where they were going. Transcontinental flight always amazed him. In early days it would take a horseback rider a hundred and fifty days to go from coast to coast if he could find horses that could walk steadily for twenty miles a day. A mach two interceptor, like the F-14, could do the run in less than two hours traveling at 1,544 mph. Amazing.

They landed at Ronald Reagan Washington National Airport, where they rolled up to the transient aircraft terminal and were met by a closed van. A civilian drove and another sat in the front seat beside him with an Ingram submachine gun held casually in one hand. The gunman stepped out as the steps came down on the plane and Murdock went down them.

"Commander Murdock and five SEALs?" the gunman asked.

"Right," Murdock said and the man stepped to the side and opened the van sliding door and motioned them inside. There were seats for twelve and no windows. The man closed the door, stepped into the front seat, and the rig moved away from the plane at once.

"Feels like I'm in a cave," Jaybird said.

"You can look for girls later," Lam said.

They drove for almost an hour, and Murdock figured they were not taking the shortest route to their objective. He could see a little out the windshield. He recognized one building that they had passed twice. Then they were in a rural area and the only thing Murdock could think of was "The Farm," the historic country estate where CIA agents were given most of their training.

After another fifteen minutes they came to a stop at a steel gate. Two guards hustled out of a stone sentry box, checked the outside of the rig, then opened the door and looked inside. The uniformed guard nodded at the SEALs, talked with the driver a minute, then the steel gate rolled back and they drove through.

The rig came to a stop and the front-seat man opened the sliding door. "We're here," he said and the SEALs stepped out of the van into a pleasant country setting with two rambling buildings that looked more like town houses than dormitories. Don Stroh came out the door of the nearest building and waved.

"Right over here, men. Welcome to The Farm. You won't see much of it while you're here, but this is it. Right this way to your quarters. Murdock, you'll bunk with the men as usual. First on the schedule is wardrobe as we movie people say. You'll have two new sets of clothes, all slightly worn, all authentic Syrian civilian. You will wear them while you're here. Yes, gents, our target for tonight is Syria. So let's get cracking. We'll go from your dorm to costuming, then I.D. and then dinner. Right after that we have a three-hour session set for your introduction to the Arabic language and to the culture, and specifically to everything that is Syrian." He looked at Murdock. "Is the fishing really that good on the overnight boats?"

"Better. A month ago they were taking up to four albacore per pole. You missed it again."

They walked over to the barracks, a small building with just eight bunks, designed for small groups. They had no gear to leave there, so Stroh took them to the costuming specialists. Two of the four women were Arabs.

"These will be working-class civilian clothes, absolutely authentic and made in Syria," one of the women said. Her dark eyes surveyed the six men for a moment, then she said something in Arabic to the other woman, who left and came back with a rack of clothes on rolling wheels.

It took an hour to outfit the men with a set of clothes, and then to put together a second set for backup. They took the extra clothes to their barracks packed in Syrian small suitcases that looked as if they were made of cardboard. They were.

"Remember not to sit on the luggage," Lam said.

Dinner was in a mess hall with a serving line and trays with real dishes. The food was surprisingly good.

"Not your usual mess hall chow," Bradford said. He'd been back for seconds on the stuffed pork chops.

Stroh had eaten with them and now led them to another nearby building that held a classroom. A dark-skinned Arab-looking man stood in front of the class dressed much like they were—unremarkable pants and shirt and light jacket. The colors of all the clothes were muted in black and dark browns, with a few dark blues.

"Good evening, gentlemen. My name is Marwan Jablah. I lived in Syria for thirty years before I came to this country, thank God. I'm a naturalized citizen and am proud to work for the CIA. No, I am not a spy, but I teach many men and women how to be spies and how to fade into the crowd in any Syrian city. This is almost the last thing I'll say in English. This is total immersion; you'll be over your head in the Arabic language. You learn it fast or you don't go to the bathroom, or eat or sleep. Now, which of you speak Arabic?"

Murdock and Rafii held up their hands.

He spoke in Arabic then: "Don't help the others. Make them learn the words, the mannerisms. They might be in a situation where they can be killed if they don't know Arabic."

Bradford followed some of it. Fernandez frowned trying to get some meaning from the words. Lam and Jaybird scowled, not understanding a word or inflection.

After three minutes of talking to them in Arabic, the instructor handed out booklets.

"Now, let's get to work. First some basics. Vocabulary, words. This booklet gives you two hundred words you'll need. I'll go over the pronunciation of the words with you. Then you'll have an hour to learn the words and how to say them. Concentrate. Arabic will be as important to you where you're going as the bullets in your weapons. First page, follow me closely. I'll say the word and you read what it means. Then we'll say the word five times."

Murdock relaxed. The man knew what he was doing. Total immersion was the best way to learn a language,

but first you had to have some of the basics, and a ground-
ing of vocabulary. That's what they were getting.

The training session lasted for four hours, with a ten-
minute break in the middle. By the time the men made it
back to their quarters, they were groggy and stuffed with
Arabic.

"We'll speak Arabic in our quarters as well," Murdock
said when they were inside. "If we don't know a word,
we'll ask Ollie. He's our walking Arabic/English
dictionary."

"Is this language training gonna be worth it?" Jaybird
asked.

"If it saves your neck in some Syrian alley, it will be
worth it. If nothing else, we'll have four more men in the
platoon who speak Arabic. Knowing the world today, I
can't think of anything that will help us out more in the
future."

Don Stroh stepped into the big room and the men
started yelling at him in Arabic. He grinned and shook
his head.

"Don't know that lingo, but I hope you aren't saying
bad things about me. Otherwise I chop off your eating
privileges." The CIA man looked at Murdock. "How did
it go?"

"We're getting a start. What are we going to be doing
in Syria? They starting a war or something?"

" 'Something' is right, but we can't talk about it yet.
We're still tying down the exact location of the target."

"Target? Why not use a laser bomb?" Jaybird asked.

"Anonymity, my small friend. We don't want to ad-
vertise that we did this little deed. We don't want anyone
to know who did it. Therefore we can't have anything on
us or with us that might tie the act down to the U.S."

"Weapons?" Murdock asked.

"The last day you get weapon training. All will be with
European-made guns. H and K will be fine, but nothing
U.S.-made."

"We going in by ourselves?" Rafii asked.

"We're still working on that. There will be a field team

of CIA people with you; we just don't know how many or where they will originate."

"They the brains and we're support?" Lam asked.

"On this one we'll need all the brains we can get. But you will be backup and support. Nobody lays down a field of fire like you guys do. Our people understand that and welcome you."

"About damn time," Jaybird said, and they laughed, cutting the tension in the room.

Don Stroh turned back to Murdock. "No lie, four albacore tuna per pole?"

"Earlier in the year. Down to about one and a half to two per pole last week. Of course that's no guarantee. The best fishermen will get six or eight and most tourists will get none or maybe one if they're lucky."

"I plan on being lucky. Maybe when we get back from our Syrian vacation, I can take a run out to San Diego."

"Hopefully. What's up for tomorrow?"

"At oh-eight-hundred you get Syrian law and customs for two hours, then language for two. In the afternoon more Syrian customs and how to fade into a Syrian crowd. Then two more hours of language. After chow call at seventeen-thirty you get three more hours of Arabic. Then you hit the sack and dream in Arabic until the wake up call at oh-five-thirty."

"We're back in boot camp," Lam said.

"Say that in Arabic, sailor," Stroh barked.

"I can't, not yet. Give me three more days."

"Good, now study those Arabic/English books you got this afternoon." Stroh smiled. "Hey, I wouldn't have yelled and screamed to get you guys on this assignment if I didn't think you could handle it. Our CIA guys wanted to go in by themselves. I convinced them they needed some real fighting types along."

"Thanks a bunch, Stroh," Jaybird said.

"No thanks needed. See you tomorrow." Stroh hurried out the door.

"Is that guy for real?" Fernandez asked.

Murdock said the same line in Arabic. Then pointed at

Fernandez. "Repeat what I said. It's Arabic for what you just asked."

They kept working on the language and the book until Murdock called a halt at 2300.

"Lights out, men. We'll hit it again tomorrow."

The Arabic language and customs and culture lessons went well the next three days. Then the last day they went to the range and met their new tools.

Murdock looked at the weapons on the folding table and smiled. He picked up a small submachine gun that could be fired with one hand. It was less than eleven inches long, spit out 9mm Parabellums and could chatter off seven hundred rounds per minute.

A CIA arms specialist nodded at Murdock. "Dandy little weapon. Made in Peru, called the MGP-15. We like it without the folding stock for easy concealment. Magazine takes thirty-two rounds and is interchangeable with the Uzi magazine. We can provide you with one per man if you want them."

They had their pick of weapons. The standard H & K MP-5 was on the table in a configuration that fired .40-caliber Smith and Wesson rounds.

Murdock looked at the display. There were no long weapons on the table. He dug out Stroh. "What's with all of these short-range weapons? Does that mean that we're parachuting in?"

Stroh gave Murdock one of those "I can't tell you" looks, then took a deep breath. "Actually we're not sure yet. Getting into Syria can be a big hairy problem. Their airports and ticketing agencies are notorious for being hard to crack. We could even go over the Golan Heights and use cars to motor into the capital. We're just not sure yet. We have four agents inside Syria now who will be working with you on this project. It's high profile and top secret, if you can use those two ideas together. You find out about it tomorrow morning on your last day here. Our director will give you the briefing with the chief of naval operations sitting beside him."

"Does sound high profile. So, do we get some automatic rifles to look over or not?" Stroh pointed at another table that had a waterproof plastic cover. Two men took off the cover. The table held twelve different automatic rifles. None of U.S. make.

"Yeah, okay. I'd say we should go with the MGP-15 from Peru. I want each man to have one. Will we have any need for sniper rifles?"

"I don't know that much about the situation there," Stroh said. "Wouldn't hurt."

"Okay, let's go with two H and K PSG1 sniper rifles. The 7.62-NATO-round and 20-round magazines. We'll want them with the sound suppressor." Murdock looked over the table of automatic rifles. The rest of the SEALs came up and checked out the group.

"We might as well go with the AK-47," Jaybird said. "We know what it can do and it has a big enough slug to drop a lot of people in a rush."

Murdock looked at the others, who nodded. Bradford picked up a rifle that looked a lot like the M-16. It was a Taiwan copy, only it didn't have the carrying handle on top.

"Doesn't feel right," he said, putting it down. "Let's do the AKs."

Stroh had men uncover the third table. It had more than twenty different small hideout weapons on it.

"I want every man to have an ankle hideout," Murdock said. "Pick the size and caliber you want. I'd go with the revolvers for reliability. No matter how much dust and dirt you wade through, the revolver is going to revolve and fire on demand. A sleek little automatic might jam up on your just when you need it."

Murdock picked the Astra Cadix from Spain. It had a two-inch barrel and in .22-caliber there were nine chambers to hold rounds. No safety, so he'd keep the ninth chamber empty. Beat five full chambers on a six-gun.

Two of the men chose the Welby RIC with a two-and-a-half-inch barrel and packing six chambers of .45 heavy-hitting slugs. When they all had made their picks, the men behind the tables gave each 250 cartridges for his hideout weapon. They would pick up the rifles and sub guns the next day along with the ammo.

Stroh looked at the language coach, Marwan Jablah. "Now, gentlemen, if you will follow me to the classroom, we'll get back to our language study." Jablah said it in Arabic and all but Jaybird understood the thread of what he said. Jaybird grinned and followed them.

The rest of the afternoon and evening were devoted to Syrian culture, everyday customs, and the use of money.

"In Syria we use the Syrian pound, currently worth about fifty cents compared to a dollar. Two Syrian pounds equal one U.S. dollar. Remember that if you get to haggling with a merchant. And haggle they will." He had said all of this in Arabic. They had learned the words for haggle and pound before. Now they understood the system a little better. At 2200, Jablah closed his book. He reverted to English.

"Gentlemen, it's been interesting working with you SEALs. You do things most men just dream of doing. I hope our sessions here have been a help in giving you some tools to use in completing your mission in Syria, and in saving your own lives. I wish you good fortune, long life, and that all of you will return from this mission alive and well."

Murdock shook the man's hand, then turned to Stroh. "Come on, CIA big shot. Tell us what we're going to be doing over there."

Stroh wouldn't budge. He shook his head, put on his game face, and waved Murdock off. "Tomorrow morning is your briefing. Then you'll fly out tomorrow afternoon. Now get a good night's sleep and be ready for what's going to be facing you in the next week."

Jaybird snorted. "Hell, Stroh, we figured out that much. You won't tell us anything else, so I'm putting a Jaybird double whammy on you, so you won't catch a single fish the next time you come out to Lotus Land."

5

Murdock and the five other SEALs, wearing their Syrian outfits, sat in the conference room in a large office building and waited for the admiral to appear with the CIA director. Don Stroh hovered over the six like a mother ruffed grouse, reminding them to sit up straight, not to speak unless spoken to, and to leap to attention when the admiral came into the room.

"Stroh, we been doing that stand-up thing for a hundred and fifty years," Jaybird said.

"Just don't forget."

Stroh wiped his forehead with a linen handkerchief, walked to the door, and came back. The conference room was one he seldom was in. He wasn't in high strategy sessions that went on around the twelve-foot polished oak table. Pens and pads of paper and glasses of water perched at each place around the table, waiting to be used. Bradford had used his already, sketching Jaybird in his Syrian outfit. It was in ballpoint pen but a remarkable likeness.

"Teen-hut!" Jaybird barked. The SEALs jolted to their feet and stood stiffly at attention. Two men walked into the room. One a civilian, short, thin, with a nearly bald head and piercing eyes that swept the room, concentrating on Murdock. He smiled and Murdock gave a curt nod.

"As you were," came the gruff voice of the most recent chief of naval operations, Admiral Alonzo H. Hagerson. The admiral was six-four, had played tight end for the Navy football team and turned down three pro contracts to stay in the Navy. He was considered by all who knew him as a team player with a sharp temper and a wary stance on anything not Navy.

"Be seated, gentlemen," Admiral Hagerson said. "You'll be standing up and running enough before long." The director of the CIA sat as well but Hagerson remained standing. He moved to a display pull-down immediately behind the conference table. Don Stroh remained standing at the back of the room.

Hagerson reached for the pull-down, then stopped and turned and looked at the SEALs. "SEALs of Third Platoon SEAL Team Seven, I welcome you to Washington and Arlington. I've asked you to do some difficult work in the past two years. Now it's time to go to the well once more. The Navy and I appreciate your efforts, and are contrite when you suffer losses. Welcome." He turned back to the chart and pulled it down. It was an eight-foot-wide map of central Syria, showing the capital, Damascus, half of Lebanon and Haifa, Israel. The map also extended out into the Syrian Desert almost to the Jordan border.

"We have a tremendously dangerous problem with Syria. Have you men ever heard of the E bomb?" He looked over the SEALs. "Commander Murdock, what is it?"

"Sir, that would be the electromagnetic pulse, an EMP, similar to that generated by an atomic detonation."

"Yes, quite right. Only now we, and some others, have taken the idea a step farther. Mr. Stroh. Would you ask Professor Ingles to come in."

A moment later a tall man with gray hair and a ramrod in his back marched into the room and to the front.

"Gentlemen, let me introduce Professor Dr. Conrad Ingles of the Massachusetts Institute of Technology, and an advisor to the President's Board of Science. Professor, would you sketch in for us the basics of the EMP and the FCG?"

Professor Ingles went to the center of the room and faced the SEALs. His dark hair showed touches of silver, but his eyes concentrated on the six men with a thirty-year-old's intensity. "It all started back in 1925 when physicist Arthur H. Compton was studying the atom. He demonstrated that firing a stream of highly energetic photons into atoms that have a low atomic number causes them to eject a stream of electrons. This is the Compton Effect and it was fundamental in breaking into the secrets of the atom.

"In 1958 scientists detonated a hydrogen bomb high over an atoll in the middle of the Pacific Ocean. The explosion resulted in a burst of gamma rays that, when striking the oxygen and nitrogen in the atmosphere, released a tsunami of electrons that spread for hundreds of miles. This force blew out streetlights in Hawaii and radio navigation was messed up for eighteen hours as far away as Australia.

"The scientists latched on to this EMP, electromagnetic pulse, development in an attempt to harness this energy and make a new class of weapon. We have made adequate progress in this field, although most of it is classified. The general thinking is that our best minds are now using high-temperature superconductors to create intense magnetic fields. What worries many of us is that some small nations, or even terrorists, could take an idea that the U.S. has discarded and make out of it a practical, cheap flux compression generator.

"This has been described as a poor man's E bomb. It is amazingly simple. It consists of an explosive-packed tube placed inside a slightly larger copper coil. It works this way. An instant before the chemical explosive is set off, the coil is energized by a bank of capacitors. This creates a magnetic field. The explosion in the tube starts at the rear and moves forward. This makes the tube flare outward so it touches the edge of the coil. That creates a short circuit.

"The propagating short has the effect of compressing the magnetic field while reducing the inductance of the coil. What happens then is that the FCG produces a rampaging current pulse, which breaks before the final disintegration of the device. This can produce ramp times of tens of hundreds of microseconds and peak currents of tens of millions of amps. The pulse that shoots out makes a lightning bolt look like a flashbulb.

"This pulse radiates in all directions. It can make fluorescent lights and television sets glow brightly even though they are turned off. Electric wires will arc and short out, and telephone lines will melt. Laptop computers will overload their batteries and fail, and every bit of data on your computer and the set itself will be totally destroyed. Internal combustion engines with electronic ignitions will stall and roll to a stop. Aircraft with electronics will flame out and crash to the ground. Even ships with electronic and computer steering will turn to toast and the ship will go dead in the water. Only diesel-engine cars and trucks will be able to run.

"In effect, all military operations within the FCG area, say a hundred-mile diameter, would be totally blasted out of operation and we would be back in the stone ages throwing rocks at each other instead of missiles.

"One more goodie here for the bad guys. Call it the slo-mo EMP effect. When the original detonation knocked down all communications, the EMP that surged through the electrical systems created localized magnetic fields. When these fields collapse after about fifteen minutes, they cause electric surges to travel through the power and telecommunication infrastructure. This will create strings of explosions and meltdowns hundreds of miles away from the original pulse."

Admiral Hagerson stood. "Professor, how difficult is it to build one of these flux compression generator bombs?"

"Not difficult at all. Almost any competent physicist with a small lab and the needed tools and equipment could make such a device in two or three weeks. There are no hard-to-get materials, no special machine tools needed."

"And what would the cost of such a device be?"

"Some experts say one could be built by terrorists for four hundred dollars. I assume that would be for the basic materials. A lab, three physicists, and a willing government could do the job in less time than three weeks. It really is not all that difficult. When contrasted with building a nuclear warhead, the warhead would be over two million times as hard to build as a pulse bomb."

"Thank you, Professor. Outside you'll find a car ready to take you to a jet to get you back home."

When the professor had left, CIA Director Whitley L. Covington stood and pulled down another display. This was a grainy photo of a one-story building surrounded by a semi-desert.

"Gentlemen, our agents in Syria report that they have confirmed that Syria is building, and may already have completed, its first flux compression generator bomb. We're not sure where this FCG bomb is, or if or when they are going to use it. We do know what their laboratory looks like where they build the weapons. This is it, but we don't exactly know where it is. That is your job. To enter Syria covertly, to make contact with our agents in-country, and to determine the exact location of the laboratory. Then you will attack it and destroy it and any scientists who are working on the project. We expect total obliteration of any additional weapons in whatever stage of completion, and the destruction of all materials and devices needed to make such bombs. Questions?"

Murdock held up his hand.

"Commander."

"Sir, has it been determined yet how we are to infiltrate the country?"

"Not entirely. We've had only six days lead time on this one. We're scratching. You came in on day two. Haifa, Israel, will be your base and control point. The carrier *John C. Stennis CVN 74* will be a hundred miles off Israel's shores to insure that no pulse reaches them, if this is a fifty-mile-radius weapon that Syria is making. It could be larger or smaller, we just don't know. Israel is the logical target. Your ingress into the country could be partly by chopper over the Golan Heights, meeting a car for transport north to Damascus. Or it could be an airdrop with ground transport the final leg into Damascus. This is all in flux at the present time. We're working on it in a minute-by-minute scramble."

"Sir?" Jaybird had his hand up. "What about explosives? This sounds like a smash-and-bash operation and we're going to need heavy amounts of C-5 or TNAZ and primer cord."

"Israel has promised us they can supply as many explosives as you can carry. We do believe that the desert location is somewhere east of Damascus. That area is actually a semi-desert with considerable sheep grazing in selected areas. We assume that the location is to protect the population in case of any accidental explosions or pulses."

"Will we have a general location by the time we meet your operatives in Syria?" Murdock asked.

"We hope so. Half of our men are on the problem right now. We're calling in all of our favors in Baghdad."

"Will we have the use of a SATCOM?" Bradley asked.

"Usually we don't let SATCOMs go into hostile environment countries. Is this a vital concern?"

"Mr. Director," Murdock said. "We've been hung out to dry by diplomatic standoffs several times, and twice we have had no SATCOM to communicate for a possible pickup or even for air support. It is against our fundamental operating guidelines to function in adverse situations without at least one SATCOM."

The director nodded. "Agreed. You have one. We can change the encrypting if it gets captured."

"Before it would be captured, it would be totally destroyed," Bradford said. "Our SATCOMs are prewired for that event."

"Good." The director hesitated and looked at a paper on the big table. "Now to last-minute preparations. You have your clothing and a spare set and old suitcases. You have your weapons selected and will pick them up in fifteen minutes. You have your well-used Syrian I.D. cards, resident papers, and work places. They are all authentic, so there should be no problem being stopped.

"Each of you will receive two thousand Syrian pounds, that's about a thousand U.S. A chopper will take you to the airport at one-fifteen. Have a good meal, and I'll see you off at the chopper pad."

"Will Mr. Stroh be going to Haifa with us?" Murdock asked. "He is tremendously helpful in these situations."

"Yes, he will be your control."

"Thank you, sir."

Admiral Hagerson stood and the SEALs leaped to attention. "Good luck, gentlemen. I'll see you off at the chopper pad." The admiral and the director walked out the door. Don Stroh came up and grinned.

"Couldn't get along without me, right?"

"Right," Murdock said. "Now, where do we go to get our weapons and our ammo? I've felt naked long enough."

6

Near Buraq, Syria

The desert heat rose in waves and shimmers on the dirt road ahead of the army staff car. Dust devils spun along the road, then darted across in front of the car and momentarily blinded the driver.

"Slow down, idiot," a voice shouted from the rear seat. General Mahdi Diar had no time for incompetents. He tried to relax. This was to be the start of his ten days of glory. Ten days to crush the hated Israelis and smash them into the sea. He tipped up the ice-cold drink from the cooler near his feet and drank. Pure lemonade, he told his staff. But they knew that it always contained a generous portion of vodka.

The car's air-conditioning purred quietly, gushing cool air to counteract the harsh reality of the desert's oppressive temperature outside the car.

"How much farther, Sergeant?"

"General, sir, we have covered thirty-two kilometers. We should have only five or six to go."

General Diar settled back in the plush seat and let his imagination run wild. The test would be a dramatic success. The schedule would be moved forward two weeks and all preparations would continue unabated. Then the day of revenge would come. Then Israel would go down, mortally wounded, and would gladly turn over the northern half of itself to Syria, including the rich city of Haifa. With this great victory Diar would have no trouble taking over the reins of government and proclaiming himself president and commanding general of the army. He smiled just thinking about it. His round face flushed for a moment, then returned to normal. He brushed back his black hair just starting to show signs of gray. He would color it again within the week. There could be no hint of age or of slowing down.

The car stopped and the driver got out and swung open the rear door. A blast of hot wind drove into the car, making General Diar gasp. "Idiot, did I tell you to open the door?"

The sergeant held the door open, knowing better than to reply to an angry question from the general. Diar groaned, pushed over to the side of the car, and stepped into the desert sand. The building ahead was low and squat, one story high with a flat roof. In front there was a small door and Diar could see no windows whatsoever. Good. Windows were dangerous.

Diar marched toward the door. Just as he got there someone from inside opened it and waved him in.

Abdul Jabrin stepped back, letting the general come into the small front office of the laboratory. "General, it is good to see you. We are almost ready for our grand experiment."

Diar frowned as he checked the small room. He'd never been here before but had almost daily talks with the workers here and the manager, Jabrin.

"Yes, yes. Do you have anything cold to drink?"

"We do, General. Do you wish to sit on the sofa and relax after your long trip?"

"No, get me the drink, then I'll have a tour of your production facility. You say everything is ready?"

"We have only a few more placements to make. Our men are in the field now and will report by radio when everything is set."

The drink came in an insulated tall mug and the general took a long pull at it, then waved Jabrin forward.

"Now let's see what I've been spending so much money on out here in the damned desert."

They went through two doors and into a laboratory, machine shop, and workroom all combined.

"In this section we fabricate the parts we need—the

tubes, the coils, the capacitors. Nothing exotic or expensive. The explosives we use are common and plentiful. We make the parts here, and put it all together on the tables in the next section."

They moved forward about twenty feet. "Here, General Diar, we assemble the parts. The tube filled with explosives is inserted into the slightly larger stator copper coil and positioned inside the outer canister. You see the whole FCG bomb is no more than six feet long. We have four in the process of assembly here. Two have been completed and we'll use one of them this afternoon in the test."

"So we have only two complete and ready to fire?"

"Yes, sir. These four more will take about a week to do the final assembly. We work carefully, double-checking every part of the process so we won't have any failures."

"Who are the people?"

"All are highly skilled and trained. As you know, General, it took us nearly two months to find the right physicists to spearhead the project. Once we convinced them that this particular bomb would kill no one, and could have the effect of saving thousands of Syrian lives by a quick surrender of our enemy, they came to work. The first flux bomb took longer, because we were experimenting with materials and size and shapes. Now that we have the technique down, the average FCG bomb will take us about four working weeks to complete, start to finish."

"Yes, yes. Now let's see the test. I'm anxious to see how it will go."

"We still have two men in the field. We can check by radio as we drive to the test area. We have taken all of our electronic equipment, including computers and cell phones, and all of our radios out of the laboratory and have driven them fifty miles beyond ground zero. They should be safe there."

"Jabrin, I don't want to know the technical details. I don't have the slightest idea how this new bomb works.

I just need to know that it does and will do the job on call, when I order it to be done."

"Yes, General Diar. We can leave now. Ground zero is only five miles away, farther out in the desert as you specified in your stipulations. We're sixty-five miles from the outskirts of Damascus, so all should be safe there. There is one small town behind us, about twelve miles away. Ordinarily it would be affected, but we have positioned the device against a sheer stone wall nearly a hundred feet high. It will deflect and channel most of the pulse to the east, away from the town of As Suwayda'. They may experience a few outages, but most electronics there will not be affected."

Outside, they drove in the general's air-conditioned car. At the test site stood a square-wall tent with the front flaps open. Two men worked with a long silver tube perched on a pair of sawhorses. Both men had on ear protectors. When the car stopped, one of the men ran up and gave the manager and general the earmuff-type protectors. They held them in their hands.

"General, we'll pull back a couple of hundred yards in your car. It is a diesel so it has no electronic engine components. Good. Your car radio will go out but you can have that replaced."

"How do you set it off?"

"We send an electronic signal that activates a starter circuit in the bomb that energizes the stator coil creating the magnetic field. We'll hear a sharp crack like lightning. No blast, a small explosion, but no mushroom-shaped cloud."

He used the radio and the two men at the bomb hurried away on bicycles. They came toward the general's car. One handed Jabrin a small box with two red buttons on it.

"When you're ready, push both red buttons and that will set it off," one of the men said. Then they bicycled away from the area, toward a small building a hundred yards to the left. General Diar and Jabrin entered the big car and the driver rapidly moved them back two hundred yards, then both men stepped out of the car and put on the ear protectors.

"Ready, General?"

"Yes, I'm ready. Let's get it done."

Jabrin held up the black box and pushed both of the red buttons at the same time. At almost the same instant the jolting crack of a lightning strike blasted into the area. General Diar looked where the sawhorses sat. Now he saw only a few pieces of shattered wood and some scraps of aluminum.

Jabrin took out a cell phone and held it. "Hot to the touch," he said. "It's fried. Will never work again. Now let's get in your diesel-powered car and go check our test area." They asked the driver to turn on the radio. He did but it didn't respond.

Jabrin beamed. "So far, so good. The local electronics are fried and out of business. We have laid out a test track down this straight road into the desert to the east."

At a sign that read "One half mile," they found a display of battery operated radios, laptops, computers, and other handheld electronic devices. Jabrin went from one to another testing them. Some were hot to the touch. None of them worked. All had worked just before the test.

They found the same results at mile markers two, four, and ten. At ten they found the first automobile, an old Citron that had served the lab workers. Jabrin got in and ground the starter for two minutes. The rig would not start. The electronic ignition was blown out.

They stopped again at test sites at twenty, thirty, and fifty miles. All of the electronic devices were burned up. None of the cars with electronic ignition would start. A diesel-powered BMW at thirty miles started on the first try.

At sixty miles two of the gas-powered electronic ignition cars started and two didn't. At sixty-five miles out, all three cars started and the laptops and other electronic devices all worked. Jabrin picked up one of the handheld radios and made a call. He had an instant response.

"Jabrin here. The test is a total success. Bring back to the lab all of our electronic gear. We can get back into production." The manager of the project looked at the general. "So, we have a total success. You have the only other complete device in a safe storage area outside of Damascus. What else do you need from us?"

"I need you to finish those next four flux bombs as quickly as you can. We may need them for backup, or for additional strikes. Now I must get back to my headquarters and get the final step of the plan in motion. Your country thanks you for what you have accomplished here. You'll go down in the history books. Finish those other four as quickly as you can, then get four more on the benches. No telling how many we might need in the next few months."

Riding back to his headquarters outside of Damascus, General Diar celebrated the success of the weapon with more lemonade. This time he doubled the vodka. Tonight he would give the order. Tomorrow the preparations would begin. Day after tomorrow the bomb would be planted and then the attack on the hated Israeli state would start. Syria's success in the first fast push would gain quick approval by the other Arab nations, who would rush to Syria with aid, and those Arab states on Israel's borders would also attack in the big push to shove the Israelis into the sea. Yes. It would happen, and soon.

Rahat Air Base
Near Haifa, Israel

The Gulfstream II VC-11 landed at Rahat Air Base just after 1230 local time. Murdock had set his watch so many times on the zone changes that he had no idea how long they had been flying. He knew they had stopped twice for fuel, but he wasn't sure just where. Murdock stood and yawned. He figured he'd had seven or eight hours sleep on the trip.

"On your feet, SEALs. Time to rise and shine. It's just after noon and we have some work to do. Gather up your gear, your weapons and packs, and we're moving."

A new crew chief lowered the steps and the men straggled out. A lieutenant colonel in a jeep sat on the tarmac waiting for them. Murdock stepped in front of his men and saluted. "Sir, Lieutenant Commander Blake Murdock, U.S. Navy SEALs, reporting as ordered."

The colonel returned the salute and stepped out of the jeep.

"Commander, good to have you on board. We don't have a lot of time to waste. You'll meet two of your countrymen soon. We need to swing by ordnance and outfit you with anything else you need. I understand you'll want C-5 and primer cord. We're well stocked. You have your weapons and ammo. I see you have on the uniform of the day, for Damascus."

A pickup pulled up to the spot. "It's a short ride. Get your men in the pickup and we'll be moving."

An hour later they sat in a small hangar at the edge of the huge airfield. Two CIA agents were there and would be going into Syria with them.

"Hi, I'm Al Trenton, with the Company. My buddy here is Mark Haddad. We're pretend Syrians, but Mark is the real item. Born and raised there and spent twenty years before he got out. We'll be hitchhiking into Syria with you. Did they tell you how we're going to get in?"

"Not a word," Murdock said. "I don't think they had decided before we left. I hope you men know."

"We do," Haddad said. "We'll go in two choppers over the Sea of Galilee down on the south end, then up and over the Golan Heights. Not a lot of action down that way. We'll drop in on a small village called Nawa. That's about ten miles from the main north-south highway."

"No border troops, spotter planes, radar?" Murdock asked. "Is that border that open that we can just fly in?"

"We'll be in low-flying birds grazing the ground, hopefully well below the radar. It's not an easy area to protect, but usually there is little risk down there. If we run into anything military, we'll try to avoid it and hide from it. If we can't, then we're authorized to use our weapons. But that will open a whole can of unhappy snakes we don't want to get involved with."

"Say we make it in with no problem," Jaybird asked. "What happens then?"

"Two of our locals are supposed to meet us at Nawa.

One will be in an old Chevy station wagon, and the other man has a small panel truck with no windows. The problem is, you don't see ten men of our age in a group taking a pleasure ride in Syria. Even the local cops would get their noses out of joint. So we split up and move north. Two in the Chevy and seven of us in the van."

"Do we have a location yet on the lab where they are working?" Lam asked.

"Not for certain. We have two possible locations. Our agents in Damascus have promised we'll have the firm location before we fly out today as soon as it gets dusk."

"How far do we move?" Bradford asked.

Haddad took the question. "Remember this isn't Texas. We're small countries over here. From the sea to the eastern Israeli border here it's only about forty miles. From the Syrian border into Nawa it's only another twenty miles. Then moving north to the capital it's another fifty miles. I know, Los Angeles is larger than this whole area. It's what we have to work with."

"Closer the better," Fernandez said.

"What's next?" Murdock asked.

"We've arranged an early chow call," Trenton said. "They promised me steaks and mashed potatoes and veggies and all the coffee we can drink."

The food was good and then they hurried back to the small hangar where they had left their equipment, weapons, and explosives. A guard on the door guaranteed everything was still there.

A half hour later, two Israeli choppers came in. They had different markings but Jaybird promptly labeled them as H-19 Chickasaws. "We use them a lot for anti-sub duty," Jaybird said. "Seat twelve, so we can have a gunner at both doors. They're not barn burners but they can do a hundred mph flat out, and move over four hundred miles without a drink of petrol."

Don Stroh and the Israeli Air Force light colonel who had met them the first day drove up in a car.

"Hey, Stroh, we get in on the choppers, how do we get back?" Jaybird called.

Stroh looked at the colonel, who shrugged. He faced the SEALs and two CIA agents.

"You have a SATCOM. Mine will be on twenty-four hours a day and monitored. When you're ready to come out, give me a call. We can't penetrate into Syrian airspace any farther than you'll be in tonight. So get near the border somewhere."

Murdock frowned. "You remember a time or two before we've had promises like this."

"I know, I know. Those were extraordinary circumstances. This time there's no problem. Israel will bail you out when it's time. How long will it take?"

"If we spend more than forty-eight hours in Syria, I'd be surprised," Murdock said. "All we need is that firm location and we just go in and do the job and get out."

"How long to lift off?" Lam asked.

The colonel looked at his watch. "Usually it's near dark here by eighteen-thirty. We've got a half hour."

"No machine gun in the door?" Rafii asked.

"You probably won't even see any Syrian military, let alone get in a shoot-out when you land. Their troops are scattered pretty thin down in this region."

Murdock used the time to check every man. He went over the equipment, clothing, and ammo. They each had an ammo bag they would take with them as long as possible. He checked the names on the I.D. and made each man repeat his Syrian name ten times.

"Don't forget those names. It could be your ticket out of Syria, or seat of honor on a funeral pyre."

They loaded on ten minutes later and the birds lifted off. Both the CIA men had the small Peruvian submachine guns. Trenton was anxious to get back.

"I was undercover here for two years, then they pulled me out. It will be good to get back and see the changes they've made. None for the better, I'm sure."

Murdock watched out the open door as the choppers flew as close to the ground as practical. Seldom were they more than a hundred feet over the landscape. Then they buzzed the Sea of Galilee and lifted up to go over the Golan Heights. When they dropped down on the other side they were really in Syria and almost to their destination.

The birds went single file. Murdock was in the first. They landed five hundred yards from a small cluster of lights that he figured was Nawa. When the second chopper lifted off, Murdock gathered the men together.

"What now, Trenton?" Murdock asked. The CIA agent had dropped to the ground and stared toward the lights in the distance. Then they all saw it, a blinking light. Once, twice, three times. Before Murdock could stop him, Trenton used a pencil light and flashed back three times.

"That could get us killed," Murdock whispered.

"No sweat, it's the way we always signal in here. The way the blinks came, this has to be Kayf. Only name I've ever known him by. He's Syrian and a schoolteacher by day. We should go meet him halfway."

They did. Kayf was a small man, five-two, thin and wiry-looking in the pale half moonlight. He and Trenton chattered in Arabic. Murdock caught most of it. Long time no see. What the hell you been doing? How's the wife and daughter? Then, where the hell is the car and truck?

They left quickly hiking across a field that had been cultivated, but Murdock couldn't tell what had been grown. They came to a dirt road and found a sedan, more like a French Citron than a Chevy, and a panel truck that looked ready for the junkyard. "Jaybird and Fernandez in the sedan," Murdock said. "The rest of us in the van. Let's move it. Trenton, we have a positive location on our target?"

"Yes, we do. I'll be in the van with you. We don't go toward Damascus. Instead we take the road out of Nawa east to a village called As Suwayda'. From there we turn north on a secondary road that runs to Suwayda'. Secondary in this country usually means gravel or dirt and not in good condition. Up the road twelve miles from As Suwayda' is a turnoff without markings that wanders to the east again into some low hills. The laboratory is down that dirt lane about three miles and can't be seen from the road."

"Let's do it," Murdock said.

The van passed through the sleeping town of Nawa a little after 2000. Murdock was glad for the empty streets. The van kept a half mile behind the sedan so it didn't look like a caravan. They met only three cars going through the village. Murdock figured it had no more than a hundred residents.

At the next town, Lzra‘, they went across a four-lane roadway that angled north and south. "The main drag into Damascus," Trenton said. He paused, then held his hands over his ears. "Yes. Yes, I receive. Will do." He turned to Murdock. "A small change in plans. Up to yesterday the lab had been unprotected. Today they put up a fifty-man army unit surrounding the site. We couldn't get in there with a crowbar tonight. We have been diverted to the next town, As Suwayda‘, to wait out the night and work out new plans for tomorrow or tomorrow night. We have an agent there, a woman who had been married to a Syrian. She married him in the States, then went back to Syria when he returned to run his family business in Damascus. Her husband died in a car crash three years ago and she stayed to run the firm. It's doing quite well. We recruited her two years ago. She's good, has connections, and is a solid favorite of some of the top men in the government."

"You have a safe house where we won't be noticed?"

"We do. It'll give us time to recon the lab and see what additional help we might need."

"If we had the Bull Pups with us, we could handle fifty men with no trouble. Not with our two sniper rifles and our AK-47s."

The road turned worse, and travel speed dropped to an average of 25mph. It took them over two hours to make the twenty-five miles from the last town to their hold point.

The town was larger, had a business section and houses around the center. Most of the buildings were stone or stucco. The van went past the middle of town and up a dark street, then turned in a driveway and parked behind a two-story structure.

"Bring all your gear, ammo, and weapons," Trenton

whispered. "Somebody may check out the van. The car we left on the street two blocks down. Don't make a sound. We go in a back courtyard and up steps to the second floor. Absolute quiet."

Jaybird had charged a round into his sub-gun, and now he loaded up his gear and ammo, then pushed off the safety. They moved out of the van and up the stairs like dark ghosts. Once on the second floor, they went into two different rooms. Mattresses covered half the floor of each.

"Okay, get some sleep," Murdock said. "Hard telling when we might get much more. We might get into action tomorrow and we might not. I'm going to check with the brass."

He found Trenton in the hall and they went downstairs to the house's living room. It was well furnished. A woman rose from a sofa as they came in. Murdock sucked in a sudden breath. She was tall, dark, with waist-length hair and the most perfect face he'd ever seen. He kept thinking of a twenty-year-old Elizabeth Taylor. She was striking, no makeup, and smiling.

"Good evening, Commander Murdock, and welcome back, Al. I'm Barbara Salman. Welcome to my friend's home. For tonight it's my little corner of the world. Something big is going on out at that lab, and I don't have a hint of what it is."

"We know," Murdock said. Then he told her about the EMP principle and the FCG bomb that the Syrians were building.

"I had no idea. My control here in Syria didn't think I needed to know. Wait until I see him again." She smiled. "Can I get you something to drink? I know this is a dry nation, but there is all sorts of booze available if you know the right people and the right places and have enough money. Fortunately I have all three."

"A beer would be good," Murdock said. She left the room and Murdock and Trenton watched her walk away. It was a lesson in anatomy and of a body in motion.

"Oh, yes," Trenton said. "I've met the lady before but never when she looked like this."

She came back with three bottles of cold beer.

"The bastards are actually making these devices. They could sell them to terrorists all over the world. It's a wonderful nonlethal way to knock out a government before it knows what has happened. Aren't there any defenses against it?"

"Some say they can seal electronic components in airtight boxes, but I'm not sure that would do much good," Murdock said.

"Isn't there anything we can do?"

"You could bring me about fifty RPGs in the morning," Murdock said. "We have a twenty-millimeter shoulder-fired weapon I'd love to have right now. It's U.S.-made so we couldn't bring it in."

"A twenty-millimeter shoulder-fired rifle?" Barbara asked.

"Yes, an amazing weapon we can get air bursts with. We have seven of them, but they're all a continent away."

"What else?" Barbara asked. "How much time would you need at the factory to blow it into rubble?"

"An hour at the most. If we can just walk in and plant our bombs, it wouldn't take more than fifteen minutes."

"You have plenty of C-5?"

"Yes, more than we need. We always like to plan ahead."

"I can give you the hour you need and pull half of the troops off the lab site," Barbara said.

Trenton frowned. "How in hell can you do that?"

"I still have a few friends in town here. This is the seat of government for the province, like a county seat. It has a small army detachment, usually three to six soldiers." Barbara stopped and walked around the room, then came back and faced the two men.

"What would happen if there was an attack on the military post here in town? Maybe a charge detonated at the rear of the building knocking it down. Then a sniper attack at the front. Wouldn't the locals scream for help? They know there are fifty troops only a dozen miles or so away. Wouldn't that commander of the guard unit send at least half of his force into town to defend the military post and try to hunt down the culprits?"

Murdock grinned. "Barbara, are you sure you didn't go to Annapolis or West Point? Your military strategy is sound."

Trenton did a pace around the room, his hands clasped behind his back. When he stopped he smiled. "It could work. The commander of that unit would have radio contact with everyone in the area. We could use one sniper to miss hitting any of the soldiers in the post. Give the impression of a concentrated attack."

"We could have our men in position for an attack on the laboratory," Murdock continued. "If half of the soldiers raced away to town, we would take on the rest of them. Cut them down with our silenced sniper rifles before they knew we were there. If any were inside we would take them out in the blasts. We figure if the place isn't more than eighty feet long and half that wide, we can take it down with charges placed against the outside walls."

"Then go inside and mop up what is left of the devices, supplies, and people," Trenton said. "You know this has to be a black flag operation."

Barbara looked up, curious.

"Oh, black flag," Murdock said. "Goes back to pirate days. When a particularly vicious and hated enemy was encountered, the attacker flew the black flag, meaning no quarter—if they lost, every man fighting against them would be killed. No prisoners taken."

"That would have to be the case here," she said.

They all sat down on the soft chairs and sofa, worked on their beers, and looked at each other.

"All right, we agree this is about our only option," Murdock said. "What about timing? We do our best work after dark."

"To catch the scientists and workers who made the devices, you'd have to hit them before four in the afternoon. Most of them live here in town. They start early, leave early."

"Daytime it is. Say we hit the military post at thirteen-hundred," Murdock said. "That's one P.M. The relief column should be leaving the laboratory by one-fifteen, and we can attack at two P.M."

"Barbara. Do you have any people here who could set the charges and do the sniping?"

"I'll do the charges, and I have a local who has an AK-47 who would love to do the shooting. I can convince him not to hit any of the soldiers."

"Your talents just keep expanding," Murdock said. She smiled and nodded, then looked away.

"If you could find us four more AK-47s, we could arm our two drivers and Mark and me. That would give us ten guns at the lab instead of six. Would you object to that, Commander?"

"All the help we can get."

"Four AK-47s. I could get them in Damascus. Here, I'm not sure. I know of two. Let me make some phone calls." Barbara put down her half-empty beer and left the room.

"She must be a great help to your work here in Syria," Murdock said.

"She is, but she's been walking a razor's edge for the past year. She takes chances she shouldn't. A dozen times she's been a deep breath away from a firing squad. She's fearless, like placing the bomb tomorrow. We can't talk her out of it. She's convinced that the auto wreck that killed her husband was a deliberate act by the Syrian Secret Police. She thinks they suspected that her husband was a spy for the U.S. because he had lived there for several years and came home. It's getting close to time we're going to have to send her back to the States, whether she wants to go or not."

Murdock waved. "I better keep my troops up to date. I'll see you in the morning."

Murdock went to both rooms and quietly told those awake what the score was for the next day. "We'll go in hard and fast, use our silencers as long as we can, then open up with all the AKs we have and hope to put down the rest of the guards. Then we blow the building from the outside, move in and blast the rest of it, and haul ass for the border."

"Only one road in and out of here," Jaybird said.

"That could be a problem, but we won't borrow trouble. If it happens, we'll fight our way through and keep going."

"What about the woman?"

"She'll probably stay here for the rest of the visit with her friend. Her friend knows what Barbara does, and helps her out when she can."

Murdock found the only unclaimed mattress and spread a blanket there and pulled the other one over him. He pushed the Peruvian subgun around so it lay right beside his head. He could have it up and ready to fire in six seconds.

Downstairs there was a sudden pounding on the house's front door. Barbara's friend hurried to the door. She opened it and two angry young Syrian soldiers stood there, their rifles at port arms ready to be used and screaming at her that they had to search the house.

7

As Suwayda', Syria

Most of the SEALs heard the pounding on the door and the subsequent demanding voices. Jaybird was the first to edge the bedroom door open and hurry silently down the hallway until he could see the downstairs area. Not enough. They were at the front door. He lifted the little sub gun, made sure it was off safety and a round in the chamber, then edged down the steps. When he could see into the living room, he found two soldiers, shouting at a woman and waving their AK-47s.

Jaybird caught the Arabic words for "search" and "house." They were busted if these guys got away. Jaybird angled the muzzle of the sub gun around the corner and aimed past the woman, at the closest Syrian soldier. He fired one shot. It sounded like a stick of dynamite going off in the closed room. The round took the foot soldier in the chest, slamming the 9mm Parabellum through his heart and halfway through his spine. He jolted backward and died as he hit the floor.

Jaybird jumped out from behind the corner and centered the sub gun's muzzle on the remaining soldier. The woman had dropped and crawled away to the left. "Drop it," Jaybird said in Arabic, surprised that he remembered the phrase that had been pounded into him. The Syrian soldier stared down at his dead buddy, then at the small submachine gun aimed at him. Slowly he let his rifle down until the muzzle touched the floor, then he dropped it.

There were noises behind him, and Jaybird knew he

had some help. He darted forward, kicked the weapon away, and pushed the soldier to the floor, on his stomach. "Bracelets," Jaybird said without looking back. "Anybody got any plastic?"

One pair dropped over his shoulder and he pulled the Syrian's hands behind his back and cinched them with the plastic riot cuffs.

Murdock knelt beside Jaybird. He checked the pulse on the first man down and shook his head. "We have to find out how he knew to come here and who else knew he was coming," Murdock said. Rafii knelt next to them and turned over the live soldier. His eyes went wide when he saw a countryman staring at him. Rafii hit the man twice in the face with the flat of his hand, snapping his head from one side to the other.

The questions came fast from Rafii in Arabic. Most of the SEALs clustered around couldn't understand all of it. After a dozen questions, Rafii settled back, then suddenly pushed the muzzle of the MPG-15 sub gun against the man's forehead and began to pull the trigger. The Syrian wailed and then nodded. He jabbered for several sentences, then his voice turned into a pleading question.

Rafii looked up. "He and his partner were on regular patrol when they saw the van come into town. They evidently followed us here and watched the house. When it was obvious no one was leaving, and the van was still in the backyard, they decided to investigate. They told no one about their suspicions. They have no radio."

"Car keys," Murdock demanded of the Syrian in Arabic. The man nodded to his right-hand pocket. Murdock dug them out and tossed them to Bradford. "Probably the rig right in front. If it is, drive it to the other side of town. Take Fernandez with you for backup. Leave the car but take the keys and throw them away in some vacant lot. Go."

The two lifted off the floor, took their MGP-15s, and hurried out the back door.

Murdock turned to Rafii. "Didn't I see a lot of wells when we came in? No central water system?"

"Correct. Usually a town well every four or five blocks. The water table must be high here."

"Jaybird and Lam. Use the van. Take these two and drop them down a well in some abandoned spot."

Barbara came into the room. She looked at the dead man and then at the other one. "I know where there's a well we can use. Nobody goes there anymore; it's sour and full of iron seepage." She wore a robe. "Give me five minutes to get some pants on." She hurried away.

By that time everyone in the house was in the living room. The shades had been drawn. The two CIA men watched.

Trenton looked at Murdock. "The two bodies?"

"Black flag. We can't let this one tell anyone what he's seen here tonight. He probably knows some English, or could figure it out. He's a black flag victim."

"Agreed."

Murdock pointed to Rafii and Lam. "Get these two in the van. Out the back door." The two carried the dead man out, then came back for the live one. His eyes were wild and he was shouting Arabic. Murdock put a cloth gag around his mouth and tied it tight at the back of his head.

Barbara came into the room dressed and carrying a small automatic. "Does this change anything?" Murdock asked.

"The two will be missing. They'll find their car. There will be a search, but it won't touch us. I'll make some discreet phone calls in the morning. No, I'd say we're still on for the diversion at noon and the attack fifteen minutes later. Let me go on this burial detail."

She left the room. "There goes a strong woman," Murdock said.

"She has to be, living in a Moslem society," Trenton said. "Women have almost no rights. They can't drive a car, go to school, own property, be seen in public without a husband or a brother. She's had to struggle here. The family business is in the name of her brother-in-law, but she's the brains and the push."

"I'm keeping a man on guard outside the rest of the night," Murdock said. "What time is it?"

"Just past one A.M."

Murdock turned to Jaybird, who was wiping up some spots of blood on the rug. "Need some good cleaner. I'll get some from the owner of the house."

"Then you come out front and relieve me on guard duty. We don't want to be surprised that way again."

Outside, Murdock found some deep shadows beside the house and next to a struggling tree. He had one of the sniper rifles with a round in the chamber and nineteen more in the magazine. He checked the sound suppressor on the front. It was screwed on tightly. He settled in to wait, checking the two cars he could see, watching the one house with lights on. Nobody moved. No dogs barked. Strange, no dogs. Too expensive to feed them probably. Or they had all been served on the dining room table for supper.

Then a figure moved from shadow to shadow next to the row of houses across the street. Murdock aimed the 6 × 42 telescopic sight at the figure. Whoever it was knew what he was doing. Then a moment later Murdock spotted a second figure following the lead of the first one. The man in front, dressed in Syrian-looking civilian clothes, took a long run from one house, across a lot, and to the next structure. At least they weren't Syrian soldiers. Then Murdock grinned. Something vaguely familiar about the way the first man ran, like he had a little hitch in his get-along. Murdock relaxed. The man had to be Bradford who'd been sent to dispose of the car. Fernandez would be behind him.

The pair came almost even with the safe house, then stood and walked casually across the street, and toward where Murdock crouched. He let Bradford get almost to the side of the house, going for the back door, before he stood.

"Bang, bang, Bradford, you're dead."

Bradford jumped a foot to the side and pulled up his sub gun.

"At ease, Bradford. Those feet of yours make more noise than a team of wild horses."

"Scared the shit right out of me, Cap. Don't do that when I'm packing a loaded sub gun. Damn, that was close. I been a little jumpy on this whole hike back."

Fernandez glided up beside them.

"Get some sleep," Murdock said. "We'll need it tomorrow. Then tell Jaybird to get has ass out here. We're doing guard duty the rest of the night."

Later, after he set the guards, Murdock waited up inside until Barbara and his two men came back. Lam nodded. "Both down and in the well. No problems. We didn't even see anyone. Met one car but it was weaving all over the street. Driver must have been sloshed."

Barbara motioned to Murdock and he went over to where she sat on the couch with a drink in her hand. "I shot the soldier before we dropped him in the well. It's a bad habit of mine. In cases like this I tell the person how his government had my husband killed just on the chance he might be a spy for the U.S. He wasn't. Then I shot him."

"How many does that make?"

Barbara looked up quickly, a frown painting her pretty features. "Oh, I understand. Only three. I promised my husband on his grave that I would do ten in his name."

"Hmmmm." He paused. She looked up. "I understand you're in considerable danger, that you've been questioned before."

"True, but one of the top men in the country likes me. I encourage him once a month. He's a good lover. He helps protect me."

"You thinking about going home?"

"Not until I get my ten."

"You have your bomb ready?"

"No, lots of time." She frowned. "I know I don't have to, but a lot of the local customs have rubbed off on me. I want to ask if it's all right with you if I have Lam with me tonight. After . . . after I do one of their people, I never like to sleep alone."

"Lam isn't on guard duty now. What he does is up to him."

"Thanks. You were my first choice, but he says you're committed to some lady in San Diego."

"True." She watched him a moment, then stood and with that catlike grace walked toward her bedroom. When she opened the door, Murdock saw that there was already a light on inside.

The next morning, Murdock watched his men eat in shifts at the small kitchen table. They wolfed down eggs, sausage, hash browns, toast and jam, and lots of coffee. They met the owners of the house, Huda and Akram. Akram worked for the power company and was just leaving for his job. There had been some problems with some of the electronics at the substation. Huda bustled around the kitchen, showing that she was glad to have a lot of mouths to feed. Each of the SEALs gave Huda fifty Syrian pounds for the hospitality. She tried to push it away, but Barbara insisted that she take it.

"You do so much for our cause, and there's little I can do for you. These young men think this is only play money. So take it. You deserve it. We put you in enough danger as it is."

Huda smiled softly. "Maybe someday we can make a difference in my homeland. We appreciate what you men are doing. There is a great evil in our land. It is difficult to do anything about it."

Murdock went out and checked the van. They would need both vehicles to get to the hill behind the laboratory. One of the CIA men had told them about the hill. It would give them cover until the last possible moment.

Barbara would ride a bicycle to the military post. She was known in this small town for her bike rides. Today would be no different except she would have a backpack.

Jaybird had been working with her for an hour to get the right components for the bomb. They at last set on four one-pound blocks of C-5. It was enough to blast the back of the building halfway to the street. She looked at the timer detonators and insisted on taking two.

"Set one for ten minutes, and one for fifteen minutes. If one doesn't work, the other one will."

"They work, ma'am. I've never had one of these misfire on me. Maybe two hundred times I've used them."

"Good, then we have a guaranteed backup."

They taped the four one-pound blocks of C-5 together in pairs. She would place them side by side against the rear wall, push in the arming levers, and ride away.

"Yes, I understand," Barbara said. "I can do this. I've done everything else. This is easy compared to shooting a man." She looked away. Her face worked for a moment. "Sorry. I keep remembering my husband. He was a good man. Came to the States to get an MA in Business Administration from Harvard. Did well. He was not a spy."

Huda insisted on feeding them again before they left. She had meat cakes of some kind, vegetables, baked potatoes, and a delicious salad that Lam liked so well he asked for seconds. Huda beamed.

Jaybird took one final look at the bomb, then handed Barbara the timer detonators. She knew how to set them and activate them.

"Casual, just be casual," Jaybird said. "You're out for a ride. Don't go past the military point in your ride. Ride slowly down that alley and at or about twelve noon, put down the bomb, set the timer detonators, and cover the bomb with some trash or the backpack, then ride away. Stay casual."

Barbara chuckled. "You'd think I was a brand-new bride the way you guys are being so gentle with me. I can do this." She looked at her watch. It was a quarter to twelve. Barbara wheeled the bike out from behind the house and rode away. She went on one of the routes she often used, to avoid as many hills as possible. At five until twelve she pedaled past the small army unit building. It was an old store the military had taken over and it sat alone on the end of a block of businesses. She went around the block and came down the alley behind the army's headquarters. No one was in the alley. She stopped, pretending to have trouble with the bike. At last she laid it down, took off her backpack, and rummaged

in it as if looking for a tool. Then she shook her head and
carried the backpack over to the rear wall of the army
building. It was less than forty feet long and half that
wide. She eased into the shade there and wiped her brow.
Then she reached inside the backpack and looked at the
timer detonator. She pushed it into the hole in the putty-
like C-5 and set the timer for five minutes. She pushed in
the arming lever and stood, wandered back to her bike
and lifted it up. Just as she was about to get on the bike,
a soldier ran up carrying a rifle.

"What did you leave against the wall?" he screamed.
She ignored him, put her foot on the pedal. He called
again, then she felt a sudden hammer blow to her shoulder
and at the same time the sound of a gunshot. She stag-
gered forward. The soldier looked at her, then at the backpack against the wall. He ran toward the building and was
almost there when it exploded. The force of the blast almost knocked Barbara down. She held the bike tightly
until the surge of hot air slammed past her. Then she sat
on the bike and rode away out the short end of the alley
to the street and to the left toward Huda's house. Shot,
she thought. I've been shot. At least she wouldn't have
to worry about the soldier identifying her. That made four.
She smiled through the pain that had gushed into her
brain, nearly making her pass out. For a moment she
thought she would faint. Then she beat it down. She had
to ride and get back to Huda's house. Huda would help
her.

The SEALs and the CIA men loaded into the van and the
sedan and drove away ten minutes before twelve. They
figured it would take them a half hour to get to the spot
they needed this side of the laboratory. Then a two-
hundred-yard hike uphill to the rear slope they wanted that
would let them look down on the laboratory only two
hundred yards away.

Murdock was in the lead sedan with Lam and Jaybird.
They all had their MGP-15 sub guns loaded and ready. A
CIA man drove the car. "We go out ten miles, then turn
off on a narrow dirt road to the right," Murdock said,

reciting from memory the directions he had been given. "The lab is in about three miles. At two point five we leave the car behind a small hill and go up to the top. The lab should be just across a small gully, about two hundred yards away."

They had almost come to the turnoff when they saw three army trucks storming down the road to meet them. The drivers were grim-faced as they raced past the civilian car heading into town.

The three SEALs cheered. "Barbara must have set off her bomb and the CO there called for some help," Murdock said. A short time later a military sedan raced out of the side road and sped after the trucks.

The CIA driver wheeled into the dirt road. "Hope to hell no other rigs come out of this road," the driver said. "They might not like our being here."

"Two and a half," Murdock said. The driver watched the odometer. Just past the 2.5-kilometer reading on the odometer, they saw the hill. It was in front of them and the road turned off to the left to arc around it.

"Show time," Murdock said. The four men piled out of the car and ran up the two-hundred-foot-high hill. Jaybird looked behind them.

"The van is coming," he said. "Not more than half a click down the road."

At the top of the hill they bellied down in the rocks and sand and peered over the top. A military tent had been set up near the laboratory. Another army vehicle had parked near it. Six civilian cars were parked on the other side.

"We wait for the others," Murdock said. He had out field glasses checking the activity below. Only two soldiers paced in front of the only door on the building they could see.

"Concrete block construction," Murdock said. "If it doesn't have massive rebar in it, the thing should shatter and drop the roof right down on what's left."

"Four more troops coming out of the tent," Lam said.

"Changing of the guard," Murdock chanced. "Where the hell are the other twenty-one men?"

"Maybe they sent more than half into town," Jaybird said. "There were three of those two-ton trucks. Ten in each one would be thirty."

The van came off the road and partway up the hill, then stopped and the six men poured out of it and raced up the hill. They were winded when they slid down beside the others.

"We're here," Rafii said. "Let the party begin."

Murdock spread them out on the reverse slope. "We've got a few targets. Most must be in the tent. We do the men out front, then, Lam and Jaybird, do in all the vehicles you see. The rest of us will concentrate on the tent. I want only the silenced sniper rifles to fire first. When we're found out, we all will fire our AK-47s. Snipers, fire away."

Bill Bradford refined his sight, then squeezed the trigger. The 7.62 NATO round jolted through the shirt of the guard standing near the laboratory door, slammed him backward, and left him dying as he slumped to the ground. A second shot seconds later hit the next guard by the front door in the left shoulder as he turned to watch his buddy go down. Another shot followed, smashing into the guard's head and blasting him backward against the building. Nothing moved outside the laboratory.

Murdock whispered into his Motorola personal radio. "Snipers, put three rounds each into the tent, Bradford take the right half."

Moments later the huff of the silenced rifles sounded on the reverse slope of the hill and two hundred yards away small holes showed in the side of the tent. A scream sounded below and three men rushed out of the tent with weapons in hand.

"Everyone, open fire," Murdock said. The three men outside were cut down in five seconds. Then one of the cars in the civilian parking area exploded as a round hit the gas tank and sparked off the built-up vapor in the top of the tank. Another car near it went up in flames. Two suffered blown-out rear tires, and the rest had windshields smashed and holes bored into their radiators and engines.

Men darted out of the tent now, some making it to the

rear of the concrete block laboratory for protection.

"Body count," Murdock said.

"I see five on the ground, two more near the tent opening makes seven," Jaybird reported.

"How many around back?" Murdock asked.

"I saw three make it," Rafii said. "Another one is down near the corner and not moving. I'd say he's a KIA."

"There's got to be more than a dozen down there," Murdock said. "Rafii and Fernandez. Go up fifty yards on the ridge here, then circle past the burning cars and see if you can get a shot behind that structure. Lam and I will circle it from the tent side. Until we get in position, I want some more rounds into that tent."

Murdock and Lam ran fifty yards along the crest of the small hill, then went over the side and darted in zigzag patterns down the side of the hill to the small arroyo at the bottom where there was a four-foot-deep ditch they jumped into. They had not taken any enemy fire.

Murdock led the way another twenty yards along the cover, away from the tent, then they lifted up and looked over the edge of the dirt and rocks.

"Another twenty," Lam said and they hurried down the gully again. This time when they lifted up they could see past the back of the tent and almost to the rear wall of the lab, but not quite.

"Let's move up and see who we can shake out," Murdock said. He touched his throat mike. "Cease fire on the tent. We're moving up toward it. Any more on the body count?"

"One more," Jaybird said. "Some asshole tried to run from the tent to the front door. He didn't make it."

"We're moving." Murdock and Lam ran forward. The tent was still on their right. If no one was looking out the back, they might not have any resistance, Murdock thought. The Syrians had enough to worry about out front. The two came to another small dry watercourse halfway to the tent. Now they could see the rear of the lab. Three men cowered there, one looking quickly around the corner of the concrete block wall, then jerking back.

"Now?" Lam asked.

Murdock nodded. "I'm left," he said. They sighted in over the rocks and sand on the lip of the depression and fired almost at the same time. Murdock held up and let Lam take the next shot on the third Syrian soldier. All three were down.

"The tent?" Lam asked.

Murdock shrugged. "Hell, who wants to live forever?" They came out of the ditch and charged forward. They raked the rear of the tent with the rest of the rounds in their thirty-round magazines, quickly dropped the empty one, and pushed in a new one. There was no response from the tent. They blasted it again with half the rounds in their weapons, then went flat on the ground behind the tent itself.

Lam took out his KA-BAR knife and sliced a two-foot opening in the tent, then dropped to the ground. There was no gunfire through the slit. He lifted up and pushed the canvas aside and looked inside. "Looks like four bodies, all dead as hell. Nobody else. Let's go inside."

They slid through the opening and checked. Five bodies in all. Murdock moved to his throat mike. "All clear in the tent. Bring down the bangers."

They went to the front of the tent and looked at the laboratory door. There had been no opening in the rear or this side of the building.

"A far side door?" Murdock asked.

Lam left the tent on a run, rounded the back of the lab and vanished. He was back in two minutes. "Far as I can see there is only this front door. We got rats in a trap in there."

Jaybird and the four CIA men hurried down the hill with their load of bombs. Each had been crafted that morning. Each used two of the one-pound bricks of C-5 and the detonators already inserted. They had six of the blasters.

"Two on the front," Jaybird said. "The other four on this side evenly spaced. Set the timers for five minutes on signal from the radio. Then push in the activator and run like hell."

"Let's do it," Murdock said.

Rafii and Fernandez hustled around the front of the lab and checked in. "You beat us to them," Rafii said. "We were just about in position when we heard you firing and the three troops behind the lab went down. We on time for the blast?"

Each of the six SEALs had a bomb. They went over the orders again, then Jaybird waved them forward. They placed the bombs and checked in on the radio as ready. When Murdock heard the last one ready, he gave the word to activate.

They did and the six men rushed away from the lab. Those in the tent did the same, until they were seventy or eighty yards away from the building, then they lay down on the ground to wait the blasts.

They came in a ragged series. The two in front of the building went off first, smashing two great holes in the block wall, leaving weird skeletons of reinforcing steel rods angling upward. Then the side bombs went off, pushing in the whole wall and making way for the roof to collapse, falling nearly to the ground on that side, leaving the lab looking like a triangle lying on its back.

The sharp, thundering explosions of the C-5 in the open that way blasted through the air like a runaway atomic chain reaction, dulling the men's hearing and blotting it out for some. A huge cloud of dust billowed up a hundred feet, and rubble and chunks of concrete blocks showered down on the far side of the former building. A slight breeze blew the dust away from the SEALs, and they waited for it to clear. As it did, they saw there were no targets to fire at. Nobody tried to get out of the building. The front of the structure had remained, but the pair of holes where the bombs had been placed were each ten feet wide and almost met in the center. Curiously, the twin doors remained in place.

"Mop up time," Murdock said. The SEALs moved up slowly, ten yards apart, toward the holes in the front of the building. The first two blasts had powered whole concrete blocks, half blocks and down to gravel-sized missiles, straight back through the laboratory. The SEALs stared into the destruction from the front holes. Machines, tables, chairs, lighting fixtures, and a dozen other items littered the floor. The ceiling slanted down from right to left so the left-hand part rested on the floor. Murdock could see two bodies twisted and battered on the floor.

"Do we go in?" Lam asked.

"Will it fall down?" Murdock asked. The SEALs stared at the debris and destruction. Bradford edged inside and pushed on the section of the roof. He couldn't budge it.

"Perfect triangle," he said. "Looks as solid as a square set in a mine tunnel. Safe as your sister's virginity."

Murdock stepped in first. He used his penlight in the gloom. To the left he found what could have been assembly tables against the far wall, where there was still eight-feet of overhead. A body in a white lab coat lay twisted and mangled on the floor under a table. On top of a table still standing he found an aluminum canister a foot in diameter and six feet long. It had split open and inside Murdock saw something that looked like the drawings of the pulse bombs he had seen.

"Check for any more like this one," he said. "I have a body count in here of three. There should be more. Look for them." The others looked and worked back through the clutter and rubble as far as they could go.

"Two bodies back here," someone called.

"Got one canister back this way," Lam said.

"Bring it forward," Murdock said.

They found two more canisters in various stages of completion. Jaybird came up with his backpack of explosives. "Pile them up. We'll give them a half pound. That should bust them up into a million pieces."

"Then we use the WP grenades and burn this sucker right down to the last concrete block," Murdock said. "We might not have much time before the rest of the guard force here comes back. So move it."

They found two more bodies for a count of seven. That matched the cars outside. The SEALs left the rubble of the building and Jaybird set the timer on the half a block of C-5 and they ran for cover. The explosion was muted compared to the others, but when they looked inside they realized that the C-5 had set off the explosives in each of the pulse bombs, but not in the right sequence, so they didn't create the pulses. There wasn't much left inside the slanted roof building.

They threw in four Willy Peter (white phosphorus) hand grenades and watched the fires start.

"Let's get out of here before we have to fight our way out," Murdock said, and the ten men took off at a trot up the hill and over it to their vehicles.

They had just driven a quarter of a mile down the main road when they met two of the army trucks filled with soldiers.

Nobody waved. The SEALs in the sedan scrunched down when the driver warned them. In fifteen minutes they were back at the safe house.

Murdock was the first one in the door. "Barbara, are you all right? How did it go?"

Huda came out of a bedroom and waved at him. "Not so good. Somebody saw her leave the package and shot her. The round hit her shoulder and she's hurting. We can't take her to a doctor here. Nobody gets shot around this area except people the army shoots at."

"You fix her shoulder?"

"Did, but I am not a doctor. She could use one."

Murdock turned. "Jaybird, front and center."

Ten minutes later Jaybird had changed the dressing, put on a binder bandage to close up the wound. The bullet was still in her shoulder and would have to come out.

"I can't do it, pretty lady," Jaybird said. "You're coming with us. Haifa is nice this time of year."

"What about my business?"

Murdock held her hand. "The CIA guys say you were overdue to be sent back to the States. Your brother-in-law will have to step up and take over. He'll do it. Why should he do the job when he had you making all the money for him? Don't worry. We'll have you out of here sometime tonight. Let's get on the road."

The van and the sedan left the village of As Suwayda' just after three that afternoon. The sedan went first, but this time Murdock, Rafii, and Jaybird were in it. Rafii was worried about roadblocks.

"Something happens like this and they'll get up their blocks and see who they can find moving. We should hide out for two weeks, then go singly toward the border. But we can't do that, especially not with the wounded lady."

Murdock wished he had a map. At least they were heading away from the smashed laboratory. Lzra' was the next town, if they got that far. He hadn't checked Bradford but he still must have the SATCOM. They hadn't needed it yet but they could. He remembered seeing Bradford with it on the chopper, then later in the van. Yeah, he had it. Now all they had to do was get through the roadblocks and they'd be in the border area and could bring in the chopper. With any luck they could be in their comfortable bunks tonight at that Israeli air base.

The CIA man driving spoke Arabic like a native. Murdock kept hoping with each turn and slight rise in the road that it wouldn't reveal a roadblock. The driver said the last sign said the main highway north was four kilometers away. "That's right near Lzra'," he said. "Once we get past that it should be clear sailing."

They rounded a small curve in the road and dead ahead not two hundred yards was a roadblock, the best kind, two two-ton trucks blocking the roadway and the shoulder on each side. No way to go around or blast through. The driver slowed and then stopped.

Murdock scowled. Nothing he could do now. It was up to the skill of the CIA man in the front seat. If they had to shoot their way through this roadblock, there would be hell to pay before they could get out of the area. He watched the guard approach the CIA driver and pushed off the safety on his MGP-15 submachine gun.

8

The Syrian guard at the roadblock came closer, looking into the sedan. "Pretend to be asleep," Murdock said softly and he and the other SEALs feigned slumber.

The guard had a submachine gun on a strap over his shoulder with the muzzle aimed downward. "Your papers," he snapped in Arabic. The driver took them out of his shirt pocket, which was where most Syrians carried their identity and travel papers. The guard stared at them a moment, and handed them back. Then he waved at the sleepers.

"A football match and we lost nil to one," the CIA driver said. "I told the men they could sleep going home."

"Where's that?"

"Up near Damascus. Town called Duma."

"Yeah, heard of it. Lost the game, huh?"

"How did you guess? We had no push up the middle and our defense was sloppy. We had two good chances and even a goal kick to tie it, but Hosni choked and couldn't get off a good shot. If you want to coach a football team, I have one all ready for you."

The guard laughed. "Not a chance I'd coach. I got my own problems. Move on through but keep your speed down. Lots of potholes up ahead."

One of the big trucks' engines started and a driver pulled the truck ahead far enough for the sedan to squeeze through. Before he moved, the CIA driver looked back at the guard. "Oh, the rest of the team on this route is behind us in a beat-up van. I won the race to the main highway." The guard nodded and the CIA man drove on through the roadblock.

When they were clear, Murdock spoke up. "How can the other driver possibly know about your football team story?"

"Easy, we use it all the time when we're going with two rigs on one mission. It almost always gets us through quick and easy. This whole country is crazy over soccer."

"Yeah, but you said football."

"That's what soccer is over here. Now we get past the big highway and we're only about ten or twelve miles to Nawa. That's where you guys bail out and call your chopper and I settle down for a long nap until tomorrow morning. Or maybe the next morning. I want things to cool down a little before I drive back up that highway toward Damascus. That hit on the lab is going to have this whole area crawling with secret police and soldiers."

Twenty minutes later the sedan pulled into the same field where the SEALs had met it less than twenty-four hours ago. They bailed out and waved good-bye to the CIA driver. He said he'd wait for the van. Murdock realized he had to wait, too. Bradford and the SATCOM were in the van. They flaked out near the side of the road.

Ten minutes later the van pulled up and the SEALs crawled out. Murdock went over to help Barbara out of the van. She had on tough-looking pants, hiking boots, and a khaki shirt with a jacket on over it. Jaybird had put her right arm in a sling.

"Well, looks like you're ready to travel, young lady," Murdock said.

"Are sure this is the best? I can stay in the van and get back home. I have two or three doctors there who will rip that slug out of me and never say a word to anyone."

Murdock looked at Trenton. The CIA man shook his head. "You have your orders, Barbara. It was either now or in two weeks, so while we have an easy chopper ride out with no hassle, let's use it. The regional director gave me specific instructions by phone just before we came in here."

Barbara lifted her brows. "So, I'm overruled again. I guess you have an extra passenger."

"We'll have a short wait, but I'll get right on the radio

and get our horses in the air." Murdock said good-bye to
the CIA contingent. The two men they came in with
would stay there, so it was seven instead of eight to go
back to Haifa. The two rigs left slowly. Murdock led Barbara over to the SEALs and then yelled at Bradford. He
already had the dish antenna out and opened up. He angled it toward where he thought the satellite should be
and turned on the set. When he got the ready beep from
the set, he pointed at Murdock.

Murdock made the call on Don Stroh's frequency. He
got an immediate response.

"Yes, Big M. How did it go?"

"Mission accomplished. Come and get us, same spot
where we were dropped off."

"Might be a problem there, Murdock."

"No problems, send in one bird, that's all we need."

The SATCOM spit out the transmissions automatically
encrypted and in a burst of less than a hundredth of a
second so it was virtually impossible to triangulate the
signal and pinpoint the sender.

"Some nut crashed a car bomb against the front gate
this afternoon. Blew up the gate and killed four military
police. The whole field is on a lockdown. I couldn't even
get the President in or out of here. The airfield CO said
if you called I was to tell you we can't move a chopper
until after oh-eight-hundred tomorrow."

"You did it again, Stroh. Next time we go fishing I'm
going to drown you. We have to stay here overnight? We
have a Company woman with us who has a rifle slug in
her shoulder. It's badly shot up. She saved our asses today. Now come and get us."

"Can't. I'll be in contact with you right after oh-eight-
hundred. Nothing else I can do, big buddy."

"This better not be a scam you're running on me."

"No scam, Murdock. Just one hell of a mess here se-
curity-wise. There's also been some rumors of a war about
to start, but a friend here said they get those rumors every
month. Just ease down there, have a good sleep, and we'll
contact you again at oh-eight-hundred."

"You did it again, Stroh. I guess there's nothing else
we can do but wait."

"Talk to you in the morning. Out."

Murdock hung up the handset and slammed his palm into the ground.

"He did it again," Jaybird said.

"Big time. Wait until I get my hands on him." Murdock looked over to where Barbara sat. "Bradford, take a look at the lady's shoulder. Do anything for it you can. Rob the other first-aid packets."

"So we wait?" Lam said.

"Yeah, we wait. We have six hours to dark. We better find some kind of cover. Lam, check out that line of brush over there and see if it's thick enough to hide us. Some of the natives might be wondering why seven people are suddenly in one of their fields."

Lam came back in ten minutes with an affirmative and the SEALs and Barbara moved as inconspicuously as possible to the brush and pushed into it. There had been a small stream there but evidently it ran only during a rainy season.

"Get as comfortable as possible," Murdock told the group. "I'm on first guard duty, the rest of you can flake out, sleep, or play tiddlywinks. Quiet is the byword." Murdock moved to the front of the brush and built himself a small OP, where he could see out but nobody out there could see him. He watched the road, and two buildings about half a mile away. He saw no one. Good. Murdock settled down to a two-hour stint of guard duty.

Five Miles at Sea
Off Haifa, Israel

Captain Hassan Khadar did not like boats or the Mediterranean Sea. He was halfway seasick in the chugging small diesel boat that moved ever closer to the hated land of Israel. He had a job to do and he swore on his own grave that he would do it or die trying. He twisted his bearded face as he remembered that General Diar said that dying wasn't enough. He must complete his mission, then if he died it wouldn't matter. He judged the coastline barely visible through the early morning mists. It was 0540 and not yet fully light. Still twenty minutes before the event was supposed to take place. He went to the stern of the small boat and signaled for the pilot to stop. He and a crewman pushed into the water a small rubber boat with an outboard engine. Securely tied on top of it was a six-foot-long device that the general had called the super bomb.

"Don't worry, it won't kill you even up close," General Diar told him. "Just put the rubber boat in the water. The engine is set to aim the craft at the coast. Start the engine and head it on its way. Then at precisely oh-six-hundred push both red buttons on this small black box."

Captain Khadar remembered the instructions. He made sure the six-foot-long cylinder was tied firmly to the rubber boat; then he started the engine and pushed it toward shore. It angled slightly forward, picked up on the morning tidal flow, and sailed toward the Israeli shore and the city of Haifa.

Captain Khadar waited, checking his watch. They followed the small craft shoreward. Now they were less than four miles from the coast. Soon the Israeli patrol boats would be working the area just off shore. The mists lifted and they saw the rubber boat ahead of them a quarter of a mile.

"It's oh-six-hundred," the boatman said.

Khadar jumped, checked his watch, took out the black box, and rested his thumbs on both red buttons. The pilot of the small diesel boat nodded. He had been given a thousand pounds to make this trip. It had to be successful.

Captain Khadar took a deep breath, watched the rubber boat hypnotically, and pushed both the red buttons. Ahead there was a sharp crack like a lightning strike. The rubber boat and the aluminum cylinder vanished in a small explosion. That was it.

Khadar looked at the boatman. "Is that all there is to it?" he asked. The sailor shook his head. The pilot of the small diesel-powered boat grinned, turned the craft north, and pushed the throttles to full. He wanted to get away from Israeli territorial waters as soon as he could.

•   •   •

In the city of Haifa, the early morning streetlights sputtered and then went out. The radio stations and the four television stations cracked and zapped and went off the air. Every traffic signal in a distance forty-five miles inland went blind. Thousands of cars on the highways and streets around Haifa and the entire northern part of Israel sputtered and died. Drivers ground the starters but the engines would not start.

A British Airways passenger liner, about to land at the Haifa airport, suddenly lost power fifty feet from the runway and came down hard. It fell fifty feet to the tarmac, smashing the landing gear and sending the big plane into a ground loop that tore off one wing and engulfed the whole craft in a jet fuel–fed inferno.

Two Israeli jets flying CAP over Haifa at twenty thousand feet suddenly lost all radio contact with the ground and with each other. Both craft flamed out as all electronic components on them failed in a smoking mass. With little lift in their short stubby wings, the planes dropped toward the ground with a hard-won glide path that topped out at forty percent. The pilots tried to restart their engines, but nothing worked. Not even the altimeter functioned, and the pilots desperately made their last move. They hugged their arms to their sides and pulled the ejection handle. The shotgun-shell-like devices exploded, which set off the solid fuel rockets that blasted the ejection seats high away from the doomed F-14 Tomcat fighters. The parachutes opened and the pilots drifted down toward Israel having no idea why their planes failed.

All over the city of Haifa and the surrounding forty-five miles inland, all telephone service failed, more than half of the electrical transmission lines were shorted out or had become masses of melted wiring. Every computer in the whole area was blown out of operation, many melting down from the cabinet to the mother boards.

Police were shocked and impotent. Gradually they found a half dozen diesel-powered cars that worked, but the streets were jammed with gasoline cars with electronic ignitions that wouldn't budge.

The police helicopters were all out of service. One news

reporting helicopter had been zapped in flight and the pilot and reporter had plunged over a thousand feet into a rest home, killing the flyers and six elderly residents.

At the Rahat Air Base just outside of Haifa, the lockdown from the previous night was forgotten as the base radio network fried in an instant and every radio and computer on the base was rendered useless. The base commander used runners to summon his top officers and they talked about the problem. A skinny young second lieutenant, usually teased as being an egghead, lifted his hand.

"General, sir. I think I know what happened here." The rest of the officers looked at him astonished.

"What, Lieutenant Baran? What has happened?"

"We've been hit with an EMP bomb. An electromagnetic pulse bomb of some kind. I've been researching them and some say they are simple and cheap to build. They spit out a stream of gamma rays that upon striking the oxygen and nitrogen in the atmosphere release a tsunami of electrons that can spread for a hundred miles. They will blow out every electronic device within the diameter of the effect."

General Menuhin scowled. "I've heard of the theory. Has it happened here?"

"It looks like it, General. We have no radio, no computers, no ignitions on our autos, no telephone, no radios. Nothing electronic works."

"Everything, Baran?"

"Well, most nonelectronic diesel engines still work. That would be diesel trucks and cars."

"Even if we have any, they can't get through traffic that is clogged all over the metro area," General Menuhin said.

"Sir, some ATVs—those four-wheel-drive recreation vehicles—are diesel. They could drive on sidewalks, around the traffic. If we sent out a dozen of them to outlying bases and had them dig up all the diesel trucks and pickups and cars they could find, we could have enough perhaps to establish some kind of a messenger service between the military bases."

"Right." The general pointed to two aids. "You and

you, go with Baran here and get this into motion. Do it now. We could have an invasion at any moment. Why disable us if somebody didn't want to invade us? We have no air power in this area. No way to tell the rest of the military our problem. Baran, send the first diesel car you find racing south to the nearest telephone that works, or the nearest base with a radio, and inform our main defense headquarters in Tel Aviv of our problem. That has to be first. Get moving on it."

In one of the officers' quarters, Don Stroh broke out his SATCOM and aimed the antenna through a window where the satellite should be. When he plugged the antenna wire into the socket on the set, he noticed that the whole black box was warm to the touch. All the switches were off. He frowned, then turned on the three basic switches. No green lights showed. Nothing happened. He jiggled them, then felt the set again. It was too warm. Something had happened to his SATCOM. Now how was he going to get in touch with Murdock? He frowned. The pilots who flew him in knew where he was. All they had to do was fly in there after the eight o'clock end of the lockdown. Yes, that would work. He went into the bathroom and flipped on the light switch. No light came on. He tried the switches in the rest of the three rooms. Nothing. Must have blown a fuse. He plugged in his electric razor, but it wouldn't work.

Stroh dressed and hurried out the door and toward the headquarters building. He saw men running all over. A dozen more rode bicycles. He didn't see a car or truck in motion anywhere. At the first street he saw six cars with their hoods up and curious drivers trying to figure out why they'd stopped. The farther he ran the more one fact piled upon another. No lights, no engines running, no radio. Haifa had been hit with a EMP bomb. If it were true, Murdock and friends would have to find their own way out of Syria. Nobody from this part of Israel was going to be able to help them for several days, maybe weeks.

9

Nawa, Syria

Murdock had taken his turn at guard around the sleeping band of SEALs and the CIA agent Barbara. Several of the men had given extra shirts they had in their packs to serve as blankets and a pillow for her. It was a chilly but uneventful night. Murdock had feared that the Syrian army would spread out through the area searching for anyone who didn't belong there.

He let the men sleep in after his six o'clock stint was over. By eight that morning he would call Stroh and the emergency would be over at the airfield in Haifa and their chopper would be on the way moments later. Then well before noon they should be back in their quarters in Haifa and Barbara well taken care of at the base hospital.

They hadn't planned on a long trip. Some of the men routinely carried energy bars with them. That would have to be enough for breakfast. He checked Barbara. She was sleeping under a half dozen shirts. He had given her a shot of morphine when she woke up about three A.M.

He went to his lookout nest and checked the surrounding area. No movement. He neither saw nor heard any vehicles. Just a quiet rural area that he hoped would stay that way.

By 0800 the sun was up and warmly greeting them. Murdock roused Bradford and had him set up the SAT-COM. When it was ready Murdock took the handset and made the call.

"Golden Boy, this is grounded, do you read me?"

He let up on the transmit button and waited. There was

no response. He made the call four times. A frown crept over Murdock's face. What in hell was going on? Stroh promised on a stack of promotion papers that he would be there at 0800. He couldn't have slept in.

Twice more Murdock turned on the set and made the call to Stroh in Haifa. Nothing. Maybe the SATCOM was broken or the frequency had been jolted off. He had Bradford check.

"Frequency shows it's right on the button," Bradford said. "Maybe we should try another frequency to make sure that we're transmitting."

"Pick a frequency."

"Go."

"C Q, C Q. This is Murdock in trouble making a confirmation call that I'm transmitting. Can anyone receive me? Please respond. Over."

They heard some static and a faint call but couldn't understand it. Murdock made the call again. This time the answer came back quick and strong.

"Murdock, you are transmitting. You are encrypted. This is Company One. You didn't hear what happened?"

"Company One, I haven't heard anything. We're at Nawa where we're supposed to be. Where is our chopper?"

"At oh-six-hundred your time, Haifa was hit by an EMP bomb. All of the communications and electronics within a fifty-mile radius of Haifa have been knocked out. No radio, no phones, no aircraft can fly. Israel expects a land attack to follow the pulse bomb. Their military has no communications. We can expect no help from Israel in getting you out of there."

"So do we walk?"

"Hold on, we have some assets in the area. Let me check. I'll get back to you on this frequency. Don't change it. Out."

"So what the hell is a pulse bomb?" Bradford asked.

"New. It kills nothing, just knocks out all electronics. That's computers, telephone, radio, everything that has electronics in it including auto engines, fighters, airliners, even navy navigation and gun sighting equipment."

"Didn't hit our radio," Bradford said.

"Then we must be more than fifty miles from Haifa. As I remember the pilot said we were about sixty miles from his air base."

Jaybird had come up and listened. "So what the fuck are we supposed to do now, climb the Golan Heights, then swim the Sea of Galilee and hike on into Haifa?"

"Probably. Get everyone up and ready. We may have to move out of here to a better defensive position."

"Company One calling Murdock."

He grabbed the mike and responded.

"Yes, we have the guided missile cruiser *Shiloh* about fifty miles off Lebanon. They have no electronic problems so evidently they were outside the range of the pulse. They have two SH-60B Seahawks on board and are well within range of your position. I've talked to the *Shiloh*'s skipper and the bird will be taking off in fifteen. After that you can contact him on TAC 4. Nawa, a village almost due east of Haifa and across from the Golan Heights. Correct?"

"Yes, not more than ten miles from the Heights."

"He'll be in touch. His call is Redeye. You'll be transported back to the ship, then we'll decide what to do with you."

"Thanks, Company One. It's a long walk out of here."

Murdock told the rest of the crew what had gone down.

"Heard about that new weapon," Lam said. "It must really work. Everything electronic. Damn, that puts us back in the Stone Age. Israel expects to be attacked?"

"She does," Murdock said. "What a terrific advantage to the invaders. The military would be operating as squads, maybe as a company if they had enough runners."

"They did it nicely in the Civil War," Jaybird said. "But it does take some overhead planning. Who will invade? Jordan or Lebanon?"

"Lebanon doesn't have squat," Fernandez said. "They couldn't invade Pismo Beach. Syria calls the shots in Lebanon. Now they do have an army and an air force. They might charge though Lebanon and into Israel from the north."

Rafii nodded. "Most likely it won't be Jordan. They are

getting settled down more now, no land takeover ambitions. Trying to get into the modern age. My vote would go to Syria."

Fifteen minutes later the SATCOM came on.

"This is Redeye calling Murdock. Can you read me?"

"You must be at ten thousand feet, Redeye. We read you loud and clear. Are you moving?"

"On our way. We have an ETA your position in forty-seven minutes. We have to go down to the Israel border with Lebanon and then slant in to your location."

"Sounds good, Redeye. When we see you coming, we'll give you one red flare on the ground. Right now we have no hostile forces and we expect none. Fly safe now, we need you."

"Do our best, Murdock. Out."

Murdock put two men in the fringes of the brush to keep a lookout, both ways.

"No sense getting surprised now that we have some help on the way." He checked Barbara.

"Heard we do get a chopper after all," she said, a half smile trying to break through. She grimaced. "Sorry. I've never been shot before. No fun, is it?"

"No fun at all. Did I thank you for that bombing? It really pulled most of the defenders away from the lab. Made our job twice as easy as it would have been."

"Glad to do it." She paused and looked up at Murdock. "Do you think I got anyone inside that army HQ?"

"I'd say you must have checked out two of them right into their meeting with Allah."

"Good, that would make six, I think."

"Then the other four you get credit for were at the lab. You count those four and you have your ten, and you're even with the Syrians even before you leave the country."

"I can count four of those?"

"I don't see why not. Nobody else has claimed them. Without your help we might not have won the war. Take them and wipe the slate clean and see what you can do for the Company back in Washington, D.C. I'd think your understanding of the Syrians and how they operate would be a big help to the Near East Desk at the CIA."

She looked up, brows raised. "You think so? I'd never thought of that."

"You'll have a debriefing when you get back. Tell them that you want to be on board and they should jump at the chance to hire you. Pay is good, and nobody is going to be shooting at you."

Ten minutes later the chopper with its "US NAVY" logo on the side chattered its way toward them. Jaybird fired a red flare and the bird sat down fifty feet from the brush line.

Exactly an hour later the SEALs and Barbara were safely onboard the *Shiloh*.

Rahat Air Base
Haifa, Israel

Don Stroh was amazed at the nearly total confusion at the air base. He'd never seen a military operation without radio communications. Runners were taking messages. Slowly the base came into a semblance of organized confusion. Guards at the entrances were beefed up tenfold, with an armored personnel carrier at each gate, their biggest guns trained on the entrances.

Messengers on diesel ATVs from the base recreation office had been dispatched before 0700 to motor as far south as they needed to, to find communications with Tel Aviv, and then relay what had happened to the Haifa area. As soon as the message got through, the air force was expected to send in replacement helicopters and fighter aircraft for defense of the northern sector. Everyone Stroh talked to expected that there would be an invasion. Nobody knew from where or who it would be. Syria and Lebanon were the most likely candidates, he was told.

Slowly the morning passed with no invasion. In town diesel tow trucks were trying to clear a lane for one-way traffic through the thousands of stalled cars on the city streets. Diesel-powered bulldozers shoved cars aside to make one-car-wide corridors through the hopeless crush of stalled cars. Police and firemen needed emergency lanes open.

By 1000 fighter planes swept in and landed at the air

force field. Soon there were twenty defensive fighters on the base, with more on the way. Pairs took off to fly patrol and CAP on Haifa, the twenty miles to the Lebanese border, and the buffer zone. The pilots brought portable radios with them for the air control tower and for headquarters.

By 1100 two transports landed on the airfield with truckloads of handheld radios and larger radio units to re-equip the airfield's headquarters and for military police. Soon radios were issued to the defensive units and infantry on base for security.

It was nearly 1600 before the base commander, Air Force General Menuhin, sat back in his big leather chair and tried to relax. A second and third transport loaded with radios had arrived and the radios were taken by helicopters to the army units in the north. By 2000, virtually all of the military units were in contact with their next higher command.

With first dark two patrols were sent out five miles into the buffer zone to sit and watch for any enemy movement. When nothing happened by midnight, the patrols were ordered to penetrate ten miles beyond the buffer zone into Lebanon, to find concealment and remain there for three days. They would be the advance eyes of the Israeli Army and must report at once any sign of a massive movement of Lebanese or Syrian tanks, trucks, or ground troops. They found their spot that night in darkness, camouflaged their position on the top of a small wooded hill, and settled in to wait the three days. Nobody in the six-man patrol would give odds that they would ever see the third day of their assignment.

Saida, Lebanon

General Mahdi Diar smiled as his air-conditioned limousine toured the back roads and fields around this small Lebanese town. He was over forty miles from the Lebanese border, and well out of the range of the pulse bomb. He had troops and tanks and guns everywhere. This morning the E pulse had hit Haifa and normal life there mushroomed into total chaos. Slowly they were recovering but it wouldn't be in time. He had sent two men into the big city on motorcycles to report back by radio. They had been outside the kill zone of the pulse. He was satisfied with the slow recovery.

All night tonight he would have his troops moving forward under cover of darkness. He would throw fifty thousand men at Israel and over a hundred tanks. His air force would pulverize any token resistance, and he expected his mounted troops and tanks would penetrate all the way to the Haifa city limits before dark tomorrow. Yes, he had the plan, the Israeli troops would be disorganized and flustered at the lack of direction and when they were hit with overwhelming odds they would shatter and scatter and race back into lower Israel.

General Diar watched the sun. Would it never set? Would blessed darkness never come? His slow buildup had been going on for two months and the Israelis had never tumbled to it. Most of the tanks were cleverly camouflaged and hidden. The men had been there on a "joint training exercise" with the Lebanese forces. He would pit fifty thousand men against Israel. He had additional men to call on. At the moment he had over 330,000 men under arms. Eighty percent of them could report for the battle if needed. His tanks would win the day. They could be slightly older than the Israeli tanks, but he had many more of them.

He cursed the sun again in its slow retreat into night. What he had worried about were Israeli patrols in the buffer zone and even into Lebanon to act as an early warning in case of an attack. Any military man would expect an attack after such a bomb went off.

He had sent special squads into the area ten miles into Lebanon, past the buffer zone. They had been in place for three days and were close enough together to spot any Israeli infiltrators. So far they had reported two groups of them. They would leave them alone until the first troops were to hit the ten-mile zone. Then the Israeli frontline lookouts would be eliminated and the troops would move on up to the initial point. The attack would begin promptly at 0530, just before dawn. Yes! General Diar motioned to his aid, a new major this week, who poured him a crystal glass of his favorite lemonade, spiced with half vodka. Yes, it was going to be a delicious war.

10

More than three hundred trucks swept south along the coast highway from Saida. They rolled like a long, jointed worm, with thirty infantrymen crammed into each truck, the men all armed and ready to do battle. Another long worm of trucks wound down the border road that swept south between Lebanon and Syria. Tanks had been rumbling south since darkness along the same roads and some secondary ones. Fifty tanks came down each side of the country, all aimed at Israel.

By midnight most of the trucks had emptied their human loads, turned, and raced back north to pick up more troops. The tanks fanned out to predesignated attack points across the twenty-eight-mile width of Israel. They would be the first wave to push off with daylight.

High on the hill ten miles inside Lebanon, Sergeant Benjamin Ranon watched the first tanks move down the country road. He counted nine of them, then lifted his radio.

"Silverstone One, this is Silver."

He had an immediate reply. "Yes, Silver, go."

"I'm at Point B. I have nine medium tanks passing me moving on toward the buffer zone. I can hear other tanks and what must be large numbers of trucks, but I haven't seen any yet. Things are moving here. Request permission to withdraw toward the buffer zone."

"Request denied. We need you there. You're our only eyes and ears. Watch for more tanks. Protect yourselves. Send out scouts on both sides for a half mile and see what they can learn. Do it now."

"That's a roger. I have a feeling we're in the middle of a massive Arab attack. No identity on the tanks, but Lebanon has few tanks."

"Move those lookouts. Have them stay in place until an hour before daylight, then rush back to your OP and report. Good luck. Yes, we feel, too, that an invasion is underway. We're doing all we can to get ready to repel it. You're helping. Out."

Sergeant Ranon looked at his four men. He chose the smartest and best soldiers of the group. "Babi and Adir. I want you to work to the sides. Babi to the west, Adir to the east. Move out a mile, and find some cover. Count any tanks and trucks you see. Also if there are walking troops, estimate their numbers. Get back here just before dawn. Headquarters is depending on us to tell them how many tanks and men are moving toward our homeland. Go. Don't fire your weapon unless you must to save your life. Now go."

Before they slipped out of their hideout, more tanks rumbled past less than a hundred yards away. The two men waited, then scurried down the sides of the hill and rushed each way from the OP. Sergeant Ranon marked down the time they had left, then added ten more tanks to his total observed and settled down to wait.

Ranon motioned for the other two soldiers to be on the alert, and he pulled a field jacket over his head, took out a map they had given him, and used his penlight to study it. The tanks would have a direct thrust into the buffer zone and on into Israel down this wide valley. Nothing would stop them. He heard trucks again, this time closer. He reached into his pocket and took out a picture of his family he'd taken where they lived far down in the southern part of Israel at Be'er Sheva. His wife and two daughters. A cold sweat broke out on his forehead and he shivered. He would never see them again. He knew that in the very heart of his soul. He was on a suicide patrol. None of them would ever come back from it, nor see the morning sunshine. It was his last day of life. He turned off the light, put the picture in his pocket. He shouldn't have brought it, but he had to. It had been with him on every patrol, every action, every bit of army life he had endured for the past three years. He looked at the other two men in the small outpost. They had no idea what was coming.

A half hour later, the radio came on again. He had turned the volume so low he could barely hear it.

"Silver, this is Silverstone. Any more tanks?"

"Yes, we've seen two groups of ten to twelve. These were slightly west of our position, but we saw them. We figure they have about thirty tanks on a line near here heading for the buffer zone."

"Roger that, Silver. Have your men left?"

"Two out, one on each side. They'll be back in about three hours, just before sunup."

"Well done, Benjamin. Your country won't forget your noble service. Stay alert."

The last transmission came at precisely the same time the rifle round slammed into Sergeant Benjamin's head, jolting him backward and spraying the other two soldiers in the outpost with his blood and skull fragments. Before the sound of the single shot had echoed into the distance, a grenade bounced once and landed at the feet of the two soldiers who were trying to scramble out of the depression so they could roll down the hill. The grenade exploded, sending shrapnel deep into the bodies of both men, killing them instantly.

A Syrian ranger sergeant worked carefully up the hill to the top and checked the three bodies there. "Three down here," he said on a handheld radio. "The other two Israelis didn't lie to us about where the lookout was. We're clear of any crossers in this section. Out."

Ten miles forward, Major Hosni Rahman brought his tank to a stop twenty feet from the buffer zone between Lebanon and Israel. It varied in width, but here his map told him it was about three miles wide. His tank and the three others in his platoon were aimed down a gentle valley that broadened when it came to Israel and continued for some ten miles. It was a perfect spearhead that he would use to dagger deeply into Israel, wiping out any resistance that the Jews might have thrown up in front of him. He knew about the pulse bomb and that the Israeli Army would be seriously handicapped in communications. He figured that most of the tanks they had were diesel-powered, and had not been harmed by the pulse. But if any of them had electronic aiming and firing mechanisms, they would be almost the same as out of action.

He stood in the tank, his head and shoulders out of the top hatch, staring with his binoculars into the night ahead of him. At first he had been surprised to see others using field glasses at night, but he soon learned that the lenses not only magnify the images in the distance, but intensify what light is available. He had begged his section chief for night vision goggles, so he could see what was out there. The colonel said tanks didn't fight at night, so he didn't need the expensive NVG.

Major Rahman had been a career soldier in the Syrian Army. He was due for a promotion to light colonel, and this fight would seal his advancement—but only if his platoon performed well and drove the hated Israelis far, far into their lands. His son would soon join the army. He had attended a military secondary school and then gone to the military academy and would graduate in two months as a second lieutenant. Yes, he was proud of his son who had wanted to follow in his father's footsteps. He would apply for the mechanized service and should wind up commanding a tank within six months.

In that time the Syrian Army could be in Tel Aviv! He savored the thought, then listened to the radio speaker in his ear.

"Red Sector. Be alert. We have reports of platoon-sized line crossers with anti-tank weapons in your area. No contact, but be on the alert."

At once the major dropped down and closed the hatch, locking it in place.

"Watch out the ports, we may have visitors," he snapped at the crew. Nothing could go wrong tonight and in the morning. Absolutely nothing. His whole future depended on it.

Ten minutes later the radio came on again. "The alert is canceled in the Red Sector. The line crossers turned out

to be a small herd of cattle that frequent the zone. Stay
alert. We have an hour and twenty minutes to our attack
time."

The darkness of time crept so slowly forward. Seconds
seemed like minutes and hours. Every five minutes Major
Rahman checked his luminous-dial wristwatch. When it
was 0555, the major roused his crew, put them through a
checklist, and made ready to start the engines. Daylight
was due at 0559. He was ready. He adjusted the earphones
on his headset, locked down the hatch, and waited for the
call on the radio.

0600 and no call. Then it was 0603.

"Tankers, start your engines. You have a twenty-second
warm-up, then we will push off and attack."

It was his section chief and Rahman knew the voice.
They were starting. He said a quick prayer to Allah, then
heard the engines start and labor a moment, then settle
down to a steady purr.

"Tanks, forward. Attack now. Go with Allah."

The tank surged forward along with the other three in
his group. No obstacles lay directly ahead, only the gentle
downslope of the valley. Further on stood an abandoned
shack and outbuildings that they would mash down as
they charged forward. The four tanks were on a line now
moving ahead at ten miles an hour as programmed. Major
Rahman knew there were two companies of infantry behind the four tanks. His tanks would blast any defenses
and plow through them and the infantry would mop up
any resistance left.

It was almost full daylight now, and he could see well
out his viewport. The last quarter mile of the buffer zone
was coming up and so far they had seen no opposition.
He scanned the landscape just ahead of him. A small ravine emptied into the valley from the left, just inside the
border of Israel, but he saw no problem. The land ahead
had been scraped down to bare earth, leaving no cover or
concealment for any soldiers. The major was sure that
machine guns had been set up to cover the area with over-
lapping fields of fire. The machine guns wouldn't hurt the

tank, and his job was to find and silence the guns so the soldiers could move ahead.

The end tank in the row had surged ten yards beyond the others and the major was just ready to use the radio to call him back into line when the tank suddenly tilted sharply forward, diving nose first into a deep ditch.

"Tank trap, all halt," the major yelled into his radio throat mike. "All reverse and hold." He watched the number four tank try to back out of the pit. Only a third of the tank showed, the rest was tracks down into the ditch, which must have been ten feet deep. It was cleverly camouflaged to hide from their air surveillance cameras and forward observers. It probably ran along here for a half mile. The major used the radio on TAC 2 and called the infantry captain behind him.

"Lance, Footloose Two, come in."

"Yes. This is Footloose Two."

"This is Lance One, we've hit tank traps. I need twenty men up here to check out the position of the ditch, how deep and how long and where it ends. On the double."

"Yes sir, Major, three squads on the way. They will probe forward, find the ditch, and set the camo on fire to show its length."

"There will probably be defensive fire," Rahman said.

They tried to pull number four tank out of the trap. Number two fastened chains on it and dug in to reverse. They lost two men to snipers as they chained the tanks together. Then after five minutes of work, the number four tank dug enough of the side of the tank trap away that the other rig could help it get out of the trap. They lost another man as they unhitched the chain.

By then Major Rahman had the length of the trap. He could see the flaming canvas that covered the ditch. It extended for almost a half mile to the left and a quarter of a mile to the right. He chose the right end and turned and charged that way, leaving the advance across the tank traps to the infantry. He told them he'd meet them back on their sector straight ahead. Now he was behind schedule. Rahman cursed the Israelis. There had been no sign of a deep tank trap so close to the border. Now a quarter of a mile down, around the end, and back to his sector. He would be at least fifteen minutes late. He led the four tanks down past infantry that had moved across the tank trap and pushed slowly forward. They also were without any tank support.

There were six tanks stacked up ahead of him at the narrow access across the tank trap. He was standing up in the hatch now, head and shoulders outside, watching everything. There didn't seem to be much Israeli infantry in the area. He dropped down. No use taking a chance like that when he didn't have to. He checked out the port and saw he was now number two in line to get across. His sergeant was moving the unit nicely.

Then right in front of him thirty yards a tank took a direct hit and exploded. He felt his own rig stop and veer to the right, away from the crossing. A round exploded where they had been moments before. Tank rounds. The damned Israeli tanks had come up and waited for a good target. He yelled at his sergeant driver.

"Get us out of here. Move us, hard right and rear, go."

Another tank round slammed into the dirt just ahead of them and the sergeant braked one track and skidded the tank back to the left and then to the right as he powered away from the danger. They worked quickly behind a small mound and for a moment they were safe.

A little more than two thousand feet overhead David "Cool Hand" Eleazar slanted down with the F-18, brought another tank into the crosshairs of his sights, and then pressed the button. The eight-foot-long Maverick air-to-ground missile, with three hundred pounds of high explosives, jetted away from the undercarriage and lanced in at the target. The lead tank in the platoon of four didn't have a chance. The missile exploded with a thundering roar where it hit just in back of the hatch, smashing it flat on one side and detonating the thirty high explosive rounds for their long gun. The whole tank shattered, sending parts raining down on the other three tanks that raced away from the spot, heading in any direction where they thought there might be safety.

Inside his tank Major Hosni Rahman never heard the

missile coming. He had just gained the safety of the hill so the Israeli tanks couldn't see him, when his world ceased to exist and he flashed into the nothingness of a dreamless sleep and a world without light or thought or anything but the blackness of an eternal void.

Northern Military Command
Haifa, Israel

Israeli Air Force General Menuhin stared at an eight-foot-high map of the border with Lebanon that hung on his office wall. It was an extremely large-scale map with villages, hills and ravines, buildings, and the bunkers, machine guns, tank hideouts, and the strength of all the frontline Israeli troops committed to defending the home border.

Jagged red lines had been drawn on the board showing incursions by enemy tanks.

"They have to be Syrian tanks," an aid said. "Lebanon doesn't have any tanks of this type."

Other markers on the board showed where tanks had been destroyed or disabled. Eighteen of the invading tanks had been taken out of action.

"One platoon of armor in the eastern section has penetrated almost ten miles," a colonel said. "They have no infantry with them and our planes have cut them down from four to two. We have a section of our tanks moving up into that area and they should contact the enemy within ten minutes."

"Our MLR has been overrun in six places, and the ground troops are moving behind tanks in a slow advance on half of the front," a colonel with infantry patches on his shoulders said. "We have lost about five hundred men so far, dead and wounded, but all have been carried back to our new front lines, where diesel trucks have been picking them up and returning them to hospitals in the rear areas."

"General, we have a real air war going on out there," a bird colonel with wings on his blouse said. "We brought up thirty fighters, but Syria has put over fifty in the air to support their tanks. Another thirty of our F-14s and F-18s have been sent up, but won't be armed and ready for another hour. Then it's fifteen minutes from Tel Aviv up to the front."

"Where can we stop them?" General Menuhin asked.

"We need control of the air. So far our F-14s have shot down eight of the enemy and we have lost two. We need to sweep the planes out of the picture."

"Do we know where they fly from?" General Menuhin asked.

"We think they come from an airfield called Dimashq, in Syria about twenty miles south of Damascus."

"Have two of our F-14s follow any returning Syrian planes and report where they land. Then put twenty F-18s on a raid to take out as many of the planes on the ground as possible and to disrupt the air base by hitting hangars, fuel dumps, launching facilities. Do that before nightfall. Go."

The air force colonel hurried out of the room.

"Gentlemen, we have about half the radios that we usually use. That restricts us. We must get more radios into the field to contact the infantry and tank defenders. Eleazar, get on a radio to Tel Aviv and have them dig up all the radios they can find that we can use, and have them flown up here within two hours. Go."

General Menuhin moved to his desk and drummed his fingers on top. "Now, what else can we do? Fly in reserves from the south, anywhere south. We need more men in the front line to blunt this charge. One captain told me he had a hundred and forty men to defend a stretch of the MLR three hundred yards across. At dawn he found three tanks coming at him and behind them more than a thousand Syrian troops stumbling over each other eager to die for Allah. He had to pull back. He lost twenty men, and now is in a holding position on a wooded hill where the tanks can't come and where the Syrian Army is unwilling to charge up the hill. We need more help for heroes like this one. Who can rattle out the most troops by chopper the fastest?"

Nobody volunteered. He looked around his staff. "Major Almon, you get the job. Get a chopper from here down to Tel Aviv and start rounding up troops. Cooks, medics, artillery—anybody who can carry a rifle. Get a thousand men up here with weapons and three hundred rounds of ammo each before dark. Go."

The general picked up his phone, scowled at the high whine he got from the line, and slammed it down. "When in hell are they going to get the lights back on and the phones fixed? Damn pulse bomb is causing a lot more problems than I figured it would." He shook his head and went back to the map where men and women had been moving the markers. He saw another incursion over ten miles into Israel along the eastern border.

"We've got to stop them before they get any farther."

11

**On the *Shiloh*
Off Haifa, Israel**

Murdock looked up, surprise washing over his face. "Stroh, how the hell did you get here?"

"The same way you did. Only I had to borrow a flown-in army radio in Haifa and call Tel Aviv. They put me through to the embassy, where they patched me into a SATCOM and I called my chief in D.C. and he called the *Shiloh*. Somebody on board sent a chopper into Haifa to get me and here we all are."

"Why? The pulse bomb has been dropped. The Syrians or somebody must be invading Israel. They have their hands full, but I don't see how we can help."

"An invasion for sure. The Syrians made two tank thrusts. One went down the coast road and penetrated over ten miles. The other one went down the east side of Israel next to the Sea of Galilee. Almost no opposition for ten miles."

The rest of the SEALs crowded around in the compartment they'd been given to use while on board.

"Don't see how that involves us," Jaybird said.

"You will." Stroh sat down on the edge of a bunk and frowned. "The drive came fast, almost none of the Jews in the area could get away. On the eastern thrust, the tanks and infantry quickly overran a kibbutz where ten American college students were staying for the summer. One of the girls was on a web site chat room with a friend and the friend in New York found out exactly where she was and who was with her in their talk. Then the whole thing fried when the pulse went out and the girl in New York knew something bad had happened. She called her father who is some biggie in the city and he called his senator and the senator . . . you know the rest."

"So we go in and bring them out," Lam said. "No big deal. Ten of them, six of us. We can get sixteen in a sixty, can't we, Jaybird?"

"Maybe, if nobody breathes. If they don't bring their two torpedoes along. They don't have any firepower. We'd have to use MGs in the doors. They can leave the sensor operator on board the ship to lighten the load a little."

"Where are the students?" Murdock asked.

Stroh pulled out a map he'd wrangled from the ship's library and spread it out. It showed just the northern half of Israel, parts of Lebanon, the Golan Heights, some of Syria, and Jordan. Stroh moved the map for better light and stabbed his finger on the paper.

"Right about here is where the last chat room conversation was made. We don't know if they are still there, if they are hiding, or if they have been captured by the Syrians. This little place is off the main north-south road and is called Zefat."

"Does the ship's captain know about this problem?" Murdock asked.

"He does. He got a redline transmission from the CNO giving us carte blanche. He's not pleased but it isn't often he gets orders directly from the CNO and he'll give us anything we need and help in any way he can. Oh, did I mention that one of the missing girls is the daughter of a U.S. senator, and one of the boys is the son of the most famous rabbi in New York City?"

"Timing?"

"ASAP."

"The rest of the SEALs?"

"They are on the way. The CNO said we might need more than six. You can't wait for them. I know you just came back from an operation on the pulse bomb factory. Good work there. That was yesterday, which is the SEALs' traditionally easy day. It's now about sixteen-hundred. Can you be ready to go in at first dark?"

Murdock looked at him and was not at all surprised.
"Tonight?

"Tonight. The ship's CO figures you can chopper in
with a sixty. They'll take everything out of it they can
and won't have any torpedoes, which should help the
speed and load factor."

"Do we get to keep the chopper there while we find the
kids?" Lam asked.

"That's a negative. The bird will drop you and fly. Too
dangerous keeping the chopper in enemy territory. He'll
be close by there south in Israel, and will come get you
when you call him on your SATCOM. But we're talking
maybe ten to twenty miles. Remember these are tiny little
countries over here."

"At least he won't be all the way out to the ship."

"We'll need resupply on ammo and materials, first-aid
kits, some field chow," Bradford said.

"No problem," Stroh answered. "You've established
that the standard twenty-millimeter cannon round will fire
in your Bull Pups. You just don't get the airburst. You
can have all of the local twenties you can carry."

"Let's get our heads together and work out a supply
list," Murdock said.

"I'll be happy to take it to the captain. We should have
more than three hours before liftoff. I'll get some special
chow set up for you. Steak is always good before a mission."

Murdock gathered the men around and Jaybird wrote
out the shopping list. Murdock realized it was mostly
ammo and first aid and field rations. Then he worked over
the equipment of each man and would replace anything
needed from the Marine detachment on board.

By 1830 they were ready and digesting their T-bone
steaks.

"Those steaks came right out of the officers' mess supplies," Stroh said. "Evidently the captain wants to keep
the CNO happy. It's always good to have friends in high
places."

The SH-60 Seahawk on the aft chopper pad was

warmed up and ready to go when the SEALs filed up to it ten minutes before liftoff time. The pilot waved at them and ushered them on board.

"Howdy. I'm Lieutenant Wilson," the pilot said. "Good to meet you. I've never had a flight before where the CNO issued the orders. Pretty high level for me. You can contact me on TAC two once I drop you off. We'll be going in below the fighting in Israeli territory and then up to that little town. Cut down our time over enemy territory. Then I ram it back south just past the fighting and find a hiding spot until you call me back in." He frowned for a minute. "We've stripped her bare of everything we could. Just hope we don't have too big a load with sixteen bodies."

Murdock took the lieutenant's hand. "Lieutenant Commander Murdock. Some of these college girls might not weigh over a hundred and ten pounds," Murdock said. "That will help. We've had bad luck lately on pickups by choppers. I hope this time we don't have any foul-ups."

"Going down like clockwork, Commander. Let's button her up and get out of here."

The flight from the cruiser to Israel, across the area just north of Haifa, and then ten miles north took only thirty-three minutes at a hundred and forty-five miles an hour, the cruising speed of the SH-60 chopper. They had skimmed over the ground, sometimes only fifty feet above the landmass. This had been over land controlled by the Israelis. Now almost at the far eastern border of Israel, the chopper turned north.

"We have to get across the area where they are fighting," Lieutenant Wilson said. "Never flown over an MLR before. There should be some firefights or something to let us know where it is. We can go low and fast over it, giving any of the Syrians only a few seconds to shoot at us, or high and slower. I pick the low and fast run. Hey, up there, I just saw a flare. There, some tracers. We're going down on the brush tops and race across. Coming up fast."

Murdock watched as the bird slammed forward at full speed. It looked faster twenty feet off the turf. Murdock

saw the outlines of a trench and what he was sure were
a half dozen muzzle blast flashes, then they were past
them and in the clear and in Syrian occupied territory.

The pilot slanted to the east a little and found the outline of the road north and followed it along the Golan
Heights. Four or five miles later a road angled off to the
left and they took it and found the small town showing a
lot of lights.

"Zefat?" Murdock asked.

"Should be. It's the only village of any size around here
according to our maps. It has lots of growing fields around
it."

Murdock watched from the cockpit.

"I'll set down just south of the place about a mile. Then
maybe they won't hear my bird. Check your SATCOM
as soon as you can on TAC two. I'll be moving south
about fifteen miles back across the MLR."

Murdock nodded. He went back to the side door and
was the first man off as the SH-60 settled gently to the
ground. The SEALs charged away from the LZ and
headed for a small patch of woods just to the left. There
they paused while Bradford angled the foldout antenna,
caught the satellite, and gave the mike to Murdock.

"This is Search One calling Skyhook."

"Yes, Search One. Skyhook and you're five by five.
Good luck."

Bradford folded the antenna on the last syllable, and
stuffed it in the pouch and hurried after the other SEALs,
who had started toward the town.

"From talk by this girl before, we know that the kibbutz
is south and west from the town itself about a mile. We're
south enough, let's move a little more west and see if we
can spot any buildings in this gloom. We sure could use
a full moon about now."

"Let's not wait," Rafii said. "No full moon for another
three weeks."

They hiked single file ten yards apart across a field,
then over a road, and angled more west. After a half mile,
Lam used his Motorola. "I've got buildings ahead. Looks
like a farm with barracks. Could be the kibbutz."

Murdock hurried up to Lam and studied the place with his binoculars. "Still a few lights on in the long buildings. Could be barracks. Let's go up softly and take a look."

The SEALs moved forward without a sound. Lam sprinted to the side of the first long, one-story building and looked in a lighted window. He dropped down and used the radio.

"Only three men in the place. All are wearing uniforms. Syrian soldiers. I'll check the house."

He was gone another ten minutes. Then his voice came over the earpieces.

"Yes, this was the place. I have with me Mr. Benazar. He runs the farm. He wants to talk. We'll come back to your position."

Leor Benazar was over seventy, stooped, with a weathered face, pure white hair, and hands as rough as corncobs. He shook Murdock's hand.

"The bastards swept in here so fast we didn't even know they were coming. We were still trying to figure out what went wrong with our telephone and electricity and our computers. Then they were shooting at us before breakfast and we tried to get to our weapons but we were way too late. They killed one of my farmhands and wounded one of the kids. One of your boys. Shot him in the shoulder. We patched him up best we could. Then before noon they hustled your ten Americans in a truck and hauled them away. I speak pretty good Arabic and I heard a sergeant tell the truck driver to take them to the police station in town. I don't know if they got there or are still there."

"How do we find the police station?"

"It's on the main street, right across from the synagogue. There's a filling station beside it."

"How far from here?"

"About two miles. Want a ride? You're not Israeli."

"No, sir. We're U.S. Navy SEALs."

"I thought they were frogmen."

"We are, but we also work on land and parachute in. That ride would be good, if it won't get you in trouble."

"These damned Syrians aren't going to be around long

enough to give us much trouble. And I see that I'll be well protected."

The kibbutz manager had a nearly new pickup the SEALs jumped into, and he drove them to within a block of the center of town. They saw only two Syrians, both standing guard near a grocery store.

The SEALs bailed out of the pickup, quietly thanked Benazar, and melted into the shadows.

"We're about a block and a half from the police station," Murdock whispered. "We'll move out until we're within fifty yards and take cover. Looks like they left almost no security here. The troops must have almost all gone forward to the fighting."

When they moved forward to the fifty-yard position, they could see only one sentry outside the police station. They watched it for twenty minutes. Only one soldier came and went inside. Nobody left. No military vehicles were in sight.

"Let's take it," Murdock said. "Bradford, one silent shot on the sentry, then we're in the door. When you're ready, Bradford."

At once a chucking sound came and the sentry on post by the police station door jolted backward and hit the wall, then crumpled to the ground and didn't move.

"Now," Murdock said and the six men rushed forward, weapons ready. Murdock and Lam wound up one on each side of the door. Murdock grabbed the doorknob and nodded at Lam. Murdock jerked the door open and Lam charged in to the left, Murdock followed him covering the right side.

They found a large office with a desk and two chairs. A lone soldier sat behind the desk with a pen in hand and no weapon in sight.

"Where are the prisoners?" Murdock asked in Arabic.

The man froze then reached toward his belt. Murdock shot him in the shoulder. The sound of the 5.56 round exploding in the room billowed around them, making it harder for them to hear for a half a minute. The soldier fell off the chair and Lam grabbed him before his hand caught his belted pistol.

Murdock repeated the question in Arabic. Lam drew the man's pistol and pushed the muzzle against his head.

"Okay," he said. "Only American prisoners. They are not here. Search. Not here. We sent them north. The colonel ordered them taken to him."

"What colonel?" Murdock asked.

"Colonel Esam Lyad. He's the commander of the East Sector."

"Where is he?"

"Five miles north on the highway, at the command post."

"Do you want to live, Sergeant?"

"If it is Allah's will."

"Allah is telling you to find a vehicle for us, a car, truck, or pickup. Get it in here now."

"But I don't . . ."

Lam pushed the muzzle of the pistol under his chin and pressed upward in the soft tissue. The sergeant stood to relieve the pressure.

"A vehicle," Murdock said, still speaking Arabic.

"I am the only one here." His eyes went wide and moved from side to side. "Yes, one vehicle in back. Through here." He motioned to a door.

"Too fast," Murdock said in English. "Could be a trap. Rafii, check it out."

Rafii ran to the door and swung it open standing against the wall. Two rounds blasted through the opening. He flipped in a hand grenade after letting it cook for two seconds. It went off just as it hit the floor. When the shrapnel stopped zinging through the open door, Rafii darted into the room.

"All clear in here. Two men with subguns. Both down and out of it. Checking the next door."

A few moments later the earpieces sounded again. "All clear to the rear door. A half-ton pickup out here, army green."

Ten minutes later the pickup came to a stop on a slight rise. The trembling Syrian sergeant pointed ahead. "There, the lights to the left. A big tent and four smaller ones. That's the regimental CP."

"Where would the prisoners be?"

"No idea."

"Get one fast or eat your own pistol," Lam said.

"Well . . . they could . . . More likely in one of the tents to the side. The rest are for the officers."

"Which side?"

"Left side, away from the lights."

"Out," Murdock said. "Park the rig over there off the road, and tie and gag our Syrian mouthpiece. We might need him again. Let's move."

Lam led the way toward the last tent, just out of the glare of a diesel-powered generator light splash. The tents were set up in a field of harvested wheat. Lam took them down a small watercourse with a swath of small trees and brush along the sides. It gave them complete cover to within fifty yards of the tent.

"I'll go up and check it out," Lam said. Murdock went with him. They walked slowly, as if they belonged there, then when behind the tent, dropped to the ground, and crawled the last twenty feet. Lam put his ear to the canvas and listened. He shook his head.

Murdock drew his KA-BAR fighting knife and cut a slit in the canvas, slowly so it wouldn't make any noise. When it was eight inches long, he leaned up, pulled the sides apart and looked inside. Two bodies lay to one side on the floor. The front of the tent had been tied shut and a guard sat on one of eight folding cots. He dozed. Murdock made the slice longer, then again until it touched the floor. He squirmed through the opening and eased up to the guard. He put one arm around his neck and jerked back enough to awaken the man. Then Murdock's other hand clamped over the guard's mouth. He came awake with a jolt, his eyes wild.

"Easy, and live," Murdock said in Arabic. "Where are the American prisoners?"

The guard pointed to the two bodies.

"Those two dead ones are two of the American students?"

The man nodded.

"Where are the others?"

The guard pointed toward the north.

"I'm taking my hand off your mouth, but if you scream or talk loudly, I'll snap your neck and you'll be dead in two minutes, do you understand?"

He nodded. Murdock let his hand come off the man's mouth. The Syrian soldier swallowed. "Easy on my throat," he said.

"Where north did they take the American students?"

"Jut inside the buffer zone is our Eastern Area divisional headquarters. The driver told me they were going up there."

"You're guarding dead men?"

"They were only wounded until an hour ago, then the second one died."

Lam looked at Murdock, who nodded.

"Can you tell us why they took the American students north?"

"For prisoner exchange."

"You heard nothing about ransom?"

"We're soldiers, not terrorists."

Lam had taken his KA-BAR out of its sheath, and when Murdock nodded the second time, he plunged the sharp blade into the Syrian's side, slanting it upward under his ribs into his heart. The Syrian's eyes went wide. He gave a muffled cry, then slumped off the cot he had been sitting on, his hands twitching and spasming, as the muscles failed to get enough blood and his brain triggered a dozen alarms, just as his lungs stopped working. He slumped to the floor dead, sprawled near the two dead American students.

"I.D.?" Lam asked.

"The Syrians would have already stripped everything from the students' bodies. Let's choggie."

They checked out the slot in the tent, found it all clear, and slid out, then ran bent over into the darker shadows they had come from and into the brush.

As they jogged back to the pickup, Murdock told the others what he and Lam had found. Rafii started the engine and wheeled it up the road to the north. They kept the police office captive with them. They passed within fifty yards of the regimental headquarters, but there was no guard or military on the highway. Down a short side road they saw a tank and three trucks with a dozen soldiers milling around beside them. None of them even looked up as the pickup powered past to the north.

Jaybird started it. "Just how the hell do six of us get eight American students out of a division field headquarters? They will have more protection around that place than Fort Knox."

"Maybe. First we look it over, let Lam have a look and then maybe take our little Syrian buddy here with us and have him get the information about where the American students are being held. Can't be anything solid up here, just tents and more tents. Give us an edge, don't you think?"

They drove six miles to find the glow of lights ahead. They parked the pickup and took the Syrian with them this time. They left his hands tied behind his back and his gag on, but untied his feet.

"He's yours, Rafii. Keep him with us, and then tell him what we want him to do when we figure it out. It's a hike from here. Lam, go out forty and be careful. They must have some security out around a divisional HQ."

They worked ahead a cautious yard at a time. Lam went slowly, made certain before moving. So far they had encountered no security patrols or interior guards, but that meant nothing about what might be ahead. The men edged forward over a low rise and then into a small valley that led directly to the brightly lighted camp ahead. Murdock could hear the chugging of what had to be four or five diesel generators that supplied juice for the lights.

They had just crossed an open space when Lam saw a patrol of eight soldiers working toward them. "I've got eight bogies bearing down on me," Lam said. "Maybe thirty yards away and moving toward me and you guys. I could get half of them in the first burst, but that would make too much noise. Any suggestions, Commander?"

12

Murdock scowled. "How close?"

"Maybe forty yards."

"You have your silenced MP-5. Pick them off one at a time from your right side. I'll send Bradford up with his silenced sniper to get some of them from the left. Go."

Bradford heard his orders on the radio and sprinted forward. Lam had been fifty yards ahead of them so the sniper went prone after a forty-yard dash and peered into the darkness. He heard a soft cry ahead but couldn't see anyone.

He waited with his finger on the trigger. The shapes came out of the gloom slowly. He saw only six. He worked the left end of the line of men five yards apart. He sighted in on the last one and fired. Then he worked the bolt, gently jacking a new round in. By that time he had sighted in on the next in line, and he dropped him with a chest shot like the first.

Another one vanished on the right end of the line. Now there were three. He fired again, scratched another Syrian before one of the two soldiers left let out a screech and turned to run back the way he had come. The soldier stumbled and fell and didn't get up. Bradford had sighted in on the last man to the left, who turned to look at his buddy. The round hit him in the middle of his back, cracking his spine into two parts and killing him in seconds.

"Commander, sir," Lam said. "We have a body count of eight down and dirty. You're welcome to come to my fish fry up here."

"That's a roger, we're on our way."

They worked forward past the corpses, until they could see two sentries walking posts near the edge of the light splash along the outside of the tents. Murdock counted sixteen tents, and there were probably more. Chances were the American students were in one of the them.

Murdock looked at Rafii. "Go back and get a uniform from one of those men we just dispatched. Bring it up here and put it on. You and our Syrian friend here are going to take a walk into the lion's den and pull some teeth."

Rafii grinned. He ran off and came back in five minutes wearing the Syrian camo uniform with a soft hat and patches on both shoulders and sergeant's chevrons on his sleeves. He carried an AK-47 and gave his MP-5 to Jaybird and his combat vest to Fernandez.

"I just promoted myself," he said with a grin.

"Good. Over there looks like a gap between the two roving guards. We need to do this quickly before that patrol is missed or somebody finds it. I've timed out these two walkers. There is a four-minute period when neither of them can see that section up there halfway between those two nearest tents. You'll need to crawl up to that scrub brush staying out of sight. When both are gone, you slam across to the tents, then find somebody to question about the American students. Everybody in camp should know about it. Our Syrian friend here must understand if he tries to give you away or yell for help, that you will ram your KA-BAR through his heart and leave him dying for nothing. Tell him now, and remind him about the KA-BAR every step of the way."

Rafii drew his KA-BAR and showed it to the Syrian as he talked to him. He paused in Arabic and spoke in English. "He says his name is Jamil." Rafii went back to Arabic. Slowly Jamil nodded. He shivered when Rafii placed the point of the knife over his heart. After three more minutes of threats and easy talk, the two moved up as far as they could in the darkness, then dropped down and crawled forward to the struggling bit of greenery that looked like sage.

Murdock watched intently. On the first pass by the

guards, he saw Rafii prod Jamil up and they both ran for the tents. They made it with no outcry or gunfire. Murdock breathed a little easier.

Rafii pushed Jamil down when they hit the shadows between the two tents. They crawled to the front and looked out. Six tents in a fair row. Rafii figured they were infantry housing. Across a thirty-yard open space loomed four more twenty-man tents. One of them had a guard out front with a submachine gun. He didn't bother anyone who walked by, but getting into the tent would be another matter.

Rafii punched Jamil in the shoulder. "We're going to walk out there like we belong. We'll go up this street and find someone to talk to and locate where the Americans are being held. I'll do the talking. You just look stupid. Understand? Or do you want to die right here and leave your wife and family alone?"

"No, no, I will go with you and not give you away."

They found a soldier staring at the sky two tents up.

"Stargazing?" Rafii asked the man.

"Oh, yeah. I used to know the constellations."

"Learn them again, they're still up there. You hear about the Americans we captured?"

"Hear about them, I captured half of them. Shot one. We brought them up here."

"They all in that same tent over there?"

"Yeah, so that's where they put them. Only tent in the whole place with a guard outside, except the colonel's of course."

"See if you can find Taurus, the bull. He's up there."

The soldier thanked them and wandered away. Rafii and Jamil headed the other way, toward the prisoner tent. Not for sure the students were there, but it was a try.

The two men walked briskly up to the guard, who brought his weapon up to port arms.

"Soldier, they told us the American prisoners are here. Is that right?"

"Not for me to say. I'm just a guard."

"You better say. The colonel told me to come and get them. He has found a good translator who speaks perfect

English and he wants to interrogate the spies."

"Say something in English for me."

"You blow-headed bastard, you can't understand me anyway, now shut up or shape out."

The guard chuckled. "Sure sounds like English. Okay, look inside."

"You have them tied up?"

"No."

"Do they at least have leg irons on?"

"No, just their hands tied behind their backs."

"Okay, you go in first and I'm right behind you."

The guard frowned, lifted his brows in surrender, then untied the flap on the tent and pushed it aside as he went inside. A single bulb burned in the center.

The eight Americans sat or lay on folding cots. Some of them were sleeping. "On your feet," Rafii snapped in English. The young men and women groaned. "Stay unhappy. I'm here to help you. Get up but be unhappy, you understand?"

"If we do?" a young man said.

"If it works right, we get you out of here and into a navy chopper and fly you out of here. Come on, we don't have a lot of time."

Rafii turned to the guard and slammed the butt of the AK-47 he had taken from the dead Syrian hard against the side of the man's head, jolting him to the ground. Then he drew his KA-BAR and sliced a four-inch slit in the rear of the tent. He turned as Jamil headed for the door. "Stop him," Rafii said. One of the young students tackled him and they rolled over. Rafii tossed the kid riot cuffs. "Tie him up, hands behind his back and ankles, then gag him. I thought you kids were tied up."

"We untied them right away. Bad knots." A girl maybe twenty said it. She looked out the slot in back. "Nothing out there but dry land and some shrubs."

"Good," Rafi said. He slit the rear of the tent open five feet high and lined up the students. "Is anyone hurt or wounded?" There was no reaction. "Good, we go out of here at a walk, don't run. Not much light gets back there. We fade into the darkness. You got that? If anyone runs, we attract attention. In the dark they won't know who is who. So they will shoot us. Understand that? We keep five yards apart. Everyone ready?"

He looked around. They were all grinning. The same girl spoke up. "An Israeli sergeant was giving us close order drill once a day. We can do it."

He put the two men in front, then the four girls and the other two men in back. He brought up the rear.

"Let's go. Five yards, and walk. If anybody starts shooting at you, run like hell generally around the tent lights and to the south. Move."

It seemed to take forever to get all eight of them out of the tent. Then Rafii followed the last boy, the one who had done the tackle. Already he couldn't see the ones in the lead. As the lights behind them faded, he pushed the rear of the line forward until they were closely bunched. He took over the lead and they did a slow trot southward.

"Hey, Commander," Rafii said on the Motorola. "We're out and moving south. I have eight chicks who want to come home to roost."

"You're out with them? We didn't hear a shot. Nothing. How did you do it?"

"Later, Commander. Give us a landmark. This bull-dozed land all looks the same."

"Head south and to your left. I'll put Lam out to listen for you. Any of the kids hurt?"

"Not that I know of."

"We find you, get the kids on the truck, and we move two-point-five miles south between the two camps and call in our chopper. Should work. Lam, anything?"

It took them a half hour to find each other in the black Syrian night. Then the kids jammed onboard the pickup and one of them drove as they headed south at ten miles an hour. The SEALs jogged along behind at their six-minutes-to-a-mile pace.

The girl who had talked before leaned out of the cab and called to Murdock.

"You must be the commander. Isn't that a navy rank?"

"Yes, miss, it is. We're Navy SEALs."

"On land. Good. Whatever, I'm glad you found us. What about Harry and Mike?"

"The two men you left behind. I'm sorry—we found them, but they are both dead. We can't do anything about them now. We'll have to wait until this little war is over."

"Why can't we get them and take them with us?"

"Far, far too dangerous. It would be compromising your safety. They won't mind waiting awhile."

"This odometer is in kilometers, Commander," the kid driving said. "I let it go to three, isn't that about two miles?"

"Close enough. Murdock saw some brush and trees ahead to the left. "Drive into those trees. No ditch here to worry about. Get the rig in as far as you can."

Murdock called to Bradford, who was unfolding the dish antenna. Quickly he had it situated and gave Murdock the mike.

"This is Search One calling Skyhook. I say again, Search One calling Skyhook."

As soon as he let up on the send button the set talked.

"Yes, Search One. Been waiting. This is Skyhook. I'm about twenty below where I dropped you. Things are heating up. Where's my LZ?"

"We're about seven and a half miles almost due north of our original LZ. We're up the north road. We'll hear you coming. You'll get one red flare at the LZ. Anticipate no ground opposition. We're between two Syrian camps but there's little activity. Most of the troops must be at the front. Your ETA, Skyhook?"

"About twelve minutes, Search. I'm lifting off now. Set your countdown watch."

"Roger, out."

Lam had cut some branches from the small trees and hid the rear of the pickup, which stuck out from the brush. Murdock called them all together.

"Hey, guys, and ladies. We're in a tough situation here, but help is on the way. In ten minutes a chopper should land in here and we'll be heading for the first leg of getting you home. Have any of you ever ridden in a helicopter?"

A few hands went up. "This one won't have side doors on it, so I don't want anyone falling out. We may have to all stand up or sit on top of each other. The point is we'll be moving toward Israel and on to a ship just off the coast."

"A Navy ship, sir?" one of the boys asked.

"Yes, a cruiser with a chopper pad. We need to get away from these trees. Jaybird, find us an LZ."

Five minutes later, Jaybird called on the radio. "Troops got a good one, nice and level for a change. Come south about sixty yards or so and stumble onto me. One red flare for the chopper, Commander?"

"That's a roger. We're moving."

The SH-60 came whirling in right on schedule and landed near the flare. Jaybird stomped out the burning flare and Murdock handed the girls on board, then the boys jumped in.

"Getting crowded in here," a girl said.

Murdock decided it was like a Japanese subway when they all got onboard. Only fifteen and they were all standing. Murdock didn't know what he would have done with two more. He stood at one door, and Jaybird guarded the other one.

"Let's move, Lieutenant," Murdock yelled and the pilot lifted off and headed south. He kept low as he worked almost due south. Murdock had been standing facing the side door with hands on the sides as a human safety strap. He turned around to face the rest of them and found a young woman almost nose to nose with him. She must have smiled but in the blacked-out bird Murdock could barely tell where she was.

"I'm Kathy Burnett," she said. He recognized the voice as the one he had talked to before. "I'm a senior in Marine ROTC and I'll be going into the service next spring."

"I bet you've been holding this bunch together. Are they all pretty tough?"

"Most of them are now. The last two days have not been fun. I hate it that we lost those two guys. Mike was trying to protect us when they shot him."

"We'll get them back, but it's going to take some time.

There's a chance this invasion will be thrown back."

Murdock felt the bird climbing. They had been yelling to make themselves heard. Now Murdock watched the ground fade into blackness.

"We're probably climbing to get over the frontline action," Murdock told the group. Some of them heard him. A moment later he heard something hit the outside of the Skyhawk. Then another hit.

"Ground fire?" Kathy asked.

He nodded, then he felt the slap of a round that hit his shoulder. The blow knocked his left hand off the side of the chopper and he swung inward. The girl caught him.

"You're hit," Kathy said. "You hang on to me. Somebody else is holding me so we shouldn't fall out."

Murdock fought down a wave of giddiness. Just a little rifle round. What the hell was he going to do, pass out in this civilian woman's arms? He blinked then shook his head and heard the engine change its throbbing tune.

Slowly the rise of the chopper slowed, then stopped, and it began to head downward. At first it wasn't rapid, then it increased. The engine revved and then revved again and the blades overhead continued to sing their lovely tune. Murdock tried to look outside. He couldn't.

"Are we near the ground?" he asked the girl . . . Kathy.

"Not sure, we must have taken a round in the engine. It sounds real ragged, like it could stop almost anytime. We're doing a controlled descent, that's what they call it. Let's hope we get low enough before anything gives out." The mini-second she said it she knew she shouldn't have. That's when the engine quit and the rotors were on freewheeling trying to lower the eighteen thousand pounds of machinery slowly to the ground.

"Hang on," Murdock shouted in the sudden silence. One girl screamed. Then they hit. Murdock felt the landing gear crumple and the body smash into the ground. The big fuselage teetered a moment, then rolled slowly to the right as the long rotor blades slashed into the ground and shattered into pieces.

Murdock felt himself lying on top of other bodies. He knew he had to get up. From below someone pushed.

"Commander, can you get up to the door?" It was Kathy. "It's almost over the top of us. The other door is in the dirt. We have to get out of here."

He struggled to lift himself, then the chin-ups came into play and he rose enough to grab the side of the door, lift himself up, and belly over the aluminum. Then the pain in his left shoulder crashed in on him. He turned and slid to the ground. The pilot and copilot crawled out of the smashed cockpit and hurried around to help the rest of them out the one side door. SEALs lifted the students as high as they could, and the pilot and copilot reached up, grabbed them, and lifted them out. Murdock sat on the dirt and rocks. This area looked as if it had been burned off lately to prevent anyone from using the grass and shrubs as cover. His arm drilled pain into his brain.

Someone knelt beside him and pulled the first-aid kit off his combat vest. He could see her in the faintest of moonlight.

"You've done this before?"

"First-aid course, yes sir. Not on one who was bleeding. Catsup we used then. Hold still. The slug must still be in there. Probably from an AK-47. The Syrians use a lot of those NATO-round weapons. I'll tie it up so you don't bleed to death. Then we'll figure out how far we are from the front and to Israeli lines."

"Are you sure you're not twenty-eight and a major in the Marines?"

"Sorry. I'm twenty and I'll be a senior next year." She paused. "If we get out of this one alive, that is, I'll be a senior. There, that's better. Now stay put while I talk to the pilot."

They had all the passengers out of the chopper. Bradford came to find the commander and frowned at the bandage.

"You take a round, sir?"

"Afraid so. I was playing door. How far are we from the bad guys?"

"Not the slightest. I'll ask the pilot."

"Kathy already went to talk to him. She's in ROTC. Might come in handy. Anyone else hurt in the crash?"

"Not that I know of. The kids are pretty shook up, but they're young, they can take it. What do we do now, walk?"

"First we get away from this bird. It could blow up at any time. I smell leaking fuel. Help me move everyone south a hundred. Then sit down and wait. I'll find the pilot."

The pilot stood beside his craft shaking his head. "We didn't pick up any ground fire through there before, none at all. They must have called out all the men and waited for us to come back. Sorry as hell to lose my bird. We aren't anywhere near the MLR. At least nobody got killed."

"We better move south, Lieutenant. Get away from here. Gonna be troops looking for it any second now."

They moved. Kathy found them on the walk.

"The pilot says we're just into Israeli territory. We're maybe five miles from Zefat, and about fifteen to twenty to the front lines of fighting. It surges back and forth."

They had just found the rest of the SEALs and students when Lam stood up and frowned. "Skipper, I heard something a while ago and didn't get it for sure, but this time I've got it. Oh, oh, look over there. See that searchlight? It's almost for sure attached to the chopper I can hear that must be searching for our sixty. That bird with its stream light is heading directly for us here in the open."

13

"Listen up, everyone. That chopper is hunting us and the downed bird. Scatter, don't be within ten yards of anyone else. Lie down and be absolutely still if the light comes anywhere near you. Cover up any white or light clothing. Go, now. Move, move, move."

The students and SEALs spread out and huddled on the ground. There was some grass here, but mostly rocks, sand, and some small shrubs. Three SEALs curled around shrubs, making the plant look larger. Others went into a fetal position to look like a rock. The chopper swung toward them, then turned at right angles and covered an area a half mile away, then it turned back toward the SEALs. By the time it reached them it had angled fifty feet beyond the nearest SEAL, and it soon turned again and flew away from them. At the far end of its sweep, Murdock got the people on their feet and jogging away from the area.

They moved generally south, keeping the highway in sight but not using it. They saw several military convoys also going south to the action. Both the chopper pilot and copilot had hideout weapons that they now carried. A short time later, Kathy found Murdock and checked his arm.

"You have a penlight?"

He gave it to her and she looked over his wound, then bandaged it again, unbuttoned his shirt, put his left arm inside, and buttoned it again. "Works almost as good as a sling. If I had on panty hose I'd take them off and use them. They work great for an arm sling."

Murdock frowned. "You're Kathy Burnett, you said.

Don't I remember a Senator Burnett, maybe from Colorado?"

"Not that I know of. There is a Senator Burnett from Idaho. He's my father."

"Your daddy carries a lot of weight in Washington. I'm glad he does. Now, with all of your military training, how the hell do we get past the Syrian front lines and then through the trigger-happy Israeli fighters without getting ourselves shot to pieces?"

"First you get me a weapon."

"Can you shoot?"

"I'm on the rifle and pistol team in my unit. I've fired everything from a twenty-two to a forty-five and most of the automatic rifles including AK-47s, M-16s, your MP-5s, and I love to throw hand grenades."

"I give." Murdock reached to his left ankle with his right hand and pulled out the .38 six-gun with a two-and-a-half-inch barrel and handed it to her. "Five rounds, hammer's on the empty chamber. Don't lose it."

"Any more rounds?"

"You have any pockets?"

"Most jeans have a dozen."

He reached into his combat vest and handed her a new box of .38 rounds. "This should do you unless we really get into trouble."

"Thank you, Commander."

Lam came up beside Murdock. "What about a farm truck, Skipper? We're in Israeli territory, they should be friendly."

"So how do we get a truck through the fighting? Better we keep off the road and watch for an opening in the lines somewhere. How far to the front line?"

"I heard some heavy explosions a few minutes ago. Tank guns probably. The Syrians don't have any one-five-fives down here. I'd say we're maybe four to five miles away."

"Kathy, how are the other girls holding up?"

"Fine. Well, mostly fine. Monica is a bit of a wimp. But she was the one on the Internet chat room, and I hear that saved our asses."

"Watch her. We're as fast as our slowest person, who probably is Monica. Shepherd her if we hit trouble. Your assignment, Lieutenant."

"Yes, sir." Kathy went back with the main group and found Monica.

"So how do we get through the fighting?" Lam asked.

"Best we do it at night. Our only chance. Outside of that, I don't have the foggiest. We play it by ear and see what develops."

"Maybe steal a Syrian six-by and drive right through their lines."

"Sure and give the Israeli gunners a real target. We wouldn't get halfway across no-man's-land."

Twenty minutes later, Monica sat down and refused to move another step. "Why did they shoot down our helicopter? We should be on the ship by now, not traipsing around out here in the cold and maybe getting shot at any minute. Damn, I just want to go home."

Murdock heard about the mutiny and walked up close enough to hear. He continued until he stood in front of Monica.

"I understand you don't want to walk any farther, Monica."

She looked up, frowned in the darkness, and nodded. "Oh, yes, mister frogman, you have that right."

"Fine with me. Let's move. The rest of us are getting out of here. If you want to stay and take your chances with the Syrian Army, that's your right. You have a nice evening."

Murdock walked forward and everyone else followed him. They were all fifty yards away before Monica screamed at them, jumped up, and ran to catch up. "Bastards," she shouted. "You fucking bastards. Just wait until I tell my dad about this."

Murdock heard the rumblings of war ahead of them. "Monica, if you're lucky, when you tell your dad, he might just think that you're too old to spank. I don't agree, but he might think that way."

Jaybird came in from the left flank nearest the road where he had been a lookout. "Skipper, there's a big con-

voy coming down the road. At least two tanks, a whole
pot full of infantry. They're sure to have security out on
both their flanks. We probably should veer off to the right,
away from the highway for at least a half mile."

"Agreed. Lam, head us out at a forty-five to the right
and we better pick up the pace. Lam, how far to the
fireworks?"

"Two miles, top, Skipper. I can hear small arms now."

"Roger that, Lam. SEALs, I want all of you on the left
side of our little band. Let's string out into a column of
twos, and stay five yards apart. Kathy, help us on this
with the kids."

They were barely a half mile from the road when the
convoy and the troops came by. Lam put his people in
the dirt, silent and still as the flankers roamed within two
hundred yards of them. When the Syrians were well past,
Murdock decided to keep his squad farther from the road.
They hit some cultivated fields then, and farm buildings.
But they were too close now to consider any transport.

"Skipper, I've been thinking," Lam said on the radio.
"We've got two twenties and a pot full of ammo. And the
sniper rifle. And then the rest MP-5s. How can we set up
a diversion or a simulated Israeli attack that would pull
troops out of a frontline position and leave it temporarily
undermanned?"

"Yes, Lam. Good. Easier to do if we knew what was
in front of us in the Syrian line. There might not be a line
at all, just a series of units without much lateral support.
That we have to scout out and pin down. Let's get up
within about eight hundred yards from the MLR and hun-
ker down and see what we can find out in front. I'll go
with you on the scout. Nothing else to do back here. How
many rounds do we have for the twenties? Fernandez,
how many on you?"

"Skipper, I have fifteen rounds. What we started out
with. That makes thirty between the two of us. We can
raise a lot of hell with fifteen even without airbursts."

"How many for airbursts?"

"I only have three," Fernandez said.

"I have four, the rest are Navy contact type. Good

enough. When we get up there, Jaybird, you have the con. Keep everyone in the area, spread out enough for safety, and keep up a guard especially out front. How close now, Lam?"

"A little over a mile, I'd say. We can leave anytime and let Jaybird take the company up to the half mile."

Twenty minutes later, Lam and Murdock lay in a growth of tall grass in front of a line of trees and brush, and checked what they could see of the front Syrian lines. There were shadows of men moving along the tree line.

"Must be a river of some kind there," Murdock said. "Looks like the Syrians are on this side. What we need is to find one of their command posts. Some spot that the officer in charge can call in some of his men on his flanks to help protect the CP."

"No way we can find that without enough light to see the place by."

"All we need is a big bunker, an old building, lots of troops around," Lam said.

Murdock scowled again. He'd been doing that too much lately. "Let's go downstream and get closer and see how thick these Syrian soldiers are along here. They sure don't have anybody in reserve."

They worked closer, silently, taking advantage of some clouds crossing a sliver of a silver moon to move in the darker times. Murdock figured they were less than forty yards from the river now, and they could hear some rifles firing. Lam grinned.

"Yeah, I've got three guys talking almost dead ahead. Can't tell what they're saying. One soldier coughs a lot. Must not be any officer along here, or these three would be spread out ten yards from each other."

"How about our firing six rounds of the twenties into the line down along the river, say three hundred yards away. Make it look like a night attack from the Israelis. Then hope these guys will get called down there. If they don't, we go in with Rafii and his knives and he clears the way for us to get into the river and find some safe spot on the other side."

"We'd make a lot of noise going over the river," Lam said.

"Not if we move slowly and angle downstream a little. Worth a try. Otherwise we're sitting mallards if we stay on this side until daylight."

Murdock used the Motorola and called up the troops and students. "Be absolutely quiet. No coughing or throat clearing, no talking, no jangling jewelry. We're talking about staying alive here, guys. Jaybird. Bring them up due south, a tad to the right. Lam will be out two hundred to show you in."

Lam nodded and headed back toward the rest of the group. Murdock watched the front lines again. This had to work. Otherwise they could get caught in a crossfire between the two sides, and both sides would think the other one was attacking.

Murdock kept watching ahead. He heard some more talk, but it was muted, maybe from downstream. He turned and Lam was just behind him. Murdock hadn't heard him coming.

"Got them," Lam whispered. "The squad's got them quiet and scared, which is good. Not even any complaints from Monica."

"I want the twenty up front," Murdock said softly into his throat mike. He and Lam picked out the target. They were on a small rise and the river made a slight turn away from them upstream just over two hundred yards. There would be some troops on the bend.

Fernandez slid in beside them. "We shooting?"

"Yes, upstream. Use contact rounds. Keep it simple. We put two rounds each into them there, then two more each about fifty downstream."

"Right, Skipper. Ready when you are."

Murdock sighted in on the bend and fired. A second later Fernandez fired. The explosions of the 20mm rounds in the stillness of the Israeli darkness came as a jolting surprise to that sector of the MLR.

The second group of four rounds hitting farther down brought some shouts and quite a bit of return fire aimed across the river.

Murdock waited five minutes, then he and Lam crawled forward and looked for the Syrians. There hadn't been time to really dig in. Some places they found shallow slit trenches. They checked a twenty-yard stretch where it looked like there had been troops, but now they found only one man. Lam used his silenced MP-5 and dispatched the Syrian soldier with a round to the chest, then another one to the head.

"Move up," Murdock ordered. "Jaybird, bring them single file, five yards apart and move them quickly. I'll stay here. Lam is going across the river. Not deep. Doesn't look more than knee wet, we'll see."

"Roger that, we're on our way."

Lam checked the shore both ways, then stepped into the cold water. It came just over his knees almost to the middle of the forty-foot-wide stream, then he went in up to his waist and waded silently on across.

"We have waist-deep water," Murdock told the SEALs on the radio. "Warn the civilians that they will get wet to their waists. Once across we'll try to dry out and find a safe spot until we can touch the Israeli lines."

Five minutes later, Murdock ushered the last of the students into the water. The girls gasped, then kept quiet and waded across. All wore slacks or shorts and they made it easily. The SEALs and the two pilots were the last ones over. Murdock knew it was taking too much time. His arm hurt like fire but he beat down the pain and kept watching upstream. That's where some of the Syrians could be coming from. He was in the middle of the water when he saw three men walking down the trail along the river. They were out for a stroll. Murdock aimed a 20mm round ten feet in front of them and fired. The round exploded and sent a storm of shrapnel slashing toward the three Syrians. None of them had a chance to survive. Murdock hurried then and got out of the water just as a flurry of rounds slammed into the far bank a hundred yards upstream.

Jaybird had moved the group fifty yards into the brush and trees along the river and due south away from the enemy lines. The Israelis had to be out there somewhere.

But Murdock asked himself how they contacted the friendlies without getting their asses shot off.

Jaybird had an idea. "Cap, we have the girls sing 'God Bless America.' What could be more us?"

"How close are we to their lines?"

"Lam is out taking a look. He said in here it would be murder unless they could get all the way to the river. He spotted some small hills just behind us. The Israelis might be holding the high ground there and in the morning will be using some tanks to blast the MLR down here just across the wet."

"Sounds reasonable. How are your charges holding up?"

"That Kathy is a wonder. She's pumping them up, talking them out of feeling sorry for themselves. She's the only one of the kids with a gun and they know that she's ROTC."

"We'll put her in for a medal if we get out of this mess," Murdock said. "You've got security out?"

"Front and back. I'm no tadpole here, Commander."

Murdock snorted. "Hell, you eat tadpoles for lunch. Any sprained ankles or twisted knees?"

"Not that I've heard about. If there were, Kathy would have them talked out of it before they decided it hurt. Now, there is a girl."

"She's too young for you."

"She's just right for me." Jaybird snorted. "Of course once we get out of this mess, I'll never see her again."

"Count on it," Murdock said.

Without warning and without making a sound on his approach, Lam dropped down beside them. "Jaybird was right, the Israelis have the high ground. I got within about twenty yards of them and could hear some low talk. I'd guess machine guns up there and at least one tank."

"How close can you get the girls?" Jaybird asked.

"You going to let him try this, Skipper?"

"Sounds like it might work. They sing, I yell, and maybe we can get some free passage."

Lam shook his head. "Skipper, I want to place everyone we have under cover, especially the girls. Do you agree?"

"Absolutely. This is no time to be taking chances. Let's get to it before we run out of darkness."

Five minutes later Monica rebelled. "I won't sing. I think that's a sappy song. I have a thing about singing in public anyway. I won't sing."

Kathy stood nose to nose with her. "Fine, Monica. Fine. I'm sure your father will really like it when he hears about this." She turned to the four boys. "Any of you tenors? We could use a couple."

Kenny stepped forward. "I used to be a boy soprano, now I'm a man tenor. Yeah, I can keep up with you. If I can remember the words."

"Easy, we'll go over them now a dozen times."

Jaybird came up a few minutes later and helped Lam place the singers behind small trees and one big boulder. He nodded. "Any time you're ready, maestro."

Kathy grinned and hit a note. Then they all sang loud and clear. "God bless America, land of the free. Stand beside her, and guide her through the night with the light from above. From the mountains, to the prairie . . ."

A shot slammed over the heads of the singers.

"Israelis on the high ground," Murdock bellowed in his best parade ground voice. "We could use a little help down here. Cease fire and listen. Are you listening?"

"Right, listening and sending for our lieutenant. What the hell, man, you got women down there?"

"Yes, we're Americans."

"Oh, yeah. Who holds the football when Charlie Brown kicks it?"

"Lucy holds it, only she jerks it back just as he kicks."

There was a silence that stretched out.

"Hey, Israelis. You still there?"

"Right. We're not going nowhere. Hey, I was raised in Brooklyn, then we came over here. Got me some army time. How you get girls in the front lines?"

"College kids in a kibbutz up by Zefat."

More silence.

"Americans, you really down there with some girls?" The voice was different. "Lieutenant Shamma up here with the Twenty-first."

"Yes, sir, we are. Lieutenant Commander Blake Murdock, U.S. Navy SEALs, requesting permission to come into your lines with two chopper pilots, eight American college students, and six SEALs."

"I'll be damned." This time Murdock could hear two or three people talking.

"You armed, SEALs?"

"Always, even when we sleep and eat."

"Hold your position. I'm sending down a six-man patrol to check you out. Don't fire on us. You understand? Don't fire."

Just over an hour later Murdock stepped into the cab of a two-ton truck that bumped over a field, bounced through a ditch and hit a gravel road.

The Israeli driver kept staring at Murdock. "Pardon me, sir, but I've never seen a U.S. Navy SEAL before. You really brought those four girls through the Syrian lines?"

"It was too far to go around."

"What's that weapon, sir? Never seen nothing like it before."

"It's a twenty-millimeter shoulder-fired rifle."

"You're trashing me. Can't fire no twenty-millimeter cannon from your shoulder."

"This one does. The Syrians thought you were hitting them with tank fire."

"Blessed be."

"About the size of it. How long before we get to Haifa?"

"Over these roads, sir, about two hours."

In the back of the big truck, Kathy Burnett sat beside Jaybird. Ten minutes after the ride started she made a little mewing sound, put her head on Jaybird's shoulder, and promptly went to sleep.

14

Haifa, Israel

Murdock awoke twice when they hit bumps in the road and his shoulder jammed against the door. He rode out the sharp pain and felt wetness down his side. He was leaking again. He could make it another half hour into Haifa.

When they stopped just inside the gate at the Rahat Air Base, for the guards to sort out the passengers, Kathy stormed up to the lieutenant in charge and demanded an ambulance for Murdock. He had remained seated in the cab, and when the Israeli officer came, he tried to get out but Kathy stopped him.

"Look at his left shoulder," she demanded.

The officer looked at Murdock's shoulder that was now wet with blood. He made a radio call and less than three minutes later an army ambulance with red lights flashing pulled up to the side of the truck.

Kathy watched them put Murdock on a gurney and lift him into the ambulance. She jumped in before they could stop her, and the lieutenant shrugged and closed the doors.

At the hospital they asked her to leave the emergency room, but she put on her silent rage face and demanded to stay with Murdock until he was treated. Two doctors showed up at once and cut off the sleeve and examined the wound.

"Miss, he has a slug in his shoulder. Well below the bone and not all that serious. We'll operate, take it out, and he'll be almost as good as new in a week."

The doctor smiled. "Yes, in a week. Now, we need you

to go to room A-12. The rest of your student friends are there and you all will get a quick check for any problems, before we can release you to the American representatives."

"I'm fine."

"I'm sure your are, miss. Nurse Sharon here will take you down to the others. Now, I have to operate on the commander."

It took the medics less than an hour to check over the eight students. They found several scrapes, some bruises, and gave Monica a shot to calm her down when she showed a mild case of hysteria.

The truck sat outside the hospital. The guard lieutenant from the gate didn't know what to do with the heavily armed SEALs.

"Give your General Menuhin a call," Jaybird said. "We're working for him on a special assignment."

The Israeli officer hesitated. "I can't just call the general."

"Then call your officer of the day or whoever else is in charge around here. Find out if an American CIA man named Don Stroh is on base. Come on, get some action. I'm tired of sitting around in these wet pants and I could do with a big steak dinner."

The lieutenant grinned and made a radio call to his CO.

Ten minutes later two jeeps drove up and the SEALs were taken to the same quarters they had used when they were on the base before. A redheaded sergeant poked his head in the door.

"Gentlemen, Base Commander General Menuhin offers his congratulations to you on your successful mission. He says that you're to relax here and clean up. A special chow call will be held for you in an hour at the mess hall three buildings down. He says a Don Stroh is on his way here from the American cruiser off the coast. He should arrive within an hour. Oh, he also said that the students you rescued are all well and will be kept here overnight. In the morning they will be met by an embassy officer who will issue them passports and arrange transportation home. You take care now." He popped a salute, did a quick about face, and went out the door.

Jaybird looked at the other SEALs. They were all watching him. "Since when did I get command here?" he asked. "So, let's wash up and go get some chow. We can't change clothes, that's for sure. At least we can brush off the grime. Wonder if they'll have any steaks for us."

Two hours later Don Stroh arrived, ordered them new cammies from the Israelis, and left them cleaning weapons and flaking out. He checked on Murdock in the hospital. He had come out of the operating room and recovery room and lay in a bed with his heavily bandaged left shoulder on a pillow. He watched a soccer game on a portable TV.

"How did they get the TV stations broadcasting so quickly?" Stroh asked.

"Yeah, and good morning to you, too, Don Stroh. Thanks for asking. No, I didn't get hit bad. I'll be up and back in uniform in two days. Nice of you to be concerned about my little scratch."

"Okay, okay. I talked to the medics. Just don't do any pull-ups for a while. Now. How did they get the TV stations back on the air so fast? I thought the whole broadcast system was fried into next Thursday."

"They are still destroyed and they aren't broadcasting. I hear one radio station has jury-rigged a broadcast setup. No TV. This is a portable flown in from Tel Aviv and a tape through a VCR. You see the kids?"

"Yeah. Looks like everyone made it through the ordeal fine except Monica. She's still mixed up and does a lot of crying. There's one girl who seems to be the leader and is holding them all together. Oh, yes, she gave me this to give to you." Stroh held out Murdock's .38 hideout.

"You better give it to Jaybird to hold."

They looked at each other for a few seconds and Stroh glanced away. "Sorry about that chopper getting shot down. At least we got the bird in to you. No high and dry this time."

"We were hung out to dry, but not by the good guys.

The bad guys did it to us. You hear how we got into the Israeli lines?"

"I did. The kids were talking about it. Bright of that girl."

"Her name is Kathy. She's the daughter of a U.S. senator from Idaho."

"The connection."

"One of them." He paused. Hell, it wouldn't hurt to ask. "When are we going home?"

"You're not enjoying the Israeli hospitality?"

"I can't even get CNN. How can I find out how the war is going?"

"Right now things are looking better. The Israelis have put enough planes in the air the shoot down or chase back most of the Syrian fighters, giving them control of the air. So they blast the Syrian tanks, bomb and strafe the convoys coming down from Syria with supplies. All the time the Israelis are trucking more and more troops and rushing tanks and trucks up into the dead zone."

"They calling Haifa the dead zone?"

"More correctly, the electronic dead zone."

"That damn pulse bomb sure shot Haifa back into the Stone Age, didn't it?"

"Until they trucked and flew in enough radios. I bet every base in the southern half of Israel is working with one or two radios. The rest were stripped out and flown north." Stroh watched Murdock and Murdock began to fidget.

"So why the long stare?"

"Just trying to figure out how far I can trust you. Oh, you might be interested. As soon as you went into the war zone, the CNO had the rest of your platoon into a plane to fly in. They should be here sometime tonight."

"So you want the JG to take over the platoon?"

"What I'm trying to figure. Just a scratch in the shoulder, you said. Yeah, I saw the pictures. You won't be able to lift your arm over your shoulder for two weeks."

"Want to bet? I had a friend who had a rotator cuff operation. Made a three-inch slice in his upper arm, went in, and stapled a couple of tendons back together where he'd tore them apart. It was an outpatient procedure. In that morning at five A.M. They did the operation and booted him out about seven. Gave him this potent pain medication and told him to take it before the pain hit him. He waited. Never did take the damn pills. Not much pain at all."

"Was that you, Murdock?"

"No, a baseball player I know. It ruined his overhand fastball, and he never pitched again, but the arm didn't hurt him either."

"Two weeks."

"Two days. I'm getting out of here in two days. Just don't schedule any missions for us before then. Why did the CNO think we needed the rest of the platoon?"

"He said you usually worked best as a unit. Now the rest of your guys might come in handy."

"You mean we have some more missions coming up?"

"Must be, or the CNO would have sent the six of you home rather than sending the rest of the platoon over here."

Murdock threw off the sheet and swung his feet out to the floor as he sat up. He felt just a little woozy for a moment, then he grinned at Stroh. "Been waiting for you to get here so you can get me the set of clean cammies they put in the little closet over there. Now, Stroh. Bring me my pants. I'm getting out of here."

A nurse came in just as Murdock finished buttoning his cammie shirt. Her eyes jolted wide open.

"Commander, you are supposed to be in bed."

"Thank you, Captain. But I've had enough bed rest. There are some small tasks I have to take care of. You tell the doctors that I'll be back in once a day for them to look me over."

She stood back and chuckled. "You damn Americans. I'll never understand you. But we love you. If you go straight down this corridor, there's an exit that will put you in the parking lot. Did you find all of your things?"

She took the Bull Pup out of the closet, his combat vest, and a plastic sack that had been filled with the ammunition and goods from the vest. "This must all be yours. Could your friend here help you carry it?"

Stroh had talked someone out of a jeep and he drove Murdock and his gear to the building where the SEALs had flaked out on their bunks.

"Well, look who decided to join the party," Jaybird said.

"About time," Murdock said. "A ship without a rudder . . . Anybody else wounded on that little hike?"

Nobody responded.

"Good. Yeah I'm not a hundred percent yet, but I can outhike any of you government-issue types. Stroh said anything about what he has working for us next?"

"Nary a word, Commander," Lam said.

"So who has the training schedule? You guys think you were going to sit on your big fat asses all day?"

"I gave them the rest of the day off, Murdock," Stroh said. "You work for me, so I'm your boss, so I said they should take it easy and eat four times a day."

"Oh, yeah, let's make him our CO." Fernandez said.

"Five will get you fifty our glorious leader didn't have a medical okay to leave the hospital," Bradford said. He looked around. "No takers?"

"That's a sucker bet," Jaybird said. "We all know this guy."

Stroh's beeper sounded and he looked at his cell phone. He frowned. "Gentlemen, I need to get to a radio and talk to someone on the cruiser. I'll be back if I find out anything important."

"Make it after chow," Rafii said. "I could use another square meal with seconds."

Don Stroh was back in the SEAL quarters less than an hour later. "Nothing tonight. Might not be anything at all, but you need to know about it. We have a carrier steaming toward us. She's still about six hundred miles away. There is a report coming out of a marina here in Haifa that a hundred-foot luxury yacht is overdue. She was scheduled to dock this morning and has not been heard from. This is understandable since her radio could have been fried in the pulse. If so, she not only is without communications, she is without any steering ability, since most modern yachts have electronic steering and computer-controlled instruments and navigation."

"So, she's bobbing round out there on the Mediterranean," Jaybird said. "Must be fifty or more boats in the same fix. Won't the Israeli Navy power out there and rescue everyone?"

"That will take time. This boat is slightly more important than many of the others. The U.S. vice president, his wife and two daughters, and the ambassador to Israel are on board. The Navy is launching a search. The two choppers from the *Shiloh* have been searching now for two hours. Their range is limited and so far they haven't found a thing. There is a huge chunk of water out there to check. The pulse reached out fifty miles on land, so it will go that far over the water. That means there is a half circle out there fifty miles in three directions from Haifa, north, south, and due west. That's one hell of a big playpen to search."

"The fourteens off the carrier can reach the area, but they won't have a lot of time to search until they get short on juice," Lam said.

"Refuel them in the air," Fernandez said.

"So what if they find the yacht and it has drifted sixty miles off the coast?" Jaybird asked.

"Easy chopper run for the sixty," Rafii said. "We fly out, take a swim and see what we can do to help. Why not winch up the vice president and get him back to the cruiser?"

"Can't do that because the SH-60 doesn't have a winch," Jaybird said.

"The vice president?" Murdock asked Stroh. "Doesn't he have Secret Service protection?"

"Sure and plenty of it. And radios and backups and backups for them. But they all must have been fried. The Secret Service can't do anything out there." Stroh put his hands in his pockets, walked the length of the room, and came back. His expression now was grim and his eyes flashed.

"There is one other factor. My boss says we have heard

that Syria knows the veep is out there and that they have a good idea where he's at. They are preparing to send out high-speed patrol boats to snatch the vice president off the yacht and hold him for ransom."

15

Murdock looked at the CIA man. "What the hell is the vice president doing on a private yacht with no real protection? A couple of Ingrams isn't worth shit against a gunboat with fifty-caliber machine guns and probably some twenty-millimeter cannons. What the hell were those people thinking about?"

"Friendly waters, and a two-day cruise. It was supposed to be on some good fishing grounds and the veep is a nut about fishing. Anyway it was a birthday present to him by the ambassador. How do you say no? Enough of this. How do we find him and get to him before the Syrians do, and how do we rescue him?"

Jaybird rubbed his nose, then scowled and looked at the wall.

"Damn big ocean out there. What assets do we have? Any AWACS unit in the area?"

"Hadn't thought of that," Stroh said. "Might be a land-based AWACS close by. If not, the carrier should have a Hawkeye. They can scan a two-hundred-mile circle and should be able to find a big ship like a hundred-foot yacht. I'll see how far away the carrier is. Yeah, good idea. Let me get to my SATCOM that works. New one I brought from the cruiser." Stroh took off running for the door to get to his quarters.

The SEALs shook their heads and thought about the problem.

"Fucking big lot of water out there, that Mediterranean Sea," Bradford said. "Our best hope is to find the yacht first."

"The carrier can send out fourteens and eighteens in a search pattern, but a half circle fifty miles in radius is a sweet mother bunch of water to look at," Jaybird said.

"The cruiser should steam off Lebanon watching for any Syrian patrol boats heading for the open sea," Murdock said. "That might cut off the attempt by the Syrians."

"Could, if they aren't already twenty miles to sea," Fernandez said. "The cruiser could put up their two sixties and scout for the patrol boat and the yacht at the same time."

"How long has it been since the pulse hit?" Rafii asked.

"This is the third day of the war," Murdock said. "So it's the third day the yacht has had no power, no steering, no refrigeration. Food might be getting scarce."

"Drifting," Lance said. "How much current is there off shore here and which way does it go?"

"No idea," Jaybird said. "We'll have to ask the Israelis."

The door popped open and Senior Chief Petty Officer Sadler stepped into the room. "Yeah, this must be the place," he said, dropping his gear. "Hear you guys been loafing around over here in the sunshine while we been working our tails off on the O course."

The rest of the SEALs from Third Platoon streamed into the large room and began claiming bunks. Lieutenant (j.g.) Gardner came in last, showing a slight limp. He saw Murdock and frowned at the bandage.

"You go and get yourself shot up on a little walk in the park like that?" he asked.

"Just a scratch, JG. Where did you get the limp?"

"Been kicking ass so long on the O course and the hikes we've been taking, then yesterday I damn near busted it on Howard's hard butt." He sat down beside Murdock. "We got anything cooking?"

Murdock told him about the veep.

"Sounds like that guy. Good time Charlie. When I run for office, things gonna be different."

"Yeah, I can see a plank in your platform," Jaybird called. "Golf and fencing lessons for every seventh-grader in the country."

"Golden idea, I was concentrating on mahjong and bridge lessons, but I'll have my campaign committee check that out."

"You guys get fed recently? Any sleep needed?"

"We're ready to go with five minutes to get our combat vests up to snuff," Gardner said. "How are we for ammo on the twenties?"

"Low on the laser-aimed. We can get all the regular HE twenty we need, but no airbursts with them."

"We brought ten rounds for each of our five twenties."

Stroh came slanting in the door. Murdock didn't remember ever seeing him move so fast. He grinned as he skidded to a stop in front of Murdock.

"Oh, Gardner. Welcome to Israel, JG. Checked with the CO on the *John C. Stennis CVN 74.* She's about fifty miles north of Haifa and ten miles off the coast. She had her Hawkeye in the air directing her CAP, and now she's searching the rest of the fifty-mile radius off Haifa. The original report was that there are more than thirty ships in the general area. They will need to be checked out. Freighters, a few military craft, the *Shiloh,* and a whole shit pot full of fishing ships. She can tell the size of most of them, but not all. They will have Tomcats check out the ones they can before dark. We only have about a half hour of daylight left."

"Are they watching for patrol boats leaving Lebanon?" Jaybird asked.

"Yes, they certainly are. They had one preliminary report that two patrol craft in the eighty-foot range left port there, but they lost them in some strange interference. They're wondering if it's a hangover from the pulse."

"Could be," Murdock said. "But it doesn't seem reasonable after two and a half days."

"So, we're in dry dock until they find the yacht," Mahanani said.

Mediterranean Sea
Eighty miles off Haifa, Israel

Vice President Arthur Harrington Milrose stared out to sea. He'd been doing that for three days and found nothing to encourage him. They were dead in the water and drifting but he didn't know which direction and how fast. Were they heading away from Israel or toward her? All of their electronic gear was fried into mush and they had no steering, so their perfectly operating diesel engines were useless.

He stretched his long legs across the deck and watched the U.S. ambassador to Israel talking with the captain of the pleasure craft. The *Inspiration* out of Haifa was 112 feet long, beautifully appointed and a true luxury yacht, with eight cabins, a wonderfully designed and decorated salon, and all the conveniences and luxuries of the rich and ill informed. But what good were gold-fitted bathrooms when the dead electric motors wouldn't flush the toilet?

He would gather the passengers together again just before sunset for a pep talk. This two-day cruise with the chance for some good fishing had turned into a disaster. The vice president of the United States was nearly six-feet four-inches and had been an outstanding tight end at the Air Force Academy. He was still in good condition and worked at it with tennis, handball, and marathons just for the fun of it. He was forty-two years old and had three kids in college and a beautiful and talented wife. Whatever had happened onboard this floating vacation stumped him. He had no idea what occurred to make all of the electronics on the yacht go out at precisely the same second. How could it happen? Computers, electric clocks, the whole electronic navigation and steering system trashed beyond repair.

Somewhere in the back of his memory he remembered something about the EMP, the electromagnetic pulse principle, but that was associated with nuclear bombs. Had Israel been hit with nuclear weapons? He didn't know. His two Secret Service men kept test firing their weapons just to be sure they still worked. Twice a day they tested the Ingrams, and each time they worked fine.

Ambassador James Epstein slid into the deck chair beside the vice president and looked over the stern at the calm water.

"So damn peaceful here I wonder if we're still on the right planet," Epstein said. "Maybe when our electronics went out we were zapped into another dimension, another universe somewhere, and our electronics conflicted with their electronics in a kind of antimatter showdown." Epstein was fifty-five, twenty pounds overweight, almost bald, with fringes of graying hair. He had a large nose between piercing brown eyes and a sharp mind that had powered him into a fortune in the stock market before he retired just before the big downer of 1999. He had flushed himself out of the market with more than a billion and a half solid gold dollars.

"You've been reading too much science fiction," Vice President Milrose said. "Whatever it is, probably half the U.S. Navy is hunting us right now. I'm surprised they haven't found us yet. Our job is to keep the guests from shooting each other, and be sure the crew feeds us from the stores of canned goods. The propane stoves still work. We can do without refrigeration and air-conditioning. How is Franklin getting along?"

"He's still mad as hell that his VCR doesn't work. I told you we should have left him in Haifa. He's a clod and a clown. He thinks he's somebody just because he has a few million."

"Remember that a batch of those few million made it into our campaign coffers in the election a year ago," Milrose said.

"Yeah, there's that. His wife still down?"

"Yes, not sure what her trouble is. Partly her heart, but there's something else. My Millicent is a nurse and it has her puzzled. My wife can usually diagnose a patient as well as a doctor, but not this time."

"Nobody has gone overboard, so we should have ten passengers and a crew of five. The captain said we were drifting south and out of the normal shipping lanes. It could be weeks before a ship finds us."

"What about the AWACS spotter planes, that fly up at forty thousand feet and search two or three hundred miles at a time? Why can't they find us?"

"Those are land-based planes," Epstein said. "I don't know if we have any in the area."

"Does Israel have any?"

"I don't know. I've only been on the job for two months."

"You think Franklin is going to settle down?"

"He worries me. I also wonder where the goddamned U.S. Navy is. Why haven't they found us?"

"First somebody would have to report us overdue at Haifa," the vice president said. "That could take a day. Then who knows, maybe there was a nuke dropped on Haifa and they can't be worried about sixteen people on some rich guy's yacht."

A man came up from the cabin. He wore only swim trunks and carried flippers and snorkel gear. He was in his fifties, suntanned, with a flat belly and a firm upper body. His red hair was shorter than the usual business cut. He frowned at the two men in the lounge chairs.

"Damn couch potatoes. I'm going swimming."

"Franklin, we're drifting. You might not be able to get back to the boat."

"Hell, I do the La Jolla Rough Water swim every year. No sweat."

"No, Franklin. Don't get in the water." Vice President Milrose barked the words in his best National Guard command voice.

Franklin laughed. "Hell, big assed veep, you think you can order me around? Stick it up your ass, hot shot."

"Franklin, you're drunk. If you go over the rail you could drown."

"Yeah, and if the vice president had wings, he'd fly."

Before either of the men could grab him, Franklin took two steps forward and dove into the Mediterranean four feet below the luxury yacht's stern rail.

"Man overboard," Ambassador Epstein bellowed. Two crewmen appeared on the stern of the ship within seconds. Right behind them were the two Secret Service men with their Ingrams out and up.

"Bill, he said he was going swimming," Milrose said to the taller tanned crewman.

Crewman Bill nodded, ripped off his shirt, and kicked
out of his shoes, as he watched the man overboard, who
was treading water as he put on his snorkel mask and air
pipe. "Get the trail line out, Wally," Bill said, then dove
cleanly into the Mediterranean.

Wally threw into the water a coil of rope that had one
end tied to the ship's rail. It stretched out floating in the
water until it trailed two hundred feet behind. Bill came
up from his dive almost at once and stroked quickly toward Franklin, who had drifted twenty feet behind the
boat. Franklin finished putting on and adjusting his face
mask. The two Secret Service men put down their weapons and watched.

Bill swam up to Franklin, who looked at him surprised.
"I want to swim alone," he shouted.

"You're getting back on board," Bill said. "Too dangerous out here without any power on the boat."

"Eat shit, sailor."

Bill slammed his fist into Franklin's jaw, spinning the
face mask off with its snorkel tube and dumping Franklin
backward into the water. At once he sank below the Mediterranean. Bill grabbed him and jerked him to the surface,
put his arm across Franklin's chest in a lifesaving towing
position, and swam fifteen yards to the side, where he
found the trailing safety rope that floated in the water and
stretched out ahead now thirty yards to the yacht. Bill
grabbed the line and shouted. "Pull away."

Wally knelt at the rail, grabbed the line, and pulled the
pair foot by foot back toward the ship. Vice President
Milrose knelt on the deck beside Wally and took turns
pulling in the rope until the two men in the water touched
the stern.

"Hold them right there," Wally said, then rushed away
and came back with a folding aluminum ladder he anchored on the rail and let down until it went a foot into
the water. Wally went two steps down and grabbed the
hands of the still unconscious Franklin and hoisted him
upward. Milrose and Epstein leaned over the deck and
caught Franklin's hands and pulled him up higher. The
two Secret Service men came and helped. It took the six

of them another three minutes to tug and shove and heave
Franklin over the rail. He was still unconscious. They
rolled him on the deck, where he wheezed and spit up
water and struggled back to consciousness. He looked up,
blinking at the ring of faces over him.

"What the hell?"

"You were almost there, Franklin," Vice President Milrose said. "Hell, I mean. Don't you have any common
sense at all, or are you still drunk?"

"Huh, what?"

"You just went swimming."

"The hell you say."

"Then why do you have on a wet swimsuit and feel
like you swallowed half of the Mediterranean?"

Franklin rolled over on his stomach and coughed and
then vomited a bile green mess onto the polished deck.
He tried three times, before he at last sat up. None of the
men moved to help him. He groaned. "Oh god do I feel
like hell." He looked up, his pudgy face contrite, eyes
puffy, his nose running. "Fuck, I musta been smashed out
of my gourd drunk. Shit."

"You can say that again."

"Shit."

"These two men saved your life. You've got a big
drinking problem, Franklin. You better get some help fast
before you risk the lives of anybody else. Stay up here
and sober up. I'm going to check on your wife."

"Louise? Is Louise sick? What do you mean?"

"She's been sick all day, didn't you notice? We're not
sure what's the trouble but it could be serious. You stay
up here in the fresh air."

Down in the second stateroom, Louise lay on the big
bed, her eyes wide with pain.

"It hurts, darlin'," Louise said. She was in her forties,
light skinned and now pale. Her short blond hair needed
a touch-up and her face without makeup looked fragile to
the veep. Bright blue eyes looked at him.

"Sorry to be a party pooper, Mr. Vice President. It just
hurts."

Millicent nodded at her husband and pointed out the

door. She was tall and slender, dark with short black hair and bangs that framed her face. Her eyes were gray, and high cheekbones and a beautiful face had earned her work as a model when she was a teenager. But nursing had called her.

"You take it easy. Millicent is as good as most doctors. You just hang on and we'll be right back."

In the hall Millicent talked softly. "Well, I should have caught it quicker. Pain around her belly button, no appetite, nausea and vomiting. What we don't want is for the pain to shift to the lower quadrant and become continuous. She's also had a little bit of coughing and sneezing but not serious yet. I should have seen it hours ago. Louise is having an attack of appendicitis."

"At her age? I thought this was a kid problem."

"Usually, but people of any age can get it."

"And if it bursts?"

"Then we're talking about Louise getting peritonitis and dying within a few hours."

"Any way to figure out how far away she is from that point?"

"None. All we can do now is monitor her."

Milrose watched his wife for a beat. He had to ask the question. "Can you take out her appendix?"

"Arthur, you can't be serious. I've watched dozens of operations, but we don't have anything sterile and no scalpels or disinfectants . . ."

"But she could die."

Millicent's eyes went wide, her mouth came open. "Oh, my. If nobody comes in the next few hours . . . Oh good Lord, I don't know if I could do it or not. I've seen it done, I know what has to be done, but we don't have a scalpel, sutures, bandages, sponges . . ."

"I'll check the ship's first-aid locker. They should have a lot of material."

Five minutes later Wally showed him what they had: bandages, lots of antiseptic, tape, some sterile pads. No scalpels, sutures, or medical sponges.

The vice president went to the galley. The cook was working on dinner.

"You have an oven that works?"

The chef nodded.

"Can you sterilize some bandages for me? And some of your sponges? Use brand-new ones and cut them up into two-inch squares?"

"Sure. Why?"

"We may need to do an operation. Oh, do you have any really sharp knifes that can cut flesh?"

"You ain't kidding, are you? Yeah, some fish filleting knives you could shave with. I'll get three of them sharpened and sterilize them in boiling water. When you want this stuff?"

"As soon as you get it ready. Then keep it sterile until we need it. We might not need it. I hope not." He found a crewman and the laundry room. They tore a sheet into bandages and squares to use for sterile pads. He took it all to the cook.

He found Millicent just outside the cabin where Louise moaned in a soft, regular rhythm.

"She any better?"

"No, a little worse. It doesn't seem to be progressing a lot. The pain is still near the navel, which is good."

"Sutures, that's just a fancy name for thread you stitch with, right?"

"Yes, but I don't have a needle to use." Her face brightened. "Hey, didn't we bring a sewing kit with us?"

Two hours later it was dark. The only lights on board the *Inspiration* were candles and some Coleman gas lanterns. Four candles glowed in the second stateroom, where Louise lay on top of the sheets. Her eyes had fallen shut but she was not sleeping.

Millicent waved her husband out of the room. "She's worse. There's a mild fever now, maybe one-oh-one or two. But the major pain still is near the belly button. That's good. I found the thread and a curved fabric needle I can use if I have to go in."

"Go in?" her husband asked. "You're starting to sound like a doctor again."

She flashed him a smile and kissed him on the cheek.

"Thanks, sweetheart. I just hope that I don't have to play doctor. Let me check Louise again."

The vice president waited in the passageway as Millicent went in the stateroom. She was back in two minutes, her face troubled by a frown.

"She's worse. The pain is moving to the lower quadrant. If it continues this way, she'll have to be operated on before morning."

16

Haifa, Israel

JG Gardner shook his head. "It's almost dark and they haven't found that yacht yet? I don't believe this. We have the best recon operations in the world with the Hawkeye. Why can't they find one luxury liner?"

"Big bunch of water," Jaybird said.

Murdock watched the men. They were antsy, getting nervous just sitting and waiting. He looked at Stroh. "Shouldn't we at least be on the *Shiloh* where we can jump on a sixty if and when they find the yacht?"

Stroh had brought back his SATCOM and had the antenna set. He called the cruiser where the search had been centered.

Captain Caruthers on the cruiser bumped them on up to the admiral on the carrier. "The *Stennis* has taken over control of the search," he said. "Better give him a call."

Twenty minutes later the SEALs trooped on board the SH-60 helicopter, squeezed in with their gear, and took off for the *Shiloh*.

"At least we'll be closer to any action that goes down," Murdock said. They left Stroh in Haifa on his SATCOM updating Washington, D.C.

When the SEALs landed on the cruiser, Captain Caruthers met them. "Just got off the air with Admiral Warnick on the *Stennis*. He says they have identified all but eight of the large vessels they have spotted with the Hawkeye. F-14s are still in the process of trying to find the others. It should be easier now, since the yacht we want won't have any lights on board, with the exception of some candles, gas lanterns, and gas lamps. Of course that also will make it harder to find them in the dark. We keep hoping."

"What about the Syrian patrol boats that were heading out into the area?" Murdock asked. He moved his left arm backward and the pain drilled through him like a firebrand. He had to remember to keep it forward.

"We found them and a dozen rounds of twenty-millimeter cannon fire across their bows, turned them back toward shore. The fourteens followed them until they docked. So they aren't a worry anymore."

"Now all we have to do is find the blacked-out yacht in the middle of the Mediterranean on a night with damned near no moon," Murdock said.

"About the size of it," Captain Caruthers said. "Let's get some coffee and stand by the radio."

High over the Mediterranean, Lieutenant Marsh "Lowblow" Arlington finished a negative report on the third large ship he had checked out from coordinates provided by the Hawkeye. Now he logged in the numbers for the fourth try. He had no idea how far from the carrier he was. All he was interested in was finding that ship with the nation's vice president on board.

He flew the bird toward the next hot spot that the radar had shown on the surface and waited. He had dropped down to a thousand feet so he would be able to identify any ship he came toward. The last one had been a luxury yacht, maybe a hundred feet long, but it had about a thousand light bulbs on it, all burning brightly. He needed a yacht shrouded in darkness.

Now he watched the screens as he approached the position. From a half mile off he could see the lights. Another bummer. He hit his mike.

"Hunter Home, this is Hunt Four. I have my fifth vessel and it is brightly lighted. Looks about the right size. You want me to buzz it and try for a name on the bow?"

"Negative, Hunt Four. No chance our target yacht could have any lights. Proceed to next suspect."

"Roger that."

He punched in the new coordinates relayed from the

Hawkeye. Three fourteens were searching out these blips being shown on the radar screens high overhead. Lieutenant Arlington hoped that one of them would strike gold pretty soon. Without any electricity, the yacht would have no refrigeration. Food might be a problem. If a storm came up, a craft that size with no power and no steering could be in serious trouble. He flew on to the next ship.

On the *Shiloh* Murdock took the handset from the radio operator and pushed the send button. "Yes, sir, Admiral Warnick. This is Lieutenant Commander Blake Murdock."

"Murdock, yes. I have some orders from the CNO about you. We're still fifty miles from Haifa and about twenty off the landfall. If one of our fourteens finds this yacht, you're going to be closer to it than we will if it is drifting south. We'll send out our S and R chopper as soon as we have a definite location, but you'll be there first. Do what you can for the people and assure them we're on our way. We'll have the *Shiloh* tow the yacht since it's really dead on all its electronics. That's about it. If all sixteen of you can't get in the bird, take your best men. We'll get to the spot as quickly as possible."

"Will do, Admiral. We're waiting for a call from the fourteens."

They monitored the channel the F-14s used to talk to the carrier. Three of them made a total of five more contacts before they had good news.

"Hunter Home, this is Hunter Four. I might have our target. She's on the coordinates, almost blacked out except for some pinpoints of light that could be candles or lanterns. I'll buzz them to let them know I'm here and see if I get any reaction."

"Right, Four."

A short time later the radio came on again. "Yes, Hunter Home. This must be the ship. I'm getting an SOS from a light source that could be a big flashlight. They definitely are blacked out, not moving and signaling for help."

"Roger, Hunter Four. Those coordinates put you about sixty miles from shore and some thirty miles south of

Haifa. Will send a SH-60 to the spot. Fly CAP on the spot until you see the chopper arrive. *Shiloh,* are you reading this?"

"Yes, Hunter Home. Reading. We have one sixty warmed up now. It will be airborne in seven with the SEALs."

"Roger, *Shiloh.* We're launching S and R now, but we're about a hundred miles from the ship."

"Roger, Hunter Home. Standing by on this frequency."

"Move it," Murdock shouted at the SEALs in their compartment. "We're taking a ride. Up to the chopper pad on the double. No combat vests but bring your weapons. Bradford, be sure you have the SATCOM. Move now."

It was eight minutes before the SH-60 lifted off the cruiser's deck and raced away to the south.

"We should have to go about fifty miles to find them," Jaybird said. "At a hundred and forty-five miles per hour in this bird, we should be there in twenty minutes." Murdock had planned ahead and stashed on board the chopper two inch-thick ropes fifty feet long. He tied one securely to each of the door posts.

"Everyone has his gloves? We'll rope down. Just don't burn your hands up. Mahanani, be sure you take your med kit. They might have some injuries down there."

"We going to find any dead bodies?" Wade Claymore asked.

"Doubt it," Murdock yelled over the noise of the chopper. "Maybe food poisoning or a broken leg if the ship got pushed around by the waves. Having no power and no steering on a ship that size is a scary thing at sea."

"Everyone has a big flashlight," Gardner said. "We're going to need them down there. Remember, these are civilians, and some important ones."

Murdock went to the cockpit and watched as the pilot zeroed in on his target and circled.

"Looks like it," the pilot said.

Murdock looked down and saw an SOS from a flashlight.

"Got to be it. Come in on the fantail where we can rope down. You've done this before?"

"Aye, Commander. I get where you want me and hold her rock steady while you drop down. No problem, there isn't a breath of wind out there tonight."

Murdock went back to the door and waited as the chopper came in from the stern and crept slowly over it about forty feet above the deck. The pilot hovered the sixty and held it. Murdock pushed out one coil of rope and the JG the other one.

"Let's do it," Murdock said. He went down first on his side and Jaybird first on the other side. Murdock slid down the rope, careful not to go too fast. He kept his left arm low and with the rope under his arm to help slow him. The pressure on the shot-up shoulder hit him like a sledgehammer. He gasped and held on tighter with his right hand but wasn't ready when his feet hit the deck. He skidded, then gained his balance. He kept his left arm at his side as he hurried toward the steps leading down to the cabin. A man stood there with a flashlight.

"Hold it. Secret Service here. Who the hell are you?"

"U.S. Navy SEALs," Murdock said. "You've been waiting for us.

Another man came up behind the first one. "It's all right, Hank. They are friendlies. SEALs, good to see you. We've got a problem, a sick woman. She has appendicitis."

"How bad?"

"Getting worse. My wife is a nurse. Oh, I'm Art Milrose."

"Good to meet you Mr. Vice President." Murdock turned. "Mahanani, this way now," he yelled. The corpsman came running up from where he had just left the rope.

"Somebody down?" he asked.

Two minutes later, Jack Mahanani shone his flashlight on Louise. She watched him with wary eyes. There were six candles burning in the cabin and two mantel-type gas lamps. The fever had come back, stronger this time, and Louise said she hurt all over.

A tall woman beside the bed held out her hand to Mahanani. "I'm Millicent Milrose and I'm a nurse. Louise is in an advanced stage of appendicitis. She has a fever, the pain has moved to the lower quadrant and is continuous and often severe. She's been coughing and sneezing, which aggravates it. There is rebound tenderness over the appendix."

Mahanani motioned out of the room and Millicent went with him. In the hallway, Mahanani shook his head. "I'm not a doctor, but it sounds like she's starting to go into peritonitis."

"It's been getting worse. Can't we get a doctor here?"

"We can call for one from the carrier, but it would take at least an hour and a half."

Millicent bit her lower lip and her face went hard. "Call them. Get a doctor here as quickly as possible. But you and I have to operate. If we don't cut out that appendix within a half hour, Louise will die. I'll help you."

"Operate? I'm just a corpsman."

"And I'm just a nurse. I've seen it done a hundred times. Let's get washed up and try to set up a sterile field. We have some sterile bandages, sponges, and knives. What else do we need?"

"A doctor," Mahanani said. Millicent grabbed his arm and pulled him back into the room.

"Everyone out," she said. "Arthur, bring those materials we got ready. This fine young man and I are going to operate. What's your name?"

"Jack"

"Fine, Jack. You have any chloroform in your med kit?"

"No."

"What about morphine?"

"Yes, ampoules."

"Good. Ten milligrams?"

"Not sure, tens I think. The kind I always use. We can use one ten without slowing her breathing too much. Correct?"

"Yes, a ten should be fine. That won't stop the pain but it will help."

The vice president came into the room with the bandages, sterile pads, and a sheet with a hole cut in it. He put the sterile goods down on the sheet.

"The sheet was baked in the oven with the other bandages and pads, so it should be fairly sterile," he said.

Murdock had gone back to the deck and used the SATCOM to call the carrier. He told them the situation and asked for a doctor to be rushed to the site.

"She's too ill to be hoisted into a chopper. The doctor will have to come here. Peritonitis is a real danger." They said a doctor would be inbound within ten minutes. No estimated time of arrival.

Back in the stateroom, the two got ready to operate. Mahanani put the shot of morphine into the woman's arm, and watched her. Her eyes fluttered but she stayed awake.

Millicent's mouth was a hard line. Her eyes were steady but cold now and angry that this had happened to Louise. She whispered to Mahanani. "When we start, the pain is going to be severe, and it probably will make her pass out. Which will be good. Then we can work quickly."

"You going to cut?" Mahanani asked.

"Never have."

"Me too." Mahanani sighed. "I better do it. Those knives look sharp. Use a pen and mark where I should cut."

They had pulled up Louise's nightgown and spread the sheet again so the opening was on her lower belly. Millicent looked at the area and used the antiseptic to bathe the whole belly twice. Next she made a two-inch line on the tender flesh. She looked at the hospital corpsman.

"Cut just through the skin first, so we can see where we are. There will be a layer of fatty tissue just under the skin. You'll cut through that next. Then I'll push that aside and separate the muscles in there until I get into the cavity and find the appendix. I've seen it done dozens of times. It takes a doctor about five minutes to do the whole job."

Mahanani looked at the patient's face. Her eyes flickered then closed.

"She might pass out," he said. "Let's do it."

They both had washed their hands in hot water from the kitchen and now bent over the bed. Mahanani took a deep breath and used the sharpest knife. He made a delicate cut on the woman's belly. It didn't go through her skin.

"You have to press hard and firmly," Millicent said. "The human skin is really rather tough."

He tried again and this time the knife sank into the flesh as he drew it down two inches. Louise screamed and lifted up in bed, then fainted and fell back. Blood ran out of the cut. Millicent soaked it up with the sponges and spread the wound.

"Now, cut again, a little deeper. See the layer of fatty tissue? We need to get through that."

Mahanani felt sweat beading on his forehead. He used the knife again and cut through the fatty tissue. Millicent spread the tissue apart. Mahanani looked in awe at the inside of the woman's body. He could see a section of intestine. Millicent probed into the area with her fingers, pushed more tissue aside, then separated the muscles until she found what she wanted.

"Here it is, the appendix. Now, all we have to do is cut off that little extension. First, I'll tie it off with a double knot below and above where you cut. That stops any bleeding and keeps the vile stuff in the appendix from leaking into the body cavity. You cut it off, and I'll hold it and lift it out. Then I'll be ready with my needle and thread and sew up any ruptures." Millicent sweat as she reached in with the sewing thread and made the two tie-offs using double knots, and leaving a quarter of an inch between them. She wiped off her hands, then blotted her face and looked at Mahanani. "Ready?"

He nodded, put the sharp blade between the two thread tie-offs, and looked at the nurse. She nodded. Mahanani took a deep breath, steadied his hand, and sliced between the ties. Millicent held on to the end of the appendix as he cut, and then she quickly took it out of the way. She sponged the area with fresh sterile sponges, then using the curved needle from her sewing kit, she made six cross-stitches on the small area just behind the thread tie and cut the thread with a pair of scissors. She sponged the field around the intestines again. "I want to pick up any foreign matter that may have been introduced here," she said. Then she finished and pulled the muscles and fatty tissue back in place and stitched it all together neatly. To finish she used more thread and made several stitches, pulling the incision skin back together where the corpsman had cut through it.

When she was done she wiped the whole area with the antiseptic twice and put a sterile bandage over the incision and taped it in place. Then she looked up at Mahanani and hugged him. "We did it, we did it. I think we saved Louise's life."

Back on the fantail, Murdock used the SATCOM again to talk to the chopper pilot, who had pulled fifty yards away.

"We're secure here, SH-60. Check with your CO for orders."

"That's a roger, SEALs."

Murdock called the carrier and told them that the emergency operation was over and seemed successful. The doctor should continue to the yacht and check out the patient. Half of the SEALs had sacked out on the fantail. They had no idea what they were supposed to do. After all of the rush, rush, this had turned into a letdown for most of them. Not for Mahanani.

"You should have seen me. There I was operating on this woman. Blood spurting out everywhere. We were down to the last chance to save her life. I wielded the razor-sharp fish filleting knife and made the final cut to remove the diseased appendix."

"Sure you didn't vomit in the cut-open body when you saw that blood?" Jaybird called.

"Barfed? No way, not our glorious medical corpsman," Miguel Fernandez said. "He couldn't—he'd passed out the second he took that fish cutter in hand."

Mahanani grinned. He'd done good and he knew it and that was all that mattered right then. Yes, he'd done a surgery. Those months of training had at last paid off.

Murdock came back from talking on the SATCOM. "Just had word from the carrier. She's working a patrol pattern now instead of moving our way. The *Shiloh* will rendezvous with us. The doctor is still on the way in an

S and R chopper. He'll come down by hoist and remain with the patient. The cruiser should get here before daylight. It wasn't clear how far away from us she is. When she arrives she'll put on a tow rope and haul us back into Haifa. No rush in our leaving the yacht, so we're on light duty until we hit port."

"Unless Don Stroh calls with another strange mission for us," Gardner said.

One of the crewmen came up to Murdock and spoke quietly with him. He grinned and left.

"Now here's some good news. The chef on board said he just found enough spaghetti and canned sauce to whip up a whole bunch of pasta, if anyone is interested. Should have enough for everyone, including some garlic toast and soft drinks."

"The passengers and crew eat first," Murdock said. "The SEALs will be at the end of the line."

"Story of my life, end of the line," Canzoneri said.

Bill Bradford came from around the bow of the ship with a grin. "Hey, Skipper. You told me to monitor the SATCOM. I sure as hell did. Somebody wants to talk to you. Your old buddy Don Stroh and he sounds so excited that he can hardly talk."

"Here we go again," Jaybird said. Murdock hurried to the bow to take the call from Don Stroh.

17

Haifa, Israel

Less than twenty hours after the spaghetti dinner on board the yacht *Inspiration,* Murdock and his top planners sat around a table at the Rahat Air Base. Israeli Air Force General Menuhin greeted them and turned the meeting over to Don Stroh. Murdock hadn't had a chance to talk to Stroh before. He and the rest of the SEALs didn't know what was coming next.

"Gentlemen, we have a problem, as one of our astronauts said a few years back. We could be facing a serious breach of top secret knowledge, skill, and training. We don't want that to happen. You know about the EMP and the pulse bomb that put Haifa back into the Stone Age for a few hours. The city still hasn't recovered from the effect of the electronic blowout.

"As most of you know, the United States abandoned the flux compression generator type of EMP bomb years ago. We're so far past that that our top men in the field hardly remember it. One of those top men is Ronen Kugel. You may think that's a German name, but it isn't. It comes from the old-time Jewish Ashkenazi, Jews of central or eastern European origin. The point here is that Ronen is an American scientist who had been visiting with his brother's family here in Israel."

"He got himself overrun by the Syrians," Jaybird said.

"Correct, just like the college kids. He's extremely high up in the physics field where the government is working to develop ultra-high-temperature superconductors to create intense magnetic fields. If any of you understand that, please explain it to me later.

"Right now Ronen is somewhere in northern Israel behind Syrian lines. We want him back unharmed and in his right mind. He is a national asset that we can't afford to lose, or to have captured and utilized by the Syrians."

"So we go in and bring him out," Murdock said. "Any idea where he might be, where he has been, who he might be hiding with?"

"No, no, and not really," Stroh said. "We know that originally he was in Karmi'el, that's about twelve miles below the buffer zone between us and Lebanon. Yes, well above the line the Syrians moved to on the first day of the invasion. His wife had been with him but went to Haifa the night before the invasion for a meeting with friends. She talked with him by cell phone that evening, and he said he would stay there for another week and then join her in Tel Aviv. That was our last contact with him. His cell phone was blasted into mush like everyone else's."

"Where are the front lines of the battle zones now?" JG Gardner asked.

One of the army generals at the table went to a large-scale map on the wall and using a pointer showed how the magnetic markers gave a visual depiction of the MLR.

"We have regained much of our lost territory," the general said. "However in this central section where Karmi'el is situated, we have run into intense opposition. Our MLR around that central zone is still well over fifteen miles into Israel."

"Do you now control Zefat?" Murdock asked.

"We do and most of the territory north of there to the buffer zone."

"Did you bring out the bodies of the two American students killed near Zefat?" Murdock asked.

"We did, yesterday if I'm correct on that," the general said.

"So how do we get across the MLR?" Lam asked.

"I understand you men are good at doing that," the general said.

"Only when we have to, sir," Murdock said. "This time we won't have any pretty girls to sing for us."

"Chopper in, chopper out the only way," Jaybird said.

"Officially we're not part of this war," Don Stroh said.

"So make it a black op," JG Gardner said. "Paint the I.D. off a Sea Knight. Fly it in here from the *Stennis* and we're in business."

"That would be a way in," Murdock said. "We fly Israeli territory up to Zefat and then cross the MLR and drop in as close to Karmi'el as we can get and start our search. Somebody there must know where he is or where he went."

General Menuhin looked at Stroh. Stroh looked back at Murdock. "Hell, Stroh, a black op is nothing new to you or the carrier. You can stash the Sea Knight back at Zefat for a quick retrieval and we're back in the barracks in time for morning chow."

"I'd have to talk to Washington."

"You already used the SH-60 into enemy-held land," Gardner said. "What's the difference?"

"Nine college kids with important fathers, that's the difference."

"One other difference," Murdock said. "That was an Israeli sixty, not one of ours. It was shot down, remember, and the pilots were Israelis."

"Yet this man is a high-up biggie in the pulse bomb department and you won't even pop one Sea Knight to get him back?" Senior Chief Sadler asked.

Murdock shook his head. "Stroh, tell the CIA if they want Ronen back, they are going to have to risk some assets besides sixteen SEALs. We can't function on fumes. We need some go power."

Stroh hesitated. "Can you guarantee that the bird won't be shot down?"

"I'll guarantee it, Stroh," Gardner said. "Of course my guarantee isn't worth a cent when the Syrians start popping away with their AK-47s. Just one of those NATO-sized rounds in an oil line or a fuel tube and that bird is history. You know that. The CIA knows that. How bad do you want Ronen back in safe territory?"

General Menuhin held up his hand. "We can help here. We can give you solid support right up to the MLR on the ground, then do some intense attacks with tanks and infantry where you want to cross the main line of resistance. You'll do it at night, so there shouldn't be a lot of action from the MLR. Still a five-minute firefight right at your crossing point should give you enough cover to get into the occupied zone. Can you inform Washington about that, Mr. Stroh?"

Don Stroh nodded. "Can and will. Actually I've been given carte blanche on this problem. I can use any assets we have as long as I don't sink a carrier. We'll bring in two forty-sixes, the Sea Knights, from the carrier. Base them here. Can we get fuel and resupply for them?" Stroh asked, looking at the general.

"Anything you need."

"Then I'll get right on the horn and fly in two forty-sixes, one for backup. What time is it?"

"A little after sixteen-hundred," Lam said.

"I'll have the forty-sixes here in two hours. Let's plan on going in as soon as they are ready after that, say eighteen-thirty. Be more than dark by the time you get to your landing zone."

"Get the coordinates on that town," Murdock said. "You SEALs, let's get back to our quarters and work over equipment and check on ammo. We will need some. General, who can our chief see about ammo?"

"I'll send a man to your quarters," the general said and then stood. The rest of the men shot to attention. "Gentlemen, good luck, and call me if you need anything."

"Special mess?" Jaybird asked.

"I'll call the mess hall nearest you," one of the Israeli colonels at the big table said. "Be there at seventeen-hundred."

Stroh walked with them back toward their quarters.

"Looks like we're flying blind again," Murdock said. "A real search and rescue mission. I like it a lot better when we can pinpoint where we're going and how we get there."

"Hey, I got you two choppers. No high and dry this time."

"At least you keep us employed," Jaybird said. "Better than sitting on our asses for six months on some carrier fucking around the South Pacific or the Persian Gulf."

"Yeah, how do we get out of that duty?" Rafii asked.

"The CNO told your captain to take your platoon out of the rotation list," Stroh said. "I thought you guys knew that."

"Most of us did," Murdock said.

"Have you got a picture and description of this Kugel jasper?" Gardner asked.

"Actually I do. One taken just last year. In my kit. I'll get it right now and meet you in your quarters."

"Ronen Kugel," Murdock said. "You say he's about fifty. We're going to need chapter and verse on him. We don't want to snatch the wrong guy."

"I'll have it. Get suited up and some chow and I'll meet you well before takeoff. I've got to get those two Sea Knights in here." Stroh turned and walked quickly away toward his own quarters.

It was old hat to the experienced SEALs. Get back from one mission and turn around fast and go out on another one. The newer men were still a little surprised by it all. Mahanani got his gear ready quickly and took his medic kit to the base hospital. He told the officer in charge what he wanted.

"I can't just give you those supplies," a captain with medical insignia said.

"Sure you can. Call Colonel Rothman over at General Menuhin's office. The general said to ask if we wanted something. I can make the call. Oh, no phones yet. So use that radio over there. I bet you can raise the colonel."

Mahanani grinned as the captain talked to Colonel Rothman.

"Yes, sir. An unusual request. Yes, I understand. Anything he wants that he can carry. Right, sir. Thank you."

The captain put down the radio and laughed. "Well, you do know people in high places. Right down here. I'll let you talk to Lieutenant Tamar. She'll be able to get what you want."

Five minutes later the nurse looked at the list. "Really? You must be figuring on doing an operation in the field."

He told her about the appendectomy and Lieutenant Tamar paled.

"I don't know if I could have done that." She nodded. "All right, yes, you do need a small bottle of chloroform. It's easy to use. Directions on the label. And some morphine, you should use tens. What else is on your list? Yes, two scalpels and two sizes of sutures, and this thing you'll call a needle."

Mahanani got back to the quarters five minutes before chow call with a grin an acre wide on his tanned face. "I'm loaded, man, am I loaded. I dare one of you fuckups to get shot bad so I can play doctor."

The SEALs were on the tarmac waiting five minutes before the pilots finished their walk-around ground check on the forty-six chopper. They boarded and the bird took off just after 1835. It was already starting to get dusk. Murdock had showed Ronen Kugel's picture to all of the men. They memorized his face, and his description: forty-nine years old, five-feet-eight, slight build, former boxer, 150 pounds with clothes on. Lots of dark hair he let grow a little long, dark eyes. Usually wore a thick mustache but no beard. They would find him.

Murdock went up beside the pilot and looked outside. Nothing but darkness, a few lights, and more black Israeli countryside.

"You know where that spot is that they're going to start a firefight on the MLR up there somewhere?" Murdock asked the pilot, shouting so he could be heard.

The pilot nodded. "Yeah. We're all zeroed in on a definite spot in the line where the Israelis will make their attack. They'll use tank artillery, machine guns, and infantry fire. When I give them the word on the radio that we're within a mile of their position, they open up. We get across in the confusion and noise and tank rounds going off in bunkers. I come back out five miles south, where we do the same thing. Should work."

"You tried it before?"

"Not in this war. It's a damn good idea. Covers up the sound of our chopper, and the Syrians don't know we're loose inside their lines. Hard to sneak a chopper like this across an MLR without some covering noise."

Murdock worried about the radio frequencies matching, but they must have worked that out and tested it before they moved out of Haifa.

"We're coming up on Zefat," the pilot said. "From there we turn a hard left and head for the MLR, which runs along there about five miles out. We'll be a little north of Karmi'el on purpose. That's where the shelling takes place." He tuned the radio frequency and nodded at Murdock. "This is Highboy looking for some Action," he said.

The pilot waited a moment, then repeated the call. His speakers were in his earphones, so Murdock didn't hear. The pilot nodded. "That's a roger, Action. In thirty seconds. We're moving your way."

The pilot waved at Murdock. "Get them at the doors. I'll touch down and then lift off in about twenty seconds. Get your men out and gone as fast as possible."

Murdock waved. "We've done it before under fire thirty or forty times." Murdock stepped back into the ship and motioned the men to the doors. One squad lined up at each side. Murdock would be the first one out. Gardner would make sure everyone was out and be tail-end Charlie. Murdock felt the craft speed up, and at almost the same time he could hear heavy tank rounds exploding somewhere ahead. Then the craft slanted lower and charged forward. Murdock could see the ground. They were no more than thirty feet in the air. A good-sized tree would knock them out of the sky. But there were no trees, and the SH-46 jolted through the night, just over the chattering machine guns and blasting rifles as the tank rounds continued to slam into enemy positions across the MLR.

Moments later they were past the firefight and bending to the south just a bit, then Murdock heard the sound of the motor change and the craft pitched slightly forward and hovered, then settled to the ground. When the landing gear touched down, Murdock yelled. "Go, Go, Go," he bellowed over the pounding noise of the chopper engine and blades.

Murdock jumped the two feet to the ground, ran forward forty feet, and went prone, his weapon pointing outward. Within ten seconds all the Alpha Squad had hit the dirt near him. The chopper's engines had revved up and it lifted straight up, then pivoted and raced back the way it had come, only to the south more, where there would be another short, sharp firefight.

Murdock touched his Motorola mike. "Check in by squads—everyone here?" He listened as his squad members all reported in, then Gardner's group. "Anybody see any lights? There should be a town around here somewhere."

"South and west," Jefferson said. "I can see some lights through the trees on that little hill."

"Lam, go," Murdock said. "Alpha Squad in a diamond formation ten yards apart. Let's choggie. Bravo, come behind us. Keep watching, there must be some Syrians in this area somewhere. Let's see them before they see us."

Murdock had his squad up the low hill almost to the top when Lam came back to them. "Little town just over the hill. Must be the place. There's a Syrian Army bivouac on this side with a few tents, two trucks, and what looks like a kitchen. We want to stay silent on this one?"

"Right, for as long as possible. How many troops down there?"

"Not sure, doesn't look like more than maybe fifty. Must be the kitchen to supply the front line troops with hot food. Do they do that?"

"I hope we don't find out. Okay, SEALs. The rest of you come to the brow of this little hill and hold. Keep ten yards in a line of skirmishers along the ridge. Lam and I are going to do a recon on this place and see what we have and if they have ever heard of a man called Ronen Kugel." By the time he said it, Lam had turned and moved silently into the darkness over the brow of the hill and down the other side. Murdock hurried to catch up with him, then eased up and followed him by ten yards, the best combat interval between men.

It took them twenty minutes to go around the soldiers and come up to the town's first houses. They found three with lights on and Murdock went up to the first one and knocked on a side door. Nobody answered. He knocked again, five easy raps that could not be interpreted as a military roust. He heard movement inside and then the door opened a crack.

Murdock heard three words he didn't understand, Hebrew probably.

"Do you speak English?" he asked.

"Yes. Who are you?"

"I'm an American looking for the American man who was staying here with his brother. Do you know about him?"

The door edged open more. "Inside, quickly. Sometimes they send patrols around the street. Most of the Syrians are still on the front lines about six miles south and west."

Murdock stepped into the dark room. He approved. No silhouette of a man in a lighted doorway.

"The American's name is Ronen Kugel."

The shadowy form of the man in front of him nodded. "We have heard of him. My sister may know where he is. Come."

They went through a door into a softly lit room with no windows. Two women sat in chairs reading. They looked up, startled by his appearance.

"A friend," the man said. "An American. The man from America visiting the Kugels. Is he still here?"

The older woman looked at him critically. "You're an American soldier?"

"No, ma'am. I'm a United States Navy SEAL."

"Heard about you men. No water around here." She stopped. "But then you work sea, air, and land. I know." She stopped and closed her book. "The American scientist, he told us what happened to our radios and TV sets. A pulse, he said. Electrons fried them. He knew all about it. He told us that somebody would invade us, and they did. He and his brother went into the hills when the Syrians were close. His brother, Yaron, said he knew a place that would be safe. We figured the war would be over in two days. It's been three or four now. We hope they don't destroy our little town in the fighting."

"A safe place, you said. Does Yaron's family know where that is?"

"They might. Their house is just four down the street. I can go bring her here."

"I'll do it," the man said. He shook Murdock's hand. "Call me Benyamin. I've been admiring your weapon. Two barrels and one looks huge. Never seen anything like it. I was in the army when I was younger. You'll have to explain it to me when I get back."

"I will. But let me come with you. Time is vital. We need to be gone before daylight."

Benyamin stared at him a moment, then nodded. "We must be careful, use the shadows. But I bet you know how to do that better than I do. How many of you are there?"

"Enough in case we run into trouble. We hope we can get in and get out quickly, with Kugel."

"He must be an important man if they sent you behind the lines." He nodded to himself. "Now, quickly, this way, out the side door. You must have a buddy out there covering for you."

They picked up Lam but didn't stop for introductions. They ran to the alley, then down past two houses. Benyamin stopped near the third and looked at the next residence. It had bright lights showing in every window.

"Not right," Benyamin said. "Wasting electricity. Yaron would never do that."

"I'll check the front," Lam said and faded into deeper shadows around the house and moved toward the street.

"Could there be Syrian soldiers inside?" Murdock asked.

"Might be. If they found out about Ronen and that he was a scientist. They might be looking for him."

Lam came back quickly. "There's a military jeep with a driver in it out front, and another soldier on guard at the front door. Let me check the back door." He vanished again without a sound.

"We have to go in," Murdock said. "How many people live in the place?"

"Usually just three. If Yaron is gone, there would be only two, his wife and his daughter."

"Good. Now, do these houses have fuse boxes on the outside? Where you can pull a switch and turn off all the lights?"

"Yes, like my place. On the other side."

Lam slipped back beside them. "One soldier on the back door. He's smoking, weapon slung over his shoulder. He'll be easy."

"Let's move up," Murdock said. "Benyamin, we'll take out the guard at the back of the house, then you go past us and turn out all the lights. As soon as you kill the light, hit the ground and stay there. We don't want to shoot you by mistake."

Benyamin touched the silencer on Lam's MP-5 and nodded.

"Yes, I can do that."

"Let's move," Murdock said. "We only have until daylight to find our man."

18

The three moved up step by slow step until they could see the Syrian soldier guarding the rear door. He lit one cigarette off the old butt and sounded like he hummed a song. Murdock pointed to Lam, who patted his silenced MP-5. Murdock nodded.

"Do the women speak English?" Murdock whispered to Benyamin. The answer came back with another whisper that they did. Lam went prone and lifted the little gun to steady it, moved the fire selector to single shot, and sighted in on the soldier fifty feet away. He relaxed, sighted in again, then slowly squeezed the trigger. The round hit the guard in the chest, near his heart, and he went down clawing the ground. His rifle banged on the dirt of the alley. They waited. No one came to his aid. Lam ran forward with his KA-BAR out, and when he saw the man was still alive, he slit his throat from one carotid artery to the other. Blood pumped out in twin surges every time the fading heart beat.

Murdock and Benyamin ran forward. Murdock paused beside Lam, who was at the rear door testing the knob. Unlocked. Murdock moved his fire selector to the 5.56 barrel and on single shot and gave Lam a thumbs-up then pointed his finger at him. They waited. Lights began going off in sections of the house. Yells sounded inside. Someone pounded toward the back just as the last lights faded inside.

The door jolted outward and a shadowy figure ran through. Lam was on the knob side and swung his KA-BAR out and the Syrian soldier ran into it. He bleated, and turned his head as he was falling. Lam ripped the blade out of the man's chest. The Syrian died as he writhed on the ground. Murdock pushed around the door where it had slammed into him. He pointed at Lam again and the scout slid inside the dark room. Murdock came right behind him. They had out their penlights and checked the room. It was a utility and storage area. No one was there. A door in the center stood open.

When one of the penlight beams darted across the opening, a shot blasted from inside. A slug whispered past Murdock and hit the rear wall. The two SEALs edged forward, one on each side of the door.

"Ladies, if you can hear me, close your eyes tightly and put your hands over your ears. Big explosion coming but it won't hurt you. Do it now."

Lam pulled the pin on a flashbang grenade and rolled it into the room. Murdock and Lam ducked their heads, closed their eyes, and muffled their ears with their hands. The six cracking explosions blasted through the house, followed by six piercing, blinding strobes of light so bright they stabbed at Murdock's eyes right through his hands, even though he was in another room. Lam and Murdock powered into the room as soon as the last strobe faded, using their small lights. With only the faint beams, they stumbled over two Syrian soldiers rolling on the floor and holding their ears. Lam tied their hands behind them with riot cuffs, as Murdock looked in the next room. Two women crouched on a sofa, hands still over their ears. On the floor nearby one Syrian officer tried to open his shocked eyes.

Murdock knew the man couldn't hear anything. He chopped the man's chin with the butt of his Bull Pup, then bound his hands behind him. One of the women peered out from in back of her hands.

"I can't really see you, but you must be there."

"Yes, ma'am. We are. Let us take care of the two Syrians at the front door and we'll be back."

When Lam had cleared the next room, he could open the front door. There was no one there. The jeep and the sentry near the front door were gone. He told Murdock.

"Ladies, we need to get you out of here. The Syrians will come back with lots of weapons and they won't be kind. Come with us. Benyamin is just outside. He sent us here. We can go to his house."

"You must be an American," the younger woman said, trying to get her ears working.

"Yes, miss. Now please, hurry with us. We don't have much time."

Five minutes later in Benyamin's house, the older woman told them what she knew.

"Yaron never really told me everything about the cave. It was a hideout, an emergency shelter and bomb shelter if we were ever attacked. We didn't have time to get all of us up there, but he and Ronen went. My Yaron said we should stay here. I don't know who told the Syrians that Mr. Kugel was staying with us."

"Your last name might have helped, ma'am," Murdock said. "How can we find the cave?"

"I'll draw you a map, but Benyamin will have to show you. It's not easy to find."

"How far is it?"

"Maybe five miles north. The Syrians are still in this whole area."

"I've got fifteen men to help us get there," Murdock said. "Please draw the map quickly so we can get moving. If I have a map, and we get separated, I'll still have a chance to find it."

"Six men in town know about it. I think two or three of them may be up there." She drew a map with a ball-point pen on a piece of lined paper and gave it to Murdock. It showed north and south, a settlement, two roads, and some hills. Benyamin had changed clothes, into jeans, hiking boots, and an old leather jacket and felt hat. He carried a rifle, and a box of shells showed out of his pocket.

"Let's go," he said. "You two Kugels keep hidden. We've got a basement storage under the rug. Better get down there now. There are candles and food and water. The Syrians are going to be searching every house. They lost a few men up there. They won't be happy."

Benyamin's wife smiled. "I'll take care of the women-folk. You men get moving. It's a good hike."

Ten minutes later the three men topped the small hill where the fourteen SEALs waited. Lam worked up to within four feet of Gardner before the JG knew he was there.

"Damnit, Lam. I never heard a sound. How do you do that?"

"Show you sometime. We're moving north. We've got a line where our boy might be stashed."

"Column of ducks, platoon, moving north," Gardner said on the Motorola. "Let's go, Lam. Get us caught up with our leader."

The platoon worked north with Lam out front. They had gone less than a quarter of a mile when Lam came back from his scouting position.

"We've got something up front I don't like, Skipper. Come take a look."

Murdock, Gardner, and Benyamin eased up a small hill and looked over the top. Seventy-five yards below they saw Syrians.

"A pair of bloody tanks," Gardner said.

"Looks like they are in reserve or maybe getting repaired," Lam said. "Must be more than a dozen men down there. Trouble is there's a cliff on the far side of them we don't want to climb, and on this side there's a good-sized river we can't cross."

"Yeah, bottleneck," Benyamin said. "This is one of the best routes north, and those two tanks are plugging it in case of a breakthrough by the Israeli Army."

"So we take them out," Murdock said. He used the Motorola. "Everyone up front. I want the twenties on line at this rear slope. Move it."

"Twenties?" Benyamin asked. "You have twenty-millimeter weapons?"

Murdock held out his Bull Pup. "This one, Ben. It has a twenty on top and a 5.56 below. We can even use this for airbursts." He explained how it worked as the SEALs moved into position.

"What I wouldn't have given to have had one of those thirty years ago," Benyamin said.

Murdock checked the seven Bull Pup shooters, then talked with Benyamin again. "We do need to go through here, to get farther north to find the cave?"

"Absolutely."

On the Motorola, Murdock said: "Two rounds each, airbursts. Three men on left of the line, hit around the left-hand tank. Rest of us the other one. Sight in now and use airbursts and fire when you hear my round." Murdock sprawled on the ground, lined up his target for the laser, and pulled the trigger. The round slammed out of the muzzle and almost at once, six more 20mm fragmentation rounds lanced toward the tanks.

They sounded like seven giant firecrackers exploding one after another and some on top of each other. All were airbursts showering hot, deadly shrapnel on everyone and everything below. Four men around a campfire died before they could move. Three others coming into the clearing from some brush went down and tried to crawl away. The second seven rounds stopped them dead where they lay. A small tent to the left side caught so much shrapnel that it teetered and then fell. One man struggled out of the tent only to have Bradford nail him with a round from his sniper rifle.

"Hold," Murdock said. "Drop anybody with sniper, and MP-5 anybody who moves," Murdock said. Four rounds sounded, then silence claimed the land.

"Lam, let's take a look," Murdock said. They ran down the first fifty yards, then flattened and watched. They saw nothing move. Both men got to their feet and without making any sounds came to the site. Murdock counted twelve bodies. The tank hatches were open. He dropped a fragmentation grenade in one and Lam put one in the second tank, in case any Syrians had been hiding inside.

"Clear front," Murdock said on the radio. "Bring the troops through."

When the SEALs had checked over the bodies and found them all dead, Murdock and Lam tore the uniform shirt off one man and cut it up into strips they could feed down the fuel filler on the two tanks. When they smelled the fuel soaking the wicks, they moved the SEALs north and then lit the wicks and ran upslope as well. They were less than fifty yards up the small valley when the first fuel tank exploded. That set off the high explosive tank rounds inside the shell, blowing the machine into several large pieces of junk. The other fuel tank blew a few seconds later.

"Scratch two tanks and crews," Murdock said. He looked at Benyamin. "Remind you of your army days?"

"Nothing quite this dramatic. Mostly hit-and-run in those days. We've got about four miles to go; we better hustle before the Syrians come to check on their tanks."

Lam soon found a trail through a harvested wheat field in the valley. He talked to Murdock and Benyamin about it.

"Wasn't made by Israelis," Benyamin said. "Has to be Syrians using this as a major route for ground troops to keep away from the planes that have been bombing and strafing trucks coming down from Lebanon with supplies and troops."

"They probably come at night to avoid the planes," Murdock said. "So we better get off the trail and into the fringes of brush along the edge of the valley."

"And we better see them before they see us," Lam said. He led them to the right, away from the trail.

Ten minutes later he called a warning. "Troops on the move in the valley; everyone better hit the dirt."

The growing moon played tag with scudding clouds now as Murdock watched the middle of the two-hundred-yard-wide valley. Soon he heard a motorcycle idling along. Then the machine came out of the gloom. An officer, Murdock figured. Behind him, moving at a fast march, came a string of troops, two abreast and not more than arm's length apart. One well-placed twenty would kill forty of them. Murdock didn't count, but Lam did. He came on the horn.

"Cap, I figure there were over two hundred in that batch. All had their rifles, some sub guns. Reinforcements for the front?"

"You got it, Little Beaver," Murdock said.

"Little Beaver? Who the hell is that?" Lam asked.

"Long before your time. Old comic strip from the forties called Red Ryder. A Western hero with Little Beaver, his ten-year-old Indian companion, who was always saying, 'You betchum, Red Ryder.' "

"Thanks for that, Skipper," George Canzoneri said. "I couldn't have lived another hour without that vital bit of folklore and history."

"You're welcome, Zorro."

"He was Mexican, I'm Italian."

"Close enough," Murdock said. "Lead us out again, Lam. I'm putting Benyamin up there with you. He says somewhere near the spot it gets tricky."

"Roger that."

It was almost forty minutes later when Lam called a halt.

"Skipper, you better get up here. I'm out about fifty ahead on another little rise at the edge of the valley. It peters out in another half mile, Ben tells me. Something you need to check out."

Murdock, Gardner, and Sadler made the short hike. They bellied down in the grass and looked over the crest of the little hill.

Below them about two hundred yards they saw a huge splash of light in the otherwise dark countryside. They could hear a number of diesel engines purring along that must be running generators. Lights had been strung on poles down a company street of at least ten twenty-man wall tents. Inside, ten folding cots could be set up on each side. A medium tank, like the two they had destroyed, sat with the muzzle of the 75- to 80mm cannon aimed south toward the Israeli lines. Murdock spotted three jeeps, two six-by-six trucks, what had to be a mess tent and a cook tent, and others on the opposite side of the company street, probably for offices and officers. It was just before 2200 and Murdock saw twenty men moving around, with no obvious direction or hurry.

"Ben says he thinks it's a regimental or divisional rear headquarters. He knows the area. It's about eight miles west of the major north-south highway, with a good paved road in this far."

"That will be a problem," Gardner said. "Do we have to go around them?"

"No, we won't go around them," Lam said. "Ben says this is close to the place where they had the secret cave and their stash of goods and arms. Now take a close look to the left in that open space opposite the tank." He pulled down his binoculars and handed them to Ben. "Three men have been stripped naked and tied to poles dug deep into the ground. Ben tells me that's one way that they execute deserters and killers in their ranks. Justice is quick if not always just."

"Who are the three men?" Murdock asked.

"That's the problem," Lam said. "Ben took my glasses and worked down to within about thirty yards of the poles. He got a good look at them and came back. He says he knows all three men. Two are friends of his from Karmi'el, the other one is the guy we're looking for, Ronen Kugel."

19

"What the hell are we supposed to do now?" Lieutenant (j.g.) Gardner asked nobody.

"We start earning our big bucks," Murdock said. On the Motorola he called up Jaybird, Bradford, and Sadler. "All we have to do is wade in there and bring Kugel out without his hide sporting a dozen rifle bullet holes," Murdock said. He looked at Ben. "Are they tied up there to be shot in the morning, or is this some kind of torture?"

"Most likely a torture. You know how hot the sun gets here in the daytime, and it don't look like rain."

"We've got to get all three of them out of there tonight. Did it look like they were wounded or hurt?"

"Not that I could see. No big wounds or broken bones."

"Let's pull down the reverse slope ten," Murdock said. When they were down, they gathered around Murdock just as the other three came up. Lam took them up to look at the problem. When they got back down, Murdock started it. "We have to rescue those three men. How do we do it? Assets?"

"We have seven twenties and can put down most of them away from the prisoners," Sadler said.

"We can call in the chopper who has a gunner with two fifty-caliber MGs," Jaybird said. "We use it to stage an attack on the north side of the camp. Pull most of their men up there."

"Then we take out the ones around the prisoners with silenced shots," Bradford said. "Get within thirty yards in the brush and shoot them with silenced rounds, then charge in and get the prisoners off their posts and up this hill."

"Then the bird drops down, grabs us, and takes us back near that town," Lam said. "We drop off our three Israeli guests and then charge over the MLR home free."

"We could hit the far tents with twenties to mark the target for the chopper," Gardner said. "They wouldn't know where the airbursts came from. It just might work."

"A real attack would include ground-based machine-gun fire and rifle fire," Jaybird said. "How can we fake that?"

"We can't unless we send a squad up north and then fire into the same area as the twenties hit," Lam said. "Then they would have some direction of the fire and they'd send out a company to chase down our squad. We don't want that."

Murdock rubbed his right hand over his face. He needed a shave. "If we hit them we have to be ready to bug out of here fast. That means having a chopper on our PD almost at once. So we need two choppers. How long from Haifa to get to where the other chopper should be, Jaybird?"

"Half an hour tops."

"Let's pull back a quarter click and leave Ben and Lam up here as our OP. Bradford, as soon as we get situated, get that antenna zeroed in. How do we talk to Stroh in Haifa?"

"TAC Two. He should be waiting for us."

Fifteen minutes later they were in a secure area with two guards out and Murdock made the call.

Stroh wasn't pleased with the plan.

"Look, they have your boy naked and tied to a pole. He may have been tied out there all day today or for two days, and be half-dead already. If the sun is out tomorrow, he could be dead by sixteen-hundred. You want that?"

"Hell no, but two forty-sixes?"

"We need them. Get that other one in the air pronto, have it meet the first one, and then they come across the MLR when we tell them to. Both of them with fifty-caliber door gunners. We're about six miles north of

Karmi'el. When we know they are ready to cross the MLR, we'll start our firefight down here and lead them in. Be sure we can talk to them on TAC One or Two."

Murdock let up on the send button and waited. He snorted and pushed the button again.

"You want this scientist back or don't you? He's worth a dozen forty-sixes, you know that. Now, stop squirming and worrying about what your boss is gonna say, and fly that other bird over here, now."

Another silence. This time Murdock waited. At last the speaker came on. "Yeah. Okay. One more forty-six with door gunners and fifty calibers. On the way. I'll have them coordinate with you on TAC Two when they are in position at Zefat." There were several seconds of dead air. "Murdock."

"Yeah, Stroh."

"I'm putting my ass on the line for this one. Don't let me down. I need that damn scientist."

"You got him. Out."

Murdock's watch showed 0100 before the radio came on again. He grabbed it.

"Yeah, Highboy One, this is Grounded."

"We're at Zefat on the ground waiting your go. We have contacted Israeli Action and they are ready to get us in and out with a fierce bombardment on the MLR just to the west of here. Give me the word. We are about ten minutes from takeoff to your position. Questions?"

"None. We'll be hitting some tents in a divisional headquarters with twenty-millimeter airbursts. Should give you a beacon to come in on. We'll also put in some WP rounds to light up the target. One of you work over the far end of the tents. Nothing on the south end, that's where the prize package is. Your attack should help pull the troops up there and away from our scientist."

"That's a roger, north end of burning tents. Got it."

"Then we want the second chopper to come in south of the camp. We'll be on a low hill and set up an LZ with a flare on some fairly level ground. If that second chopper isn't on time, we're toast. We won't be able to communicate then, we'll be charging away from the hill. You'll have your go in about five minutes. Grounded, Out."

Most of the SEALs heard the talk on their personal Motorolas. Now they got up, checked their weapons, and went with Murdock up to the hill. He spread them out as before, with Lam taking four MP-5 shooters down the hill to within forty yards of the edge of the camp. They would use silenced rounds so they didn't attract attention to their position.

"Ready," Lam said.

"I want two WP and the rest airbursts. I'll do one WP, Mahanani the other one. Then we put in measured rounds for three or four minutes. I'm waiting until I can hear the choppers before we open fire. Bradford, you set up?"

"Yes, sir, ready."

Murdock used the mike. "Highboy One and Two. This is your go. I want Highboy Two to come in a hundred yards south, that is south of the lighted camp. We'll have out a flare for his LZ. Got that, Highboy Two?"

"That's a roger, Grounded. We're in the air. Hit the MLR in five and you in another five."

"When I hear your engines, I'll start firing. Just head for the biggest light show in this end of Israel. Electric lights all over the place. But fire into the north end of the tents only."

"That's a roger, Grounded."

"Hold steady, SEALs. When we hear the choppers, we fire. Not before. We could overplay our hand. Lam. As soon as you eliminate hostiles in that immediate area of the posts, take your four men in there with KA-BARs and cut free and carry out or let run out with you those three men. You might shoot out some of the floodlights while you're at it. Bradford, good job for you. Get as many in this end of camp as you can." Murdock paused, listening for the choppers. No indications they were near.

"Everyone on board? Check in." Murdock waited while both squads checked in, by patrol order.

"Roger that, platoon. We're all here. Now listen for those birds."

It was six minutes by Murdock's watch before he heard

the choppers. "Here they come. On my round twenties. We'll do the first salvo, then a round every ten seconds. Space them out. Bradford, you do those lights and help on Lam's crew. Here we go." Murdock sighted in on the farthest tent with his WP round and fired. It hit midway in the canvas, tore through, and exploded inside. The second WP round hit a short way toward the front and moments later the whole tent was one big bonfire. Then the airbursts began and rained death down on the men who scurried out of tents along the line. Some had weapons, most didn't. Murdock saw the first chopper slanting in and the .50-caliber rounds tearing up the last three tents in the line. The bird swung around and raced back out of rifle range and hovered somewhere out of sight, blasting the area with the long-range .50-caliber machine guns.

Below, Lam sighted in on a guard who paced near the last tent in the row. He was thirty yards from the prisoners. He heard one floodlight shatter, then saw another go dead. Two more guards moved toward the prisoners, looking at the dead floods. Lam's men cut down all three Syrians and watched for more.

"Two more bad guys on the left, just coming out of the shadows," Donegan said. Both went down with two slugs in each one. Bradford had killed three floodlights in the same area. Lam watched for more Syrians. He saw three more run into the scene from behind the row of tents. Bradford must have nailed one; the MP-5s stuttered out three-round silenced bursts and the last two men hit the dirt and didn't get up.

"Donegan—you, me, and Rafii, let's go in and get those guys. On the double, be ready to shoot anyone you see in there." Before they were to the edge of the camp, two Syrians ran around one of the officers' tents. Lam saw them coming and drilled them with a three-round burst. They jolted to the ground and one tried to crawl away. Donegan saw him moving and nailed him with three more rounds.

Lam got to the first prisoner and sliced his rope ties. He was barely conscious. Lam draped him over his shoulder and ran for darkness out of the camp and toward the hill. He heard more silenced rounds. Behind him. Donegan shot a Syrian who had wandered toward them looking up at the dead floodlights. Donegan cut the bonds of the third man. He was conscious, angry, said he could walk, and he and Donegan ran for the darkness.

Rafii was last to get to his man.

"Yes, yes," the man shouted. He was ready to run when Rafii got him cut loose, and they both sprinted for the darkness. Rafii heard firing behind him, felt the wind of a bullet zipping close to him, and rushed forward out of the light into the darkness. He stumbled and stopped.

A body. A SEAL. He turned the man over. Donegan. Rafii bent and picked up Donegan, who weighed more than he did, and began to work with him up the hill. Lam almost had his man to the top of the hill when the choppers hit the tents again with another sequence of .50-caliber machine-gun fire. One of the forty-sixes swept in closer, then slanted back out of rifle range and blasted the tents with the .50-caliber fire. Some men still ran from the tents; most had guns now but couldn't see the choppers killing them.

Murdock had watched the men below as one by one the prisoners were cut loose and helped up the hill. When all three of the prisoners were free, he saw one of the SEALs go down. Was he shot or did he fall? He didn't get up. Another SEAL stopped and picked up the wounded man and worked up the hill. Murdock sprinted down the hill and took the weight off the much smaller Rafii and they hurried up the hill. Lam had his man over the ridge last. Jaybird had run down the hill on the reverse slope to find an LZ. A minute later, Murdock saw a flare go off marking the LZ location. Bradford didn't have the SATCOM working, but the bird flyer knew what he was supposed to do.

"Everyone down to the flare," Murdock said on the Motorola. Murdock checked the prisoners; the two up and moving were the Israelis. Lam had the package. "Is he hurt bad?" Murdock asked.

"Don't know, Skipper. He can't walk, hasn't said a word. He was unconscious when I cut him down. Didn't see any obvious wounds. I don't think he's been shot."

"Get him down to the chopper. I'll get two men to help you." Murdock hurried the two Israelis down the way toward the flare.

"Mahanani, we've got a customer for you. On Lam, and me now. We've got Kugel, but he's almost out of it. He's coughing, and he has a fever. I don't know what's the matter, but it isn't good."

Murdock gave Donegan to Howard to carry down the hill. He was dead and Murdock didn't know how it happened. A stray round or one aimed at the rescuers? He helped Lam with Kugel. Murdock tried to talk with him but got only gibberish back.

He had left Fernandez and Canzoneri on the top of the hill as a rear guard to discourage anyone who tried to get up the hill to fire at them. Now he could hear the weapons on the hill chattering off rounds. It took them only three minutes to get everyone down near the flare. It had almost burned out. Murdock looked into the darkness. Where was the other bird? Not again.

Then he heard it coming. It swept over the small hill to the west and settled to the ground twenty feet from the flare. By the time Murdock got there, half the platoon was on board. He bellowed at Fernandez and the two rear guard men raced down the hill intent on getting to the flying bird before it took flight. Lam found a place on the floor to lay Kugel. Two of the men took off their shirts and wrapped them around the naked man. The two Israelis were chattering, crying, and singing.

"We knew we were dead," one of them said. "We thought we were safe in our cave, then they pulled in with that regimental headquarters and sent out troops to check every hill and bush and they soon found our cave. Nothing to eat for three days. Almost no water. Put us in the sun yesterday morning. Kugel couldn't take the sun. He's in a bad way."

Fernandez and Canzoneri clambered on board and Gardner called it. "All accounted for, Commander," he shouted.

"Get out of here," Murdock yelled at the pilot and they

lifted off just as two rifle rounds slanted off the outside plates. Ten seconds later they were up and over the protective hill and heading for the village of Karmi'el. Murdock moved over beside the scientist lying on the floor.

"Not sure what's the matter with him," Mahanani said. "Could be sunstroke or heat exhaustion, but must be something else or something more. I feel so damned stupid not being able to figure it out."

Yaron knelt down beside them. Two flashlights played on the sick man. "He didn't take well to the heat. Hated it. Kept mostly indoors. Two days in the sun could do it. Canteens? Let's cool him down, can't hurt. Pour the water right over the shirts. That might help enough."

They poured water over the prostrate man and Mahanani said it seemed to calm him down at least. The fever was still there, but to the corpsman's trained hand it seemed a little lower.

Five minutes later they set down outside of the village of Karmi'el and the three Israelis stepped out. Murdock thanked them. They hugged the SEALs, and then the chopper lifted off and headed for the same MLR spot it had come across on the way in. Murdock saw a black shape against the clouds and recognized the other forty-six flying forty yards to the right. Everyone accounted for.

The tanks were still blasting the Syrian positions. Machine-gun fire and rifle fire peppered the same targets. There was some counterfire but not much.

Before Murdock could even locate the actual lines of the two sides, they were past them and into the darkness and quiet of the Israeli countryside. The worst was over. Now it was just a chopper ride back to Haifa.

Murdock went to the cabin. The pilot spoke on his radio. "Yes, Haifa, mission accomplished. We're across the MLR and on our way south, then to the west."

Murdock touched the pilot's shoulder. "We have one sick man, our package. Have a gurney and doctors at the hospital chopper pad when we can get there. Our medic says he looks critical. Tell Haifa that."

The pilot nodded and Murdock went back to talk with

Mahanani and to watch Kugel. "Don't let him die on us,
Mahanani. We didn't come all the way in here and lose
one man KIA just to have Kugel die of sunstroke. Keep
him alive."

Murdock used his flashlight and looked at the other
body on the chopper's floor. Tracy Donegan's head
wasn't marked. Murdock felt his shirt. The cloth over his
heart was soaked with blood. He used his flashlight again
and opened three buttons on the cammie shirt. Two round
black marks showed on Donegan's white chest. One was
directly over his heart, the other three inches to the left.
He had died instantly. Murdock buttoned the shirt and
closed the dead man's eyelids.

He looked at the silent face that had been Donegan.
They had been on a few missions together. He had been
a good SEAL. Murdock wiped his hand over his face.
The chopper was not full of SEAL talk, as often was the
case coming back from a mission. They all knew about
Donegan, and probably were making silent prayers that
the bullets hadn't found them. Murdock frowned trying to
remember. Was Donegan thirteen or fourteen? He
couldn't remember. Was he getting so callous, so de-
tached from reality, that he took the deaths of his men as
a matter of course?

"Casualty report," Murdock bellowed to get over the
chopper noise. "Anybody else get hurt?"

"Something's been squishing inside my left boot," Rafii
said. "I don't remember walking through any water."

"Where are you?" Mahanani shouted. "You've been
shot, son, but you're going to live."

Murdock watched Kugel. His breathing had evened out.
They poured more water on him and he shivered. His eyes
blinked now and then, but he was still unconscious. Murdock touched his carotid artery. A strong pulse, and regular.

Twenty minutes later the chopper came in at the
brightly lighted helicopter pad just outside the Israeli military hospital on the Rahat Air Base and six medics waited
there with a gurney. Three SEALs moved Kugel to the
edge of the chopper and then eased him out with infinite

care until he was on the gurney. Someone took Kugel's pulse, another his blood pressure as they ran forward wheeling him directly into the emergency entrance.

Murdock told Gardner to take the men back to their quarters. He sat in the chopper with Donegan. The pilot came back.

"I heard," he said. "We better take him to the morgue around in back of the hospital. We call it Graves Registration. I'll go get somebody to come out."

Murdock put both hands over his face and didn't try to stop the tears from coming. He had wiped away the wetness by the time the pilot came back with a gurney and two attendants.

"Sir, there's some paperwork we'd like you to fill out," one of the white-coated attendants said. "It'll only take a few minutes. He's a SEAL, I understand. Damn fine fighters. I'm sorry that you lost him."

"Donegan, damnit. His name is Tracy Donegan, Signalman Second Class from Andersonville, Illinois." Murdock closed his eyes and slid out of the forty-six.

"Sorry, it's been a rough night. I'll be glad to fill out the paperwork that you need. Hold the body for shipment to the U.S. It should be within a day or two."

As he followed the rolling stretcher into the hospital, Murdock remembered. Fourteen. Goddamnit, it was fourteen.

20

Nahariyya, Israel

General Mahdi Diar sat in the coolness of the oceanfront home he had commandeered as his field headquarters and sipped at his vodka-spiked lemonade as he studied the latest field reports. A colonel and two majors fussed around an eight-foot-long situation board, changing symbols as new reports came in. He hated the jagged line that the MLR had become. Early on the second day he had kept his lines almost even for better lateral support and so none of his flanks were exposed. Now there were ten places where he had little flank protection for his troops.

His position there at the coastal town of Nahariyya was secure. He had a company of tanks dug in and well hidden from Israeli aircraft. He also had five hundred seasoned troops in the immediate area and a crack regiment down the road about four miles, where the Israelis had pushed up the coast. But they were stalled now at some low hills with Syrian gunners holding the high ground.

The war had not gone as he had expected. There had been no help whatsoever from other Arab nations surrounding Israel. His call for a holy war to push the great evil Jews into the sea had failed miserably. He had counted on at least two nations to help him. Not Egypt, but surely Jordan and Iraq would send assistance in material and weapons if not troops. How had he miscalculated? Had the pulse bomb been too extreme? It had not killed a million people the way it could have if the bomb had been nuclear. Or had he misjudged the tenor of the times? Perhaps after generations of hatred for Israel, and

the goal of its total annihilation, the urgency had become
diluted and the resolve muted. Still there were dedicated
suicide bombers and men who gave their lives to hurt
Israel. Had he misjudged that faction?

He looked at the symbols again on the battle situation
board and the ragged line across the twenty-mile front.
The Israelis had pushed his men back almost to the buffer
zone on the far eastern front. His Syrian Army still held
good positions in the center of the line, but there were
deep dents in it the farther he moved to the west. On the
coast the Jews had retaken 'Akko, and were a mile north
of there. His staff had estimated Syrian losses at far more
than what he had expected. He wondered if the figure was
accurate. They said he had lost seventy-five of his one
hundred tanks. He knew that had to be impossible. Of the
fifty thousand men he had poured into the fight, his staff
reported that there had been three thousand dead and another eight thousand wounded and evacuated.

The trucks that were the lifeline of a forward moving
army had faltered in their mission. Jewish planes strafing
and bombing had reportedly destroyed over two thousand
trucks. The general rubbed his reddish face and scowled.
How could so many be gone? He had planned every detail. Air power. He hadn't counted on the skill of the Jew
pilots. They had simply outflown his pilots and shot most
of them down. He scrubbed his flattop black hair and motioned the men to continue working on the board. He went
down a short hall and into the first bedroom. The master
bedroom by the looks of it. It was at least twenty-four
feet square, with a large bed and a couch and a double
bath off it. He closed the door and smiled at Samira. She
was sixteen, well developed, and lay on the bed watching
Israeli TV, which they had somehow begun broadcasting
again. She wore nothing but a thin veil across her lower
face.

General Diar sat down beside her and she squirmed into
his lap and put both his hands on her breasts.

"May I please you, my favorite general?" she asked,
her voice low, enticing, filled with a thousand and one
promises.

"Soon. I have had bad news and I must think what I can do next. Can you help me with that?"

"Send a thousand naked Syrian girls into the front lines to seduce the Jew soldiers. Then our glorious troops can march right into Tel Aviv."

He laughed and bent to kiss one of her breasts.

"Not quite that simple. I had planned on using another pulse bomb on Tel Aviv, but the day before we set off the first one, some raiders blew up our laboratory and destroyed the other four bombs we had almost completed. They killed our scientists, too, and now we would have to start over from the first raw idea of the bomb." He shrugged and began undressing.

"In five days I was sure that we would be in Haifa and on our way to Tel Aviv. I need a striking success, a bold stroke that will demoralize the Jews and allow our troops to surge forward in a great victory."

He kept talking, not so much for Samira to hear, as to convince himself he was doing the right thing. But what? Tanks. The only way to drive forward quickly. He had more than twenty-five, he was sure. A slashing, charging thrust with all of his tanks in a surge from near the coast and shooting their way right through the suburbs and into Haifa's business district, where he would blow up every building over four stories high.

Yes. He would do it. He would risk the last of his fighter squadrons. He knew he had sixteen planes still ready to fly. Some had been sent to airfields far away for safety. He would bring them back to make morning strikes, to battle the Israeli fighters and to protect his tank column. He would get with the tank commanders now and lay out the plan. They would have no infantry support at first. Trucks would follow directly behind them when possible and provide infantry when they could. The infantry would mainly hold the corridor a mile wide down through Israel and into the homeland. Yes, it would work. The Jews would be surprised. They thought he was on the run, when instead he would be running right down their throats.

He dumped the nubile girl off his lap and hurried back to his large situation board.

"Hanieh, get me an up-to-the-minute report on all the tanks we have that are manned and ready for action. I want only those tanks that can carry at least half of their normal load of rounds for their cannons. I want it in fifteen minutes. Colonel Adar, do the same on trucks. I mean the big ones to haul troops. Also check on supplies of ammunition for the troops, and field rations. Where is that topographical map of northern Israel? Numan, I want you to help me pick the fastest and easiest route from the center of our MLR directly into Haifa. Yes, gentlemen, we are going on the offensive. We are going to drive a tank column with infantry support right into Haifa."

"General Diar," Colonel Adar said. "It's now thirteen-hundred. When do you want to start the attack?"

"We will begin to move forward across the Jews' MLR at precisely nineteen-hundred today, so get your asses in gear. We have a war to fight. Praise Allah."

"Praise Allah," the men in the room shouted in unison, then they scurried out to get to their assigned tasks.

Major Numan rolled out a large-scale topographical map. He used wipe-off markers and traced a line down from Karmi'el.

"General, we can assemble our tanks here at Karmi'el and have a good thrust due south. We charge across the weak MLR there, and continue for three more miles, then we turn due west. We charge through this valley and over a pair of low-lying hills and we should be in the outskirts of Haifa before they can move any forces to stop us. We'll go at night so their aircraft will be seriously limited in finding any targets. The trucks will drive without lights. In the darkness they won't know anything but a column thrust through their MLR. They will be blind until dawn."

"I don't see any roads in there, Numan."

"Not many, but enough that we can use the dirt roads to meet the tanks at designated spots and discharge troops to act as security for the corridor."

Diar studied the area for a moment, looked over the route and the few roads he saw on the map, then grunted.

"Good, write out instructions for the tankers. We'll use our secure radios to reach the tanks. Give them as much warning as possible about the dash to Karmi'el, and then the plunge into Haifa. All tank movements will be after dark."

"Yes, sir, General. I'll write up the orders at once and send them by radio."

General Diar looked out the window, at the view of the Mediterranean Sea and the small cove nearby. Idyllic. He wished Syria had a longer coastline. It was only about eight-five miles long. Someday he'd have a villa there, right on the beach, or on a cliff overlooking a bay with waves crashing into the rocks. He sighed. He'd been a soldier for a long, long time. With the stumbling they had done on this invasion, he had suffered his first doubts about ever becoming president and head man of all Syria. He knew he needed a smashing victory to prove himself to the people and to the powerful band of army officers who ran the country. Without that support, he was just another general looking forward to retirement.

He heard a door open behind him and turned. All the army men had left the room. He looked back and saw Samira standing in the door wearing the small thin veil and nothing else.

"Busy?" she asked.

He turned and rose from the chair. He loved her full breasts and the way they bounced and rolled when she walked. Her sweet little behind was another pleasure zone he never grew tired of. Diar smiled as he walked toward her. She pushed one hip out at him and made her breasts bounce.

"Oh, yes," Diar said. "A man has to have some time for recreation." He grabbed the girl by one breast, pulled her into the bedroom, and closed the door.

Major Nabil Shamalekh stood beside his tank in the first bunker dug into the Jewish soil just below the commanding general's headquarters. They had destroyed a house to dig the protective bunker and then camouflaged it with boards from the wrecked residence. He had his orders. As soon as it was dark he would lead his four tanks away from the coast and plunge cross-country to meet more tanks almost in the middle of northern Israel near the small town of Karmi'el. It was all in Syrian-held territory. He had studied his maps and knew the best route. Down a country road for a mile, then over a small rise due west, then down a valley to a crossroads. The road would take him directly into the rendezvous point. He figured it would take about twenty minutes if he didn't run into any mounted Israeli patrols. All of the area was in Syrian hands, but line-crossing patrols had been moving into the area to harass them lately. He went over the route again.

Major Shamalekh had not even had time to polish the new gold oak leaves on his shoulder. A major. He had dreamed of leading a platoon of tanks into battle. He just hadn't thought it would come so quickly. His platoon commander and two men above him in date of rank had been killed in the second day of fighting, when the Jew fighters had pulverized the Syrian tank battalion. He sighed. He would much rather be at home with his wife, two sons, and his small daughter, than in this fight. His family was safe in Hamah, far to the north in Syria. One of his men came up asking how many rounds of the heavy shells they should load.

"All we can carry, and we'll plan on shooting every one of them. Maximum on the machine-gun ammo supply as well. We're going all the way into Haifa." The sergeant saluted, and hurried back to the tank to take stock.

Nabil looked down at his gold oak leaf. A rank he often wondered if he would ever attain. Now it was here. He had been promoted in the field by General Diar himself yesterday. Now he was at war and had his best chance to move up another notch in the officer corps of the fairly small armored division. He took out a folder he kept in his right breast pocket. No wallets or identification of any kind were permitted, but he had brought the plastic folder along. It had two pictures. One of his sons and baby daughter. What a little jewel. She was precious. The other picture was a portrait photo of his wife. She was so beautiful he wanted to cry. So wonderful. Worth fighting for.

He would fight and come back and be the best husband he could be and raise his sons to be true men and to love the army.

He went to the tank, slid inside, and flipped on the radio. It was a half hour to dusk. He would be on alert for an early leave. He checked. All his ammo was in place and his crew inside. They were ready.

The call came ten minutes later.

"Major Shamalekh, move out your platoon. Lead them in your approved route to the meet. Go with Allah."

"Go with Allah," he said in response. Then on the same frequency, "Red Platoon, start your engines. We move out in thirty seconds."

Five minutes later the five tanks rolled down a Jewish dirt road that led to two small hills to the south and east. They would be easy. No timber to speak of, mostly brush. No rocky cliffs or sudden drop-offs. Almost too easy.

The platoon came off the road following Major Shamalekh up the first gentle slope. Too late to fire the machine guns, the major saw the Jewish infantry patrol break from a patch of brush and rush behind the slope.

"Infiltrators on the left," the major radioed. "Number five, swing over that way and bring them under fire. Six men I saw, nothing heavier than a machine gun."

"Received, Red Leader, I'm on it."

The sound of the machine guns firing came over the radio before it cut off. Major Shamalekh checked the front and saw they were at the brow of the small hill. He slowed the tank and stopped so he could recon the area below. Surely the Jews had not pushed up this far from the MLR. It was supposed to be three miles on south.

He scanned the landscape looking for fires or men smoking or any other sign that there were considerable numbers of Jew fighters in the area. He saw nothing.

"Hit three of them with the MG," the radio said. "The others have scattered. Should I get back in formation?"

"That's an affirmative, Five. Move now."

The five tanks soon tipped over the ridge and powered downward toward a small stream and a single building. It could hide a squad of Jewish infantry. Then also it could be a resting place for wounded Syrians on their way back for medical aid. He left the building standing and made his left turn along a gravel road wide enough for only one car or tank at a time. The rest strung out behind him thirty yards apart.

He led the tanks down the road, watching through the faint light for any opposition. There should be none, but that's often when it appeared . . . and killed you. He saw nothing. The radio chirped.

"Red Platoon Leader, come in."

"Red Platoon here. We're on our final leg, due west toward the town. ETA about five minutes."

"Right, Red PL. Keep it moving. Fifteen tanks already in position. You are to take the lead of the column. We want ten men to ride each tank until you come under fire or need to maneuver sharply. Understand?"

"Yes, sir. Ten hikers on board. Will I pick them up at Karmi'el?"

"Right, Red PL. You have seven minutes to get in the lead of the force, pick up your riders, and move out on your designated compass course toward the target. You will be the column leader. Good luck. May Allah sing praises to your name."

"Look sharp now, crew," the major said. "We're almost there. We'll go just south of the town and meet the other armored units. Yes, there they are. We'll go to the head of the pack."

"Right, sir, to the head and beyond," the driver said.

When they pulled into position, the major opened the hatch and stood so he could get the larger picture. He saw some of the crews out of their tanks. He went on the net at once. "This is Red Platoon Leader. Every tanker will be in his vehicle within thirty seconds or answer to me. We pull out in two minutes. You know our objective. As ordered, we will present a three-tank front, with the rows behind the first tanks at forty to fifty yards. Please maintain your distance. Infantry get on board and hang on. The MLR is about four miles distant, and we'll be firing at it as we race through. Our men have given us a one-hundred-yard open zone on our side, so we won't crush any of them. We pull out in one minute. Infantry get on board. Drop off if we take heavy tank counter battery. That's it. Good luck and may Allah ride with you. Now, first row, move out."

Major Shamalekh kept his position standing in the hatch as the tank churned across a harvested grain field and down the valley. The MLR was just this side of the low hills, and he hoped they would hit it quickly and with such a punch that they would be through it and well into Israel before the Jews knew it. A mile from where he could see small arms fire, he buttoned up his tank and drove for the center of the one-hundred-yard-wide opening in the Syrian lines. He knew that the Jews had a lot of tanks across the front somewhere. He just hoped that they didn't have a concentration of them at this point.

He could see rifle fire now coming at them from the other side. The tanks raced over narrow trenches where the Syrians had dug in, and charged into the one wide swath between the lines. He could see tracers to the sides. Small arms. Good. No sign of any tanks. When they were fifty yards away from the Israeli MLR, he fired his big gun. The round rammed into a bunker on the Israeli side and then he heard the other tanks in his row pounding the line with rounds. His gunner got off three rounds before they rolled into the Jewish positions, crashed through makeshift bunkers, over trenches, and were through. He had not seen or heard a single tank. They were into the rear areas within five minutes, encountering no opposition. They used a road to race up and over the low hills, then came down into a larger valley and kept moving south. After three miles, he turned his column of twenty-six tanks due west and began the drive straight into Haifa.

Ahead five hundred yards he saw a tank or an artillery piece fire. The belching flame gave away the position and he fired a few seconds later directly at the muzzle blast. He knew the round hit true when he saw it detonate, then the huge blast of a secondary explosion. To the far left he saw more heavy rounds going off, but none of them came toward his column. Was it going to be this easy? The map showed that after he turned right, he should have

only fifteen to eighteen miles to the heart of Haifa. Tonight they would push the Israelis into the sea. His heart
beat faster. He didn't know if he still had infantry on
board or not, but he didn't care. He was leading a tank
thrust deep into enemy territory, and so far it had been
with almost no opposition.

Ahead, he saw lights of a small town. He fired two
rounds into it, watching the HE rounds explode and start
two fires. He swung the column around the town and on
west. Where was the enemy? Where were the Jew tanks
that the Israelis had bragged were the best fighters in the
world?

He used the net radio again. "This is Red Platoon
Leader, is everyone through the MLR? Anyone still not
through sound off." There was only silence. "Good. We're
on the second leg, moving west, don't miss the turnoff.
Key in on the tank ahead of you. Keep your three-unit
front as we swing toward Haifa. No real opposition yet,
but things could get tougher at any moment."

Just as Major Shamalekh finished talking, he heard a
roar and the tank on his right erupted into a huge ball of
flames and a thunderous explosion as every round in the
machine must have exploded when it was hit by an enemy
round.

"We're taking fire in the front row, disperse to a hundred yards but maintain your forward motion. Maintain
your advance at ten miles an hour. No sign of what fired
the round. No lights or gunfire visible to the front. Keep
driving hard."

A moment later the tank on his left vanished in a jolting
explosion that rocked his machine from side to side. His
second tank had suffered a direct hit.

"Zigzag—all tanks take evasive action but maintain
forward speed and direction," the major shouted into the
radio. He had to find out where the rounds came from that
had just killed eight of his good friends and two of his
tanks. If he didn't nail it down fast, he could lose half of
his column in a matter of minutes.

21

Haifa, Israel
Rahat Air Base

Four Star General John Bildad listened to the radio reports from his tankers in the field. He was sixty, small, built like a lead pencil with muscles, and worked out every morning. His head was shaved and his brows stood out starkly on his otherwise hairless head.

"Sure, we can slow them, but the problem is, can we stop them? We knock out two of them and they keep coming. Twenty-four left. We only have six tanks out there on line."

"General, we have the high ground and our laser-aimed guns," a bird colonel said. "We have to see them before we can hit them, but we're doing well so far."

General Bildad stood and paced. "Our first intel was when they broke through our MLR. Then we lost them. The bird overhead, that Hawkeye spotter, really saved our onions. The U.S. Navy loaned it to us. We called it in and it pinpointed the movement of the tanks. So we moved up as many as we could to block them from the high ground and here we are. What's next?"

"The Hawkeye reports the twenty-four tanks are advancing but slower now, down to about five miles per hour they figure or maybe they have stopped. They couldn't be sure." An officer with a headset on made the report.

"Could the Hawkeye pinpoint them enough for our F-18s to go in and hit them in the dark?" General Bildad asked.

General Menuhin shook his head. "Not a chance. Those anti-tank missiles aren't any good if they hit ten yards off target."

"What about artillery?" another bird colonel asked. "We could lay down a pattern that would certainly hit some of them."

"We have one-fifty-fives within range," General Bildad said. "Yes, worth a try. We have the coordinates, call in a fire mission now to those one double nickel and let's see how we do." The calls went out and the men waited.

"What about the six tanks we have here?" General Menuhin asked. "I know their electronics were fried, but they will still run and the guns will still shoot. We could get in some rounds with trial and error. Line-of-sight aiming."

"How fast can you get them revved up and out to that line we have ten miles to the east?" General Bildad asked.

"An hour to roust out the crews and load the ammo, another half hour to get to that line."

"Do it. We have to get this done in the dark or they'll be in town before daylight."

"What would come in handy are a dozen U.S. B-52s that would do pattern bombing and tear up every inch of a swath a quarter of a mile square," one of the bird colonels said.

"Dream on. We've got to do this ourselves and before daylight."

"Infantry anti-tank?" General Menuhin asked.

"Yes, we have the Dragon, a medium-range, shoulder-mounted anti-tank guided missile. But you have to be within a thousand yards to use it." He turned to his aid. "Major, get on the horn and see where our nearest teams of Dragon men are and how soon you can get them here. We'd need at least twenty-five. And we want men who can hit the tank they aim at. Go."

They had a report from the artillery then. The big guns had zeroed in on the coordinates and sent out twenty rounds. The colonel who commanded the battery talked to the general.

"Sir, we made the fire mission, but we don't know if

we hit any of the enemy tanks. We'd need an FO in the area who could give us corrections for the next salvo."

"We don't have time for that, Colonel. Tell your guns to fire twenty more rounds left a hundred and up a hundred and we'll call it a night."

"Yes, sir, General."

The faces around the table were growing longer. "There's got to be some way," General Bildad said. "How long before those Dragon shooters can get to us?"

"Half of them are in anti-tank defensive positions about fifteen miles east along the MLR. The captain said he had two eight-man squads he could detail to us, but they would need twelve hours to get operational."

"Thank the captain for us and tell him we'll have to find another way." The men looked at each other.

General Bildad rubbed his face and swore softly. "If our tanks try to advance, they'll be in a dangerous situation?"

"Yes, sir. Then they'll be in the open with no hills between them and the Syrian tanks, which are protected by some low ridges. There's no good way to outflank them. Again, bad terrain. If we move, they fire star shells and blast us. We had one tank damaged the last time we tried to run up over the ridge and fire at them."

"So we have a tank stalemate. They run the same risks if they try to advance any farther, right?" Heads nodded. "Then we have to find another way to blast those tanks before morning. Come daylight they will throw the rest of their fighter aircraft into close support of the tanks. We'll have to answer with our fighters and the stalemate will be doubled. What in hell else do we have?"

"What about the SEALs?" General Menuhin asked. "They have those new shoulder-fired twenty-millimeter rifles. A pair of twenties on the tracks of those tanks would put them dead in the water."

"Where are the SEALs?" General Bildad asked.

"On base, just back from an operation. But I can get them."

"Do it. We'll truck them up as far as we can." Bildad frowned. "I've heard about that weapon. Isn't supposed to be available for field use for three years yet."

"They have them, and they are laser sighted."

"Get them, now," Bildad said.

Murdock took the radio call from Stroh shortly after 2100. He had been ready to watch a war movie on the VCR in the SEAL ready room. He squinted a moment, then nodded. "Yes, sir, we can be ready for your transport in twenty minutes. Seven guns, twenty rounds per man. We're on the way."

Murdock looked around their quarters. "Everybody with a twenty front and center. We're employed again."

It was almost an hour later when the six-by-six truck dropped the seven SEALs off at the end of a narrow valley more than ten miles east of Haifa.

"Just over this hill should be our tanks," the driver said. "You work past them and the Syrian tanks are stalled about a mile beyond that. We've got the high ground, and when one of them pokes his turret over the ridge, he gets a round up his ass."

"Roger that," Murdock said. He stepped out of the truck, which turned around and moved slowly without lights to the rear. Murdock looked at his team: Gardner, Jaybird, Lam, Fernandez, Canzoneri, and Claymore. "You know the routine. We get close enough to the tanks to see them and hit them with HEs on their tracks and try to put them dead in the water. Remember they probably have machine guns that can fire in any direction. Doubt if they pop any one-oh-five rounds at us but they might. We'll keep dispersed. We hit the tanks closest to us, then move ahead and get those in the middle and on the other side. It might take two or three rounds to kill a tread. Take your time. Work in pairs. I'm the odd man out. Let's go."

They double-timed with their heavy load of rounds in chest bags that fit over their heads. They didn't have their usual combat vests, which cut down the overall weight.

Murdock set the pace, went around the Israeli tanks he could see on the reverse slope. Now and then one fired a round to the east.

They hiked past the friendly tanks, keeping a quarter

mile away from them, then angled to the right a little watching for any muzzle flashes ahead. Murdock saw one. He figured about three thousand yards. They kept moving.

Murdock found the first tank edging up to a small rise. He sent the rest of the squad forward to look for more. They kept in touch with the Motorolas. Murdock watched the tank. He was a little over five hundred yards from it and decided to move closer. There was a little cover here and he found a gully he used for a hundred, then looked over the rim. The tank had moved closer to him and eased up the reverse slope again looking for a target. Murdock pushed on the twenty lever and sighted in on the fuzzy outline of the tracks. He closed his eyes and tried again. A momentary shaft of moonlight broke through the clouds and outlined Murdock's target. He heard a twenty round fired somewhere farther east. A moment later he fired and saw the round jolt into the tank just over the tracks. He worked the bolt for a fresh round and this one exploded on the front of the tracks. In the brief flash of light he saw part of the track blown away. The tank tried to move. It spun around in a circle and Murdock grinned and moved straight ahead. There might be another tank on this small hill waiting for a target.

In his lead tank, Major Shamalekh had called his thrust to a stop after he lost two. He directed them to find cover from the enemy tanks that must be out front. They couldn't risk charging forward into what could be forty Israeli tanks lined up hip to hip waiting for them. They could even have night vision scopes on their aiming devices. He had to wait. He popped up over a slight rise and fired one round at what he thought might be the tanks' position, then rolled back down before any counterfire could come.

He hated this waiting. What could he do? Fire a star shell high over the enemy, roll up six tanks, and fire at whatever they saw? He liked the idea. He had just told the six tanks on the front line the plan when he heard a strange sound. Nothing too large, a rifle of some kind, no more like a small cannon.

"Major, I'm hit." The voice came from the third tank in his old platoon. He knew the voice. "Something hit the side of the tank and bounced off, then seconds later I took a round on my right track. I'm doing circles, dead in the water here."

"What hit you?"

"I don't know. Big enough to rip the right-hand track off."

"All right, the same orders with our five guns. Captain Fahd, fire that star shell out about a mile. When it bursts, we roll up fast, find a target, and fire and roll back. Fire, Fahd."

Claymore heard the tank fire and looked up surprised. It was less than fifty yards directly ahead of him rolling in and out of the deep shadows of a tree. As soon as the tank fired, it rolled back into the cover. By then Claymore had his twenty zeroed in on the churning tracks and he fired. The first round slammed into the back of a track just as it started making the turn around the power rollers, and whipped it off.

"Got one," Claymore said on his Motorola.

Jaybird had slid past the first tank he saw and headed for the second. They were lined up like on a parade. He nailed the second tank track with his second round, then had turned to fire at the tank he had bypassed when its machine gun chattered and hot, angry slugs cut a swath through the grass six feet from him. He rolled four times the other direction, then aimed and fired for the tank with the MG working. It fired again just as Jaybird's round hit one of the tracks in the middle on top and blew it apart.

"Two down," Jaybird said. He heard more firing then, the familiar slapping sound of the 20mm round as it left the muzzle of the Bull Pup.

"Anybody keeping count?" Murdock asked on the net.

"That makes seven reported," Lam said.

Murdock told them about the first line all rolling up at once. He wondered what results they had.

Major Shamalekh heard more of his tankers report that their tracks had been blown off. He hit the side of the tank with his hand. It couldn't be anti-tank weapons. They were small shoulder-mounted missiles that would blow up the tank, not just knock off the tracks. So far he'd lost seven of his tanks. That and the two blown up made nine. He had only seventeen left.

He waited for the star shell to glow ahead and the tank rolled up. He forced his eye to the scope and checked. He could see three Israeli tanks about a mile and a quarter away that were gunning backward down a reverse slope. His tanks fired but he knew they were too late. All five of his gunners got off rounds, but they did little more to the Israeli position than dig up dirt.

Who was killing his tanks? Retreat? Could be shoulder-mounted weapons he knew nothing of. Men in the grass.

"All tanks. Use your machine guns and spray the area around your rig. Especially those not hit yet. Some kind of infantry weapon out there is hurting us. Spray out a couple of hundred rounds covering as much area as you can."

Murdock heard the first machine guns fire, dodged behind a rock, and hunkered down safe from the tank nearest him. Then the tank on the other side began firing. Soon the area was a wildfire of bullets and tracers as the tank machine gunners drilled thousands of rounds into the ground to the sides and rear.

"Hold steady and take cover," Murdock said on the Motorola.

"They know we're here?" Jaybird asked.

"They know somebody is here disabling their tanks. They can't know who it is or how we're hurting them. If any of you are close enough and can see any operating tanks, take them out with your twenty. But don't get yourself killed."

Murdock checked his area. He could see two tanks well ahead of him firing their machine guns, but he wasn't close enough to be able to sight in on the tanks' treads.

He heard slugs hit the rock he hid behind, then move on past him. Maybe they should pull out? They had cut down seven of the monsters, but there must be fifteen or more healthy ones out there ready to charge into Haifa.

They had to wait for the MG fire to quit in any case.

"I shot myself a tank tread," Canzoneri said. "He won't be going anywhere but in circles for a spell."

"Yeah, I nailed another one," Fernandez said. "That should be nine we've put down and dirty." They waited. Murdock checked his watch. The machine gunners tired of their work and one after another the guns went silent. When there was no more hot Syrian lead flying toward them, the SEALs moved on looking for more tanks.

Lam came on the radio. "Do believe I've disabled another one to make ten." Moments later reports of two more tank tracks knocked off came over the Motorola. They had stopped a dozen Syrian tanks.

"Let's get out of here," Murdock said on the radio. "Silent movement, and keep away from the front of these tin cans. They have viewing ports. I came with six healthy bodies. I want to go back the same way."

It took them a half hour to move to the side they came in on, and Murdock collected them in a small depression out of the sights of the Syrian guns. He let them wind down a minute before they headed back to their truck.

"The Syrian tanks are moving," Lam said. "Listen to them."

"If we killed a dozen tanks, there must be at least three men to a tank. Are they riding back on the other machines?" Murdock asked.

The seven crawled up to the top of their protective small rise and looked over it. In the bit of moonlight they could see the tanks now in ghostly shapes as they turned and headed back east and then somewhere north, to the Syrian lines.

"Some airbursts would be good about now," Jaybird said. "We might catch a few men riding on top of the tanks."

"Good idea," Murdock said. "Two rounds each lasered for airbursts. Take your pick of tanks."

They bellied down on the little rise and soon fired. The explosions twenty feet in the air over the tanks were spectacular. The SEALs could hear the shrapnel whining off the metal. The rounds didn't slow the tanks, but if there had been any riders on the back of the beasts, they might find a lot of new holes in their hides.

"Let's choggie," Murdock said. The SEALs moved into a column ten yards apart and hiked back toward where they had left the truck. With any luck the driver would still be there. He wasn't. Murdock had left a Motorola with him just in case.

"SEALs calling our favorite truck driver. We're here, where are you?"

A reply came quickly. "Didn't know how long you'd be, Yanks. I'm burning up the brush getting to you. Give me about ten."

The truck dropped the SEALs off in front of the general's office. "They told me to bring you back here," the driver said. Murdock told him to take the rest of the SEALs to their quarters. He and Gardner went in to talk with the general and his staff.

It was almost 0140 but the staff had assembled again.

Murdock and Gardner came to attention at the side of the big table and General Bildad looked up frowning.

"How in hell did seven of you turn around a column of twenty some tanks and send the survivors racing back to the Syrian lines?"

"We work best in the dark, General," Murdock said. "There should be a dozen of the tanks disabled out there on those fields. You might want to send out tank retrievers and bring them into your house. All of them should be in good shape except for the tracks on one side."

"All with those damn twenty-millimeter rifles? I want to look at one of them."

Murdock took two steps forward, worked the bolt, cleared the chamber, catching the unfired 20mm round, then dropped out the large magazine. He handed the Bull Pup to the general. The general looked at it, checked the laser sight, and nodded.

"Yes, I see. It must have an efficient recoil system. Can I keep this one?"

"Sorry, sir. If I lose one of my seven, I get busted down to seaman recruit for the rest of my hitch."

The general chuckled. "We don't want that to happen. I'd like a demonstration of the twenty tomorrow. I'll let you know where and when. Now give me a full report on your trip out to the tanks and how you got close enough to disable them."

Five miles behind the MLR and well into Syrian-controlled land, Major Shamalekh spread the remaining tanks out along the main line of resistance and then drove his tank back to General Mahdi Diar's headquarters in the small Israeli beach town. He backed the tank into the defensive position just below the expensive home they had taken over and started up the walk to the front door.

Two soldiers with submachine guns aimed at him jumped out of the shadows.

"Are you Major Shamalekh?" one of them asked.

"Yes."

"You're to come with us. The general wants to see you."

The tank commander felt a tremor pulse through his body. He thought coming back that he'd at least have the rest of the night to get his arguments ready about why the tank thrust didn't work. Now it was happening. The two soldiers led him into the house and to the master bedroom, where they rapped on the door. One of them opened it and slipped inside.

A minute later he was back. He held the door open and a sleepy-eyed General Diar, wearing a robe and with bare feet, stared at Major Shamalekh. He had both hands behind his back.

"Major, what the hell went wrong out there?" he roared.

"I told you everything in my radio report, General. It just turned sour. Everything went wrong. They brought up six tanks on line that they must have trucked in from the south. Their electronics were working. I lost two tanks before I knew they were shooting at us. Then we forced them back."

"The other part, Major. The mystery force that knocked the treads off a dozen of my tanks. What did that? How could that happen?"

"I still don't know, sir. It wasn't the shoulder-fired missiles the Israelis are getting. It had to be something else."

"You don't know what?"

"No, sir. I'd have to inspect the blasted treads."

"Then what use are you to me? You're no use. You're a traitor to Syria. You're a disgrace to our military uniform." General Diar brought his right hand from his back, lifted the revolver he held, and fired three rounds into Major Nabil Shamalekh's chest before the tank commander could move. The major grabbed his chest as he jolted backward from the force of the rounds. Two of the slugs ripped into his heart and he died as he slumped to the polished wooden floor.

22

Rahat Air Base
Haifa, Israel

Murdock and his six gunners slept in until 1000 the next morning. The only reason they got up then was that Don Stroh was pacing up and down in the squad room. At last he went in and bounced Murdock in his bunk.

"Hey, sailor. What'n hell you think this is, CIA boot camp where you get to sleep in until noon? Rise and shine, swabby, we've got some water work for your boys to take care of."

Murdock came awake instantly and kicked his bare feet to the floor. "Water work?"

"Yeah, you know that wet stuff you guys like to play around in when you aren't working." Stroh came off his manic mode and sat down on the end of the bunk. "You boys did good work last night. The old general was shitting marbles trying to figure out how to stop twenty-four tanks with his six. I'm gonna bust my balls to get you six more Bull Pups. Tell the brass you need them for evaluation."

"Water work?" Murdock said, pulling on his socks and boots.

"Yeah. The general is putting on a push up from the south on all the bulges in the MLR. He wants a diversion to pull half the Syrian troops off the MLR and rush them over to the coast."

"Water work?"

"Right. He'll tell you all about it. We've got an eleven-hundred meet with him and the brass. Better get some new cammies on and look like you're awake."

"Did the Israelis retrieve those twelve Syrian tanks?"

"That they did, my boy. That they did. Brought all twelve of them back with tank retrievers. The general told me that with new tracks on one side they'll be good as new. For that I told him we'd be billing him for five million a tank, which seems like a bargain price. That's sixty million, which will just about pay your salary."

"Good. Have Donegan's parents been notified?"

"I took care of that. We sent a Navy chaplain and a captain out to his parents' place in Osceola, Nebraska. I had the body shipped back this morning."

"I'll write them a letter as soon as we get back stateside." Murdock yawned and stretched. He was testing his shot-up shoulder. It still hurt but not as bad. He'd never let the pain show. "I hate to go to bed and then I hate to get up. Doesn't make sense." He looked at Stroh. "You said eleven-hundred. Who will be there?"

"Bring your planning staff: Jaybird, Lam, and Gardner. How is the new JG working out?"

"Good. He's been there before on command. He hasn't had a lot of combat yet, but he's flowing in nicely with the platoon. I think I'll keep him."

The meeting in the general's conference room was much like the others. Half a dozen colonels and a couple of majors, and the air force general and General Bildad, the overall military commander from the Army side. The four SEALs sat down next to Don Stroh, and Murdock watched three Israeli Navy officers walk in.

"Good, we're all here," General Bildad said. "The fighting along the MLR has stalemated. We can't push forward to where we want to be. So, we're going to throw a surprise at the Syrians and hope it fools them. Captain Dagen will lay out the plan he's proposing. Captain Dagen."

The man who stood could have been a fisherman. He had a sea-weathered face with pockmarks, a nose that had been broken more than once and never quite set right, bushy brows over deadly earnest green eyes, and a mop of dark hair that he had to cut every month to keep it within regulations. His mouth twisted a little, then he looked each man there in the eye before he spoke.

"My planning group thinks that this will work, and that it can do what General Bildad needs done. We suggest that we stage a mock amphibious landing along one section of the twelve miles of our northern coast that the Syrians still hold. There are enough flat beaches up there above Nahariyya that we can fake an amphibious assault. We want to do this at night. We'll have a good concentration of our ships just off shore, including a couple of landing craft and several patrol boats. At one point they will circle and then head for the beach.

"Before the fake landing there will be a naval bombardment of the coast. We'll keep the rounds on the beach or just in back and avoid hitting any houses or buildings if possible. An important part of the operation will be our landing about forty men on the beach to plant explosive charges. The underwater specialists will plant the charges, then go with small arms fire and swim away from the beach and set off the charges. We want the fifteen SEALs from the U.S. to lead the way, followed by twenty-five of our underwater specialists to do the same task. The bombardment will continue from the offshore guns almost until dawn. By that time we hope that the Syrians will have pulled ten to fifteen thousand men off the MLR to meet this amphibious landing they will have to assume is going to come at daylight. Are there any questions?"

Murdock stood. "The charges we plant on the beach. Do we set timers on them, then swim out to the boats?"

"If that works best for you, Commander. We could set them off electronically, but with the water, it might be safer and more reliable to use your regular timer/detonator system."

"Can Syria move large numbers of troops that quickly?" an army colonel asked.

"Syria drove about a thousand trucks into the area they occupy. We destroyed a lot of them with air attacks, but they still have plenty of transports to move a lot of men the short distance that's required. That's a yes."

"Could we send in an agent to warn the people in the

area and give them time to evacuate away from the beach?" an air force light colonel asked. "I have relatives around that town."

"It's already been done," General Bildad said. "We sent them in this morning through the lines. If we hear no major objections and no problems we can't solve, we want to get this operation underway and move our ships north at first dark. Our attack time with the first naval bombardment will be twenty-two-hundred."

"How big will the charges be?" Jaybird asked.

"We'll use C-5, and each charge will be two pounds," an army colonel answered. "Enough to blow down the average house, and set in the open on the beach, it will make a tremendous sound and visual display."

"How do we coordinate the beach blasts?" Gardner asked.

"When the underwater men have the charges set, you will fire one red flare," the navy captain said. "At that point each man will set his timer/detonator on the charge for thirty seconds, activate it, then reenter the water and swim for the landing craft off shore."

"What if we get enemy fire as we set the charges?" Lam asked.

"We will have three patrol boats just off the surf line watching for any enemy activity," an Israeli navy commander said. "If they see any enemy movement, or if anyone fires from that section of the shore, our boat machine gunners will open fire and give you close support. They will know exactly where you are. No friendly fire problems."

"Timing?" General Bildad asked.

"Good with us," Murdock said.

"We can have the corvettes *Eliat* and *Lahav* on station within two hours. Both are here in Haifa. The patrol craft on station in one hour. We'll use two landing craft that will follow the corvette out of port and stay seaward of it."

"Where do we pick up the charges?" Murdock asked.

"You'll get them on board the *Eilat* when you board her," an Israeli commander said. "You should be at the dock at eighteen-hundred."

General Bildad looked around the table. No one else had any questions. "We're done here," he said and stood.

"Teen-hut," one of the army majors bellowed. The rest of the men shot to their feet and stood at attention as the two generals walked out of the room.

Later, in the SEAL quarters, Murdock explained the operation.

"So that's about it. Not exactly a barn burner but it should make one hell of a bang when eighty pounds of C-5 goes off almost at once."

"What do these guy want from us?" Senior Chief Sadler yelled. "First we drop sixty million dollars' worth of tanks right in their hip pocket and now they want us to play sapper on the beach?"

"About the size of it," Gardner said. "Let's get our wet gear ready. We'll have a full layout inspection in fifteen minutes."

That evening at 1800 the fifteen SEALs were on a dock in the Haifa harbor waiting for an Israeli Navy launch to take them out to the corvette. Murdock looked over at the senior chief. "Sadler, we have the EAR with us on this trip?"

"Yes, sir. I had a hunch you might want it along on a silent operation like this, so Rafii is packing it."

"Good."

Claymore stared out into the harbor. "What the hell is a corvette? I thought that was a Chevrolet."

Jaybird bristled. "Claymore, you shit-eating knuckle-head. You're on your second hitch in this man's Navy and you don't know what a corvette is? So I'll tell you. It's often a smaller country's largest naval vessel. Smaller than a destroyer but much larger than most patrol boats. Most of them are about two hundred and fifty feet long with a displacement of around a twelve hundred tons. A destroyer is over five hundred and sixty feet with a displacement of about nine thousand tons. Get the picture? In between are the frigates, four hundred and fifty feet and about thirty-five hundred tons displacement. You got that, Claymore? I'm giving a test in ten minutes."

"I'd guess they have enough guns to protect us," Claymore said.

Jaybird laughed. "Right, Claymore. They have missiles like the harpoon and SAMs and torpedoes and three-inch guns and twenty-five-millimeter Vulcan cannon. Yeah, they have guns."

Five minutes later the launch arrived and the SEALs stepped on board. After a short ride they went up a ladder to the chopper pad on the stern of the corvette. They waited on the empty pad for an ensign to come and lead them to a small compartment where they met the twenty-five Israeli underwater specialists. One of the men came over to Murdock and held out his hand.

"I'm Lieutenant Joseph Marnin."

Murdock gave his name.

"Looks like we'll be setting off some charges. I hear you guys have underwater personal radios. How in hell can they work?"

Murdock showed him the waterproof earpiece, the throat mike, and the waterproof unit on his belt. "We kept prodding Motorola until they made this latchup. Not sure if it's commercially available, but I bet they would work up a bunch for you. Have your people give them a try."

"Going to do that. We almost lost a man on a simple operation last month. With a radio like that it wouldn't have happened."

"How long a ride we have tonight?" Murdock asked.

"Not long, maybe an hour. Depends how fast they move. She can make thirty-three knots if they crank her up."

The loudspeaker cut into the words. "Divers to the fantail. All divers to the fantail."

"Must be us," Murdock said.

They sat on the chopper pad, waiting for their signal to move into the landing craft. Each diver had his package of two pounds of C-5 and the waterproof timer/detonator. The SEALs all carried their weapons over their backs.

Ten minutes later the corvette eased to a near stop off shore from a sparkle of lights from some small town.

"Our beach is two miles north of this town," the Israeli

diver told Murdock. "Why are they stopping here?"

Murdock listened. "Patrol boat that probably isn't one of ours," Murdock said.

An officer came to the fantail with a pair of large binoculars and scanned the sea shoreward. Murdock figured they were only two miles off the beach.

The officer let down the glasses. "God, it's a Syrian patrol boat headed right for us. How can we get past him without his seeing us? We can't put him down. If we fired now the whole north beach would be on alert."

Murdock touched the man on the shoulder. "We can put him dead in the water without a sound," Murdock said.

The Israeli officer snorted. "Sure and my grandma wears dive fins. How in hell can you do that?"

"We've got a weapon that can do it. Shoots out a concentrated enhanced sound that will break windows, but it also knocks out anyone within fifteen or twenty feet of it. Puts them down and out for four hours. They wake up with a slight headache but that's all."

"Damn thing works?"

"Been using it for two years now."

"Let me talk to the captain." The man hurried away and came back with another officer.

"A damn ray gun?" the new Israeli asked.

"No, sir, Captain. We call it an EAR, enhanced acoustic rifle. Rafii, bring up the EAR."

Rafii worked through the SEALs and handed the weapon to Murdock. "This is it. We need to be within four hundred yards, and then it's beddy time for anyone on board that patrol boat."

"We were about ready to scrub the mission. We'll ease in toward him. Keep the ship totally black. No smoking, no talking," the captain said. He hurried away.

Murdock felt the craft work slowly forward, then toward the sound of the patrol boat. He watched through the night but still couldn't see the craft. It took five more minutes of moving shoreward before Murdock spotted the lights of the craft. It was small, maybe sixty feet.

Lam was beside him, watching now. "Cap, I'd say the

range is about six hundred." The patrol boat, which had been idling its engines, either listening or working its radar, suddenly gunned the motors and headed straight at them.

"Call it, Lam," Murdock said. He was prone with the EAR angled toward the oncoming boat.

"Five-fifty, Cap."

They waited. "A little under five. Still coming."

Another few seconds, then a half a minute.

"Cap, she's at four hundred. Fire when ready."

The whooshing sound of the EAR came at once and they watched the patrol boat. Murdock counted down the ten seconds until he could fire the recharged gun again. The boat continued at them, only not quite so fast now.

Murdock fired the EAR again. This time the patrol craft slowed and then coasted toward them on the same course. The engine cut to an idle. She slid through the water and came to a stop less than twenty feet from the corvette's rail.

"Everyone on board should be fast asleep," Murdock said. "When the Syrians find they have lost radio contact with the craft, they'll send another one out to investigate. By then she may have drifted on shore or down the current ten miles."

The Israeli captain grinned, shook Murdock's hand, and ran back to the bridge to continue the mission. The big ship edged forward, then came up to ten knots and worked its way up the coast and closer to shore. Five miles north it slowed and then stopped. A landing craft that had been shadowing the corvette on the seaward side slid up to the stern and tied on. The ensign who had met them came back.

"Time to load into the landing craft," he said. "We have two. They will take you within two hundred yards of the shore. When you hit the beach, send up a green flare and we'll start our bombardment. We can cause a lot of trouble in there but we hope not to smash up too many buildings. After all, it is Israeli territory." Murdock found the Lieutenant Marnin he had talked to before and gave him his backup Motorola. He fastened it on the man and explained how it worked.

"Give me a call," Murdock said, turning his back on the man.

The call came through and Murdock gave the Israeli a thumbs-up. "When you get all of your bombs planted and ready for the red flare, call me on the radio and we'll shoot the flare," Murdock said. The Israeli grinned, thanked him, and went to load with his men.

The SEALs climbed into one of the craft, and the Israeli specialists into the other, and they moved toward the silent, dark shore. Jaybird had the Colt M-4A1 to fire the flares.

At two hundred yards the two boats went dead and the men began dropping over the side. The SEALs kept together, then moved as a group toward the beach. They had been assigned the left-hand side, so they swam that way. The breakers were easy compared to those off Coronado. They surfed in on them, then let the waves move them toward the sand like beached logs where they lay. Murdock gave the Israelis another two minutes. "Lieutenant, are you ready on the beach for the shelling to begin?"

"Ready on the right," came the answer over the net.

"Jaybird, fire that green flare and aim it well out to sea. When ready."

The rifle made a sharp report, but the surf drowned out most of it. The green flare arched up and then burst into brightness well out to sea. Within twenty seconds they could see the guns firing off the corvette and hear the rounds coming over.

"Three incher," Lam said. They made a good-sized explosion when they hit on shore.

"Let's get our bombs strung out," Murdock said on the radio. "Ten yards apart, move it, now. Check in when you have your units in place on the top of the wet sand. Move slowly, so we don't attract any attention. Let's do it."

The SEALs spread out on each side of Murdock and soon covered almost two hundred yards of the sandy beach. They eased up forward, out of the water, and crawled slowly up the wet sand until the breakers stopped hitting them. There they set down the two-pound bombs. They were so small it always surprised Murdock how much power they contained. He pushed the timer/detonator into one of the soft blocks of plastic explosive and set the timer for thirty seconds. But he didn't move the activator lever.

He waited and then used the radio. "How we doing? Check in with your squad leader when you're all set and ready to activate. Don't activate yet. Wait."

He took calls from five of his six men, then Jaybird chimed in.

"I had the farthest to crawl," he said.

"Good, now hold." Bravo Squad had waited for Alpha to finish, then they checked in. All were ready.

Murdock watched the explosions on the land. He heard some of the 25mm rounds hitting and slashing overhead. Time to get out of there. He used the radio.

"Israeli frogmen, are you ready with your plants?"

A moment later the earpiece spoke. "Everything done and done here, mate. Let that flare rip whenever you're ready. As soon as it flares, we'll push the arming levers and swim like crazy out into the deep water."

"We're ready. Stand by. Shoot it, Jaybird."

The red flare arched up high overhead and burst into a bright pinkish light that drifted slowly south.

"Go," Murdock said on the Motorola. The SEALs and the Israeli frogmen pushed down the arming levers on their bombs, stood, and raced into the surf, then swam straight out to sea.

Murdock had counted down in his head the thirty seconds. When he got there he stopped swimming and treaded water as he watched the shore.

The sudden eruption turned the blackness into daylight as the crackling roar of the blasts showered sand and water a hundred feet in every direction and sent a shock wave through the air to break out all the windows within a quarter of a mile. It wasn't just one blast; they came like a string of firecrackers, some doubling on each other, some far down the beach, some close at hand—until all forty of the huge bombs had detonated and slammed the shock wave time after time into the mostly rural Israeli countryside. There were more shells from the ship at sea, and then the noise tapered off and faded out and Murdock turned and stroked easily toward the dark hull of the landing craft he spotted fifty yards to sea.

"SEALs, the right-hand boat is ours. Do you all see it? Sound off?"

One by one the SEALs checked in, then Bravo Squad tallied in. A moment later the Israeli came on. "What a hoot that was. We gave any Syrians around this part of the country a welcome. Our men are approaching our landing craft. I can't count them yet, but we should have all of our lads with us. I understand the ship will stay on station and fire into the countryside every half hour or so to convince the Syrians that something is afoot up here."

Murdock hit the side of the landing craft and lifted up and was pulled over the side by hands above. Then he helped lift in the rest of the SEALs until everyone was accounted for. His left shoulder burned with every tug on a SEAL, but he ignored the pain.

"Marnin, you get all your men back?" Murdock asked on the Motorola.

"Waiting for one, he's our slowest swimmer, but he's in sight. You can take off for the ship whenever you want. We'll see you on board. I understand the ship's mess is going to put on a special feed for us."

"Sounds good, see you there." Murdock stretched out his left arm. Hurt like hell, but he'd never admit it. He felt like a wild animal. They tried never to show that they were injured or hurt in any way, because then they would become the target of any predator in the area. He flexed the arm again and Jaybird grinned.

"You say a word, little friend, and I'll squash you like a lop-eared grasshopper on the sidewalk."

"Me? What? Just wondering what we'll have for chow."

23

The SEALs arrived back at the air base later that same night and sacked out. Stroh had some words for Murdock and Gardner.

"Good job on the fake landing. We have reports of a massive movement of troops toward that area. The generals think that's going to swing the balance. Already some Israeli forces are moving forward into positions vacated by the Syrians. By tomorrow night the war situation should be going the Israeli way big time."

"So when do we fly out of here?" Gardner asked.

"General Bildad wants you to stick around a couple more days. Not sure what might turn up. He's been thankful that you were here to help out."

"That's why we get the big bucks," Gardner said.

"Hold that thought."

"Then we can actually get some sleep time?" Murdock asked.

"Be my guests," Stroh said. "But remember the old Stroh proverb: he who sleeps to noon has a short morning." The CIA man grinned and slipped out the door.

The next morning Murdock heard that the war front news was good. The Israeli forces were advancing on all fronts except that one nearest the ocean where the fake landing had been. There were still massive troop concentrations there. The frustrated Syrian generals were probably trying to figure out what happened.

At 1410 Don Stroh popped back into the SEAL quarters. He found Murdock cleaning his Bull Pup.

"Get it clean, you're going to need it."

"I thought we'd already won the war for the Israelis," Jaybird said.

"Almost, but not quite. The friendly troops are advancing on all fronts now, except the beach property. Recon shows that the concentration of troops that were rushed there last night have been pulled out and sent to the other fronts, but they got there too late to do much good and now half the army is in a rout heading for the buffer zone and Lebanon."

"So let's go home," Jaybird said.

"Not so fast, Machine-Gun Mouth," Stroh said. "We know where their GHQ is for this romp. It has the commanding general in it, a professional soldier by the name of General Mahdi Diar. He's in a luxury home overlooking the sea near the small town of Nahariyya. That's about four miles north of where you guys hit the beach last night."

"Sure and he's probably got about two thousand guards around him," Murdock said. "You know how these generals are."

"Maybe yesterday, but today the Israelis have a man in the area with a radio and they say he's down to about twenty guards, he's sent everyone else to the front."

"So?" JG Gardner asked.

"So he wants you guys to go in with sixteen Israelis and do a HALO jump and take out the general and his staff."

"Just like that?" Murdock asked.

"How else? It's what you guys do best. The Israelis will send their elite jump team from their special forces. They are good."

"How high?"

"Talking about twenty thousand, not too chilly."

"Stroh, you've never jumped into cold air up there," Gardner said. "That high it'll freeze the old gonads off a brass monkey."

Stroh chuckled. "Haven't heard that phrase for thirty years. Thought it died out in the fifties—well, the seventies."

"So when's the meeting?" Murdock asked.

"At fifteen-hundred, usual place. Bring four."

"We'll be there."

Murdock was pleased an hour later when the meeting got underway. They passed around digital pictures of the luxury house. There were four views of it, showing three sides.

"These pictures were taken this morning by our man there with his digital camera," General Bildad said. "He then sent them by his cell phone with special modem in it to our phone and we printed them out."

The Israeli Air Special men talked with the SEALs. Their leader, who had been introduced as Captain Lansky, had the floor.

"We come in from the sea at about twenty thousand, and then fly north a half mile. There's a south breeze blowing today and it's supposed to continue tonight. If we bail out at twenty, and free-fall to two thousand, we shouldn't drift much. Once our chutes open we can control them and come in on the beach about a quarter of a mile from the objective."

"Can we start it as a silent operation?" Murdock asked. "We can silence half of our weapons, then go with the rest of the guns when we need them."

"Sounds good," Captain Lansky said. "We'll have half our submachine guns silenced," the captain said.

"Timing," General Bildad said.

"Anything around oh-one-hundred would work for us," Murdock said. "Guards tend to let down about then."

The Israeli captain agreed and they looked back at the general.

"This is a bit of a sensitive situation. The mansion we're going into is owned by an influential man high in the Israeli government. We want as little damage to the building and furnishings as possible. That's why we haven't called in a missile strike on the GHQ. Don't use grenades or other explosives, and try to limit your weapons fire to single shots if it can be done that way."

Murdock scowled. "General. I won't risk my men's lives to save some antiques or fancy furniture. My men are worth a lot more than this house. Maybe you should leave us out of the mission."

General Bildad frowned. "Commander. I may be a little rusty on my American military discipline. But I always thought a lower rank officer did as he was ordered."

"You're quite right, General Bildad. However, we are U.S. Navy personnel, and answer to the highest ranking American naval officer on post. Which I happen to be. We are here at your request, not our own. In the field, when I am on the direct orders of our President, which I am in this case, I outrank anyone in the mix, which would include you, General Bildad. If you need us for this mission, my men and I will take all due caution to preserve the property. However, if it is a choice between a blasted dining room or a dead SEAL, that dining room will indeed be blasted. Do I make myself clear on this matter?"

"Yes, Commander. Totally clear. I didn't mean to imply that you endanger your men to save the house. However, it would be appreciated if you could complete the mission with as little structural and internal damage as possible. If it can't be done that way, we still want this Syrian general to be eliminated."

Murdock hesitated, looked at the general, then nodded. "Yes, General Bildad. We'll do the job with as little damage as must be done."

"Good, we're all on the same page. The plane will take off oh-thirty. I suggest you SEALs go to our parachute building to check on the harness and operation. These chutes may be a little different."

"Will we have masks and oxygen bottles?" Gardner asked.

"From twenty thousand we usually don't use the oxygen," Captain Lansky said. "We're through the cold zone in two minutes and then the oxygen is sufficient. We can provide them if you want them."

"You're right," Murdock said. "At twenty we usually don't use them either on a HALO. Do we need to coordinate on the kind of weapons we take?"

"We'll get together on that right after this meeting," Captain Lansky said.

"How do we get back?" Lam asked.

"Thirty men," Murdock said. "I'd suggest a pair of SH-60s could do the job, if we have a secure beach LZ."

They all looked at the air force general. "Yes, we can send in two sixties. We call them UH-60 Blackhawks when they're on land. They can each lift out fifteen men. We need to send in a pair of chopper gunships to assure that the LZ is secure."

Murdock grinned. "General, I like the way you plan a mission. The gunships are a must. How do we call them in when we're ready?"

Captain Lansky looked up. "We have radios that work on TAC Two with the planes. We'll call them in. We always have three radios for backup in an operation like this."

Lam rubbed his neck the way he did when he was unsure. He frowned and looked at the generals. "How far will we be from the MLR? How far would it be if we have to fight our way back into friendly territory?"

General Bildad looked at one of his aids. A colonel spoke up.

"Sir, right now we have pushed the Syrians back to within about five miles of that GHQ."

"Be a hell of a lot easier to swim back," Jaybird said.

"Not for us," Captain Lansky said. "I haven't swam a mile in twenty years."

"Then we'll be sure to get the birds in there," General Bildad said. "And two gunships will guarantee a safe LZ. Now, are there any more questions?" There weren't any.

Outside Captain Lansky talked with the SEALs.

"On jumps we mostly use the Uzi. We've customized ours with sound suppressors, but that doubles the weight."

"If you could bring half of them suppressed, that would help," Murdock said. "We'll have a sniper rifle suppressed and eight H and K MP-5s all suppressed. We take one, sniper rifle with scope, a machine gun, and the rest will be the Bull Pups with twenty-millimeter and 5.56."

"I've heard you have those," the captain said. "I'll look forward to seeing them. Sound like a fantastic infantry weapon."

"Turns a dogface into a walking artillery piece," Gardner said. "They are simply fantastic for anything long range."

"How are you fixed for ammo?" The captain asked.

"Not sure," Murdock said. "If you could send one of your men with us, we'll check and then he could take us where one of our men could get the needed ammo."

"Done," Captain Lansky said. "First let's go to Building 412 to check out your chutes. I think you'll find them pretty standard."

The chutes were almost exactly what they used in the U.S., and the ammo supply was replenished. Later the SEALs followed Murdock from the tarmac at 2400 into a plane he had never seen before. It had a fixed high wing with jump doors on both sides and turbo prop power. Murdock shrugged—just so it flew.

It did. They leveled off at twenty thousand feet and the pilot then moved slowly a half mile inland and a half mile north of the target. Then the red light changed to green and the SEALs and the Israeli jumpers went to the doors holding the rip cords in their hands. Murdock took a deep breath and stepped out first on the SEAL side into the cold blackness of the Israeli night. It was always a shock to the senses and the system that first step into nothingness. Then as he fell he moved his arms so he was fairly flat and sailed toward the cluster of lights he saw far below and south. Without realizing it, Murdock had held his breath when he jumped, and now a minute and a half later he let out the air. The cold air slapped his lungs but was welcome. The cold didn't worry him. He'd been colder lots of times. He wasn't aware of the rest of the SEALs, but knew they had to be slightly above him. All had their Motorolas on and he touched the throat mike.

"SEALs, check in." He heard the fourteen men make the radio check in the usual order. "Good. Lam and Jaybird, call out the two-thousand-foot level and we'll pull. No automatic openers on these chutes. We do it the old-fashioned way. When we land I'll use a light stick so we can get together. Generally we go south."

He watched the lights come closer, and the ground. He could soon see the dark blobs below.

"Coming up on two thousand," Jaybird said. "In ten. Count it down." Murdock counted, then pulled the rip cord and tried to get vertical before the harness lines snapped him up short from his free fall. "Damnit," he shouted as the harness jerked him sideways then upright. He looked up and forgot the pain as the beautiful chute billowed out. It was the directional kind and he watched the ground coming up slower now. A house up front. The lights of the village they were aiming for vanished behind a small hill.

Then the ground rushed up at him and he pounded his boots on the field in a run that countered the forward motion of the chute. He stopped and pulled the chute down and unsnapped the harness.

"Down, SEALs, have a blue color tube on. Anybody see it?"

"Got ya," Jaybird said.

"Coming," Mahanani said.

"Captain, are you down and can you read me?"

Murdock had given the Israeli one of the spare Motorolas to keep in touch.

"Down, but I'm afraid I have a small problem, Commander."

"Where are you? Can you see my light stick?"

"Yes, you're to the west of me. I broke my leg. Four hundred jumps and not a scratch, now this."

"We'll find you, Captain. Hold tight."

Murdock gathered up his men as they moved east. They found the white blobs of parachutes on a cultivated field. Soon Lam spotted the captain and some of his men.

It took them a half hour to gather up all of the men.

"Who is your second?" Murdock asked Captain Lansky.

"Sergeant Lot. A good man."

"Sergeant Lot, front and center," Murdock called.

The man ran up and saluted. "Lot here, sir."

"I'm Murdock. No more saluting. You have the command of your men. First, detail two to carry the captain with us. Our medic has checked his leg and splinted it and given him a shot of morphine. We'll be moving up now. Keep your men spread out at ten-yard intervals."

Murdock turned to his radio. "Lam, what's ahead?"

"All clear. I'm out about three hundred. Don't see any Syrian troops at all. Looks like we're about a mile from the lights."

"Captain, give the sergeant the Motorola. Jaybird, rig it on him so he can use it. We're moving, troops."

They went in diamond formations forward, with the Israelis in the middle and slowing them with the aid to the captain.

After a half mile, Murdock called. "Lam, what's out front?"

"I've got a road, not much traffic. We have to cross it. Fields on the other side. We're nearer the coast now. I saw a jeep down on the hard sand. Don't know where it went."

"Find a spot to leave the captain and a guard. We're behind schedule."

Mahanani had been watching the captain. "He's hurting, Skipper. Not much more we can do. No more morphine for another hour."

"Watch him. We're almost there."

They went across the road in two bunches. They missed a military jeep by a hundred yards, then hit the dirt and didn't move for five minutes.

"Clear," Murdock said. "Let's get to the target."

A quarter of a mile later, they went up a small rise where Lam waited for them. "Better take a look, Cap."

They bellied down in the grass at the top of the rise as they had done so many times in the past. Murdock grunted as he stared downhill forty yards.

Outside the target house there had been set up a twenty-man wall tent. A jeep and a six-by sat in front of it. More than a dozen soldiers idled around the tent and the trucks.

"Where the hell did they come from?"

"More protection for the general," Senior Chief Sadler said.

"Okay, get spread out at ten. Sergeant Lot, put your

men along the top of the hill on the reverse slope. We've
got at least a dozen men below. We'll take out the trucks
with our twenties. Then everybody cuts down anybody
who moves."

"That's a roger, Commander."

"Move up."

Murdock called on Howard to do the jeep; he would
take out the truck with an engine shot.

"As soon as the twenties go, work your single shots on
the troops. Watch out for the house windows. When
you're ready, Howard."

The two 20mm rounds fired at almost the same time
and exploded on target half a second later. The truck
sprouted a flame that burned through the engine and then
the fuel tank blew, showering parts of the truck on the
house roof only twenty yards away. The jeep disinte-
grated.

Silenced shots and unmuffled ones cracked in the stillness after the original explosions. Rafii tracked one running Syrian and dropped him with a lead shot. Canzoneri
drilled two surprised soldiers before they could move
from the front of the tent. The tent caught fire from the
exploding gas tank and revealed a dozen cots inside with
blankets that quickly caught fire.

Three men ran for the house. Jaybird cut down one of
them and Bill Bradford nailed the other two with his
sniper rifle. The whole firefight lasted less than fifteen
seconds from when the twenties fired. The Israelis worked
the far end of the tent and dropped three men trying to
slip out of the flaming canvas.

"Sergeant Lot, take your men and run around to the
front of the house and don't let anybody come out and
stay alive. Move!"

"Roger, moving."

Murdock checked the scene below. One man crawled
toward protection. A silent round stopped him dead in his
crawl. The rear door to the house had a small porch. Murdock figured the place was no mansion, maybe twelve
rooms, around four thousand square feet.

"Gardner, cover us, we're going down. Alpha, move it.

Half on each side of that door. Gardner, fire at anyone who fires from the windows at us. Let's go."

Alpha Squad lifted up and charged down the hill. Murdock and Jaybird were ahead. Murdock pasted himself at the left-hand side of the rear door. Jaybird was on the right.

Murdock took out a flash-bang grenade and showed it to Jaybird who nodded. Jaybird, reached for the knob and tried it. Unlocked. He looked at Murdock, who nodded. Jaybird opened the door six inches; Murdock rolled the grenade through the door. Jaybird pulled the door shut and covered his ears with his hands.

The pulsating sounds jolted through the house and splattered out the windows and walls, then the piercing, blinding strobes of light put lightning to shame as they tore through the house.

When the last light faded, Murdock kicked open the door and raced inside taking the left hand half of the room. It was large, with tables, supplies, and two soldiers writhing on the floor. Murdock shot one in the head and Jaybird hit the other one with a heart shot, and the SEALs ran ahead ten feet to the next door. It was closed. As Jaybird turned the knob, two rounds jolted through the thin wood. Murdock slammed three rounds of 5.56 through the same door, then Jaybird unlatched the panel and jammed it forward.

A huge black dog the size of a small pony, with a wide-open mouth, lunged through the door directly at Jaybird. Murdock reversed his grip on the Bull Pup and swung it like a club, mashing the heavy stock into the dog's head. The blow jolted the animal's large head backward, snapping his neck and leaving him dead as he slammed into Jaybird, knocking him down. Jaybird crawled from under the spasming dog's body and found his MP-5.

Both men looked around the door into the room. A naked woman stood in the center of a living room, wearing only a thin veil over her lower face. She held a submachine gun with her finger on the trigger. The weapon centered on Jaybird. He swung up the MP-5 and hesitated a fraction of a second. Murdock put three rounds from the 5.56 barrel into the woman's chest, one through her left breast, the other two in her heart.

"Come on," Murdock said and Jaybird snapped out of his trance and cleared the rest of the room. "Clear one and two," he said for those SEALs behind him. The men darted to the next opening that led into a hall. Murdock pointed to the left and to Jaybird. He had three doors on his side of the hall. Murdock had three on his side.

They were about to open the first doors when the next door ten feet down the hall opened, and a hand reached out and tossed a hand grenade toward them. There was nowhere to run. There was nowhere to hide. The deadly grenade bounced on the wooden floor and came a foot off the deck and straight at Jaybird.

24

Jaybird's eyes went wide in the milliseconds he had between the grenade bouncing toward him and his decision. Then he took half a step and kicked. His right boot hit the grenade in the center and pounded it down the hall in the other direction almost to the end of the forty-foot-long corridor. As soon as he kicked it, he and Murdock dropped flat on the floor. The grenade exploded just before it hit the far wall and stabbed hundreds of shards of steel into the walls, ceiling, and floor. Only a few came as far as Murdock and Jaybird and they dropped harmlessly to the floor.

The same door opened and a head peered out. Jaybird had been waiting. He put a round through the surprised man's forehead and he slammed backward and out of sight. Murdock eased up to the first door on the left and pushed it open. No reaction. From floor level, he peered into the room. A bedroom, with luxurious furniture and a four-poster bed. Nobody there. He moved to the second door. Jaybird checked past the dead man. A luxury bedroom with no one else in it.

The third and fourth rooms on each side held no one. By the time they retraced their steps to the living room, Gardner had sent two men up the stairway to the left. It was half-open, vanishing partway up toward the ten-foot ceiling. Rafii was in front, with Fernandez covering for him. Raffi made it to the top and looked over the carpet on the short hall. He shook his head, flattened on the floor, and slid down to the first door on his left. Before he got there two men with submachine guns jumped out of the end room and began firing. He fired back, the rounds from his MP-5 cutting one man nearly in half and knocking down the other one. When neither man moved, Rafii opened the door to the room. It was an office with computer and bookcases and a big desk. No one there.

On the lower floor, Murdock and Lam investigated the wing to the left. It was only one story. Murdock heard firing at the front of the house, then a machine gun chattered off six bursts of ten rounds.

Lam pushed open the first door and waited. No reaction. He looked inside. It was a den, with a fireplace, carpet, weapons on the wall, a large TV set, a pair of soft chairs, and a long sofa. A man sat in one of the soft chairs, holding a pistol aimed at the side of his head.

"I am General Diar. I demand to see your commander."

Lam kept him under his MP-5 and called Murdock. The man had two stars on his shirt's shoulder. He was clean-shaven except for a thick mustache.

"I demand to see your commander," the man said in Arabic.

Murdock edged into the room and heard him. "I'm the commander of this group. Who are you?"

"I am General Mahdi Diar, commander of all Syrian forces. I wish to surrender."

Murdock heard more firing from the front of the house. He stared at the man. He had no way of being sure this man was who he said he was. "Put down the pistol and we'll talk," Murdock said in Arabic.

The man shook his head. "Then you will kill me. This way you won't kill me, because I might shoot one of you, and you want to question me."

"You are not Diar. He has a red face, a big nose, and a close-cropped military haircut. You are thin, light-skinned, and with a short nose and hair too long to be a general."

"No, I am General Diar. I planned the attack. I had the pulse bomb built in the desert. I almost won. I didn't count on such good Israeli pilots."

"If you are General Diar, where are your body guards? You had twenty-five men protecting you."

The man in the chair waved one hand. "They ran away. What could I do?" He waved the pistol and then brought it down and tried to fire at Murdock. Murdock jumped to the side when he saw the weapon coming. He fired two shots before the man in the chair could pull the trigger. Both rounds hit the man in the chest and he died before the dropped pistol hit the carpet.

"He's not General Diar," Murdock said. Murdock frowned as he heard more gunfire from the front of the house. He headed that way.

Sergeant Lot had taken his fourteen men around to the front of the big house, keeping back thirty yards. He found protection for his men, then settled in. He thought he heard shots inside the house, then it was quiet. A moment later one of his men cried out: "I've been shot— shoulder."

Sergeant Lot had not heard a weapon fire. "Silenced shots—stay under cover. Watch the windows. Return fire if you see any movement in the windows." Lot checked the area again. A military sedan sat ten feet from the back of the ground-floor door. He could see no one in it. A road of sorts ran from the back of the house to the street half a block over, and another track led toward the beach fifty yards to the right.

He lifted up a moment from the large boulder he had hidden behind. A fraction of a second later a rifle slug zinged off the rock and ricocheted away. Another silent round. Now he could see that the rear door was open to the inside. A screen door hung on the outside. He lifted his Uzi and drilled three rounds through the screen.

A moment later two hand grenades were lofted toward Lot's squad, but didn't get to them. At the same time the blasts came, three figures dashed from the rear door into the sedan. It started and raced away. Ten Israeli guns slammed rounds at the sedan and the tires. One rear tire went flat but the car kept going fifty yards to the beach, then made a hard turn south and soon raced out of sight behind a stand of trees that screened the ocean.

"Three men just ran out the back and left in a sedan," Lot said on his radio. "They went down to the beach."

"Chase them," Murdock said on his radio. "Follow them. We're clear in here. Go get them. We're right behind you."

Murdock and the rest of the SEALs charged out of the empty house and down the trail to the beach. They could see some of the Israelis forty yards ahead. Nowhere did they see a sedan.

The Israelis had grouped at a street that ran up from the beach to the rest of the streets. Murdock and his men came up to them.

"Gone," Lot said.

"Maybe not," Lam said. He took his penlight and shone it on the wet sand where it met the pavement. "Look at the tire tracks in the wet sand. That's tread like I've never seen before. Memorize the pattern. I'll make a sketch." He did.

"This isn't a big town," Lot said. "Maybe two hundred people. We scatter, and hunt for a military van with olive drab paint and tires that look like this and one flat tire. It's plenty dark enough that our uniforms won't look that much different from any Syrians if we see any soldiers."

"Let's do it," Murdock said. Now he wished that he'd put Gardner and Bravo Squad watching the back door. If he had, it probably would have all been over by now.

They worked up to the first street and two Israelis went down it. The next street Murdock and Lam took. They alternated SEALs and Israelis so the SEALs could contact the Israelis if they needed to get together or move or attack something.

Murdock and Lam jogged down the street. The first block they saw no military sedans. At an intersection they saw a Syrian Army jeep on a roving patrol. The driver and his passenger never even looked at them. The next block Lam held up his hand. Ahead fifty feet sat an olive drab military sedan. The left rear tire was flat. As they came up on it, Murdock could see three bullet holes in the rear panels. The car sat in front of a small store with a residence above it. There were steps leading up from the street. Murdock did a quick check inside the car and found bloodstains.

They took the stairs one step at a time, with feet placed on the very edge of each runner, near the wall so there would be no squeaking. At the top they found a small landing, with two doors leading off it. Murdock whispered to Lam, who stepped back out of sight. Murdock knocked on one door. He knocked again and the door came open slowly just a crack.

An old man stared out. Murdock asked him in English if he'd seen some Syrian soldiers. The old man's eyes went wide and he nodded and pointed to the other door, then held up three fingers. He smiled, patted the weapon Murdock held, and then closed the door softly.

Murdock brought Lam up. He took two steps back then jumped at the door kicking hard with his right boot next to the knob. The door latch splintered open and the door slammed inward. Murdock and Lam went in right behind it. They found a large room with a man lying on a couch and two men bending over him. Two Syrian soldiers stood behind the couch. They had pulled up their submachine guns but they were too late. Murdock and Lam fired, killing both Syrian soldiers and making the men kneeling at the side of the couch duck down. They looked up in fear.

"Speak English?" Murdock asked.

"Yes, this man is wounded, hurt bad. I'm not a doctor but I know some first aid."

Murdock moved up and looked at the man. He had a red face, black closely cropped hair, and looked to be about fifty. He wore a Syrian army blouse with major leaves on his shoulders.

"Do you know who this man is?"

The Israeli who spoke before nodded. He was about forty, with almost white hair and a long nose. He rubbed his face and bobbed his head. "Oh, yes. He's been in town for a week, yelling at everyone. He had two of our people shot because they didn't get out of the way of his car fast enough. He's the big-shot Syrian general, the guy who led the attack on us. I don't know why he has major's insignia."

"He's hiding. How is he wounded?"

"A bullet through his back, lodged somewhere in his

chest. I'm no doctor for that kind of work."

Murdock turned to Lam. "Call in the troops. Tell them we have him. Send most of them back to the beach. Meet downstairs with six of our people. Find the car keys in the pockets of one of the two bodies over there. We'll take the general for a little ride."

"We don't have a hospital here," the Israeli said.

"I wasn't thinking of taking him to a hospital."

It took them almost an hour to get the two Syrian soldiers' bodies out of the apartment over the store. The owner of it said he was a pharmacist, that was why they brought the general to him. There was no doctor in the small town.

Diar was conscious, but not talking as they carried him down the steps. He took a swing at one of the SEALs, who promptly spit in his face.

They dumped him in the car's backseat. Murdock sat guarding him while they drove the car back to the beach near the house he had taken over as his headquarters.

Gardner had called in the UH-60s a half hour before and both came whirling in and landed on the wet sand. The two helicopter gunships hovered nearby but had no targets.

They carried the general out to the chopper and told him where he was going.

"General, you wanted to get to Haifa, I'm told. The target of your invasion. Well, we're going to make your dream come true. You'll be in Haifa in about twenty minutes. But you'll be in a hospital prison ward until the authorities have questioned you all they want to. Then I'd think a firing squad if you survive the Israeli bullet that's in your chest. Sound like a good deal?"

Murdock had told him this in his not perfect Arabic, but the soldier got the idea. The choppers took off, the injured Captain Lansky in the first one with his troops, the SEALs in the second one with their prize prisoner.

"Hey, Skipper," Canzoneri said. "I didn't think we ever took prisoners."

"For a two-star general, we'll make an exception," Murdock said. "Think what this is going to do to the invasion forces once they learn that their commander has been captured and is in prison in Haifa."

The chopper pilot must have told Haifa who the prisoner they had was, because when the birds set down on the chopper pads, twenty officers and six cars had pulled up to meet them. A stretcher came first and a gurney, then General Bildad talked to the hurting general a moment in Arabic before sending him to the hospital.

General Bildad came over to Murdock and his SEALs.

"Commander, you do good work. Never in my wildest dreams did I hope that you could capture him alive. Now we have a big bargaining chip to use with the Syrians. Their war is over. We'll demand compensation for the war and for the economic hit we took when our electronics went down. Estimates are somewhere around fifty billion dollars in equipment alone, not counting the economic loss. Yes, Syria will remember this day for a long time in the future."

Don Stroh met them in their quarters. He frowned. "Murdock, you lied to me. You said it was good fishing year round in the kelp off La Jolla. I talked to them at Seaforth today and they said they only had eleven fishermen on one half-day boat for twenty sculpin, six sand bass, and twelve mackerel. Now, that is not what I'd call good fishing."

Murdock felt drained. He shrugged. "Hell, Stroh. Everybody knows fishing falls off a little December through February. So sue me."

"I might. You're done here. I got the word from the CNO while you were gone. You fly out tomorrow afternoon. So get some sleep. You earned it on this trip. Congratulations on bagging that general. I'd say that's a first for you guys."

Murdock nodded. "Yeah, a first," he said, then headed for his bunk.

25

NAVSPECWARGRUP-ONE
Coronado, California
Lieutenant Commander Blake Murdock kicked back in his
tiny office at Third Platoon of SEAL Team Seven and put
his feet up on the small desk. He couldn't remember how
long it took them to get home from Israel. The Navy had
been in a flat-out rush to get them over there, but coming
home had been the opposite: from slow to stop. Most of
the time they hitchhiked on military planes going their
direction. They wound up at Miramar Marine Air Station
north of San Diego, and Master Chief MacKenzie sent a
Navy bus to bring them the last leg of the journey. That
had been a 1000 arrival and Murdock had promptly given
the men a three-day leave. It was nearly noon and he
hadn't been home yet. He figured that Ardith didn't know
when they were arriving. She had lost her Washington,
DC, inside information pipeline. He'd surprise her when
she got home from her new job. He knew that high on
Ardith's agenda would be looking for a different apartment. They had just started to search when his orders
came to jet out to Israel.

Lam caught a ride with Jaybird as far as his apartment
building.
   "Hey, how about me taking your Hog out on a ride?"
   "Never happen, boysan. Not until you get your biker's
driver license. You don't have one."
   "Yeah, but we're buddies. How about on some deserted
parking lot somewhere?"

He had put off Jaybird and went directly to the small storage area in the parking garage where he had hidden his bike. He hadn't thought a lot about the murder of the old store owner just before they left for Israel. He had fully expected the master chief to have a warrant for his arrest as soon as he came over the Quarterdeck that morning. He didn't.

Lam unlocked the storage door and grinned when he looked at his Harley Hog. What a great machine. He'd wanted one for ten years. Now it was all his. And all paid for and insured. He sat on the bike but didn't roll it out. He had a lot of thinking to do. Should he go to the police with the names of the three men who had killed the old man? He'd written them down that night of the killing just so he wouldn't forget them. The three would at once implicate him and probably say he was the one who did the stomping. Three to one. Who would the cops believe? Then he'd be indicted, and a trial set and in jail and thrown out of the SEALs and probably discharged from the Navy as well. Damnit.

What had he told them? He said he was a SEAL. Okay, there were well over three hundred SEALs in NAVSPEC. How could they spot him out of three hundred? Yeah. That made him feel better. He polished the bike, then closed the storage door and locked it. He went toward his apartment. It was on the second floor with an outside access. As he passed the office, the manager waved at him and came outside. His name was Marion Jones and everyone called him Jonesy. He was the manager, not the owner of the thirty-six-unit building. Jonesy was about fifty, with a potbelly and a belt that got lost somewhere under it, graying hair, and he wore large black-rimmed glasses.

"Mr. Lampedusa, could I see you for a minute?" Jonesy called from the door of the small office.

"Yeah, sure. What's up?"

"What's up is exactly what I want to know. When I didn't see you for a few days, I figured you were off on another of your trips. I still don't understand where you go or what you do. But that's not important. Three days after you left, your neighbors reported a lot of noise in your apartment about three A.M. They told me about it the next day. I figured I should go and check. I hate to be the one to tell you, but the inside of your apartment has been ransacked, totally trashed. Almost everything you had in there has been smashed . . ."

Lam ran out the office and down to his steps and took them three at a time. He fumbled with his door key, and when he pushed the door open, he stopped. "Them sonsof-bitches. How did the fuckers know where I live?" He didn't even give them his last name, did he? He couldn't remember. Yeah, figures he did. But how could they . . . He wasn't listed in the phone book. They would have no way of knowing . . . There wasn't any chance, no way they could have found out where he lived. But they did.

How in hell had they done it?

He tried to think as he stepped over what was left of his living room. His stereo had been smashed beyond repair. All of his CDs had been broken into pieces, the case that held them splintered. Even the pictures on the walls had been taken down and crushed, the books and book-cases splattered over that end of the room. His TV had the picture tube smashed and the guts inside pounded with a hammer into an electrical mine field. His one good sofa had been sliced and ripped to shreds, the small table broken, legs smashed off chairs. He didn't have the will-power to look in the kitchen.

Jonesy stood at the door looking in. "My god, some-body must really hate you. An ex-wife or an ex-wife's boyfriend?"

"Nothing like that."

"Some enemy you made in the service?"

"Oh, no. These guys were civilians. I think I know who did it. I just don't know what I can do about it."

"You want me to call the police? They should know about this."

"No. No police. I'll take care of it myself." Lam looked at the walls and the carpet. "Doesn't look like they hurt the building itself much. Just my stuff."

He looked into the kitchen, then the bedroom. The same all over. The kitchen was the worst, with dried milk, catsup, and mayo splattered on everything that had been trashed. He doubted if there was an unbroken dish or bottle or jar in the place.

He'd bought the furniture on a rent-to-own deal going back two years. Most of it was paid off. He checked the bedroom closet. All of his clothes he had hung up had been slashed and ripped into small pieces. His one good suit, that he had bought for his sister's wedding, was in at least twenty different shreds. Nobody would ever sleep again on the mattress that now rested on the floor where it had been dumped.

Lam wondered about his emergency fund. He had stashed two one-hundred-dollar bills in the bottom of a five-pound bag of sugar in the kitchen. He remembered: The sugar had been sifted over everything else when they were done. The sugar paper sack had been crumpled to one side. They had found the two hundred.

Lam went back to the front door. "I won't be staying here tonight," he said. "Not a chance. They break the lock to get in?"

"They did. A crowbar, I'd guess. I've seen it done before. Where will you be?"

"At a cheap motel. Then tomorrow I come back and see if I can clean up this mess. Could you have one of the trash bins moved close by so I won't have to pack the trash so far?"

"Yes, seems the least."

Lam thought to call Jaybird. He could bunk with him. When he looked for the phone he found it smashed into pieces and the wires pulled out of the wall.

At least his bike was safe. Lam frowned. But for how long would it be safe? The three of them probably took turns standing watch waiting for him to come back. One of them might be watching right at that moment. He nodded to Jonesy and hurried out. He'd get on his bike and ride over to Jaybird's place and tell him what happened.

His hideout.

He went back into the far end of the living room where the books had scattered. He found the volume he wanted. *The Complete Works of William Shakespeare*. It had fallen near the far wall. He picked it up, dusted off the top, and opened it. Most of the interior had been hollowed out, leaving room for a .32-caliber automatic with eight rounds in the handle. He pushed it and a box of rounds into his pants pocket. He needed an ankle holster. He'd be armed from now on 24-7.

Jaybird lived less than a mile away. He wasn't going to bring his bike out until he knew more what had happened to the murder case. He thought of the papers, but the paperboy automatically stopped the paper if two piled up by the door.

Lam left his apartment, pulled the door shut. It wouldn't latch. He looked carefully around, saw no motorcycles, or cars that didn't look like they belonged. He went out the back drive, then through an alley, and paused at the far end watching and waiting. After five minutes he figured that no one was following him. He jogged on to Jaybird's house and caught him in the shower.

"Got a heavy date," Jaybird said through the steam. "What the hell you doing here?"

Lam helped himself to one of Jaybird's beers, and spelled out the trashing as soon as Jaybird turned off the shower.

"Hey, I didn't do it. I got an alibi." Jaybird frowned. "Must be something you're not telling me. Give, buddy. Who did you get so mad that they trashed everything you own?"

Lam told Jaybird the whole thing from the afternoon at the motorcycle dealership and the ride and the stomping.

"Man, you are in deep shit. You try to turn in these guys and they all say you did it. In the meantime they know you're a witness because you saw it and ran. Hey, I know how they found you. Your license plate. You had a permanent plate on when we saw your bike at the parking lot. They traced you by the plate."

"They remembered my plate? I don't remember theirs."

"They might have got it from the dealership. Point is they know where you live. So now you live here. I scrunch you down when we come out of the parking lot every day and when we go to work in the mornings. First we get some help and clean up your place. I'll make some phone calls. We work on it tonight. We'll all have hide-outs. Three of them won't bother six or seven of us."

"What about your heavy date?"

"Hell, she's just a bimbo. I can get out of it."

Lam rubbed his face with one hand and frowned. "Hell, I don't want to get anybody else involved."

"We won't tell our guys why you got trashed. They won't ask. You know our guys. They'll pitch in. We're a team."

That night five SEALs worked in Lam's apartment. They stood up the bookcase and put back the books that weren't ruined. Jaybird brought a garbage can from his place and they carried it time after time to the Dumpster, filled with ruined clothes, dishes, pictures—anything they could lift.

"Whoever the hell did this has got to answer to me," Canzoneri said. "I'd like to get him one-on-one for about ten minutes."

Jaybird had been right, Lam thought. Not one of the other three SEALs asked why Lam's place had been at-tacked. By midnight they had a semblance of order. The bed could be used. They propped up one side with a wooden box and turned over the mattress. It had been slashed only on one side. They found one shirt and one pair of pants the trashers had missed. The rest of Lam's clothes went into the garbage can and then into the Dumpster at the side of the complex.

"They must know that you're home," Jaybird said. "Bet they have somebody watching right now. Say we all fade out, and drive off. We wave at Lam here on the porch. Then we sneak back through the alley and set up a watch in the shadows. Plenty of hiding spots around here. Hey, we're good at an ambush like this. Bet the farm they will storm the place again once they know we're gone. They want your ass, now that your place is trashed."

"You don't have to do this, guys," Lam said.

"Hell you say," Bradford barked. "You'd do it for us."

A half hour later they quit, had beers Jaybird had brought, and made some noise leaving. Lam turned off the lights, closed the door as well as he could, and sat there in a broken chair with his .32 automatic in his hand waiting. He could imagine the four guys slipping up on his apartment.

Outside, Jaybird settled down with his back against the wall, one apartment down, in a small alcove that was totally dark. He watched the steps leading to the second-floor unit and waited. He was about twenty feet from the stairs with an open field. Jaybird knew where two of the other SEALs were, but he hadn't spotted Bradford. The guy was getting good.

An hour after the SEALs had left the apartment, two late model cars wheeled into the parking lot easing along on a recon. They turned at the end of the narrow lot and came back. Both parked near the steps. One man left the car. He was dressed in black bike leathers but without any insignia. Only his face showed white. He went up the steps three at a time and knocked on the door. Three more men eased out of the cars and moved to the bottom of the steps.

A moment after he knocked, the big man with red hair at Lam's door kicked it hard, popping it open. He stormed in. From ten feet away, Lam turned on the lights and leveled the .32 at the man's head.

"Cooley, isn't it?" Lam said. "You're the fucking red-head in the murderous trio. Don't say a damn word. Just lean out the door and wave for your guys to come on up. You do anything else and I shoot you in the balls—you got that, sucker?"

Cooley's widened eyes came back to normal. He nodded slowly and backed up to the door. Without looking out, he waved the others up.

Jaybird came out of his crouch and charged the twenty feet, slammed a shoulder block into the first man on the second step, smashing him off the wood and into the swatch of green grass. Jaybird immediately bounced to his feet and planted a kick into the man's midsection, stopping his try at getting up. This was Downfield, Jaybird figured from Lam's description. He surged up to his knees and Jaybird powered his own knee up hard, slamming into

Downfield's chin, pitching him to the side. He struggled to his hands and knees and then came to his feet. He charged Jaybird.

Jaybird sidestepped the charge, pounded his fist as hard as he could downward on the back of Downfield's neck, and saw the thin man sprawl on the grass on his belly. Jaybird dropped hard on his back, splashing half the air out of his lungs. Then Jaybird lifted Downfield's head by his hair and slammed it into the hard ground three times.

At the same time Jaybird attacked Downfield, the other two SEALs hit the second pair of leather-wearing bikers.

Bradford tackled the one who had to be a health nut. He was trim and lean in his black leathers. Bradford rolled him over and pounded one fist into his jaw, slamming his head to one side.

"What the fuck you doing?" the man bellowed. Bradford hit him in the throat, not hard enough to crush his larynx but enough to keep him from talking for at least a day.

"I hear you like to trash apartments, you bastard." Bradford hit the prone man again in the face, breaking his nose and splattering blood all over his face and the grass. Bradford rolled him over on his back and sat on him.

Canzoneri caught his man as he tried to run up the steps. The SEAL grabbed the runner's back foot and twisted it, spinning the biker over the rail and landing hard on his shoulders. Canzoneri was on top of him a second later. He pinned the big man to the grass like a wrestler. "Who the hell are you?" Canzoneri asked.

"Who the fuck wants to know?" the black-leather-clad man snorted. Canzoneri rolled him over and pounded two hard fists into the biker's belly, doubling him over. Canzoneri cocked his fist and then slammed his elbow into the biker's cheek, breaking cheekbones and maybe his jaw. The biker collapsed, holding his face and keening in pain.

In the apartment, Lam motioned Cooley to turn around. "Okay, badass, lace your hands on top of your head before I get impatient and shoot you in your balls just for the fun of it. I don't like people messing with my things. You owe me twelve thousand dollars. You ready to pay up?"

"Eat shit, Lampedusa."

Lam slammed the butt of the pistol into Cooley's right kidney. The biker bellowed in pain and bent over almost double. As he did, Lam slammed the weapon into the kidney on the other side and Cooley fell to the floor whimpering and pulling his legs up into a fetal ball.

"So talk to me, asshole. You killed the old man, and you think you can intimidate me? Hell, I can tell the DA so much you three will join each other in a triple party in the gas oven. Twelve thousand you owe me for my apartment furnishings. You remember that?"

Cooley looked up at Lam and tried to sneer. It never quite got there. "Lampedusa, you bastard. I'll get you for this." Lam hit the seated man so fast with a pair of jabs that he never saw them coming. His hands went to his eyes just as Lam jolted him with a wild right-hand round-house that landed on his jaw and slammed him into the carpet. Lam looked outside, saw the three bikers on the ground. He went back and kicked Cooley until he stood up.

Below in the parking lot, the fight was over. The three would-be trashers were down and not moving. Bradford snorted and pulled his KA-BAR. Jaybird shook his head, but Bradford just grinned. He ran to the cars and slashed the tires on both rigs until they had eight flat tires.

Jaybird found a hose at the front of the apartments. He turned it on and hosed down the three bikers until they sputtered back to consciousness.

"Get in your cars and get the hell out of here," Jaybird told each of them, not raising his voice. "If you come back here, the next time we'll kill you. That's our job, killing assholes like you. One more time your face is in this lot and you're stone-cold dead assholes. Now move."

Jaybird ran up the steps and found Lam pushing the last of the quartet of raiders out the door. Jaybird angled him down the steps, tripping him on the last one so Cooley's face skidded on the concrete walk.

"You better get in your car while you still can," Jaybird said. He repeated the warning about killing them if they came back. Cooley looked as if he could barely control his pain. He glared at Jaybird, then crawled into the nearest car. Both rigs' engines started and they moved a half dozen feet and stopped. The drivers got out and looked at the tires. They swore and got back inside. Jaybird lay the barrel of his hideout .38 on the first driver's open window ledge. "You boys better drive, or you won't ever be able to drive again."

Both cars moved with caution toward the exit. Each had flapping rubber on the flat tires before they got to the street. Five miles an hour would be their top speed.

The five SEALs sat on the steps talking in hushed tones.

"Those four won't bother you anymore," Bradford said.

Jaybird shook his head. "Oh, I think they just might. I'll rig a flash-bang grenade to go off if the apartment door is opened. Then Lam stays at my place."

"Let's give it a try," Lam said.

Two days later Lam felt safe enough to ride his bike to the SEAL parking lot. Nobody would mess with it there. That night he came away from a hard day of training and headed for Jaybird's. He always went a different route so he could check to see if anyone was following him. This time he was two blocks from Jaybird's when he saw the same new yellow Mazda turn when he turned. It was the third turn the Mazda had made with him.

Lam speeded up, darted down an alley, came out on the other side. The Mazda driver had guessed which way Lam would turn and was half a block behind him. What next? He could always pull in at the Coronado police station; the Mazda wouldn't turn in there he was sure. But the thought of talking with cops scared him. He turned toward the ramp leading to the San Diego–Coronado Bay Bridge. He knew a spot in National City where he could lose whoever drove that Mazda. If he could get there before the driver rear-ended him. He gunned onto the entry ramp and accelerated. All he needed was a three-minute lead time. If he could get it. The damn yellow Mazda was fifty yards behind him and gaining.

26

Lam kept watching over his shoulder. The Mazda was getting involved with traffic and couldn't gain on him. Soon they hit the slowdown on the bridge and Lam wove in and out between cars and gained fifteen car lengths on the yellow Mazda. Then he came off the bridge and swept down the 5 South freeway, where he blasted up to ninety miles an hour and left the Mazda eating exhaust. He slipped onto an off ramp, cut his speed to make the corner, and headed for a section of woods and water and a bit of wilderness right there on the outskirts of National City. He'd ridden a rented trail bike there before.

The Mazda's driver spotted him on the off ramp and followed. The guys in the car must be sure now of the kill. Lam rode as far into the woods as he could and hid his bike, then circled back so he could watch the Mazda. It parked at the edge of the woods but nobody got out. They must be talking. Then three men stepped out and he recognized Cooley's red hair. One of the other men in black leathers limped and the third one had a bandage on his nose. Three of the same bikers they had pounded around before.

The three bikers hurried into the woods where they'd seen his bike vanish. Lam waited until they were well inside the growth, then he sprinted out to their car and reached for his KA-BAR knife. It wasn't there. He used a stick and let all the air out of all four tires, then ran back into the woods. He slipped up on the three men as they tried to track him. By following the tire trail in the woods, they soon found his bike. Lam grabbed his .32

hideout pistol off his left ankle and fired one shot over their heads. In the thick woods it sounded like a rifle shot. The three bikers ducked and scattered.

"You three guys are dead, you know that?" Lam bellowed at them. "I know where you are. You're on my turf now, hotshots. Who wants to die first?"

Lam kept quiet then and moved up on the nearest biker. He was Cooley, and he had backed up against a foot-thick tree and pulled out a switchblade, waving it in front of him. At least he didn't yell anything and give away his position. He didn't have time to. Lam went around him and came up in back of the tree. He slid his belt off, bent low, and whipped the buckle around the tree a foot off the ground, catching it on the far side of the tree and cinching it up tight before Cooley knew what had happened.

"Hey, bastard. What the hell you doing? Let me go."

Lam reached around the tree and slammed his fist into Cooley's right hand that held the blade. Cooley screeched in pain and dropped the weapon.

Lam drifted around the tree and snorted at Cooley. "Look, Mister Hot Shit, take off your jacket."

"Hell no. Untie me."

Lam picked up the blade, tested it, grabbed one of Cooley's arms, and made a thin blood line down the back of his hand.

"Take off your jacket or I'll cut your little finger off."

Cooley's eyes went wide and he shivered. "You ugly bastard, you'd probably do it. Hell, what you want my jacket for?"

"Just take it off."

"He's over here," Cooley yelled.

Lam knocked down one of Cooley's arms with his left hand and slammed a hard knuckled fist into his jaw. Cooley slumped to the right, then straightened.

"Okay, okay, the fucking jacket. Hey, I'm taking it off."

He unbuttoned it, peeled out of it, and threw it to Lam.

Lamb grabbed it and went behind the tree.

"Where the hell are you?" Cooley demanded.

Lam came from behind the tree, pushed the jacket over Cooley's chest, threw one sleeve around the tree, and caught it on the back side. Then he crossed the arms in back of the tree and pulled them tight. He tied the arms in a hard knot and faded away into the heavy growth without a sound.

"Hey, what the hell?" Cooley shouted. "Why the fuck you tie me up?" He was silent a moment. "Woodward, Johnny, you guys better get over here."

Lam hovered in the dark green growth listening. Both the other men were to his right, maybe thirty feet. One of them came back toward Cooley, but he moved a step at a time with caution and quieter than Lam expected.

"What the hell. Where are you guys?" Cooley called again.

Five minutes later, Lam spotted the tall, thin one, Downfield, slip behind a tree and wait. He peered out, looked all around, then took three steps toward Cooley, only to step onto a dead branch, which snapped under his weight. He dropped in place and didn't move. Lam grinned. This one had some woods smarts about him. It wouldn't save him, but he'd last longer.

Lam waited as Downfield stepped carefully past him only ten feet away. Downfield watched ahead now. Lam moved in behind him one silent step at a time. The next time Downfield stopped and crouched to look to both sides and ahead, Lam brought the butt of his .32 hideout down smartly on the man's head. Downfield grunted, half turned, then his eyes glazed and he pitched forward into a patch of brush.

Four minutes later Lam had stripped Downfield's belt off and used it to tie his hands behind his back. Then he pulled his shoelaces out and tied his ankles together with the hardest knots he could remember. Lam used Cooley's switchblade and cut long slices down each of the black leather jacket sleeves, then slit Downfield's pants down each leg. As a parting gesture, he used the knife again and made a two-inch blood line down his cheek, cutting the skin just enough to make it bleed.

Lam moved ten feet away from Downfield and fired

one shot from his .32 into a tree. Then he ran, crashing brush over near Cooley. He stopped in front of him and showed him the gun.

He held it at Cooley's head a moment.

"Oh god no, don't shoot me," Cooley screamed.

Lam moved the weapon to the side and shot into the tree over his head. Then he faded out of the area, got his bike, and pushed it out of the woods as silently as possible. He would have loved to stay and see Woodward find the other two. He'd untie them, scream at them for being so dumb, and then hurry them out to the Mazda.

As he came to the Mazda, Lam stopped. "Hell, why not," he said out loud. He popped the hood and grabbed three spark plug wires and ripped them out. Cars still needed spark plug wires, even with the fancy electronic ignitions they used these days. He carried the wires with him as he started the bike and rode out to the street. He threw the plug wires into a drainage ditch and headed for Jaybird's place. He still didn't feel safe going back to his apartment.

Jaybird put his fists on his hips and frowned when Lam walked in.

"Where the hell . . ." He stopped when he saw the expression on Lam's face. "Okay, what happened? They make another try for you?"

"Yep."

"But you used your skills as a paid United States black operation double-covert sub-rosa killer and you dismantled them one body part at a time."

"Almost." He told Jaybird what happened, as they ate the Rice-a-Roni Spanish rice that Jaybird had just finished cooking.

"I bet that redhead shit his pants," Jaybird shouted. "Damn I'd have liked to see his face when that shot went off."

"I saw his crotch get all wet." Lam shook his head. "I don't like this, Jaybird. I'm tired of being a target all the time. I've decided I have to go to the district attorney and tell him what happened up there above Descanso. I've got to do it."

"You could be in deep shit, man."

"I know, and if that's what happens, it happens."

"No, first we talk to the commander, and see what he says. Let's let him make the call. He should have a say in this."

Lam closed his eyes and shook his head. "Tomorrow, right after we get off duty, we'll buy him a beer somewhere and I'll spell it out in detail."

Lieutenant Commander Blake Murdock was feeling ill at ease and a bit anxious. They had been home a week already from Israel and they still hadn't found a man to replace Tracy Donegan. The two men who had been interviewed by both him and JG Gardner just weren't the type of man they wanted. The master chief said he would send three more over the next day. Murdock hated this limbo situation. He needed that man slotted into Bravo Squad today so he could get integrated into the team action, so he would be a team player. He had to know how the man in front and in back of him would react in every situation. The process was difficult and wasn't done overnight.

Murdock kicked his feet off the desk and stood. They had to find the right man tomorrow. Enough for today. Ardith would be coming home about six. She said she waited to miss the bulk of the rush hour traffic. She worked in one of the big towers in the Golden Triangle in the University Center area. He closed up and headed for home.

Murdock had just finished his shower when Ardith walked in. He flapped a towel around his waist and met her in the living room. She was as tall and slender and blonde and beautiful as ever. More so today with the gorgeous smile glowing on her pretty face.

"I found the perfect condo," she said. "Just perfect for us for years and years. It's three bedrooms and on the second floor and is in just the farthest edge of La Jolla. The best part, it's in our price range and I want to show it to you."

"Maybe I should get dressed first."

"Oh, yes, there's that. This is just perfect. Not too big, but big enough for three or four of us. You said you wanted . . ." Ardith stopped and watched him. "You still do want one or two?"

"Yes, of course. How well within our price range is it?"

"Only three hundred and twenty, less than we'd have to pay for a house almost the same size, and no lawn to worry about or gophers, or fertilizing . . ."

"Or scooping snow off the sidewalks," Murdock finished the usual patter they had worked out. "Yeah, let me get dressed, then I'm taking you out to dinner—if I like the condo."

He liked it. The only thing La Jolla about it was the address. It was on one of those streets half a block away from the Ocean Beach imaginary boundary. It wasn't La Jolla upscale, it wasn't gated, and it had Fords and Chevys and Buicks in the parking garage and not Ferraris and Cadillacs and Lincoln Town Cars. The building had been there for fifteen years but had been immaculately maintained.

"Probably," Murdock said over the salmon steak.

"We've got two days to decide, then he'll talk to the other people."

"Yeah, two days," Murdock said. "Are you having dessert?"

The next day was wet training. Murdock and Gardner had interviewed two possible candidates for the spot in Bravo Squad. Gardner was high on a kid named Derek Prescott.

"He's big, six-three, played football, so he can take the work load, he's a radioman second class, and he's from Idaho. I just like the way he comes across."

Murdock looked at the man who sat in the squad room waiting. He'd been the second one interviewed. "Okay, Chris, he's your boy. Call Master Chief MacKenzie and tell him to put through the paperwork. He's been in Team One, so he gets a transfer. From now on let's keep two

SATCOMs in the field with us at all times. You might have Prescott pack the one in your squad."

That afternoon they went for a swim. Ten miles with fins and full gear. They came back tired, and Murdock realized that it had been some time since they had done a ten miler with weapons and their equipment. Murdock put his wet suit on the drying rack and stashed the rest of his gear in his locker. Then he dropped into the chair behind his desk. More paperwork. He was just getting started on the pile when Jaybird and Lam came in. Lam had a strange look and Murdock sent up his warning flags. Jaybird carried the ball.

"Hey, Cap, got a little situation here you need to know about. Could we buy you a beer and talk about it?"

Murdock stared at Jaybird a minute. He was serious. Lam's expression swayed Murdock. He dropped his pen and grabbed his floppy hat.

"We were thinking maybe in civvies, sir," Jaybird said.

Murdock frowned. This was sounding more serious by the second. Somebody was in trouble here, and it probably wasn't Jaybird. Lam wouldn't look him in the eye. Murdock nodded and took a deep breath. "Yeah, civvies, and the beer is on me. Give me five minutes and I'll be with you in the parking lot."

Jaybird and Murdock drove their cars down six blocks to a bar and Lam rode his Hog, parking it between the two cars.

They set up beers and took a booth. Murdock looked at Lam. "Okay, Lampedusa. Time to come clean. I want to know what this is all about."

Fifteen minutes later Murdock closed his eyes and shook his head. "You understand that by law you were with them, so that makes you guilty of murder right along with the other three."

"But I never touched the old man. I got out of there as soon as I saw them start kicking him."

"Doesn't matter, you were with them. The law is extremely clear in this regard. Now, what the hell can we do?"

Jaybird put down his beer. "Lam says he wants to turn

himself in and give evidence against the other three."

Murdock nodded. "About the only thing you can do. But not before you get a good lawyer, I'm talking about a five-thousand-dollar fee up front. A criminal lawyer who can bargain with the DA. What you need is total immunity from prosecution for your testimony that will convict the other three."

"Will they do that?" Lam asked.

"If your lawyer is good enough, and if the DA wants the other three guys bad enough."

Murdock ordered another round of beers. "Sounds like you beat up these guys pretty good."

"We had a couple of go-rounds with them, yes, sir," Lam said. He rubbed his face and took a pull at the beer. "This will be like on those lawyer shows on TV where they make a deal with the DA?"

"Exactly," Jaybird said. "Let's see, five big ones divided by sixteen SEALs is about three hundred and fifteen per man. I'll be the collector. Now, how do we find a good lawyer we can trust, who will get Lam on the case, but not charged with a crime, so he won't get booted out of the Navy?"

"I know a guy in JAG who can help us. It won't be a Navy case, but he can help us put it just the right way to the civilian lawyer and to the DA so we should be able to keep Lam from being charged. I'll talk to him tonight, and try to get a meeting set with him for tomorrow night. Will that work with you, Lam?"

"Oh yes. This is the best news I've had since we got home. Now if he can just keep me from being charged, and call me as a witness, not a participant, that will be great."

Outside they walked to where they parked and Lam bellowed in protest. Three men in black leathers were trying to start his Harley Hog.

"Let's take them," Murdock barked and the three SEALs charged the bikers, who looked up in surprise. It was too late for them to run. Woodward whipped out a motorcycle bike chain. Cooley pulled an eight-inch knife. Downfield grabbed a two-foot-long crowbar and the three stood there with their backs to each other waiting for the SEALs to rush them.

27

"I'm right," Murdock said.

"I've got the left," Jaybird answered.

"I'm on the guy in back," Lam said. They spread out, and Lam circled the trio until he faced the man in back.

"Now!" Murdock shouted and the three charged the bikers.

Murdock darted forward, watched the fit-looking biker start to swing the two-foot-long bike chain. Once it's started, it's hard to stop. Murdock jolted to a stop, ducked under the swinging chain, and drove forward, catching Woodward at the waist in a pro-football-style tackle and blasting him backward into one of the other bikers. All three went down in a heap. Murdock caught the stilled chain, wrapped it around the biker's neck, and began to tighten it. Woodward clawed at the chain with both hands, then tried a backward elbow punch that missed. Murdock surged upward, bringing Woodward with him. He spun him around and blasted a tight fist into the biker's midsection, then another one into his jaw. The thin man gave a little moan and passed out. Murdock let him fall to the ground and turned quickly looking at the other bikers.

He and Woodward had knocked down Cooley when they crashed backward. Cooley didn't have time to get up before Jaybird kicked the knife from his hand, blasted another kick into the biker's belly, spun him around, and put a half-nelson hold with his forearm around the man's throat, pressing inward until Cooley began to cough. Jaybird eased up on the chokehold and threw Cooley to the parking lot, where he sat on him, driving his face into the pavement.

Lam had more trouble with Downfield and his crowbar. The biker knew how to use it, didn't make wild swings, kept it close waiting for the right chance. Lam jolted forward twice and then back when he saw the feint wasn't working. He could see no weapon nearby to use to counter the crowbar. He bent and pulled his .32 pistol and aimed it at Downfield's crotch.

"Put it down, idiot, or I'll blow your balls off."

Downfield snorted. "One shot and there'll be a dozen cops swarming all over this place."

"Maybe so, idiot, but you'll be shooting blanks out of your cock for the rest of your life. You want that?"

Downfield squinted at Lam. "Hell, you'd probably do it." He shrugged and started to drop the bar, then he charged forward swinging the deadly steel shaft. Lam sidestepped but not far enough. The end of the bar hit his right hip and glanced off. That gave Lam the opening he needed. He surged forward and hit Downfield in the chest with his shoulder, blasting him backward. The two fell with Lam on top, driving the other man into the pavement. Downfield gasped and then gagged trying to get his breath. The fall had knocked the wind out of him and he writhed on the pavement trying to suck air into his lungs. Lam pulled plastic riot cuffs out of his pocket and bound the biker's hands in front of him.

It had all happened fast, in thirty seconds, Murdock figured. Not time enough to gather a crowd. One man going to his car stopped and looked at the scene.

"Saw the whole thing," he said. "Them bikers were trying to steal that Harley Hog. You want that I should call the cops on my cell phone?"

Murdock walked him away from the scene. "Thanks, sir, but we've got them down. They can't hurt anyone now. We'll take care of it, thanks a lot."

By the time he got back to the group, Jaybird had cut off half of Cooley clothes. "Turn these bastards loose bare assed and running," Jaybird said. "Serve them right." He slit the biker's shirt and pulled it off, then cut off his pants and shorts.

He tossed the captured blade to Lam, who did the same to Downfield. He came partly out of his lack of breath and yelled.

"What the fuck you doing? I paid fifty bucks for that shirt."

"Fortunes of combat, asshole," Lam said. "You start a war, you gonna get splattered by some of the fallout. Have a nice time naked in Coronado."

Five minutes later they had the three naked bikers hidden behind Murdock's car. By then all of them were conscious and swearing.

"You can't do this," Cooley bellowed. "Our car is a dozen blocks from here."

"Car won't help you, man," Lam said. "Because you don't have any car keys. Now, get out there and get running or I'm gonna call the cops."

The three looked at each other, then headed for some shadows in the alley behind the bar. Lam looked at his bike. It didn't seem damaged. They'd been trying to jump-start it without the key. He slid into the saddle, turned the key, and the Hog started on the first try.

Murdock walked up. "I'll call my JAG friend tonight and see if he knows of any top local criminal lawyers. We'll find one. Then tomorrow I'll get him to come over and we'll go over the situation and see what he thinks we can do."

When Murdock arrived at his apartment, Ardith had dinner waiting.

"You must have been held up in traffic," she said.

He smelled the cooking and lifted the top off the big cooking pot. "Stew, oh yeah, you can't miss with a great stew."

"I'm trying to win you over to buy that condo. I've got forty thousand I can pull out of my 401K retirement plan. You said you had some savings. If we can get sixty thousand down, that would make a much lower monthly mortgage payment."

Murdock shivered. "Hey, lady. I've never owed anybody more than five thousand dollars in my life. You're talking about a debt of two hundred and sixty thousand dollars?"

Ardith reached up and kissed him, then again. She looped her arms around his neck and pushed hard against him. "Something like that, maybe a little more with the points. But we can handle it. I earn more than enough to make the mortgage payments."

"And I'm not going to be sensitive because you make twice what I do, right?"

"Yes, right. You're terribly adult and sensible about that."

"I convinced you about that, right?"

"Convinced yourself. Now, let's have some stew. I made it nice and soupy so you can put it on a plate and mash up the potatoes in the juices. I have eight kinds of vegetables in there. Some of them are so cooked up you can't tell what they are."

After dinner they sat in the living room and looked at the pictures of the condo. "If we buy this place, does that mean we're getting married right away?" Murdock asked.

Ardith moved over on the couch and kissed his cheek, then his lips. "Actually I was thinking about one step at a time. The condo so we'll have enough room. And then, later . . ." She grinned. "Like a week later we get married."

"You are one sneaky female."

"It's in my genes."

Murdock held her with her head against his chest. "Hell, an officer is supposed to be able to make decisions, sometimes in the heat of the moment. Like now. Okay, Ardith, okay. Let's buy the condo. I can come up with about thirty thousand. I had some good stocks and got out just before the last crash."

Ardith stood and grabbed his hand. "Let's seal the deal," she said, pulling him toward the bedroom.

The next day, Murdock and his JAG lawyer friend, Commander Lewis, talked with Lam for two hours. At the end of that time the commander put his notepad away.

"Yes, I'd think that the right lawyer can get you total immunity to prosecution for your testimony. It has to be good. It has to be enough to put these three away for a long time."

It took Murdock a week to find the right lawyer, J. Bascomb Tretter. He said if he could make a deal with the DA for total immunity, his fee would be $4,000. If the DA wouldn't go for the deal and charged Lam with the others in the murder, his fee would be double that. Jaybird did his figuring again.

A week later lawyer Bascomb and Lam went to talk with the DA. The assistant DA had been briefed and knew what it was about. The lawyer leaned heavily on what Lam did for a living, all of the covert operations they went on, that they were directly assigned by either the president or the chief naval officer in the Pentagon. Even the assistant DA was impressed.

Lam told his story and said he would testify against the three. When they got approval of the deal from the DA, Lam gave the names of the three bikers. The DA said the cops wouldn't have any trouble finding them. The next day Lam gave a formal deposition in front of a judge, a court stenographer, and a video camera. In case he was out of the country when the case came up for the preliminary hearing to see if it would be bound over for trial, they would use his deposition.

It had been three weeks since they came back from Israel. Prescott had blended in nicely with Bravo and with the platoon. He was strong and funny and easygoing, an expert marksman and swam like a salmon going upstream. The condo was a done deal. They would move in when the current owner moved out in a month. Ardith was starting to look at furniture. They'd take what they both had but they would need something new for a new house. He thought about it just after they sweat their way through a tough training schedule.

The phone rang. "Seal Team Seven, Third Platoon, Murdock."

"Get your buns over here, Commander," Master Chief Petty Officer Gordon MacKenzie said. "We've got orders and I don't think you're going to like this mission even a little bit."

"What is it, Master Chief?"

"Get over to the Quarterdeck and you'll find out."

Murdock grabbed JG Gardner and they hurried up to the Quarterdeck.

SEAL TALK

MILITARY GLOSSARY

Aalvin: Small U.S. two-man submarine.

Admin: Short for administration.

Aegis: Advanced Naval air defense radar system.

AH-1W Super Cobra: Has M179 undernose turret with 20mm Gatling gun.

AK-47: 7.63-round Russian Kalashnikov automatic rifle. Most widely used assault rifle in the world.

AK-74: New, improved version of the Kalashnikov. Fires the 5.45mm round. Has 30-round magazine. Rate of fire: 600 rounds per minute. Many slight variations made for many different nations.

AN/PRC-117D: Radio, also called SATCOM. Works with Milstar satellite in 22,300-mile equatorial orbit for instant worldwide radio, voice, or video communications. Size: 15 inches high, 3 inches wide, 3 inches deep. Weighs 15 pounds. Microphone and voice output. Has encrypter, capable of burst transmissions of less than a second.

AN/PUS-7: Night-vision goggles. Weighs 1.5 pounds.

ANVIS-6: Night-vision goggles on air crewmen's helmets.

APC: Armored Personnel Carrier.

ASROC: Nuclear-tipped antisubmarine rocket torpedoes launched by Navy ships.

Assault Vest: Combat vest with full loadouts of ammo, gear.

ASW: Anti-Submarine Warfare.

Attack Board: Molded plastic with two handgrips with bubble compass on it. Also depth gauge and Cyalume chemical lights with twist knob to regulate amount of light.

Used for underwater guidance on long swim.

Aurora: Air Force recon plane. Can circle at 90,000 feet. Can't be seen or heard from ground. Used for thermal imaging.

AWACS: Airborne Warning And Control System. Radar units in high-flying aircraft to scan for planes at any altitude out 200 miles. Controls air-to-air engagements with enemy forces. Planes have a mass of communication and electronic equipment.

Balaclavas: Headgear worn by some SEALs.

Bent Spear: Less serious nuclear violation of safety.

BKA, Bundeskriminant: Germany's federal investigation unit.

Black Talon: Lethal hollow-point ammunition made by Winchester. Outlawed some places.

Blivet: A collapsible fuel container. SEALs sometimes use it.

BLU-43B: Antipersonnel mine used by SEALs.

BLU-96: A fuel-air explosive bomb. It disperses a fuel oil into the air, then explodes the cloud. Many times more powerful than conventional bombs because it doesn't carry its own chemical oxidizers.

BMP-1: Soviet armored fighting vehicle (AFV), low, boxy, crew of 3 and 8 combat troops. Has tracks and a 73mm cannon. Also an AT-3 Sagger antitank missile and coaxial machine gun.

Body Armor: Far too heavy for SEAL use in the water.

Bogey: Pilots' word for an unidentified aircraft.

Boghammar Boat: Long, narrow, low dagger boat; high-speed patrol craft. Swedish make. Iran had 40 of them in 1993.

Boomer: A nuclear-powered missile submarine.

Bought It: A man has been killed. Also "bought the farm."

Bow Cat: The bow catapult on a carrier to launch jets.

Broken Arrow: Any accident with nuclear weapons, or any incident of nuclear material lost, shot down, crashed, stolen, hijacked.

Browning 9mm High Power: A Belgian 9mm pistol, 13 rounds in magazine. First made 1935.

Buddy Line: 6 feet long, ties 2 SEALs together in the water for control and help if needed.

BUD/S: Coronado, California, nickname for SEAL training facility for six months' course.

Bull Pup: Still in testing; new soldier's rifle. SEALs have a dozen of them for regular use. Army gets them in 2005. Has a 5.56 kinetic round, 30-shot clip. Also 20mm high-explosive round and 5-shot magazine. Twenties can be fused for proximity airbursts with use of video camera, laser range finder, and laser targeting. Fuses by number of turns the round needs to reach laser spot. Max range: 1200 yards. Twenty round can also detonate on contact, and has delay fuse. Weapon weighs 14 pounds. SEALs love it. Can in effect "shoot around corners" with the airburst feature.

BUPERS: BUreau of PERSonnel.

C-2A Greyhound: 2-engine turboprop cargo plane that lands on carriers. Also called COD, Carrier Onboard Delivery. Two pilots and engineer. Rear fuselage loading ramp. Cruise speed 300 mph, range 1,000 miles. Will hold 39 combat troops. Lands on CVN carriers at sea.

C-4: Plastic explosive. A claylike explosive that can be molded and shaped. It will burn. Fairly stable.

C-6 Plastique: Plastic explosive. Developed from C-4 and C-5. Is often used in bombs with radio detonator or digital timer.

C-9 Nightingale: Douglas DC-9 fitted as a medical-evacuation transport plane.

C-130 Hercules: Air Force transporter for long haul. 4 engines.

C-141 Starlifter: Airlift transport for cargo, paratroops, evac for long distances. Top speed 566 mph. Range with payload 2,935 miles. Ceiling 41,600 feet.

Caltrops: Small four-pointed spikes used to flatten tires. Used in the Crusades to disable horses.

Camel Back: Used with drinking tube for 70 ounces of water attached to vest.

Cammies: Working camouflaged wear for SEALs. Two different patterns and colors. Jungle and desert.

Cannon Fodder: Old term for soldiers in line of fire destined to die in the grand scheme of warfare.

CAP: Continuous Air Patrol.

Capped: Killed, shot, or otherwise snuffed.

CAR-15: The Colt M-4Al. Sliding-stock carbine with grenade launcher under barrel. Knight sound-suppressor. Can have AN/PAQ-4 laser aiming light under the carrying handle. .223 round. 20- or 30-round magazine. Rate of fire: 700 to 1,000 rounds per minute.

Cascade Radiation: U-235 triggers secondary radiation in other dense materials.

Castle Keep: The main tower in any castle.

Cast Off: Leave a dock, port, land. Get lost. Navy: long, then short signal of horn, whistle, or light.

Caving Ladder: Roll-up ladder that can be let down to climb.

CH-46E: Sea Knight chopper. Twin rotors, transport. Can carry 25 combat troops. Has a crew of 3. Cruise speed 154 mph. Range 420 miles.

CH-53D Sea Stallion: Big Chopper. Not used much anymore.

Chaff: A small cloud of thin pieces of metal, such as tinsel, that can be picked up by enemy radar and that can attract a radar-guided missile away from the plane to hit the chaff.

Charlie-Mike: Code words for continue the mission.

Chief to Chief: Bad conduct by EM handled by chiefs so no record shows or is passed up the chain of command.

Chocolate Mountains: Land training center for SEALs near these mountains in the California desert.

Christians In Action: SEAL talk for not-always-friendly CIA.

CIA: Central Intelligence Agency.

CIC: Combat Information Center. The place on a ship where communications and control areas are situated to open and control combat fire.

CINC: Commander IN Chief.

CINCLANT: Navy Commander-IN-Chief, atLANTtic.

CINCPAC: Navy Commander-IN-Chief, PACific.

Class of 1978: Not a single man finished BUD/S training in this class. All-time record.

Claymore: An antipersonnel mine carried by SEALs on many of their missions.

Cluster Bombs: A canister bomb that explodes and spreads small bomblets over a great area. Used against parked aircraft, massed troops, and unarmored vehicles.

CNO: Chief of Naval Operations.

CO: Commanding Officer.

CO-2 Poisoning: During deep dives. Abort dive at once and surface.

COD: Carrier Onboard Delivery plane.

Cold Pack Rations: Food carried by SEALs to use if needed.

Combat Harness: American Body Armor nylon-mesh special-operations vest. 6 2-magazine pouches for drum-fed belts, other pouches for other weapons, waterproof pouch for Motorola.

CONUS: The Continental United States.

Corfams: Dress shoes for SEALs.

Covert Action Staff: A CIA group that handles all covert action by the SEALs.

CP: Command Post.

CQB house: Close Quarters Battle house. Training facility near Nyland in the desert training area. Also called the Kill House.

CQB: Close Quarters Battle. A fight that's up close, hand-to-hand, whites-of-his-eyes, blood all over you.

CRRC Bundle: Roll it off plane, sub, boat. The assault boat for 8 SEALs. Also the IBS, Inflatable Boat Small.

Cutting Charge: Lead-sheathed explosive. Triangular strip of high-velocity explosive sheathed in metal. Point of the triangle focuses a shaped-charge effect. Cuts a pencil-line-wide hole to slice a steel girder in half.

CVN: A U.S. aircraft carrier with nuclear power. Largest that we have in fleet.

CYA: Cover Your Ass, protect yourself from friendlies or officers above you and JAG people.

Damfino: Damned if I know. SEAL talk.

DDS: Dry Dock Shelter. A clamshell unit on subs to deliver SEALs and SDVs to a mission.

DEFCON: DEFense CONdition. How serious is the threat?

Delta Forces: Army special forces, much like SEALs.

Desert Cammies: Three-color, desert tan and pale green with streaks of pink. For use on land.

DIA: Defense Intelligence Agency.

Dilos Class Patrol Boat: Greek, 29 feet long, 75 tons displacement.

Dirty Shirt Mess: Officers can eat there in flying suits on board a carrier.

DNS: Doppler Navigation System.

Draegr LAR V: Rebreather that SEALs use. No bubbles.

DREC: Digitally Reconnoiterable Electronic Component. Top-secret computer chip from NSA that lets it decipher any U.S. military electronic code.

E-2C Hawkeye: Navy, carrier-based, Airborne Early Warning craft for long-range early warning and threat-assessment and fighter-direction. Has a 24-foot saucer-like rotodome over the wing. Crew 5, max speed 326 knots, ceiling 30,800 feet, radius 175 nautical miles with 4 hours on station.

E-3A Skywarrior: Old electronic intelligence craft. Replaced by the newer ES-3A.

E-4B NEACP: Called Kneecap. National Emergency Airborne Command Post. A greatly modified Boeing 747 used as a communications base for the President of the United States and other high-ranking officials in an emergency and in wartime.

E & E: SEAL talk for escape and evasion.

EA-6B Prowler: Navy plane with electronic countermeasures. Crew of 4, max speed 566 knots, ceiling 41,200 feet, range with max load 955 nautical miles.

EAR: Enhanced Acoustic Rifle. Fires not bullets, but a high-impact blast of sound that puts the target down and unconscious for up to six hours. Leaves him with almost no aftereffects. Used as a non-lethal weapon. The sound blast will bounce around inside a building, vehicle, or ship and knock out anyone who is within range. Ten shots before the weapon must be electrically charged. Range: about 400 yards.

Easy: The only easy day was yesterday. SEAL talk.

Ejection seat: The seat is powered by a CAD, a shotgun-like shell that is activated when the pilot triggers the ejection. The shell is fired into a solid rocket, sets it off and propels the whole ejection seat and pilot into the air. No electronics are involved.

ELINT: ELectronic INTelligence. Often from satellite in orbit, picture-taker, or other electronic communications.

EMP: ElectroMagnetic Pulse: The result of an E-bomb detonation. One type E-bomb is the Flux Compression Generator or FCG. Can be built for $400 and is relatively simple to make. Emits a rampaging electromagnetic pulse that destroys anything electronic in a 100 mile diameter circle. Blows out and fries all computers, telephone systems, TV broadcasts, radio, streetlights, and sends the area back into the Stone Age with no communications whatsoever. Stops all cars with electronic ignitions, drops jet planes out of the air including airliners, fighters and bombers, and stalls ships with electronic guidance and steering systems. When such a bomb is detonated the explosion is small but sounds like a giant lightning strike.

EOD: Navy experts in nuclear material and radioactivity who do Explosive Ordnance Disposal.

Equatorial Satellite Pointing Guide: To aim antenna for radio to pick up satellite signals.

ES-3A: Electronic Intelligence (ELINT) intercept craft. The platform for the battle group Passive Horizon Extension System. Stays up for long patrol periods, has comprehensive set of sensors, lands and takes off from a carrier. Has 63 antennas.

ETA: Estimated Time of Arrival. The planned time that you will arrive at a given destination.

Executive Order 12333: By President Reagan authorizing Special Warfare units such as the SEALs.

Exfil: Exfiltrate, to get out of an area.

F/A-18 Hornet: Carrier-based interceptor that can change from air-to-air to air-to-ground attack mode while in flight.

Fitrep: Fitness Report.

Flashbang Grenade: Non-lethal grenade that gives off a series of piercing explosive sounds and a series of brilliant strobe-type lights to disable an enemy.

Flotation Bag: To hold equipment, ammo, gear on a wet operation.

FO: Forward Observer. A man or unit set in an advanced area near or past friendly lines to call in artillery or mortar fire. Also used simply as the eyes of the rear echelon planners.

Fort Fumble: SEALs' name for the Pentagon.

Forty-mm Rifle Grenade: The M576 multipurpose round, contains 20 large lead balls. SEALs use on Colt M-4A1.

Four-Striper: A Navy captain.

Fox Three: In air warfare, a code phrase showing that a Navy F-14 has launched a Phoenix air-to-air missile.

FUBAR: SEAL talk. Fucked Up Beyond All Repair.

Full Helmet Masks: For high-altitude jumps. Oxygen in mask.

G-3: German-made assault rifle.

GHQ: General Headquarters.

Gloves: SEALs wear sage-green, fire-resistant Nomex flight gloves.

GMT: Greenwich Mean Time. Where it's all measured from.

GPS: Global Positioning System. A program with satellites around Earth to pinpoint precisely aircraft, ships, vehicles, and ground troops. Position information is to plus or minus ten feet. Also can give speed of a plane or ship to one quarter of a mile per hour.

GPSL: A radio antenna with floating wire that pops to the surface. Antenna picks up positioning from the closest 4 global positioning satellites and gives an exact position within 10 feet.

Green Tape: Green sticky ordnance tape that has a hundred uses for a SEAL.

GSG-9: Flashbang grenade developed by Germans. A cardboard tube filled with 5 separate charges timed to burst in rapid succession. Blinding and giving concussion to enemy, leaving targets stunned, easy to kill or capture. Usually non-lethal.

GSG9: Grenzschutzgruppe Nine. Germany's best special warfare unit, counterterrorist group.

Gulfstream II (VCII): Large executive jet used by services for transport of small groups quickly. Crew of 3 and 18 passengers. Maximum cruise speed 581 mph. Maximum range 4,275 miles.

H & K 21A1: Machine gun with 7.62 NATO round. Replaces the older, more fragile M-60 E3. Fires 900 rounds per minute. Range 1,100 meters. All types of NATO rounds, ball, incendiary, tracer._

H & K G-11: Automatic rifle, new type. 4.7mm caseless ammunition. 50-round magazine. The bullet is in a sleeve of solid propellant with a special thin plastic coating around it. Fires 600 rounds per minute. Single-shot, three-round burst, or fully automatic.

H & K MP-5SD: 9mm submachine gun with integral silenced barrel, single-shot, three-shot, or fully automatic. Rate 800 rds/min.

H & K P9S: Heckler & Koch's 9mm Parabellum double-action semiauto pistol with 9-round magazine.

H & K PSG1: 7.62 NATO round. High-precision, bolt-action, sniping rifle. 5- to 20-round magazine. Roller lock delayed blowback breech system. Fully adjustable stock. 6 × 42 telescopic sights. Sound suppressor.

HAHO: High Altitude jump, High Opening. From 30,000 feet, open chute for glide up to 15 miles to ground. Up to 75 minutes in glide. To enter enemy territory or enemy position unheard.

Half-Track: Military vehicle with tracked rear drive and wheels in front, usually armed and armored.

HALO: High Altitude jump, Low Opening. From 30,000 feet. Free fall in 2 minutes to 2,000 feet and open chute. Little forward movement. Get to ground quickly, silently.

Hamburgers: Often called sliders on a Navy carrier.

Handie-Talkie: Small, handheld personal radio. Short range.

HE: High Explosives.

HELO: SEAL talk for helicopter.

Herky Bird: C-130 Hercules transport. Most-flown military transport in the world. For cargo or passengers, paratroops, aerial refueling, search and rescue, communications, and as a gunship. Has flown from a Navy carrier deck without use of catapult. Four turboprop engines, max speed 325 knots, range at max payload 2,356 miles.

Hezbollah: Lebanese Shiite Moslem militia. Party of God.

HMMWV: The Humvee, U.S. light utility truck, replaced the honored jeep. Multipurpose wheeled vehicle, 4 × 4, automatic transmission, power steering. Engine: Detroit Diesel 150-hp diesel V-8 air-cooled. Top speed 65 mph. Range 300 miles.

Hotels: SEAL talk for hostages.

HQ: Headquarters.

Humint: Human Intelligence. Acquired on the ground; a person as opposed to satellite or photo recon.

Hydra-Shock: Lethal hollow-point ammunition made by Federal Cartridge Company. Outlawed in some areas.

Hypothermia: Danger to SEALs. A drop in body temperature that can be fatal.

IBS: Inflatable Boat Small. 12 × 6 feet. Carries 8 men and 1,000 pounds of weapons and gear. Hard to sink. Quiet motor. Used for silent beach, bay, lake landings.

IP: Initial Point. This can be a gathering place for a unit or force prior to going to the PD on a mission.

IR Beacon: Infrared beacon. For silent nighttime signaling.

IR Goggles: "Sees" heat instead of light.

Islamic Jihad: Arab holy war.

Isothermal layer: A colder layer of ocean water that deflects sonar rays. Submarines can hide below it, but then are also blind to what's going on above them since their sonar will not penetrate the layer.

IV Pack: Intravenous fluid that you can drink if out of water.

JAG: Judge Advocate General. The Navy's legal investigating arm that is independent of any Navy command.

JNA: Yugoslav National Army.

JP-4: Normal military jet fuel.

JSOC: Joint Special Operations Command.

JSOCCOMCENT: Joint Special Operations Command Center in the Pentagon.

KA-BAR: SEALs' combat, fighting knife.

KATN: Kick Ass and Take Names. SEAL talk, get the mission in gear.

KH-11: Spy satellite, takes pictures of ground, IR photos, etc.

KIA: Killed In Action.

KISS: Keep It Simple, Stupid. SEAL talk for streamlined operations.

Klick: A kilometer of distance. Often used as a mile. From Vietnam era, but still widely used in military.

Krytrons: Complicated, intricate timers used in making nuclear explosive detonators.

KV-57: Encoder for messages, scrambles.

Laser Pistol: The SIW pinpoint of ruby light emitted on any pistol for aiming. Usually a silenced weapon.

Left Behind: In 30 years SEALs have seldom left behind a dead comrade, never a wounded one. Never been taken prisoner.

Let's Get the Hell out of Dodge: SEAL talk for leaving a place, bugging out, hauling ass.

Liaison: Close-connection, cooperating person from one unit or service to another. Military liaison.

Light Sticks: Chemical units that make light after twisting to release chemicals that phosphoresce.

Loot & Shoot: SEAL talk for getting into action on a mission.

LT: Short for lieutenant in SEAL talk.

LZ: Landing Zone.

M1-8: Russian Chopper.

M1A1 M-14: Match rifle upgraded for SEAL snipers.

M-3 Submachine Gun: WWII grease gun, .45-caliber. Cheap. Introduced in 1942.

M-16: Automatic U.S. rifle. 5.56 round. Magazine 20 or 30, rate of fire 700 to 950 rds/min. Can attach M203 40mm grenade launcher under barrel.

M-18 Claymore: Antipersonnel mine. A slab of C-4 with 200 small ball bearings. Set off electrically or by trip wire. Can be positioned and aimed. Sprays out a cloud of balls. Kill zone 50 meters.

M60 Machine Gun: Can use 100-round ammo box snapped onto the gun's receiver. Not used much now by SEALs.

M-60E3: Lightweight handheld machine gun. Not used now by the SEALs.

M61A1: The usual 20mm cannon used on many American fighter planes.

M61(j): Machine Pistol. Yugoslav make.

M662: A red flare for signaling.

M-86: Pursuit Deterrent Munitions. Various types of mines, grenades, trip-wire explosives, and other devices in anti-personnel use.

M-203: A 40mm grenade launcher fitted under an M-16 or the M-4A1 Commando. Can fire a variety of grenade types up to 200 yards.

MagSafe: Lethal ammunition that fragments in human body and does not exit. Favored by some police units to cut down on second kill from regular ammunition exiting a body.

Make a Peek: A quick look, usually out of the water, to check your position or tactical situation.

Mark 23 Mod O: Special operations offensive handgun system. Double-action, 12-round magazine. Ambidextrous safety and mag-release catches. Knight screw-on suppressor. Snap-on laser for sighting. .45-caliber. Weighs 4 pounds loaded. 9.5 inches long; with silencer, 16.5 inches long.

Mark II Knife: Navy-issue combat knife.

Mark VIII SDV: Swimmer Delivery Vehicle. A bus, SEAL talk. 21 feet long, beam and draft 4 feet, 6 knots for 6 hours.

Master-at-Arms: Military police commander on board a ship.

MAVRIC Lance: A nuclear alert for stolen nukes or radioactive goods.

MC-130 Combat Talon: A specially equipped Hercules for covert missions in enemy or unfriendly territory.

McMillan M87R: Bolt-action sniper rifle. .50-caliber. 53 inches long. Bipod, fixed 5- or 10-round magazine. Bulbous muzzle brake on end of barrel. Deadly up to a mile. All types .50-caliber ammo.

MGS: Modified Grooming Standards. So SEALs don't all look like military, to enable them to do undercover work in mufti.

MH-53J: Chopper, updated CH053 from Nam days. 200 mph, called the Pave Low III.

MH-60K Black Hawk: Navy chopper. Forward infrared system for low-level night flight. Radar for terra follow/avoidance. Crew of 3, takes 12 troops. Top speed 225 mph. Ceiling 4,000 feet. Range radius 230 miles. Arms: two 12.7mm machine guns.

MI-15: British domestic intelligence agency.

MI-16: British foreign intelligence and espionage.

MIDEASTFOR: Middle East Force.

MiG: Russian-built fighter, many versions, used in many nations around the world.

Mike Boat: Liberty boat off a large ship.

Mike-Mike: Short for mm, millimeter, as 9 mike-mike.

Milstar: Communications satellite for pickup and bouncing from SATCOM and other radio transmitters. Used by SEALs.

Minigun: In choppers. Can fire 2,000 rounds per minute. Gatling gun-type.

Mitrajez M80: Machine gun from Yugoslavia.

MLR: The Main Line of Resistance. That imaginary line in a battle where two forces face each other. Sometimes there are only a few yards or a few miles between them. Usually heavily fortified and manned.

Mocha: Food energy bar SEALs carry in vest pockets.

Mossberg: Pump-action, pistol-grip, 5-round magazine. SEALs use it for close-in work.

Motorola Radio: Personal radio, short range, lip mike, earpiece, belt pack.

MRE: Meals Ready to Eat. Field rations used by most of U.S. Armed Forces and the SEALs as well. Long-lasting.

MSPF: Maritime Special Purpose Force.

Mugger: MUGR, Miniature Underwater Global locator device. Sends up antenna for pickup on positioning satellites. Works under water or above. Gives location within 10 feet.

Mujahideen: A soldier of Allah in Muslim nations.

NAVAIR: NAVy AIR command.

NAVSPECWARGRUP-ONE: Naval   Special   Warfare

Group One based on Coronado, CA. SEALs are in this command.

NAVSPECWARGRUP-TWO: Naval Special Warfare Group Two based at Little Creek, VA.

NCIS: Naval Criminal Investigative Service. A civilian operation not reporting to any Navy authority to make it more responsible and responsive. Replaces the old NIS, Naval Investigation Service, that did report to the closest admiral.

NEST: Nuclear Energy Search Team. Non-military unit that reports at once to any spill, problem, or Broken Arrow to determine the extent of the radiation problem.

NEWBIE: A new man, officer, or commander of an established military unit.

NKSF: North Korean Special Forces.

NLA: Iranian National Liberation Army. About 4,500 men in South Iraq, helped by Iraq for possible use against Iran.

Nomex: The type of material used for flight suits and hoods.

NPIC: National Photographic Interpretation Center in D.C.

NRO: National Reconnaissance Office. To run and coordinate satellite development and operations for the intelligence community.

NSA: National Security Agency.

NSC: National Security Council. Meets in Situation Room, support facility in the Executive Office Building in D.C. Main security group in the nation.

NSVHURAWN: Iranian Marines.

NUCFLASH: An alert for any nuclear problem.

NVG One Eye: Litton single-eyepiece Night-Vision Goggles. Prevents NVG blindness in both eyes if a flare goes off.

NVGs: Night-Vision Goggles. One eye or two. Give good night vision in the dark with a greenish view.

OAS: Obstacle Avoidance Sonar. Used on many low-flying attack aircraft.

OD: Officer of the Day.

OIC: Officer In Charge.

Oil Tanker: One is: 885 feet long, 140 foot beam, 121,000 tons, 13 cargo tanks that hold 35.8 million gallons of fuel, oil, or gas. 24 in the crew. This is a regular-sized tanker. Not a supertanker.

OOD: Officer Of the Deck.

OP: Out Post. A spot near the front of friendly lines or even beyond them where a man or a unit watch the enemy's movements. Can be manned by an FO from artillery.

Orion P-3: Navy's long-range patrol and antisub aircraft. Some adapted to ELINT roles. Crew of 10. Max speed loaded 473 mph. Ceiling 28,300 feet. Arms: internal weapons bay and 10 external weapons stations for a mix of torpedoes, mines, rockets, and bombs.

Passive Sonar: Listening for engine noise of a ship or sub. It doesn't give away the hunter's presence as an active sonar would.

Pave Low III: A Navy chopper.

PBR: Patrol Boat River. U.S. has many shapes, sizes, and with various types of armament.

PC-170: Patrol Coastal-Class 170-foot SEAL delivery vehicle. Powered by four 3,350 hp diesel engines, beam of 25 feet and draft of 7.8 feet. Top speed 35 knots, range 2,000 nautical miles. Fixed swimmer platform on stern. Crew of 4 officers and 24 EM, carries 8 SEALs.

PD: Point of Departure. A given position on the ground from which a unit or patrol leaves for its mission.

Plank Owners: Original men in the start-up of a new military unit.

Polycarbonate material: Bullet-proof glass.

PRF: People's Revolutionary Front. Fictional group in *NUCFLASH*, a SEAL Team Seven book.

Prowl & Growl: SEAL talk for moving into a combat mission.

Quitting Bell: In BUD/S training. Ring it and you quit the SEAL unit. Helmets of men who quit the class are lined up below the bell in Coronado. (Recently they have stopped ringing the bell. Dropouts simply place their helmet below the bell and go.)

RAF: Red Army Faction. A once-powerful German terrorist group, not so active now.

Remington 200: Sniper Rifle. Not used by SEALs now.

Remington 700: Sniper rifle with Starlight Scope. Can extend night vision to 400 meters.

RIB: Rigid Inflatable Boat. 3 sizes, one 10 meters, 40 knots.

Ring Knocker: An Annapolis graduate with the ring.

RIO: Radar Intercept Officer. The officer who sits in the backseat of an F-14 Tomcat off a carrier. The job: find enemy targets in the air and on the sea.

Roger That: A yes, an affirmative, a go answer to a command or statement.

RPG: Rocket Propelled Grenade. Quick and easy, shoulder-fired. Favorite weapon of terrorists, insurgents.

S & R: Search and Rescue. Usually a helicopter.

SAS: British Special Air Service. Commandos. Special warfare men. Best that Britain has. Works with SEALs.

SATCOM: Satellite-based communications system for instant contact with anyone anywhere in the world. SEALs rely on it.

SAW: Squad's Automatic Weapon. Usually a machine gun or automatic rifle.

SBS: Special Boat Squadron. On-site Navy unit that transports SEALs to many of their missions. Located across the street from the SEALs' Coronado, California, headquarters.

SD3: Sound-suppression system on the H & K MP5 weapon.

SDV: Swimmer Delivery Vehicle. SEALs use a variety of them.

Seahawk SH-60: Navy chopper for ASW and SAR. Top speed 180 knots, ceiling 13,800 feet, range 503 miles, arms: 2 Mark 46 torpedoes.

SEAL Headgear: Boonie hat, wool balaclava, green scarf, watch cap, bandanna roll.

Second in Command: Also 2IC for short in SEAL talk.

SERE: Survival, Evasion, Resistance, and Escape training.

Shipped for Six: Enlisted for six more years in the Navy.

Shit City: Coronado SEALs' name for Norfolk.

Show Colors: In combat put U.S. flag or other identification on back for easy identification by friendly air or ground units.

Sierra Charlie: SEAL talk for everything on schedule.

Simunition: Canadian product for training that uses paint balls instead of lead for bullets.

Sixteen-Man Platoon: Basic SEAL combat force. Up from 14 men a few years ago.

Sked: SEAL talk for schedule.

Sonobuoy: Small underwater device that detects sounds and transmits them by radio to plane or ship.

Space Blanket: Green foil blanket to keep troops warm. Vacuum-packed and folded to a cigarette-sized package.

SPIE: Special Purpose Insertion and Extraction rig. Essentially a long rope dangled from a chopper with hardware on it that is attached to each SEAL's chest right on his lift harness. Set up to lift six or eight men out of harm's way quickly by a chopper.

Sprayers and Prayers: Not the SEAL way. These men spray bullets all over the place hoping for hits. SEALs do more aimed firing for sure kills.

SS-19: Russian ICBM missile.

STABO: Use harness and lines under chopper to get down to the ground.

STAR: Surface To Air Recovery operation.

Starflash Round: Shotgun round that shoots out sparkling fireballs that ricochet wildly around a room, confusing and terrifying the occupants. Non-lethal.

Stasi: Old-time East German secret police.

Stick: British terminology: 2 4-man SAS teams.

Stokes: A kind of Navy stretcher. Open coffin shaped of wire mesh and white canvas for emergency patient transport.

STOL: Short TakeOff and Landing. Aircraft with high-lift wings and vectored-thrust engines to produce extremely short takeoffs and landings.

Sub Gun: Submachine gun, often the suppressed H & K MP5.

Suits: Civilians, usually government officials wearing suits.

Sweat: The more SEALs sweat in peacetime, the less they bleed in war.

Sykes-Fairbairn: A commando fighting knife.

Syrette: Small syringe for field administration often filled with morphine. Can be self-administered.

Tango: SEAL talk for a terrorist.

TDY: Temporary duty assigned outside of normal job designation.

Terr: Another term for terrorist. Shorthand SEAL talk.

Tetrahedral reflectors: Show up on multi-mode radar like tiny suns.

Thermal Imager: Device to detect warmth, as a human body, at night or through light cover.

Thermal Tape: ID for night-vision-goggle user to see. Used on friendlies.

TNAZ: Trinittroaze Tidine. Explosive to replace C-4. 15% stronger than C-4 and 20% lighter.

TO&E: Table showing organization and equipment of a military unit.

Top SEAL Tribute: "You sweet motherfucker, don't you never die!"

Trailing Array: A group of antennas for sonar pickup trailed out of a submarine.

Train: For contact in smoke, no light, fog, etc. Men directly behind each other. Right hand on weapon, left hand on shoulder of man ahead. Squeeze shoulder to signal.

Trident: SEALs' emblem. An eagle with talons clutching a Revolutionary War pistol, and Neptune's trident superimposed on the Navy's traditional anchor.

TRW: A camera's digital record that is sent by SATCOM.

TT33: Tokarev, a Russian pistol.

UAZ: A Soviet 1-ton truck.

UBA Mark XV: Underwater life support with computer to regulate the rebreather's gas mixture.

UGS: Unmanned Ground Sensors. Can be used to explode booby traps and claymore mines.

UNODIR: Unless otherwise directed. The unit will start the operation unless they are told not to.

VBSS: Orders to "visit, board, search, and seize."

Wadi: A gully or ravine, usually in a desert.

White Shirt: Man responsible for safety on carrier deck as he leads around civilians and personnel unfamiliar with the flight deck.

WIA: Wounded In Action.

WP: White Phosphorus. Can be in a grenade, 40MM round

or in a 20MM round. Used as smoke and to start fires.

Zodiac: Also called an IBS, Inflatable Boat Small. 15 × 6 feet, weighs 265 pounds. The "rubber duck" can carry 8 fully equipped SEALs. Can do 18 knots with a range of 65 nautical miles.

Zulu: Means Greenwich Mean Time, GMT. Used in all formal military communications.